"We won't be sharing a bed," Glenna decreed in the dark.

She heard Jared laugh yet again and decided she didn't like his sense of humor any more than she did his views on marriage.

"We will definitely be sharing a bed." He vetoed her decree as he got into one side of the object in question. "For a while, until you're healed, all we'll be doing in it is sleeping, but after that . . . we'll get around to just about everything most other married couples do."

There was something very unnerving about that deep male voice in the dark.

"No, we will not," she answered him.

"No, we will not what?" He seemed to be enjoying her discomfort with the subject.

"No, we will not be getting around to . . ." She cleared her throat to keep up her steam. "Without feelings between us, there won't be any . . ."

"Is that right?"

"It is. You said you wanted someone to care for your house and your  . . . and that's what I'll . . . what I'll be *hire*

Dear Reader,

September proves to be another top-notch month of reading here in the Harlequin Historical line.

Victoria Pade is a writer who's equally at home writing contemporary and historical romances. This month she looks back to the 1886 Kansas frontier and follows Glenna Ashe as she answers an ad to become a rancher's wife. At first Glenna is simply eager to escape an impossible situation in Chicago, where her own family has cruelly turned against her, but once she meets the man who is to become her husband, she has another goal in mind: turn this marriage of convenience into a genuine marriage of the heart.

In *King's Ransom*, by popular historical writer Mary Daheim, Puritan Honor Dale finds herself falling in love with the handsome highwayman who stole her dowry—planning to send it to exiled King Charles, the sworn enemy of Honor's family. The warm characters and beautifully handled British setting make this a book to cherish.

Next month, look for Marianne Willman and Jo Ann Algermissen to take you on two more exciting trips into the past, and don't expect the excitement to stop there, because there's more coming up in the months ahead. Be there every month, when we bring you the best historical romances around—only from Harlequin.

Yours,

Leslie Wainger
Senior Editor and Editorial Coordinator

The Doubletree

Victoria Pade

Harlequin Books

TORONTO • NEW YORK • LONDON
AMSTERDAM • PARIS • SYDNEY • HAMBURG
STOCKHOLM • ATHENS • TOKYO • MILAN

Harlequin Historical first edition September 1990

ISBN 0-373-28653-8

VICTORIA PADE,

author of both historical and contemporary romance fiction, is the mother of two energetic daughters, Cori and Erin. Although she enjoys her chosen career as a novelist, the Colorado resident occasionally laments that she has never traveled beyond Disneyland, instead spending all her spare time plugging away at her computer. She takes breaks from writing by indulging in her favorite hobby—eating chocolate.

Chapter One

1886

Glenna Ashe's long, thin fingers were steady and methodical as she fastened the buttons up the front of the black shirtwaist she had borrowed from old Aunt Lida. Threadbare and faded, the ill-fitting mourning dress had seen better days.

But then so had Glenna.

And a disguise was what she needed to go out into the streets of Chicago this late September morning.

She took a calming breath and pushed herself up from the wing chair in the corner of the guest bedroom she and her sister Mary had shared for the past three weeks. The dress fell inches short of her ankles, but there was nothing to be done about the hem now. At least the gown was age-softened and hung loosely on her; today she doubted her battered body could stand anything formfitting.

From her valise she took black lisle stockings and went back to the chair. With her feet firmly on the floor, knees together, skirts primly down, she bent forward at the waist and reached down to put on the stockings. The action sent a stab of pain through her side and she caught her breath. Slowly she straightened. She set her jaw and waited stubbornly for the pain to subside. When it had, she yanked her skirts up all the way to her lap, brought her ankle to rest on the opposite knee and rolled on the delicate hose that way. Sometimes being a lady just didn't work.

Once both stockings were in place she flipped her dress back down and nodded her head just once, sharply, in a way that said *so there!* to no one in particular.

From the narrow bed in the corner of Aunt Lida's guest room, Glenna's nine-year-old sister, Mary, sobbed in her sleep. It was a pitiful sound, one Glenna had become all too familiar with in the three weeks since their mother's death.

And it was one of the few things that defeated Glenna.

For a moment, she sagged. Then, taking a steeling breath, she once again rose from the chair, this time going to the side of the brass four-poster to see if Mary's eyes were open.

They weren't.

Rather than attending to the task at hand, Glenna lingered at her sister's bedside, carefully pulling the crisp white sheet up over the little girl's bony shoulder, then lightly touching a thin lock of the sleeping child's hair. Mary was a delicate child, a tiny replica of their mother. Her hair was flaxen and baby-soft, nothing like Glenna's unruly, copper corkscrews. Unlike her sister, Mary didn't have a single freckle across the only feature they shared, a thin, aristocratic nose. And her eyes, so pale...so different from Glenna's odd, dark aqua-colored ones.

Glenna reached to smooth Mary's brow but then thought better of it. No sense taking the chance that Mary would wake up. She had been asleep for only a few hours.

The thirteen-year difference in their ages made Glenna feel more like Mary's mother than her sister. Now that they had only each other that feeling was stronger than ever.

As she stood at the bedside she wondered how she could leave Mary behind with ancient Aunt Lida, who slept more hours than she was awake, smelled of camphor and wasn't even a blood relation.

But she could, she told herself quickly. And she would. Because she had no other choice.

They had already gone over it. In fact, she and Mary and Aunt Lida had spent much of the night discussing Glenna's options after the authorities had come looking for her and she had been forced to hide among the cobwebs in the attic. They all knew there was nothing else she could do, no matter how much any of them wished otherwise.

So, get to it and quit lollygagging, she told herself. She went back to her dressing.

Glenna pulled on a pair of black shoes in the same unladylike manner she had her stockings. She wielded the buttonhook as if it were a saber and did up every one of the seven side buttons on each shoe in a matter of seconds.

The hat and gloves that would complete her disguise were on the bureau. Glenna had avoided that particular area of the room as she had seen quite enough of herself in the oval mirror above the dresser when she had cleaned up last night.

But she couldn't avoid it any longer.

Standing in front of the bureau, she didn't immediately look in the mirror; rather she took the hat and dusted it with her fingers. It was an old-fashioned black slat bonnet, at least twenty years out-of-date—ugly and hot.

Satisfied that it was clean, yet still stalling, she set it back on the bureau top and picked up her hairbrush. Tending the curly mass was a chore in itself and today she couldn't keep her arms up long enough to do more than brush the knots out of it. Then she pulled the hat onto her head and stuffed her hair up inside the pouchlike back.

There was no avoiding a glance in the mirror after that. She had to make sure every curl of her distinctive hair was hidden. She jerked her head up defiantly and stared full at the glass. The sight of her face stopped her breath short; she looked worse this morning than she had last night.

Glenna shook her head, puffed out her cheeks with a big breath and slowly deflated them as she blew it out. There was nothing to be done about it, and since this was the whole purpose of the hat she eagerly rolled the veil down to the tip of her chin.

Then she craned her neck around, turning her head this way and that to see just how much of her face was visible through the black netting.

More than she would have liked.

What was it Betty Majors did when she was flirting to hide that big ugly mole she had on her jawbone? Glenna dipped her chin nearly to her chest and looked up out of the corners of her eyes. That was better; at least then the bruises looked more like shadows.

Escaping her reflection, she went back to her valise for a hatpin. She might as well get some use out of what was condemning her.

Rummaging through the things left in her satchel for want of enough space in the drawers or armoire, she pushed aside dresses, a skirt, a blouse and two pairs of shoes before she finally found what she was looking for—a purple velvet box.

Her mother's jewelry box.

Glenna's throat constricted and she felt tears well up in her eyes. She squeezed them tightly closed and tried to master her grief much as she had the pain a few minutes before.

When she could open dry eyes, she did, taking the box into her lap. The top was embroidered with tiny violets and white butterflies. She couldn't help herself; for a moment she trailed her fingertips across the velvet the way she had when she was a little girl. Then she lifted the box to her nose, smelling her mother's verbena perfume.

The scent was sweet, but now the thoughts that came with it were not. She put the box back in her lap.

The top didn't slide open as easily as it had when it was atop her mother's dressing table; it was bent now. Glenna wondered if that had happened when it was thrown at her or when she had snatched it up and flung it into the bottom of her valise to take it with her to the attic.

Applying a little force, she finally managed to slide the top free so she could peer inside.

The gifts of David Stern. A foul taste came to Glenna's mouth.

Diamond drop earrings and a garish necklace to match. A diamond bracelet that had always looked too heavy around her mother's delicately boned wrist. The large ruby ring that had wedded Sybil Ashe to her second husband. A tiara—as if he had wanted the world to think she was his queen ...

Glenna roughly sifted through them. Buried beneath she found the simpler pieces given by Sybil's first husband and Glenna and Mary's father, Frederick Ashe. The plain gold chain with the small, perfectly round garnet hanging from it. The string of pearls. The simple gold wedding band. Frederick Ashe had been a dignified man, a man of taste and good breeding, and it showed in his gifts.

If only he had lived ...

Glenna pushed back the thought. Senseless, that was what it was. Her father hadn't lived. He'd been dead for eight long years now. And David Stern had taken his place....

To Glenna it was a travesty that the two sets of jewelry were mingled together—like good and evil. But she put that thought aside, too, and took out the plain silver hatpin she had been after in the first place, the one her mother had worn during her mourning for Frederick Ashe, beloved husband and father.

Feeling her way, Glenna jammed the pin into place across the top of her hat, then firmly closed the jewel box. Back into the satchel it went, before she struggled stiffly to her feet again.

Her gloves were still on the bureau. She went back there and, without glancing in the mirror, pulled them on with efficient tugs. Fully dressed and disguised, she reached for the slip of newsprint in the glass hairpin dish below the mirror. Smoothing out the wrinkles against the crocheted doily that protected the dresser top, she scanned the item for the most important information.

The Arms Hotel, room 204.

Suddenly there was a ringing in her ears. She felt clammy and light-headed. She grasped the bureau's edge to keep her balance and then took a breath deep enough to send the jab of pain down her side again.

The pain was just what she needed.

Releasing her grip on the dresser, she folded the newspaper clipping into a neat square and tucked it firmly into the cuff of her left glove.

She glanced at the bed where her sister still slept and then Glenna slipped out of the room, soundlessly closing the door behind her before descending the stairs and leaving Aunt Lida's town house.

The air outside was thick and moist from a rain the previous night. Glenna's black widow's weeds seemed to weigh a thousand pounds, but there was no relief for it. She couldn't chance hiring a carriage even had she the fare.

At the end of the block she turned to the left, making certain she kept her chin tucked all the while. Metering her pace to appear normal, she passed a boardinghouse whose white picket fence was lined with well-tended rosebushes, then the livery from which the smells of horses and leather emanated, next the noisy blacksmith's, until she rounded Dr. E. Walter Linden's corner and stepped into the center of the city.

The normal pace on these streets was fast and she was glad for the hectic bustle. Only a few more blocks and she'd be there.

So far, so good.

Passing a pie shop, she stepped around a hefty man who was gazing through the window of the bakery and found herself just behind a blue-uniformed policeman.

She stopped short.

Panic overwhelmed her and for a split second Glenna couldn't think what to do. She darted a glance to her left, then back over her shoulder in search of an inconspicuous escape route. She spotted a narrow opening, and crossed between a hansom cab and an ice wagon, barely breathing until she was safe on the opposite sidewalk.

Her relief was short-lived. A cautious glance behind her fell not on the policeman she had avoided but on a familiar face just emerging from that hansom cab.

David Stern. Her stepfather.

Glenna's mouth went dry. He couldn't have seen her or he wouldn't have been so deliberately picking coins out of his palm to pay the driver. She turned abruptly so that her back was to him and walked a little faster. Three women strolled along past the storefronts ahead and she fell into step with them, so close behind she could have been one of them—just four friends out for a morning stroll....

Maybe her stepfather had gone in the other direction. She risked a fast look over her shoulder.

There he was, several feet behind her.

Glenna's pulse raced to her throat. She pretended to be very interested in what the women just ahead of her were saying.

Then they stopped to look at a baby carriage in a store window. David Stern kept coming, the distance between them closing fast.

Glenna went cold. The sound of her heartbeat pounded in her ears. She tried to get around the women and into the shop, but two of them had moved into the doorway for a better view of the carriage.

Glenna could see her stepfather nearing, reflected in the glass. She couldn't tell if he was after her or just walking in the same direction, but regardless she couldn't let him catch up to her. Her disguise suddenly didn't seem like any kind of concealment at all. She had to get away.

Heedless now of how it looked, Glenna sidestepped around the women and hurried up the street. She needed a place to hide. A group of businessmen in broadcloth morning suits stood outside the seed and grain store. Glenna passed them and seized the camouflage of their bodies to slip into the shop door just beyond them.

The pungent, earthy smell of the place made Glenna's stomach clench. She swallowed thickly and searched for a secluded place to watch for her stepfather.

A man was paying for his purchase at the counter and another picked up a handful of grass seed and let it sift through his fingers. It was behind this second man that Glenna positioned herself, staring out the store window just to the right of him.

David Stern came into view almost immediately. Glenna's heart rate doubled and echoed in her ears.

He rounded the group of men, but before he got out of Glenna's sight one of them called to him and he retraced his steps. Accepting the businessman's extended hand, David Stern was in profile a scant few feet from the window.

Perspiration erupted on Glenna's upper lip and she pressed a gloved forefinger there to daub it. Just then the farmer who had been judging the grass seed clapped his hands together to brush off the seeds and left the store. Before the door had closed behind him the man making a purchase at the counter completed his transaction and followed him out.

Feeling suddenly exposed, Glenna spun around to find a young salesclerk watching her.

Enemies everywhere. She was beginning to see every person who looked at her as an enemy. *Get a hold of yourself, Glenna, get a hold.*

She smiled at the young man, who looked to be in his middle teens. Did he see the panic she was feeling? Once again she remembered Betty Majors's coyness and dropped her chin. When all the clerk did was continue to stare at her, she pretended to browse as if it were hats she looked at and not barrels of carrot and cucumber seeds, sacks of corn and bushels of bulbs.

"May I help you?" the boy asked in a voice that cracked with youthful manhood.

"No, thank you," she answered, ignoring his curious scrutiny.

Jars of flower seeds lined the counter top and Glenna pretended interest. Marigolds, geraniums, peonies, phlox.

"We got real tulip bulbs all the way from Holland," the boy offered. "Plant 'em now and they'll flower come spring."

Keeping her chin demurely dipped, Glenna declined. "No, I don't think so, thank you." If she'd had so much as a nickel she would have bought something—anything—just to keep his suspicious eyes off her.

"Are you waitin' for somebody?"

She should have thought of that herself. "Yes," she agreed too eagerly, and then as if to confirm her words she stole another look out the window.

Obviously David Stern had neither seen nor followed her. Now, if only he would just leave so she could get out of here and on with what she needed to do.

Stern's hearty laughter erupted outside. He seemed to be enjoying himself.

Glenna could hardly hold still. She had to get to The Arms; she might be too late already.

As she turned back to the counter the clerk pushed aside a curtain and went into a storeroom. For the second the curtain was open she caught sight of a back door. It was tempting. Very tempting.

But how would she explain that?

No, there was nothing to do but wait her stepfather out. He still hadn't seen her.

Once more Glenna dried her damp upper lip with her gloved finger. A drop of perspiration ran from her temple down the side of her face. She could feel her hair inching its way out from under the hat to her forehead.

She was alone in the shop—the clerk was still in the back room—so she carefully lifted the veil to push her hair back under her hat. But as she did, the door opened, and reflexively she jerked a look over her shoulder. A bearded man came in. At the same moment Glenna looked up, David Stern glanced through the store window and their eyes met. She saw him frown and only then remembered her veil was up.

David Stern turned toward the seed store's door. Glenna grabbed her skirts and dashed past the counter, bounding through the curtain and directly into the young clerk. She stumbled forward, he fell backward, and a basket full of tiny seeds flew all around them like black snowflakes.

"What the—"

"Stop her!" The sound of her stepfather's voice came from the front of the store.

Glenna regained her balance and made a break for the back door, fumbling with the handle and flying through the moment it opened.

Cats screeched their displeasure as she bounded into the alley. With her skirts clenched in her fists Glenna ran as if the Devil himself were after her. She made it to the end of the alleyway before anyone could chase her, but just as she was on the verge of rounding the corner a wagon piled high with empty crates pulled into the opening and stopped.

Thinking fast, Glenna bent low and scurried under the belly of the wagon, her feet very nearly sliding out from under her as she did. Once out of the alley she veered to the right, bobbing and weaving her way through the morning shoppers, businessmen and storekeepers; she had to get to The Arms.

As she ran across a street she misjudged the speed of an oncoming carriage. The horse whinnied a complaint and reared back on its hind legs, but Glenna didn't pause. On the other side of the street she headed between a saloon and a roominghouse and found herself in another alley.

A stitch in her side threatened to double her over, but before she gave in to it she looked over her shoulder; no one was after her yet. But she had no way of knowing how close David Stern might be. She paused long enough to draw three breaths and then, wrapping her arms around her middle, she headed up the alley as fast as she could go.

There was another opening between two buildings and she took it, bursting into the street directly in front of a church. She needed to rest, to compose herself, to hide until she was sure she had lost her stepfather.

Keeping hold of her skirts she charged into the sanctuary. It was cool and quiet. Glenna's labored breathing echoed softly. An old woman kneeling at the altar looked over her shoulder and then turned back to her prayers.

Glenna slipped into the confessional beside the door, pulling the curtain closed behind her. She slid down to sit on the kneeler and the sound of her heartbeat was all she could hear until she caught her breath and her pulse slowed. Then she listened.

No sounds came from beyond the confessional's curtain.

Glenna peeked through an opening in the curtain. David Stern was nowhere in sight.

For a moment she wilted.

But only for a moment, until her breathing came back to normal and the coolness of the church dried her perspiration; she knew she had to go on.

Setting her jaw, she stood and again peeked through the curtain to be sure the coast was clear before she came out. She reached up and straightened her hat, pulling the veil evenly down to her chin again. Then she slipped out of the confessional.

After leaving the church by a side door, Glenna scanned up and down the street before merging with the other peo-

ple on the boardwalk. The red stone structure of the Arms
came into view.

Her palms were damp inside her gloves, her head itched
beneath the felt hat, and her body hadn't hurt this much
since she fell from the top of the Mudrocks' apple tree; but
she kept going.

Beneath the red awning that shaded the hotel entrance
Glenna stopped. She was here, on the threshold of a future
she had scoffed at two days before when she had come
across the advertisement now folded inside her glove.

A liveried doorman held the walnut panel open for her
and waited. Glenna swallowed hard. She rubbed the tips of
her fingers into the palms of her hands. Her gaze rested on
the doorman, then the open portal; she swallowed again.

No choice.

She stepped into the cool, green brocade interior. A man
sat near a tall potted fern, reading a newspaper; another
checked his pocket watch and glared up the stairs; a couple
addressed the clerk behind the registration desk. Off to the
right was a wide archway, beyond which linen-clothed tables were visible, occupied by people eating breakfast.

Glenna moistened her lips and took the newspaper clipping out of her glove. She unfolded it to read it for what
seemed like the thousandth time.

Who would answer an advertisement like this? What kind
of woman?

This kind, she thought now, defensively.

She eyed the stairs that led up to the rooms. Each step
looked like the highest of mountains.

Folding the advertisement once more she tucked it back
into the cuff of her glove, straightened the waist of her dress
and smoothed the long sleeves down her arms. Squaring her
shoulders, she lifted her chin and took a breath.

Then she headed for those stairs.

Room 204.

And Jared Stratton.

Chapter Two

The inside of his mouth felt and tasted like he'd been sucking on a horse's hoof. But Jared Stratton was too tired to do anything about it, so he tried to ignore it and go back to sleep.

He *needed* to sleep.

What had woken him up, anyway? Didn't matter...

Then the sound came again.

What the hell was that pounding?

Damn place. Damn city. Too many damn people in too small a space.

He tried to swallow, but his mouth was so dry his tongue stuck to the roof of it.

Water. Didn't that prissy valet usually leave a glass of water on the table next to the bed?

Jared opened his eyes into slits and turned his head very slowly. His nose came up flat against the foot rail.

What the hell?

Snarling, he opened his eyes all the way. Knives shot through his eyeballs into his brain. He closed them again with a hoarse groan. *Mother of God...*

He was lying across the bottom of the bed. That meant he was actually going to have to move to find out if there was water on the nightstand. It wasn't worth it. Better to sleep...

Why didn't they stop that blasted pounding?

Maybe the place was on fire. Hell, he'd rather burn to death than move.

"Mr. Stratton?"

Just let me sleep, for God's sake....

He wouldn't answer it. Whoever it was would go away. Every knock on the door was like a fist in the side of his head. What time was it, anyway?

"Mr. Stratton."

He lifted his arms and pressed the heels of both hands into his eyes. Probably that valet bringing breakfast.

Food. That was the worst thought yet. His stomach lurched.

"Mr. Stratton?" The voice outside the door was louder now.

"Go the hell away," he growled.

The pounding again.

"Please, Mr. Stratton. I must see you," the person at the door insisted, sounding slightly irate.

This couldn't be the valet; he didn't have the guts.

Belatedly Jared realized the voice was that of a female. He groaned and pushed the heels of his hands even harder into his eyes.

Another damn woman.

"Mr. Stratton!"

With his teeth clenched, Jared reached a hand to the top of the foot rail and hoisted his carcass into a partially upright position. His head felt as if there were an ax embedded in it, and his stomach was twisted into knots. Once again he tried opening his eyes, but it was just plain agony so he squinted them back into mere slits.

The pounding again.

"Stop that!" he shouted. Sorely regretting the noise he made, he continued just loud enough to be heard. "I'll be right there."

He was either going to marry this one or kill her.

With one hand on the foot rail and the other flat against the mattress he pushed himself to his feet. Then he stumbled back onto the bed. One boot was half on, and the instep of his bare foot had found the other. Grumbling, he reached down, yanked off the boot he partially wore and threw it. It hit the wall with a loud thunk and fell. Then he kicked the other one out from under his foot. It slid through the doorway that connected the bedroom with the sitting room. The knock sounded yet again.

"Dammit, I said I'd be right there," he called through the door.

Pushing himself to his feet, he spent a moment to let his stomach settle and the hammers in his head ease somewhat. Then he felt his way to the washstand and splashed tepid water over his face. Letting it drip down his neck he hooked both his hands onto the sides of the washbowl and nearly pressed his nose to the shaving mirror above.

Matted flat on one side and sticking up on the other, his usually sun-streaked blond hair was more the wheaten color of his bushy mustache; his angular jaw was shaded with stubble. The way he squinted obliterated his eyes in creases beneath a fiercely square brow.

He was still wearing the clothes he had left his room in last night, or at least part of them. He'd lost the top two buttons on his white shirt—most likely from having tried to get it off before he passed out. His clothes were wrinkled, and probably smelled like a saloon.

Damn disreputable was his own assessment.

And it served this pushy woman right for waking him up.

"Mr. Stratton!" the voice from the hallway demanded.

Jared grumbled to himself and headed from the doorway through which his boot had preceded him. The sitting room was blessedly dark, with drapes still drawn. He crossed it to the outer door.

With his hand on the knob, the pounding came again. Standing scant inches away from the sharp raps, he felt as if they originated in the center of his skull.

He strangled the knob and yanked the door open.

The woman in the hall jumped as if she hadn't expected the door ever to open. She tipped her head way back to take in his full height of six feet four inches, and then quickly dropped her chin to her chest like a naughty child caught sneaking a peek during prayers.

Jared pinched the bridge of his long, thin nose, and squinted again to cool the burning sensation. When he found it bearable, he fully opened his eyes to take in the tenth woman who had appeared at his door since he placed that advertisement in the newspaper.

He settled his weight onto his left hip, grasped the edge of the door with one hand, laid his forearm along the top of the jamb and leaned out to take a look at her—at least as good a look as he could through vision blurred with too little sleep, too much bourbon and her standing in a hallway lit only by a single, small octagonal window at the far end.

A little crow, was his first thought.

She could have just come off the tail end of a cattle drive for all the dust that powdered her black dress. It would have taken two of her to fill it, and he wondered how many meals she had missed to leave the thing hanging like limp curtains.

The hat she wore was just plain ugly. Not able to see through her veil in the dimness of the hallway, he could only imagine what horrors it hid. Pockmarks, pimples, pores like craters, a nose big enough to shade an acre of land, crossed eyes or a half-toothless grin—he had seen them all in the past two days; but this was the first applicant who was so bad she needed to hide behind a veil.

And he was in no mood.

"I'm Stratton," he ground out through clenched teeth.

Voices sounded down the hallway, and she shot a look in that direction. As she did Jared caught sight of something that made this woman a little more interesting. A single strand of the curliest, reddest hair he had ever seen snaked out from the pouched back of the hat and stuck damply to a thin, alabaster nape.

Then she faced him again and took a step forward. In a prideful voice as if she were doing him the greatest favor, she said, "I've come in answer to your advertisement."

Her tone caught him by surprise, and made him laugh—not heartily, he was in no shape for that. But after a parade of poor, meek, broken-spirited souls who thought he was their last hope for marriage and a home of their own, this struck him as funny.

"Did you, now!" He couldn't suppress his ornery urge to challenge her.

"I did," she confirmed without hesitation, as haughtily as her initial announcement.

Jared stared at her for a long moment just to see if she'd back down. When she didn't he pushed away from the jamb and freed the doorway. "Then I guess you'd better come in."

She glided in front of him as smoothly as if she were on wheels, instructing proprietarily as she did, "Please leave the door ajar."

Silently, behind her back, he laughed again, carefully shaking his head. This one was definitely different. He did as she had ordered, but just barely, leaving about as much of a crack in the door as he had in his eyes on the way to it.

Following her, Jared watched the straightness of her back. When she hit the center of the room the little crow stopped abruptly, and turned to size him up—no doubt unfavorably.

"Sit down," he instructed in the same tone of voice she had used to decree the door be left ajar, and he motioned to a high-backed gold brocade chair.

"Thank you," she murmured formally. She sat almost as if she were in pain. Was she crippled, too?

That advertisement was surely the foolest notion he had ever had.

His mouth still felt as dusty as her dress looked, so Jared went to the bar that stood in the corner. He poured himself a glass of water from a crystal ewer. He added just a splash of bourbon. Then he took a long pull of it, and held it in puffed-out cheeks for a moment before swallowing it.

For the second time he pinched the center corners of his eyes and then turned back to the woman, who seemed to be watching his every move from behind that veil. Ignoring her, he yanked open the draperies on two large windows, grimacing as the morning light pierced his brain.

Then he went to where she sat. He stepped over the low oval table that stood between her chair and a matching settee.

"Do you have a name?" he prompted sardonically.

She didn't immediately answer him. Then she cleared her throat and said, "Glenna."

"Glenna what?" he persisted impatiently.

Again the hesitation. This time she nearly whispered. "Ashe."

"Glenna Ashe," he repeated, trying it out. "And you've come in answer to my advertisement."

"Yes," she stated firmly, and then as if remembering, dipped her chin.

The action made Jared more curious about what she was hiding behind that veil. The black netting had an illusionary effect; he couldn't actually tell much about her features and yet he could see an array of unnatural colors. Did they come from shadows cast by the veil or did they originate from underneath it?

He wondered if she was birthmarked.

It made his head hurt worse to frown, so he checked the impulse. "You're going to have to take off your hat so I can get a look at you."

This time her hesitation was obvious and extended. He saw her swallow. He heard her resigned sigh. She slowly lifted her hands to untie the ribbon that formed a bow under her chin. But when she took hold of the veil to roll it upward she seemed to change her mind. Instead, she lifted the hat off from the back, pulling it forward.

The first thing he saw was the wildest mass of red curls cascading from the bonnet's back to fall all around and down past her shoulders to her elbows. After a moment, Jared turned his attention to her face.

"Good Christ, woman, what happened to you?"

"A mishap," she answered curtly.

"A mishap!" he repeated.

"I fell."

"On somebody's fist." He didn't like the concerned feeling the sight of those bruises stirred in him. His tone of voice sharpened. "Unless I'm mistaken those four blue bruises on your cheekbone came from some pretty heavy knuckles."

When she didn't say anything, Jared studied her abused face. She had a gash from her right temple into her hairline, her left eye was black and swollen, her lip was cut and that cheekbone with the knuckle imprint was twice the size of the high, sharp crest on the other side of her face. "I've seen men come out of a Saturday night brawl looking better than you do right now."

"It doesn't matter, Mr. Stratton. Please may we talk about the matter at hand?"

"I think we'd better talk about how you got like that first."

"I fell," she insisted firmly. "I tripped on my skirt hem at the top of a very high flight of steps and I fell all the way to the bottom. I have no more control over how it looks to you than I did over the marks that were left," she recited.

Jared let silence fill the air, staring her down. Beneath the bruises and swollen flesh she could well be easy on the eyes. Hell, even with the bruises she was easier on the eyes than the women who had preceded her. And she didn't seem flighty. That was important. He didn't want a flighty woman.

But he also didn't want a woman who was running from something.

"So you fell down a flight of stairs," he mused. "Let's say I went around this city of yours asking who knew Glenna Ashe and if it was true she was so clumsy she tripped over her skirts. What do you think I'd find out?"

He saw her back go straighter. She was tempted to call his bluff; he had played enough poker to see that. But then it looked as if she thought better of it. Her aqua eyes met his squarely. "My stepfather did this."

The sound of that rang true. "Why?"

"That's my business."

"All right." He postulated again, "Then let's say I take you on as my wife and we head for Kansas. Am I going to have this stepfather of yours on my trail?"

She laughed mirthlessly. "No."

That, too, sounded honest. "Then you're a free woman?"

She hesitated again, for just a moment. "Yes. I'm twenty-two years old, I have never been married nor even betrothed and I can do as I please."

Jared continued to watch her. He had the sense that she was telling him the truth. But not all of it. He jutted out his chin and scratched the underside, his beard making a grating sound in the silence as he thought about his own situation.

He'd been gone for nearly two months now, first to Topeka and then these past two weeks here. He had to get home. There was no more time to waste. But since he hadn't done what he'd set out to do in Chicago, he had need of a wife. With women as scarce as hens' teeth in Kansas, he'd decided to take one home with him. And this one was the first he'd met who didn't repulse him.

"The last thing I need is a parcel of trouble, Miss Ashe," he warned her. "And I never learned to suffer liars kindly. If there's more behind this than just wanting to get away from a bad home, the first sign I have of it, I'll dump you in the middle of the prairie and leave you flat," he told her matter-of-factly.

"There's no more to it."

That had come smoothly. It might even be the truth.

Still he stared, wanting to see if his steady scrutiny unnerved her any more now than it had at the door.

Again, she held her ground. That impressed him and set him to thinking about the prospect of taking her on as his wife. She seemed determined, strong willed, and she had to have an even stronger constitution to be doing what she was doing in the shape she was in. Those were all assets. He couldn't take any less of a woman to the life he lived. She was on the small side, but her spunk ought to make up for that—at least it wouldn't take much to feed her. And he had to face the fact that getting a wife through an advertisement in the newspaper was a risk any way you looked at it.

"My brother Joseph and I own a six-thousand-acre cattle ranch in Kansas," he stated flatly.

He saw her swallow again and breathe as if she hadn't in the past few minutes. "The advertisement said Kansas," she agreed amiably, a slight note of relief sounding in her voice.

"Do you know anything about life on the prairie, Miss Ashe?" he asked facetiously. It was obvious by the way she carried herself that she was a city girl born and bred.

"No," she admitted.

"It's a wagonful of hard times," he understated. "Do you know what a doubletree is?"

"It yokes two horses together so they can share the burden of pulling a heavy wagon."

"On the prairie marriage is a doubletree." He let her think about that for a moment. "My house is a forty-minute buggy ride from the nearest town. Everything we eat we plant, tend, harvest, collect, slaughter or cure ourselves. There's no household help and if the ranch hands' cook takes ill you do that job, too. The chickens are yours to tend, and the pigs yours to raise. There's no Chinaman to do the laundry, or bakery to make the bread. If we run out of store-bought soap before I can get into town you make your own and if we use up the lamp oil, you make candles. When the dry spells leave nothing but a drizzle coming out of the pump you carry water a half mile from the nearest stream. You doctor the sick and prepare the bodies of the dead. And I have a year-old son that needs raising, too."

He let that drop like a rock to watch her reaction. Her eyes widened slightly, but that was the extent of it, so he went on. "I need a woman to care for my house and my son. In return I'll be a generous husband, provide every comfort I can, never gamble away the roof over our heads, never womanize and—" under the circumstances, he couldn't suppress a smile at this one "—rarely drink to excess."

She eyed him dubiously. "I wouldn't like a drunkard for a husband."

He eyed her back, still grinning. "No, I don't suppose you would." But he offered no more explanation.

Now it was her turn to stare him down but Jared was every bit as stubborn. She might as well learn right off that just as with her, it took more than a look to break him.

"Am I to believe that your present condition is due to a rare celebration?" she persisted.

Jared breathed a short, ironic laugh. "A celebration? No, I wouldn't say that."

"What would you say?"

He stared directly into her eyes for a time. What should he say? That realizing he couldn't go through with what he'd come to Chicago to do, and not knowing if he could live with not doing it, had put him nose-down in a glass rather than thinking about it anymore? No.

"I'd say that's my business. The same way the beating you took is yours. I suppose taking a mate like this leaves us both with some wondering to do about what's behind it."

He watched her ponder that, her expression showing that she was debating what his reasons might be. But in the end she settled for "Then do I have your word of honor that this is not something you often indulge in?"

He gave it without hesitation. "You do."

She seemed to accept his word with a change of subject. "How long have you been a widower?"

He closed his eyes and leaned his head back farther into the settee cushion. "I've been alone since the boy was born," he said grimly.

"I'm sorry."

After a few moments he opened his eyes again. "If I take you on I'll expect you to care for the boy as if he were your own and pledge to stay on no matter how hard times get."

She frowned back at him. "You say that like a threat. If we agree to marry there's no question about either of those, is there?"

"I want your word on it," he demanded.

"You have it."

Jared took a deep breath. He put his feet flat on the floor and sat on the edge of the settee. With his elbows on his spread knees and his hands clasped, he leaned far forward to scrutinize her. "Do you want the job?"

"Do you mean will I marry you?"

"One and the same."

She didn't answer readily. Instead she chewed on the inside of her bottom lip for a moment and looked around the room. He watched her take in his discarded coat on the floor, his vest on the table, his boot in the doorway and then, at last, him. He could tell she didn't like what she saw.

But she took a careful breath and stuck out her chin at him. "Yes, I will marry you."

He nodded just once. "What time is it anyway?" he asked as he felt automatically for his pocket watch and found only soiled shirtfront.

"About eight-thirty," she informed him flatly.

"Well, the first thing I need is some sleep. Then we'll have to get you to a doctor."

"I don't need a doctor," she said firmly, her expression about as stubborn as any he had ever seen.

This time it didn't matter that it caused him pain. Jared frowned anyway, and gave her a display of his own stubbornness. "There won't be a wedding without one."

"I'm perfectly fit," she insisted.

He bored through her with his eyes. "I can see for myself that that isn't true, Miss Ashe. But even if it appeared so, I'd still be taking you to a doctor before I married you. Advertising for a wife brings some interesting women out of the woodwork, all of them desperate in one way or another. Now, I'll grant you that maybe you just want away from a heavy-handed stepfather, but I can't take the chance that a dalliance with some beau left you in a family way and that was what riled your stepfather in the first place. I'm taking on a wife here, not someone else's bastard to boot. So I'll have a doctor's word that that's all I'm getting or I won't have you."

Her eyes flashed anger but she controlled it. Then she looked down at her lap for a moment before stating her own terms. "All right. But not here. I left home to stay with an aunt and I don't want to draw my stepfather's attention by seeing a doctor or marrying here. I want out of Chicago before he…thinks twice about my leaving and comes after me again. Joliet isn't too far away. We could go there."

Jared's suspicions rose slightly. She'd come up with that suggestion pretty smoothly, as if she had already thought it out. But in the end he decided there wasn't any harm in allowing what she asked. It didn't make much difference to him whether it was a doctor in Chicago or in Joliet that checked her over. A short time in the other city would tell him whether or not she was being followed, and he knew from coming in that the train stopped there, that he could get back to Hays City as well from there as here.

He shrugged and swung his feet up onto the arm of the settee. Laying his head on the other arm, he clasped his hands over his belly and turned only his head to stare at her. "Suit yourself," he said. "Write your address on a piece of paper and leave it on the table. I'll hire a rig and pick you up at five tomorrow morning. But know this, Miss Ashe, if I get a bad report on you you'll find your own way back here." He turned his head to face the ceiling and closed his eyes, dismissing her.

But she didn't move. He could feel her staring at him. After this had gone on for a time he opened his eyes and slowly turned his head her way again. "Is there something else?"

Still she stared at him.

Jared stared back.

"No, there isn't," she answered him curtly. Then she pulled her hat back on, stuffed that red lambs'-wool hair of hers into it, tied the ribbon under her chin and tugged the veil into place.

Jared watched her still as she followed his instructions, finding paper and pen on the round dining table placed between two chairs near the bar. She pushed his vest aside, wrote out the address he had requested and walked to the door. "I'll be ready" was all she said before she left.

Jared pushed his shoulders into the settee to find a more comfortable spot, closed eyes that burned like fire and settled in to go back to sleep.

In his mind lingered an image of Glenna Ashe. He couldn't help wondering what she would look like once all those bruises healed . . . and what had happened to get them for her.

Chapter Three

Even though the walk back to the town house was uneventful, Glenna was relieved when she slipped inside the front door. The next time she stepped foot out again it would be to leave Chicago with Jared Stratton.

But she didn't want to think about Jared Stratton, and the sound of Mary's laughter coming from the dining room was the perfect excuse not to.

She headed in that direction, on the way shedding the veiled hat and leaving it on the knobbed handle of one of Aunt Lida's canes sticking up out of the umbrella stand. With both hands, she lifted her hair off her neck, ruffled it up from where it had matted against her head and then shook it out. She hoped it was cooler in Kansas than it was in Chicago.

Just before Glenna reached the entrance to the dining room the sound of a man's voice carried to her. She recognized it instantly—the voice of Aunt Lida's grandson, Carter Lamb. Out of town on a business errand, Carter had been due back today, but he hadn't been expected until later this afternoon.

Glenna stepped into the doorway, but once there, unnoticed, she spent a moment taking stock of the three people dearest to her.

Sitting in one of four ladder-back chairs at the small, scarred mahogany table, was plump, mellon-cheeked Aunt Lida. Pale yellow yarn was webbed through her gnarled hands and she knitted feverishly. Not really Glenna's aunt, Lida was her maternal grandmother's best friend. As close as sisters, they had shared widowhood and Lida's town house until Glenna's grandmother's death a dozen years ago. Both before and since, Lida had been as much a part of the Ashe family as Glenna's own grandmother.

Carter stood at the chipped sideboard pouring himself a cup of coffee. The tall, spindly man had been raised by the two dowagers when his parents had both died in a fire. As a result, Glenna and Carter had grown up together. She felt as close to him as she would have to a brother. He was a good, kind, gentle man who used the wages he earned as a bank teller to support Aunt Lida. It was not a prosperous living, and it didn't please Glenna to think of adding to Carter's burden with the care of her sister. But for the time being she had no choice.

And then there was Mary.

The little girl held a snow-white kitten in an awkward grip against her chest. Paying scant attention to Aunt Lida and Carter's discussion of the previous night's rain, Mary swung her head this way and that like a pendulum so that the soft fur tickled the underside of her chin. Thin flaxen strands of hair fell around her delicate face and onto her narrow shoulders, which swayed with the movement. Her eyes were closed, and she looked deceptively peaceful. Glenna hated to disturb that. But before she so much as took a step into the room the child sensed her presence.

"Glenna? Is that you?" she asked, opening her sightless eyes to stare in no particular direction.

"It's me," Glenna answered, moving to the chair beside her sister and sitting down.

The air in the room suddenly thickened with tension and Mary's expression reflected it. Her grip on the kitten tightened. But she forced a small smile and said, "Do you see what I have?"

"Yes, I see. Where did you get it?" Glenna played along, herself loath to talk about the errand from which she had just come.

"Carter brought him for Aunt Lida but she said I could have him. Can I?"

"I don't know why not, if Aunt Lida doesn't mind."

"No, I don't mind. I've three of my own as it is," Lida put in quickly. A few soft white curls that didn't quite conceal her pink scalp showed outside of the dowager's cap she wore. She sat on the other side of Mary and glanced up only once to look at Glenna. Her face was as pleated as a party dress, the skin of her neck like folds of a loose bodice gathered and cinched at a narrow waist. Her head shook slightly in a tremor that seemed to match the frenzied speed of her needlework as she bent back to it.

"How are you, Glenna?" Carter whispered as he came to sit in the chair between his grandmother and Glenna. Setting his cup on the threadbare linen tablecloth, he reached over and covered her hand with his.

But before Glenna could answer him Mary chimed in with the bluntness of a nine-year-old who had been blinded since birth and took being sightless in her stride. "Why are you whispering, Carter? I can hear you anyway. I can't see but I hear very well."

Carter laughed nervously and looked to Glenna for help. She forced a laugh, shook her head and rescued her old friend. "Don't pay her any mind, Carter. I'm fine." Then she gently chastised her sister. "You know Carter never speaks loudly, Mary, and please remember your manners."

"You don't look fine," Carter insisted, narrowing his nondescript hazel eyes at her.

"Carter," Aunt Lida hushed him, glancing sideways at Mary.

"I think this is the softest cat in the whole world." Mary persisted in pretending she was oblivious to the undertone in the room. "Feel him, Glenna."

Glenna petted the animal with long, slow strokes. "What are you going to call him?" she asked, as inclined as her sister to stall.

"Thornton," the little girl said without a pause. "After our old butler, because he used to make the same rumbling sound when he napped in the pantry. That's how I knew he was in there." Still she moved her head like a slow pendulum over the cat's fur.

"Mother's explained everything to me," Carter said then, sighing through pinhole nostrils and pursing his thin lips. "I don't like it."

"Feel Thornton's nose, Glenna," Mary interrupted. "It feels so funny."

"Thornton doesn't want his nose felt," Glenna informed her sister when she had tried and the cat had impatiently ducked away.

"Glenna," Carter said a little louder than usual, impatience in his tone. "I said I don't like your thinking about marrying some stranger and going off to the wilderness with him."

"Feel his side, Glenna," Mary persisted. "He's purring for me."

Glenna obliged her sister but finally answered her friend in a purely practical tone of voice. "I don't like it either, Carter, but there isn't anything else I can do." She hesitated a moment and then added, "And I'm not just thinking about it. He's accepted me."

Mary stopped the pendulum swing of her head. The clack of Aunt Lida's knitting needles sped up. Carter was speechless.

Glenna felt the need to fill the palpably tense air with words. "Jared Stratton is in his early thirties, I'd say, and he's passably attractive." Not completely a lie. There was no need to tell them he was drunk and disorderly. What good would that do anyone? She continued to present the facts in a way that made them sound better than they actually were. "He seemed considerate enough—wanting me to see a doctor—and amiable enough to let me have my way about waiting until we're out of the city to do it. He owns a big cattle ranch and he has a year-old son...." She suddenly ran out of things she could say about her intended that, even under a rosier glow, wouldn't frighten these people who loved her.

"Will he take me, too?" Mary demanded.

"What did you tell him about...how you were hurt?" Carter said at the same time.

It was Carter whom Glenna answered, in an undertone. "I told him my stepfather had beaten me."

"Did he ask why?" Aunt Lida put in, still rapidly plying those needles.

"Yes. But I just told him it was my business."

"I don't like it," Carter decreed, shaking his head in what resembled his mother's tremor.

"Can I come, too?" Mary reiterated more loudly.

"It will be just fine, Carter," Glenna snapped. Then she took a breath. "I'm sorry. It certainly isn't what I would have chosen for myself, either, but truly, I think it will be just fine. I even managed to convince him to go to Joliet to be married—Aunt Lida said if only I could get there her friend would probably buy some of Momma's jewelry.... Anyway, he'll be here at five tomorrow morning, and that will get me out of this city, which is my only hope now. Kansas must be a good place because so many people are going there to start their lives over, and I mean to do just that...."

"What about me?" Mary's softer voice was so much harder to ignore as it crept in when Glenna ran out of steam.

She couldn't look at her sister. Instead she watched her own hands pinching the limp tablecloth into peaks in front of her. She swallowed back a lump in her throat and spoke gently, but firmly. "We talked about this last night. The advertisement said he would not accept a woman with a family, Mary. You know what we planned. You'll keep Aunt Lida and Carter company for a little while until Mr. Stratton gets used to me and I can sell Momma's jewelry. Then I'll send for you. It won't be long, I promise you that."

Mary started to swing her head against the kitten's fur again, only now it was a slow, mournful motion. Tears welled in her eyes and began to spill. "I wish you hadn't told on David. You never should have told, Glenna."

"I had to, Mary," Glenna answered in a choked voice.

"I want to stay with you...." Mary pressed her mouth into the kitten's neck.

Glenna's own eyes filled and stung. Carter clasped her shoulder but there was no comfort for her. "I know you do—" She caught her breath. "Mary, just listen to me...."

The child cut her off with nine-year-old logic. "If he has a son why can't you bring your sister? I wouldn't have to bring Thornton."

"I don't know why. I only know I couldn't take the chance that anything would make him refuse to accept me. Try to understand, Mary. I don't have any other way out of Chicago, nowhere to go, no one who can help...." Her voice dwindled off into a plea. She strengthened it and went on with a semblance of optimism. "But once we're married and I have the money for your journey and keep, it will be different. Then we can be together again."

"I don't want to wait," the little girl said pitifully.

"We'll have a fine time," Carter put in feebly. "And then when Glenna comes back for you, Thornton will be big enough to take along to Kansas, too."

"What if Glenna doesn't come back?" Mary reasoned fearfully with Carter.

Glenna smoothed her sister's hair away from her face and spoke with strong conviction. "Nothing could make that happen."

"You could die like Momma did."

"But I won't. No matter what, we'll be together again." Glenna's heart was in her throat. She tried to swallow it back and sound normal but she didn't quite manage. "And in the meantime you need to keep working with Mrs. Stidwell on your Braille and your lessons."

"What if Aunt Lida dies and Carter dies and David comes after me and tries to hurt me, too?" Mary hugged the kitten so hard it tried to get away.

It was the kitten's cry that Glenna addressed because it was easier. "Careful not to squeeze Thornton too hard or he'll scratch you."

"I want to come with you, Glenna."

"You can't," Glenna answered too sharply, her own pain and frustration making her temper short. Then she reached for her sister and pulled the delicate little girl onto her lap, cat and all. Sighing, she propped her chin on Mary's shoulder and tried explaining it all yet again. "If there was anything I could do to take you with me, I would. You know that. But I can't. If I don't get out of Chicago very, very soon, David or the police will find me and put me in jail. I don't have the money to leave on my own, let alone pay your way, too, and nowhere to go if I did. I can't sell Momma's jewelry here or they'll catch me, and that means Jared Stratton is my only hope."

"But what if David comes after me?" Mary persisted.

"You know he won't do that. You were asleep when—" Glenna sighed again. "There's nothing you can do to...bother him. It's only me he wants to pay back."

"Because you told," Mary accused again. "And it didn't even do any good."

"No, it didn't," Glenna agreed. "But what's done is done, and now all we can do is go on."

"Everything will be all right, Mary," Aunt Lida reassured.

"And before you even know she's gone, Glenna will be back for you," Carter put in.

"Do you promise you'll come back and get me?" the child asked in defeat.

Glenna hugged her sister hard and held on, her own throat constricted again. "I swear it," she whispered because this time she couldn't even force her voice to sound normal. "I swear it."

Jared scraped the last of the suds off his jaw and splashed his face with water from the basin. It was cold and brisk, just what he needed to wake himself up at four in the morning. Then he reached for the towel that hung over the lyre-shaped back of the washstand and patted his face dry.

He'd be glad to get out of this city. With any luck he'd never have to set eyes on it again.

He'd been here only once before—ten years ago with Bill to settle a small inheritance his boyhood friend had gained from a grandfather. It had been a lark for the two of them, both having grown up on the Kansas prairie, to see a place so different from Topeka or Wichita or even Kansas City. They had been two twenty-year-olds looking to have a good time in the big city. Neither of them had expected to come home with a wife. But Jared had.

He'd met Janie innocently enough at a party given by some distant cousin of Bill's. She had been just another guest who had caught each young man's eye the minute she'd arrived. She had seemed to take an instant dislike to Bill. And just as instant a liking to Jared. And Jared...

Jared had loved her, more than he thought any man could love any woman. He had impulsively married her and whisked her away from her family in Chicago to take her home to Kansas.

He shook his head to clear it of those memories and palmed his brush to rake it through his hair. Janie was gone and he'd had more than a year to learn that thoughts like these did him no good.

He gathered his shaving gear and went to the bed to toss all of his toiletries carelessly into his valise there. It was all over with, he reminded himself as he took a chambray shirt that hung over the bedpost and slipped it on.

The tails of his shirt dangled around his denim-clad hips as he rolled the sleeves up to his elbows. He scanned the room as he fastened the buttons, making sure he had packed everything. There was a stray sock sticking out from under the nightstand and he went to fetch it, throwing it into his bag before he tucked his shirt into his pants.

Now it was time to get on with his life. Simple as that.

"Simple?" he said with bitter humor. There wasn't anything simple about taking on another wife. He jabbed his belt through the loops of his jeans.

Much like the first time he'd come to Chicago, a wife was the last thing he'd figured on bringing home. But it had turned out to be the only answer.

A man alone could do just fine on the prairie; but add children and you needed a woman. So he'd gotten himself one. A new pair of boots, a new Sunday suit, a new repeater rifle and a woman. In that order.

Jared sat on the bed and pulled on his socks. The boots needed a little breaking in, but he liked them. The suit was plain black serge; he liked it well enough, too. The rifle was a honey. But he had his doubts about the woman.

Why couldn't he quit wondering what she was going to look like dressed in clothes that fit and with all those bruises and all that swelling gone? Hell, he'd even dreamed about her last night.

Maybe he should have chosen a homely one the way he had first intended. Pick a woman with a face like a fence post, he'd told himself when he placed that advertisement.

A strong back was important. A solid character. An even temper. A quiet disposition. Not a pretty face—a pretty face wouldn't get the work done. And he'd already had a pretty woman.

No, Janie had been beautiful....

With one boot half on his foot he stopped and stared straight ahead. It wasn't anything in the room he saw. It wasn't even anything in the present.

Then he jolted himself out of his thoughts yet again, finishing with one boot and plunging his other foot into the second.

It didn't matter what this Ashe woman looked like. The boy needed a mother and that was what she would be. That was *all* she would be.

He closed his valise, pulling the strap that secured it so tightly it cinched well past the last hole where the tongue of the buckle could poke through. He had to let up on it some to fasten it.

No, it didn't matter at all what the woman looked like when those bruises healed. It didn't matter that he had almost enjoyed the challenge of her stubbornness, or that he had been impressed by her stamina and determination. It didn't even make any damn difference that she had porcelain skin or straight shoulders or a soft nape or flame-colored hair. Because he had really only hired her on for a job, not much different than hiring a ranch hand or a new trail boss. He just had to marry this one to get himself a cook, a seamstress, a laundress, a housekeeper, a woman to raise the boy. And that was all there was to it.

Jared swiped up his valise and headed out of the room, nearly colliding with a sleepy-eyed maid carrying an armload of towels. He took a step back against the wall to let her by, not returning the smile she angled up at him in thanks. But even as she passed his glance stayed on her, or more precisely on the bow that tied her hair at the nape of her neck. It was a striking aqua color, the deep bluish-green that the sky turned just before a fierce spring storm. The same deep bluish-green of Glenna Ashe's eyes.

"A hired hand," he muttered firmly to himself through clenched teeth. "Nothing else."

Glenna put the last pin in the knot her hair was twisted into at the base of her neck and tried to smooth the wild wisps at her temples. Some of the swelling had gone out of her cheek, giving her face a more normal contour if not color. But today she barely noticed the unsightliness of the bruises. Today the only thing on her mind was leaving Mary.

She knew that her sister was waiting downstairs with Aunt Lida and Carter to see her off. She also knew she was purposely dawdling.

Mary would have Aunt Lida and Carter, she reminded herself. She would have her studies with the same teacher she had been working with for three years now. She would get used to Glenna's not being around. She would be fine. Just fine.

Glenna needed to believe that.

Finished with her hair, she took her brush and stuffed it into the side of her valise.

She was wearing her own clothes today, as leaving before dawn freed her from the necessity of a disguise. Unlike her cheek, however, the swelling along her side had not gone down and the waist of her plain brown traveling dress was uncomfortable. For a moment she considered wearing Aunt Lida's heavy widow's weeds again; she discarded that idea when she thought about sitting atop a wagon seat all day under the hot sun.

The muted clop of horse's hooves on the dirt road drifted up to her; Glenna froze and listened. Part of her hoped it wasn't Jared Stratton, that he would never come for her. But the more rational part of her hoped it was he, so she could get on with this.

The sounds grew louder and then a deep voice calmly called "Whoa," just out front.

She had a sudden flash of the man to whom she was about to entrust her life—drunk and slovenly, caustic, sardonic, rude...

How many times had she gone over this since meeting him yesterday morning? Too many. The list never got any better and neither did Glenna's doubts about the course she had set for herself.

"Glenna? Mr. Stratton's here," Carter called up the stairs to her. It sounded so simple, so ordinary, as if the man were coming to take her for a Sunday ride in the country.

Glenna's stomach lurched. Was he even sober today?

"Glenna? Did you hear me?" Carter said again.

She swallowed and said, "Yes," but it came out so weakly despite her effort that she knew he hadn't heard her. She cleared her throat and tried again. "I'm coming."

Actually what she wanted to do was sneak down the back stairs and out the kitchen door. For a moment she wasn't sure marrying Jared Stratton was preferable to going to jail. She doubted the place smelled any worse than his hotel room had.

But of course she wasn't going to do that. She closed her satchel and pulled on the short pelisse that matched her dress.

"Can I take your bags downstairs?" Now Carter's voice came from just outside in the hallway after a knock on the bedroom door.

Who was in such a hurry? Carter or Mr. Stratton? "Come in, Carter," she said instead, hating the tension that edged her own voice.

The willowy man opened the door and bustled in with only a furtive glance her way. "He's waiting," Carter admonished slightly.

Let him wait. "Carter?" she said to stop him just before he rushed out with her satchels the same way he had rushed in. He stopped and turned sad eyes on her. "You will take care of Mary? I know she'll be a burden, but I'll send for her as soon as I can."

Carter cleared his throat now. "She won't be a burden, and don't you worry about her. Just take care of yourself." Then he sighed in a way that made his shoulders shrug. "At least this Stratton *seems* like a decent man. I was worried that anyone who advertised for a wife would be a lout or a brute."

And he isn't? she nearly blurted out, for she considered him both. But before she could say anything her old friend went on.

"He's downstairs now reassuring Grandmother that he'll take good care of you. And I believe he will. I'll tell you the truth, Glenna, it almost seems as if this man was heaven-sent to get you out of this predicament."

Heaven-sent? Were they talking about the same man? Another thought struck her all of a sudden. If Jared Stratton was downstairs with Aunt Lida and Mary, the little girl might say something about coming with them, or about Glenna sending for her later on. "I'd better not leave Mary alone with him," she said and hurried around Carter.

Nearly bounding down the stairs, Glenna came upon a scene that stopped her in her tracks. With her hands clasped in front of her, Aunt Lida looked on approvingly as Mary stood in the center of the parlor feeling the face of a man hunkered down in front of her.

Glenna stared at the man, in profile. It was Jared Stratton, all right, but not the Jared Stratton she had met yesterday morning.

This man, who calmly and with his eyes closed allowed her sister the method she used for becoming acquainted with a person's appearance, bore only a slight resemblance to the Jared Stratton of yesterday. It was the same square brow, the same very thin, pointed nose, the same prominent cheekbones and chiseled jawline. But he was clean-shaven, save for the bushy wheat-colored mustache, which was now neatly trimmed. His golden hair glistened with streaks the shade of pale sunshine. His chambray shirt was crisply pressed, the denim trousers that molded massive thighs were clean, and his boots looked new.

He looked new.

She would certainly never have expected the man she had met yesterday to fold his tall, massive body into a crouch to accommodate a little blind girl's whim, let alone to do it in a way that made him seem so patient and gentle. Glenna didn't quite know what to do. And she definitely didn't know what to think.

"Oh, Glenna, there you are," Aunt Lida said.

Instantly, Mary took her hands away from Jared Stratton's face. The man stood and glanced over at her as the little girl listened for the direction from which Glenna was coming.

"Here I am," she answered so that Mary would know where she was, but rather than looking at her sister, Glenna kept her gaze on Jared Stratton. For the first time she noticed that his eyes were the darkest, most riveting shade of green she had ever seen.

And then Mary was in her arms, holding on to Glenna's waist for dear life.

"Good morning, Miss Ashe." There was no mistaking that deep baritone voice, though it was slightly less gravelly than the day before.

Glenna nodded just once. "Mr. Stratton," she answered, inclining her head slightly. Yesterday it had been easier to understand his need to advertise for a wife. But today he looked like a man most girls would be plotting to snare as a husband. It was a confusing revelation.

Just then Carter came into the parlor with her bags. "Shall I put these out on the buggy?"

It was Jared who answered. "I'll take them. I imagine you all have some goodbyes to say." Then with manners that had been nowhere in existence the day before, he told Aunt Lida he was happy to have met her, shook Carter's hand and ran the back of a single index finger down Mary's cheek, saying softly, "Take good care of that kitten, little one." He picked up Glenna's bags and left.

"He seems very nice," Aunt Lida breathed with a note of relief, breaking the ensuing silence. "It makes me feel much better to have you going off with a man like that."

"He liked me, Glenna," Mary said, tilting up her face to her sister's. "Maybe he would take me along after all."

Hope chimed in the child's voice and tore at Glenna. "You know what we've planned, Mary."

"But—"

Glenna cut off the plea. "I can't ask him. You know that."

Mary pulled back, letting her arms drop to her sides. "You could ask," she said in a small, accusing voice.

Jared Stratton's kindness had only made this more difficult. "I can't ask. He was very firm about not accepting a woman with a child. But you're right, he did like you, and that will make it all the easier to convince him to let you come live with us a little later on." Then Glenna forced her voice to sound as normal as if she were going on a brief holiday. "Be a good girl for Aunt Lida and Carter, and study hard. I'll write to you every chance I get."

Aunt Lida stepped up behind Mary and took her by the shoulders. "You'll be with Glenna before you know it, child."

Mary's eyes filled with tears. Instantly, Glenna's answered in kind. "It will be all right, Mary. I promise. Give me a hug," she said through a clogged throat, holding out her arms.

Mary hesitated but finally stepped back into Glenna's embrace, burying her head against her breasts. "I don't want you to go," the little girl sobbed.

Glenna couldn't say anything at all. She just couldn't. Tears rolled down her face and fell into Mary's hair. Somehow the pain of the child's hug around her abused rib cage seemed like no less than she deserved.

Aunt Lida had turned away from the scene and stood sniffling a few feet from them. It was Carter who came to them, pulling Mary to cry against his stomach instead. His own eyes were red-rimmed and cloudy. "Go, before the sun comes up, Glenna," he said softly.

She nodded but she couldn't make herself move. Instead she put her hand out for one last touch of her sister's head. "I love you, Mary," she whispered because it was all she could manage.

But the little girl pulled out of her reach, sobbing and holding on tighter to Carter. Glenna looked up at her friend. He nodded toward the front door. "She'll be fine," he mouthed. "Go on."

Glenna took a breath that rattled all the way into her lungs. She put her hand out to smooth Mary's head again but closed it into a fist before she had touched her and pulled it back again.

There was no choice.

Glenna turned very slowly, took a few steps toward the front door and then looked back over her shoulder. She couldn't make herself leave. There had to be another way.

"Glenna?" It was Jared Stratton's voice. He was standing just outside the front door as if he had come back to see what was keeping her. But his tone was soft, understanding, as gentle as he had appeared to be with Mary moments before. And then he opened the screen and held out his hand to her, big and rough and callused. "Come," he invited tenderly, in a way that made her think everything would be all right.

There was no other choice, she reminded herself yet again. She cast one more glance back at her family, at Mary.

No choice.

And then she took Jared Stratton's hand.

Chapter Four

I'll have the truth now."

The sun was just rising in the east in pale shades of summer squash-yellow and persimmon pink. Chicago was a jagged silhouette against it as Jared pulled the two-seater shay off the road and stopped just outside of the city.

Glenna had long since dried her tears and accepted her situation. In fact, as they had rolled through the streets of Chicago, each block taking her a little farther away from the dangers there, she had begun to feel the slightest twinge of excitement. Until now.

She stared out at the sunrise, not looking at Jared. "Pardon me?" she said, even though she had heard him.

She could feel his eyes on her but refused to look his way. The cool early morning air was beginning to warm up and she was suddenly aware of the fact that they were sitting so close to each other in the small rented buggy that his thigh was on top of her skirts and pressed against her own leg.

Much too much time elapsed in silence and Glenna was becoming increasingly uncomfortable. Finally Jared repeated, "I said I'll have the truth now."

"I don't think I understand."

Silence again.

Glenna didn't like it. Steeling herself for the worst, she turned and met his eyes with her own.

For a moment he held her gaze, then, in a voice that seemed to boom through the silence of the morning, he said, "You came to my room dressed like a pauper yesterday. My impression was that you came from genteel poverty, that you had been reduced to circumstances that forced you to seek out a husband through a newspaper advertisement—an abusive stepfather, most likely a family that would be glad for one less mouth to feed, yourself with no alternatives."

That story would do. Glenna raised an eyebrow at him as if to agree with all he said.

It obviously didn't convince him because he went on as if she hadn't responded in any way, reaching to finger the linen of her cuff. "These aren't the clothes of any kind of poverty, genteel or otherwise."

He waited, apparently expecting his stare to intimidate her into confessing. Glenna wished he would let go of her sleeve. The backs of his fingers rubbed against her wrist and made her all too aware of his touch.

"All right," he said after a moment more of her silence. "Not only are your clothes a surprise after the way you presented yourself yesterday, but there's your family. Your aunt and her grandson were obviously uncomfortable with our arrangement. I had the impression they were giving you up reluctantly, as if it was only because their hands were tied. And then there's your sister. It was clear that neither of you wanted to be separated. So why didn't you just leave your stepfather's abuse and live, along with Mary, in your aunt's town house? None of this adds up. And you and I aren't going one inch farther until I know why."

"Lida Lamb isn't really my aunt," she hedged. "She's just a family friend."

"But you could have stayed with her. Your sister is," he persisted.

Glenna looked at the sunrise again. "Carter supports them both on a bank teller's salary. I would have been a burden."

"You could have gotten work to pay your share. By being left behind, Mary will be just that, a burden. What are you running from, Miss Ashe?"

His use of formal address was clearly a warning. But Glenna's position was too tenuous for her to trust him with her story. "I didn't do anything wrong," she blurted out.

"Then what—" he pronounced each word slowly and distinctly "—are you running from?"

"Nothing," she said much too quickly. She could feel his gaze, as hard and cold as stone.

"That's a lie," Jared decreed. And then, without another word, he clicked his tongue at the horse and turned back toward the city of her birth.

The action brought Glenna around to look at him. His jaw was set, he stared straight ahead at the horse's rump, and he seemed as implacable as a marble statue. "No, wait!" she said in a hurry.

Jared slowed the horse to an amble and then stopped the shay smack-dab in the center of the road, facing Chicago. With the reins dangling loosely in his grip, his elbows braced on his knees, he turned his head her way. It was obvious she had better talk fast or else.

Glenna took in the frown that creased his square brow. "All right," she conceded reluctantly. "I'll tell you the truth."

"I'm waiting," he said when she didn't immediately make good on her word.

Glenna took a deep breath and sighed. "My real father died eight years ago, leaving my mother, Mary and me nearly destitute. A buggy accident just before Mary was born had left Papa paralyzed. We lost his apothecary shop and almost everything else by the time he passed away.

"It was Aunt Lida who introduced Momma to David Stern—my stepfather—just as soon as a suitable period of mourning had passed. He was a distant relation of one of her late husband's friends and he owned Stern Farm Implements. He was very wealthy, but he had had a crude up-bringing. My mother, whose family was highborn but, as you said, of genteel poverty, appealed to him.''

Pride made Glenna's voice quiet. ''By then we had literally nothing. We were living off the charity of Aunt Lida and Carter, a clothing drive from the church had replaced our worn things....'' She swallowed. Pride wouldn't allow her to go into any more details. ''Momma's own health was frail. There was no work she could do and I was too young.... So she accepted David Stern. They were married slightly more than a year after my father's death and we all moved into his grand house.'' Still low, her voice turned hard. ''They had been married only a month when he hit her for the first time.'' It was a sound Glenna would never forget, and for a moment she couldn't say anything more.

''How long before he hit you?''

''He hardly paid any attention to Mary or me. He instructed Momma to keep us dressed as was befitting his image as an eminently successful businessman, but beyond that he didn't want us anywhere around him, we weren't even allowed to eat at his table. I guess that disassociation spared us because it was only Momma that he beat. He was a strange man. One minute he could be kind and charming, the next, something as silly as a spot on his boot could provoke a rage in him. Not even Momma understood it, but she made me promise that I would never interfere or try to stop him, that the moment I knew anything was amiss I would take Mary up into the nursery and keep her safe....'' The feeling of helplessness was another harshly vivid memory that Glenna fought against. How many times had she run to help her mother only to have Sybil shriek for her to go and take care of her sister?

Glenna's gaze drifted out to the sunrise once more as she spoke softly, ''Poor Mary. I'd rock her and hold my hands over her ears so she wouldn't hear....''

She was silent again for a time before Jared prompted. "Go on."

"Besides his foul temper and the beatings, my stepfather drank excessively and flaunted an array of... women of ill repute. Regardless of the fact that he had married my mother to better himself he resented her being more educated and well mannered. He seemed to think of her as some sort of insult to him. He ranted as he beat her, more often than not raving about taking her down a peg and teaching her to respect him. And then, three weeks ago..." Glenna's voice caught and she had to stop for a moment.

She looked down at her lap before taking a deep breath, then she raised her chin stubbornly and forged on. "Three weeks ago he came home late at night, very drunk and in a blacker fury than any before. He slammed the front door so hard he broke the glass out of it—that's what woke me. I knew what was coming so I got up and was putting on my wrapper to go to Mary, when I heard Momma come out of her room. He started hitting her before she had said a word and he kept at it and at it...."

Glenna had to close her eyes at the thought and swallow back the bile that rose to her throat. "I snuck out to go to Mary. That was when I heard the banister break. He had hit her into it. She was trying to regain her balance, and he saw that. He reached out, I thought he was going to pull her back... we were on the third floor of his house, but instead... he pushed her...."

Glenna took a deep breath and drew herself up very, very straight. Disbelief and anger mingled in her tone. "He walked back out the front door without even looking at her. She was dead by the time I got to her. I ran to a neighbor and when the authorities came I told them everything. David was arrested. I thought he'd be hanged." She laughed bitterly. "But it seems that money buys some powerful friends even for madmen—one of his was a judge. David paid him to rule my mother's death an accident. I know because he bragged about it when he was let go the day before yesterday.''

"And he came after you. My guess is he didn't take too kindly to your accusations."

"Or to the money it had cost him to get out of it," she confirmed wryly. "He found me at Aunt Lida's—Mary and I had both moved there. I was alone in the house. He barged in, in fact, he kicked the front door open and broke the lock. I tried to get away, but . . ."

Glenna swallowed with difficulty, working hard to contain a shudder at the memory of the man's blows. "After he gave me a taste of what my mother had been enduring, he threw her jewelry box at me and explained what he had planned as retribution for my embarrassing him and costing him a small fortune in bribery money. It wasn't going to cost much more to persuade his friend the judge that I was a thief who had robbed my benevolent stepfather of the jewelry he had given my mother."

Glenna shook her head. "He was so arrogant. He said it didn't really matter if the police found the jewelry or not, but that he didn't want anything that had belonged to my mother in the house. He said I would spend ten years in jail—he thought that was just about enough to punish me for my meddling."

She sighed. "The authorities came not fifteen minutes after he'd left. I had run upstairs, thinking to pack quickly and leave the house . . . though I don't know where I would have gone. But they were banging on the door before I had done more than throw a few of my things in a satchel."

"How did you get away?"

"During the war Aunt Lida had the stairway to her attic camouflaged behind some paneling—just in case the Confederates invaded and she had need to hide. I barely made it there before the police came in. I listened to them search for me but they never found the stairs." She took a breath.

"And that's all of it." Or at least all of what had led her to him.

This time it was Jared who studied the sunrise. His expression was inscrutable. Glenna's heart pounded in her ears; so much was at stake.

"What happened to the jewelry?" he asked after a while.

To tell him the truth about that was to be left in Chicago. She knew David Stern didn't care about the jewelry, that it was nothing to him and he would never bother coming after her for it. But Jared wasn't likely to believe that. He would think her stepfather was bound to follow her—one of the things that would have caused him to refuse her in the first place. And to say she meant to sell it to have Mary come to live with them was out of the question. So Glenna lied. "The police must have found it and taken it as evidence. They just didn't get me."

Again he let silence sit between them like a tombstone. Then he pierced her with his eyes and said, "So you decided to try your luck with a stranger, answer my advertisement and marry me to get yourself out of Chicago before your stepfather had you locked up."

"That's the whole of it. If he could get himself out of murder, he could certainly have me put away. And as for trying my luck with a stranger, David Stern had come highly recommended by many people who knew him. Familiarity didn't seem to me to be any kind of assurance."

He stared at her and Glenna could tell he was debating whether to believe her. She didn't know what else she could say to convince him and she wouldn't grovel, so she matched his stare with one of her own.

"What about revenge?" Jared said in a way that sounded like a test. "Would you like to come back here and exact a pound of flesh?"

"How does a person take revenge on a rich, powerful madman?" she asked. "And even if there was a way, would it bring my mother back? All it would accomplish is to put me in even more peril than I've already found myself in. That seems foolhardy to me."

"And you can accept that?"

She had, because finding a way to take care of Mary was more important. "I don't fight useless battles, Mr. Stratton. I make the best of what I have."

"I'll just bet you do," he said, half to himself. For a moment he continued to study her. Then he shook his head.

The only indication that he believed her came when he lifted the reins, clicked to the horse and turned the buggy around again, away from Chicago.

"Making the best out of the hand life deals you is something you're going to have need of in Kansas."

The bride wore fading bruises and the groom a frown as Glenna married Jared late that evening in a simple ceremony in front of a Joliet justice of the peace.

It was a far cry from the wedding she had imagined for herself long ago. As a naive girl of fourteen—before the harsh realities of her mother's marriage had tarnished her fanciful thoughts—she had dreamed of this day.

She'd pictured not just a church, but a cathedral as the setting. In her dreams she had been gowned in ivory satin and French lace, with a train so long it would take four little girls to keep it straight. The air would be redolent with the perfume of flowers—yellow rosebuds and tiny white baby's breath. The angelic voices of a children's choir would serenade the hundreds of guests. And then, as she stood at the back of the church, two organs would sound an echo of herald and she would follow the music down the aisle to her anxiously waiting groom—tall and handsome and beaming with the deep and abiding love he felt for her. And when the ceremony, in all its formality and grandeur, was completed, church bells would peel from the spire in announcement and celebration.

Glenna didn't know whether to laugh or cry as she re-membered her daydreams now.

The only flowers were in the faded rug beneath their feet, the only music a discordant howl from a dog out back, the only well-wisher a dour-faced prune of a woman the justice introduced as his wife. There wasn't even a ring for Glen-na's finger. And there was certainly no joy in the room.

Throughout the ceremony Jared didn't even take her hand, but rather stood stick straight with his own hands clasped in front of him as if he were being sentenced for a crime. Out of the corner of her eye Glenna watched him watch the justice.

He hadn't said a dozen words to her throughout the drive to Joliet and she wondered if he was always this quiet. But then she realized she hadn't offered twelve words herself, and gave him the benefit of the doubt.

He was big beside her. Bigger than any man she had ever known before. That was a little intimidating and she com-pensated by standing up straighter. But it wasn't only his height. His chest was as broad as a barrel, and the fact that his waist narrowed to a V only accentuated that. She had had that long buggy ride during which to sereptitiously study his muscular thighs—they had nearly taken up the whole seat—and yet his hips were...

Glenna swallowed and concentrated on the Bible from which the justice read. How could she be standing here thinking about a man's hips?

The justice cleared his throat loudly and Glenna sud-denly realized all eyes, even Jared Stratton's, were on her, waiting. She hadn't heard a word. Her expression must have illustrated that because the justice repeated, "*Do* you, Glenna Ashe, take this man to be your husband?"

"Yes," she blurted and then amended, "I do."

She stared at the justice's sallow face then, focusing on the words she had not heard said to her as he repeated them to this stranger who was about to become her husband. Jared's answer came without hesitation in that resonant voice of his, strong and confident, but not eager.

Why wasn't he eager? she wondered. After all, he had been the one to instigate this.

But before her mind wandered any further the justice's voice penetrated her thoughts. "You, sir, may kiss your bride."

There was a moment when no one moved. It seemed as if neither of them had considered it coming to this. And then she heard her new husband give a sardonic chuckle as he turned to her. Glenna glanced up to that face of his that was all sharp angles and smoothed planes of pure masculinity. She saw an expression that gave her the distinct impression that he was going to kiss her only because it was expected and not because he was the least bit inclined to. She tilted her head upward and a bit to the side, intending to let him know the kiss meant nothing to her, either.

And then those big hands of his came up to cup her shoulders and pull her toward him, surprising her with his gentleness. His eyes met hers. So intense was his stare that Glenna suddenly felt as if there were no one else in the room. One eyebrow cocked up and one side of his mouth curved in a smile that somehow made them coconspirators. Very slowly, he lowered his mouth to hers.

The kiss was light, chaste and just long enough for his mustache to brush her skin and tickle her, before he broke the connection. But then, taking her by surprise, back he came for a second one. This time his lips were parted and his arm encircled her, pulling her all the way in to him. His body felt solid and unyielding and powerful against hers. No one had ever kissed Glenna like that and she wasn't sure what to do. Kissing him back only left her lips puckering up inside his slightly open mouth. It didn't seem quite right and so, learning from him, she let her own lips relax and part.

A new world of sensations opened up to her.

His mouth was warm and a little moist. The feel of it sent heat sluicing all the way down to her toes. The coarse softness of his mustache tickled, but in a nice way. His arms around her felt good, comforting, though nothing at all like the hugs Carter gave or the shy, inexperienced embraces of the two beaus who had kissed her before. There was something about being held like this that invited participation in the same way his parted lips had.

Glenna raised her hands to his chest and found that he seemed even more solid beneath her palms. She could feel his heart beat and the ripple of muscle from the motion of his head as he kissed her. Things she didn't recognize were awakening inside of her, tingling and tickling and very strange.

And then it was over.

He drew away from her, opened his arms and just like that, he was gone.

For a moment Glenna stared up at him, wondering about these sensations still churning in her, this yearning that made her feel as if she had an itch somewhere deep inside that needed scratching. And then she realized she was staring, slack-jawed, and clamped her mouth shut.

But she knew he had seen. One of his eyebrows dipped down in a reflexive half frown, as if he didn't know why something so simple, something that was no more than a pretense, should have affected her. The heat Glenna felt this time was pure embarrassment, which worked its way up her neck and flooded her face. *If you were so unmoved by it, why'd you come back for a second round?* she wanted to say, but of course she didn't. Instead she dropped her head and brushed an imaginary piece of lint from her skirt as if she, too, hadn't given the kiss a second thought. Or at least a third thought.

She didn't look at Jared as he paid the justice. Then, just when her insides were calming down, he took her elbow and shook things up all over again. But Glenna clenched her teeth and held her breath rather than show him any sign of how he affected her. It was fatigue that caused this response anyway, she decided. It wasn't Jared Stratton. Fatigue and nerves.

Only this time when she sat on the buggy seat she hugged the side and angled her knees outward to prevent any contact with his thigh.

Fatigue and nerves, she kept telling herself. She just needed to rest and she'd be fine. She'd be impervious to him.

Jared climbed into the shay and set the horse into motion with a murmured "Giddap."

But rest seemed unlikely when, with the turn of the buggy wheels, Glenna realized she was on her way to a hotel room with a strange man.

And for the first time she stopped thinking about what she had gotten herself out of and began to wonder what she had gotten herself into.

Chapter Five

They checked into Joliet's single hotel. Jared carried their bags up to a second-floor room and, without a word, left Glenna there.

The room was old and sparsely furnished with a small round table, two ladder-back chairs on either side, one frayed and faded wing chair and a bed. One bed. Very narrow. Covered with a brown quilt that had been patched in the corner with a triangle of green calico.

Left to her own devices, Glenna wasn't at first sure what to do. And then it occurred to her that undressing in this small space without so much as a screen behind which to hide could very well be embarrassing. She hurriedly shed her clothes, put on her plain white cotton nightgown and donned her matching wrapper as if it were a heavy winter coat that would protect her from the cold, tying it at the waist in a double knot.

She took her hairbrush out of her valise and sat on the edge of the bed. But the moment she realized where she was, she shot back up as if the mattress were on fire.

"Well, you've done your job, bed," she said to the narrow piece of furniture. "All it took was the sight of you to wake me right up."

With her hairbrush still in hand, she claimed the wing chair in the corner. Ignoring the pain of the ribs the doctor she had visited late this afternoon had deemed broken, she plucked the pins from her hair, clamping each one between her lips as she did. Then she began to brush the unruly, tangled mass, all the while watching the door.

Jared didn't knock before coming in several minutes later. It was something Glenna noticed. A small thing that made a big impression on her, more of an impression, in fact, than had hearing herself called Mrs. Stratton for the first time as they registered with the desk clerk in the lobby. Not even her mother or Mary entered her bedroom without knocking first, yet now this man, this stranger, had the right. It was his bedroom, too.

No, she wasn't a bit tired anymore.

Jared was carrying a tray in both hands. He kicked the door closed after himself. Involuntarily, Glenna's stomach growled at the sight of food. They had neither one eaten all day.

"It isn't much," he explained as he set the tray on the table. "Just some sandwiches and a little pie left over from dinner." Then he glanced at her for the first time. His gaze went from her hair down to her nightclothes and back up to her face, his expression blank. "Unless you were thinking of eating those hairpins."

Glenna snatched them out of her mouth and then looked around for somewhere to put them. There was a tiny washstand in the opposite corner, only large enough to balance a washbowl with a pitcher set inside of it. Below it was a lower shelf where she placed her hairbrush and pins before joining him at the table.

"I'm hungry," she said, feeling the need to speak and not knowing what to say. But the moment the words were out they sounded inane to her and she wished she hadn't said anything at all. What *did* a person say to a man she had just married but didn't know from Adam?

He took one of the sandwiches from the top of a stack of four and put it on a dish in front of her. "Sit down, then, and eat. You could use a little meat on your bones."

It wasn't the first time anyone had said that to her. But it was the first time it had irritated her and so she took a bite of the food without thanking him as courtesy dictated. It was a simple sandwich of beef and cheese, but it tasted wonderful.

Jared took a bite, too, and when he had finished chewing—with his mouth closed, Glenna noted—and swallowed, he informed her, "The cook had just baked the bread for the morning."

Glenna nodded in the middle of another bite and forgot her own manners to say around a mouthful, "It's good."

Jared poured milk from a jar and set that in front of her, too.

"No, thank you," she managed after swallowing. "I don't like milk."

He shrugged and took it back. As he reached for a second sandwich he asked, "How are the bandages around your ribs? The doctor said I'd probably need to help you with them."

"They're fine," she answered too quickly, and wished warts on the cold-fingered practitioner who had performed the humiliating examination. Beyond giving instructions, he hadn't said a word to Glenna, as if she had been a horse he was checking out for a prospective buyer. Then, while she dressed, he had gone into the outer room and in a voice Glenna could hear—even though she doubted she was meant to—had informed Jared that she likely had broken ribs, had sustained cuts and bruises that would cause no long-lasting effects, and possessed a maidenhead that was intact.

Glenna and Jared fell into silence again. Jared drank a whole glass of milk, in one gulp, it seemed, then wiped his mouth with a napkin. He offered her the last sandwich by pushing the plate her way, taking it himself only after she had refused it with a shake of her head.

Try as she might, Glenna couldn't keep herself from watching him. His jaw and the hollows beneath his cheekbones were shadowed by the day's growth of beard. It made him look more the way he had the morning she had met him in his hotel room, only now it didn't give him the appearance of being unclean, but only made him look very rugged and masculine. Glenna had never seen Carter or even David Stern with whiskers. Jared's mustache still looked neat, and then, just like that, into her mind popped a memory of the feel of that mustache when he had kissed her that afternoon.

She was grateful that he interrupted her thoughts. "When we finish here I'll put the salve on that cut on your temple. You've broken it open again brushing your hair."

Gingerly she pressed her fingertips there, and they came away with blood on them. "I can do it," she told him, because she'd rather he didn't get too close and she certainly didn't want him to touch her. In any way.

Jared looked around the room. "There's no mirror. You'd better let me." His appetite was apparently waning because he sat back in his chair and studied her then, turning his milk glass around and around. Glenna didn't particularly like to have the tables turned and found a watermark on the wall near the door to study.

"I've never seen hair like yours," he said after a moment.

"It's just plain hair," she answered defensively.

"It looks more like wool. Copper-pot-colored wool. I keep wondering what it feels like." Without warning, he reached across the table and took a thick strand between his fingers, startling Glenna. But even though she jumped and jerked back, he didn't let go, leaving the long tress curling around the knuckle of his thumb and stretched between them like a rope. He turned his gaze to her face. "Skittish tonight, aren't you?"

"No." She nearly spit out the word.

It made him smile as slowly as honey dripping from a spoon. The knowing expression on his face softened his features and made him all the more strikingly handsome. "You can relax," he said sardonically. "I'm only feeling your hair."

Heat shot up into Glenna's face anyway. It must have been the sight of her blushing that sent a laugh rumbling from deep in his throat. She speared him with her eyes and snatched her hair out of his hand. "You know the truth about why I'm here, but what's your reason for needing to get a wife through a newspaper advertisement?"

Jared finished off the last of his sandwich, watching her through eyes that sparkled with wry amusement. "I told you, women are hard to come by in Kansas."

"But not impossible, I'll warrant. You could also have found ways to be politely introduced to any number of women in Chicago, and to court them properly."

He seemed to think about it for a moment. "True enough. But to marry one I'd have to play at wooing and cooing and pretend to have feelings I'll never have again. This seemed like a more sensible way."

He replied without hostility, plainly, honestly and with finality. And for some reason the words offended Glenna. It wasn't that she had expected some grand, love-at-first-sight romance. But this seemed so—

"It's business." He cut into her thoughts with an explanation that put a name to what she was having difficulty describing. "People are more careful about buying a pair of boots than they are about whom they marry, and that seems pretty foolish to me. I decided it was a better method to advertise, interview and hire on someone the way I would for any other job."

"Is that how you married your first wife?" she challenged him with facetiousness.

His expression showed nothing. Rather than answering her, he tilted up the pan that held a quarter of a pie and asked conversationally, "Dessert?"

For some reason she didn't understand, Glenna wanted to push it in his face. It was disheartening to know she had married a man whose views of marriage she didn't like. "No, thank you." She waited for him to answer her question. When it didn't seem as if he was going to, she re-worded it and asked again, "Is that how you chose your first wife?"

He took a forkful of pie right out of the pan, chewed and swallowed it with a grimace of distaste, then washed it down with the last of his milk. But he still didn't answer her. Instead he said, "I've made you mad for some reason, haven't I?"

"No," she denied in a way that told him differently.

"Did you think that marriage meant instant love? That the ceremony would endow us with it like magic?"

"Of course not."

"What did you think?"

"I don't know," she shot out curtly. "And that isn't what we were discussing anyway. Did you marry before for love?"

Jared wiped his mouth and mustache for the last time and laid the napkin alongside his plate. Then he went to his valise, took a small jar from it and brought the salve back with him. As if she hadn't asked him a direct question, he opened the jar, sniffed it and then tilted her face upward with a single knuckle under her chin. He dipped the tip of his index finger in the white cream and carefully dabbed it onto Glenna's temple.

"Yes," he answered finally. "I married the first time for love. Passionate, knee-weakening love," he said with just a hint of self-mockery.

Glenna swallowed hard, trying to quell the tingling sensation that his touch aroused in her. "Did you find it to be a mistake you didn't want to repeat?" she asked bluntly. "Is that why you avoided it this time?"

Again he didn't readily answer. He finished applying the salve to her temple, combed her hair away with the backs of his fingers in what seemed like a search for more of the cut; then he closed the jar. "It's late and you're going to need rest for the trip ahead of us. We'd best get some sleep."

That said, he pulled the tail of his shirt from the waistband of his jeans and began to unbutton it.

Glenna had never felt more wide-awake in her life. Or more agitated. She stayed put and once again reiterated in a tone that demanded. "Was marrying for love a mistake you didn't want to repeat?"

Off came his shirt and up went Glenna's temperature. She tried to ignore what he was doing and stared hard at his face. Only at his face.

"I don't see what difference it makes to you," he said finally as he neatly folded his shirt and laid it over the back of the chair he had been sitting on before. Then he sat down to pull off his boots and socks. "The fact is, love wasn't involved in the arrangement between you and me. And our arrangement is the only thing that should matter to you."

"I'm curious," she declared and then proved it by losing her grip on herself and dropping her gaze to the breadth of his chest where hair the dark wheat color of his mustache shadowed bulging pectoral muscles. The moment she realized what she'd done she amended it and looked him squarely in the eye.

Again he laughed at her, a short chuckle. The sound of his second boot falling to the floor seemed to be the only answer she was going to get. And then his brow beetled and in a serious tone of voice he said, "A man's heart . . . at least this man's heart, only loves once, Glenna. This time other things were more important."

"The doubletree," she guessed with a touch of sarcasm.

"That's right. So if you have some romantic notions, you might as well get them out of your head. To say that I will ever love again would be a lie." He unfastened his pants and then seemed to think better about it. Bending over the single lamp that burned on the table, he blew it out, leaving the room in the dim white glow of the moon through thin curtains.

Glenna snapped her head away to look out those curtains as he dropped his pants. She didn't know what she had thought about this marriage, but she did know what she *hadn't* thought about, and that was the personal side of all this. The intimate side. She'd just plain been too occupied thinking about everything else. Now she realized there was only so far she was willing to go in the name of extracting herself from the dangers Chicago held.

"We won't be sharing a bed," she decreed in the dark, wondering why it gave her both relief and something else, something that she might have mistaken for disappointment if she hadn't known better.

She heard him laugh yet again and decided she didn't like his sense of humor any more than she did his views on marriage.

"We will definitely be sharing a bed." He vetoed her decree as he got into the object in question. "For a while, until you're healed, all we'll be doing in it is sleeping, but after that... We'll get around to just about everything most other married couples do."

There was something very unnerving about that deep male voice in the dark. And it didn't help a bit that he was so calm and confident.

"No, we will not," she answered him, matching his tone.

"No, we will not what?" He seemed to be enjoying her discomfort with the subject.

"No, we will not be getting around to..." She cleared her throat to keep up her steam. "Without feelings between us, there won't be any..." It was hard to find a name for something she had never in her life discussed with another living soul.

"Is that right?" he said with amusement tinging his voice.

"It is. You said you wanted someone to care for your house and your son. That's what I agreed to and that's what I'll do. Nothing else. There's a limit to what I'll be *hired on* for."

There was silence for a moment before he said, as if with a shrug, "Suit yourself." Then he added in a tone that was both amused and curious, "Your hackles are really up, aren't they?"

And his weren't—it was all the more frustrating to be answered with such calm. He seemed to Glenna to have no feelings whatsoever. For some reason she found that very insulting.

But before she said anything else he sighed and closed the subject. "There's no need to argue it more tonight. Come to bed. You need some sleep."

"I'm not tired."

Silence fell again for a moment before he sighed. "If I'm taking up too much space and you decide you're ready for bed, just push me over to one side or the other then."

Glenna heard the rustle of sheets as he settled himself. In the dark she could see by his mountainlike silhouette that he was lying on his side, but she didn't know whether he faced her or had turned away from her.

Was he watching her? She couldn't tell.

For a while she stayed sitting on the hard ladder-back chair, staring out at the night through the curtains. Before long, weariness settled over her in spite of everything, and her body began to ache all over. Without a glance at the bed, she got up and reclaimed the softer chair in the corner, resting her head against one of the wings.

And there she spent her wedding night, sitting up, madder than a wet hen at her new husband, and not altogether sure why.

Chapter Six

Spending the night in the chair, Glenna barely dozed, listening every hour for the chimes of the grandfather clock in the lobby one floor below. The train that would take them through Kansas City and all the way to Topeka on the first leg of their journey left Joliet at ten-twenty in the morning. That didn't leave her much time to get to Aunt Lida's friend to sell her mother's jewelry, and she had been fretting about how she was going to accomplish her errand without her new husband knowing. Sleeplessness hatched a better plot than she had been able to come up with before. Glenna decided to slip out just before dawn while Jared still slept. With any luck she could be back before he woke.

Dressed for the second time in Aunt Lida's old widow's weeds so as not to draw attention to herself, she cautiously slipped out of the hotel room and put her shoes on in the hallway. Once that was done she again donned the bonnet and rolled down the veil to hide her abused face.

Carter had given her ten dollars—just in case—and with that in a small sack purse around her wrist and the jewelry bundled into a kangaroo pouch she'd formed with her petticoat, she descended the single flight of stairs to the lobby and asked where she might find a hansom cab at this hour.

Joliet's streets were still deserted as Glenna followed the desk clerk's instructions and went down a block and across to the livery that housed the city's transportation for hire. Going in through the stable she found a man in trousers, undershirt and suspenders just emerging from a room in back. He eyed her suspiciously but when she offered to double the fare he hitched the horse to the cab, took the slip of paper on which Aunt Lida had written Harold Diddleblock's address and nodded over his shoulder in a gesture that told her to climb into the carriage.

The fact that she could have walked the distance in five minutes had he but given her directions left Glenna tempted to rescind the offer of double fare when she arrived at the two-story, red brick house. But in the end she paid him in full rather than raise a ruckus, sending him back to the stables instead of asking him to wait for her.

The sun was high enough by then to glare blindingly off the huge front window of Harold Diddleblock's steeply roofed house. There was no sign of anyone stirring. Glenna took a deep breath, steeling herself for the reception she would get after awakening the household.

Just rousing Harold Diddleblock wasn't an easy task. She pounded the lion's-head knocker until the blood had drained out of her arm before the beady eyed, scowling man opened the door, a shock of white hair hanging over one temple and his robe gaping above a tied sash to reveal striped pajamas.

"Mr. Diddleblock?" Glenna asked. "I'm Glenna Ashe…" She stumbled over the name, thinking as she spoke that it wasn't hers anymore. "I believe Lida Lamb wired you about me?"

He made a sound that was somewhere between acknowledgement and clearing his throat, and stepped aside for her to go in. Without a word he scuffled into an extremely ornate parlor and slumped into one of two chairs that stood on either side of a table in the far corner of the room. "Do you know what time it is, young lady?" he asked finally.

"Miss Lida didn't say you'd be coming nearly in the middle of the night."

"I'm sorry to disturb you but I've a train to catch this morning and . . ."

He waved away her explanation and loudly hawked phlegm. Then he raised those beady eyes to her as if in expectation.

Glenna knew he was waiting for her to remove her veil, but she had no intention of alarming him with the sight of her, so instead she asked, "Did Aunt Lida's wire explain that I have some jewelry . . ."

Again he didn't allow her to finish. "I'll see what you have to sell but I want no details," he told her in a disgusted tone of voice.

Glenna glanced around the room. "Is there somewhere I might have some privacy to retrieve it then?"

His scowl deepened but he pointed with a thumb over his shoulder at an archway that opened into a dining room. Going there, she slipped to one side of the arch, and with the wall between her and Diddleblock, hiked up her skirt. She wore her petticoat backward with the two ends of the waistband knotted around the hem pulled up to her middle. Her fingers were stiff with tension as she worked the tie free, but then she quickly unrolled the jewelry from its hiding place. With the waistband of her petticoat retied, she brushed her skirt down over it again and carried her cache to the waiting jeweler.

Since she had not been offered a seat, Glenna stood beside the table as he looked over each piece. It was a cursory assessment without even the aid of an eyepiece to study the quality of the gems. Then he separated the items David Stern had given her mother from the plain garnet necklace, the pearls and the wedding band that had been her father's gifts.

"I'll give you three hundred dollars for the lot of these, but those others I won't take at all." He pushed the more conservative pieces toward Glenna.

"Three hundred?" she repeated in disbelief. "Why, they're worth—"

"Only as much as someone is willing to pay for them. Look here, missy, I don't know what's going on, but it would take a dimwit not to see something about this isn't right. Urgent telegraph wires, you coming in here before dawn, keeping your face hidden behind a veil. What do you take me for? Lida Lamb's husband was a friend and because of that I'll close my eyes, buy these pieces, break them down and remake them so they're unrecognizable. But don't expect to get what they're worth in an under-the-table deal like this. Three hundred, take it or leave it."

The jewelry was worth ten times that much, maybe more, and they both knew it. Glenna hadn't expected to get the whole value, not even close to it, but she had expected a great deal more than three hundred dollars. This money was not only for Mary's train fare when the time came, it was her sister's entire future, to contribute to her room and board, her clothing, anything she needed so as not to be a complete burden on a man who didn't want her around in the first place. Three hundred dollars was a pittance for all of that.

But once again, Glenna knew she had no choice. Where else between here and Hays City, Kansas, was she going to sell elaborate jewelry like this? And to whom? How could she chance even showing them to someone who was more of a stranger than Mr. Diddleblock? Another person might just snatch the jewelry away from her and leave her with nothing.

"Couldn't you give me just another hundred dollars?" she tried.

The man glared at her. "Three hundred—that's my only offer."

"What about taking the smaller pieces as well and giving another fifty dollars?"

"The smaller pieces aren't worth more than sentiment. Three hundred or keep it all and see if you can find somebody else who'll buy them."

Glenna swallowed frustration and wondered what she had done to deserve the series of bad hands fate was dealing her these days. But once again she decided she would just have to make do.

"I'll take the three hundred."

Without a word the jeweler climbed the stairs that faced the front door, returning minutes later with the money.

"It's for the sake of an old friendship that I do this. But never again. I'm a reputable businessman."

And I'm not a thief in need of someone to bring my plunder to over and over again! Glenna wanted to say. But she held her tongue.

It seemed ludicrous to thank him when she felt cheated, but she did, perfunctorily, after he counted out the three hundred dollars and handed it to her. She folded the money and put it into her purse, along with what was left of her mother's jewelry, pulling the drawstring tight. Saying nothing to the man she returned to the wall beyond the archway, lifted her skirt and tied the purse to the waistband of her petticoat.

With her arms crossed over her middle so she could feel the bag of money against her stomach, she returned to the parlor. Ignoring his leer, she bade the man good-day and left.

When she had closed the door behind her, Glenna caught sight of Harold Diddleblock standing at the window, glaring out at her. She could still feel his eyes on her as she made her way down the walk and even as she turned onto the cobbled street. But she answered him only with straight, proud shoulders.

"Think whatever you like," she said to herself as she headed for the hotel in the early dawn light. "But nothing will stop me from keeping my promise."

* * *

"Well, well, well. What have we here?"

It was Jared's voice, deep and sarcastic, that greeted Glenna as she slipped through the door of their hotel room.

At the sound, the skin on the back of her neck prickled and her mouth went dry. She turned and faced him for all the world as if she hadn't a thing to hide.

"And dressed in your Sunday best again, I see," he went on caustically.

Morning light came through the thinly curtained window. He was sitting in the very center of the bed, his back against the wall. One of his knees was bent, making a tent out of the sheet that covered his lower half and left his chest bare. One forearm rested atop his knee, his big hand dangling carelessly. His hair was sleep-tousled, his jaw darkly shadowed with beard, and his expression was as cold and remote as any Glenna had ever seen.

"Should I believe you wore hat and veil to the outhouse?" he went on when she said nothing.

Glenna took off the hat and met his stare levelly. "Perhaps you should simply ask where I've been."

Her eyes followed the shrug of one bare, broad shoulder. She pulled her glance away and saw him nod his head curtly. "Have it your way. Where have you been before dawn in a strange city?"

"For a walk," she said, surprising herself at how smoothly the lies flowed. "I couldn't sleep anyway, and after sitting up all night I felt stiff. I thought it best to try and work that out before boarding a train. I also posted a note to my family to let them know we were married."

"And why not wear your own clothes?" he asked.

"I thought it more practical. A woman alone on abandoned streets has need for the protection of appearing to be a poor widow, not warranting the attention of whatever blackguards might be about," she recited.

"Has she?"

Glenna shrugged. "Better to be safe than sorry," she answered offhandedly. Then, as if she had sufficiently explained herself, she moved to her open valise, put the ugly hat in it and went back to the door. "I'll just wait outside while you dress and then you can do me the same courtesy."

She left then, in a hurry before he could either argue or fling the bed sheet away. But the image of him haunted her even as she stood in the hallway, and her heartbeat was a bit more rapid because of it. The man had the oddest effect on her, she thought as she tried to take deep breaths and calm her pulse.

When the door opened again some time later it startled Glenna. She turned to find Jared dressed in tan-colored breeches and a brown leather vest over a white shirt, the sleeves rolled up to his elbows. His face was shaved, his hair combed, his mustache neat and he smelled of soap. As he stepped into the hall and freed the room for her he warned, "This is the last time we play this game, Glenna. Get used to the fact that we are man and wife now. And while you're at it, get used to the sight of me and mine of you."

Glenna said nothing, instead passing in front of him and closing the door after herself. Through it he called, "I'll get us some breakfast and be right back. Make short work of this because I'm not waiting out here for you to finish."

The room was full of the scent of him and she tried not to notice as she quickly slipped out of the widow's weeds.

Arrogant, insufferable, rude man . . .

She untied her purse from the waistband of her petticoat, and took the three hundred dollars and what remained of her mother's jewelry out of it. Irately, she snatched the purple velvet box from where it was buried in her valise and stuffed both money and jewelry into it. Then she wrapped the black dress around it and jammed it back among her other things.

"Get used to the sight of me and mine of you," she repeated under her breath, mimicking his tone.

Didn't the man have any sense of propriety? They were strangers, after all. What did he think she was, some sort of light skirt?

With her traveling gown on she brushed her hair free of tangles. She tried to ignore the pain in her ribs as she fumbled to twist her curls into a knot at her nape.

Irritating, insolent...

And then he was back, coming in much as he had the previous night, with tray in hand.

Glenna remembered just how much she had at stake. She had to have a home to bring Mary to, and if that meant dressing and undressing together...

"Come and eat," he ordered.

She narrowed her eyes at him, clenched her teeth and took the seat she had occupied at the table the night before.

They said nothing over hotcakes, ham and eggs but Glenna could feel Jared watching her. When he had finished his breakfast he curved his hand around his coffee cup as if it were a glass and balanced his chair back on two legs.

"Why is it that you're twenty-two and not married until now?" he asked her then, his tone more than just curious. He actually sounded suspicious, but in a cold, removed sort of way.

"I was only fourteen when my mother married David Stern. At sixteen when other girls were coming out, he refused to pay for the same thing for me. He said it would be a waste of money on a plain girl...." Glenna paused at the jab of that old memory, but went on. "He had other plans. He was going to find me a husband who would prove advantageous to him. That didn't require an expensive debut."

She looked out the window beside the table rather than meet the eyes she knew were studying her. It was to the glass pane that she continued, "He brought three or four candidates around but I was not ... welcoming.

"I'll bet that's an understatement," Jared said sardonically. "Weren't there parties or dances you were invited to where you met other men?"

Glenna shrugged. "I'm afraid after my mother married David Stern my opinion of men was not high. There were a few parties...."

"And a few suitors," he put in.

"And a few men who asked to call," she confirmed. "But the way my mother was treated didn't leave me overly anxious to find a man of my own to do the same to me. And besides, there was Mary."

His square brow creased into a frown. "You stayed to witness your mother's abuse, and refused yourself a husband to take you away from it, all for your sister?"

"Do you find loyalty so unbelievable?" she shot back at him.

"At times. In women," he answered bluntly.

That made her hackles rise. "I have never known loyalty to be a particularly male virtue. In fact, given David Stern's peccadilloes, I would say the opposite."

His only answer to her challenging tone was to cock one eyebrow and tilt his head slightly, as if amused by her audacity.

"At any rate," she went on, "my mother wouldn't accept my help for her own sake, but there had to be one of us who could keep Mary away and safe when my stepfather was in a rage." Again she looked out the window at the sun now fully risen, hating the feeling these memories stirred of her frustration at being unable to help her mother.

"And there was never anyone who even caught your fancy?" he asked dubiously.

"No, there wasn't." Curious, she met his eyes. "Why does this matter to you?"

Jared let his chair fall to all four legs and pushed himself to his feet. "I just wondered if I had need to watch for a lover following in our tracks."

The light dawned on Glenna. "I didn't sneak out to meet someone this morning, if that's what you think."

"Did you *sneak* out?" he asked as if he had caught her at a lie, taking the salve from where he had left it on the wash-stand the night before.

"I tried not to wake you," she hedged.

Jared came to her and tilted her chin to apply the salve to her temple again. "I'm a very light sleeper."

There was a warning in his voice, but again his tone was oddly remote. It gave Glenna the impression that were he to discover this or anything else about her that he didn't like he would quite easily desert her just the way he had threatened to twice before, with nary a glance back at her or a care as to what straits he might leave her in. "I'm sorry if I disturbed you," she said.

But rather than answer her apology, when he was finished applying the salve he turned away and began packing his things. "We have a train to catch."

Wondering about him, Glenna gathered her belongings as well. Not another word was spoken between them until they stood at the door to leave. Carrying both her bags and his, Jared stopped and frowned down into her eyes.

"I've never hit a woman in my life, if it's any comfort to you," he said solemnly.

All things considered, she found little comfort in it.

Chapter Seven

They boarded the train at ten. As Glenna took the window seat Jared stowed their grips and a box lunch made up by the hotel on a shelf overhead.

Sitting down himself, Jared absently turned his head toward the window. Glenna was staring out so intently that her nose was nearly pressed to the glass.

"Something out there interest you?" he asked, trying to spot what might be garnering such rapt attention.

"No," she answered sheepishly, without budging her pose.

Jared leaned over her to get a better look outside. More passengers boarded, families bade farewells, the conductor took tickets beside the door and two small boys traded shoves just below the window. So far as he could tell there wasn't anything out of the ordinary. "What's so interesting out there?"

He heard her impatient sigh before she turned her head ever so slightly in his direction. Keeping her chin nearly to her chest, she said irritably, "I'm just tired of being stared at."

At her words Jared glanced up to a woman coming down the aisle behind a little boy in knee pants. Sure enough, from four seats away the woman's glance caught on Glenna. When the little boy began to turn into their row she put a hand on his shoulder so hard he flinched and she pushed him past, cutting a look at Jared as she did.

It wasn't the first time the cuts, bruises and swelling on Glenna's face had drawn stares and judgment. The justice of the peace had obviously had reservations—it had cost Jared an extra two dollars to get him to perform the ceremony. And the desk clerk at the hotel had gawked at Glenna. Jared shrugged the situation away now as he had the other times and stretched out his feet under the facing seat. He'd take the blame if it got him some legroom.

"For what it's worth, you look better today. Some of the bruises are starting to fade and that salve left your cut healed enough for your hair to hide it," he said, wondering as he did why he should feel inclined to try to ease her vanity.

With a final two steamy bellows of the whistle, the train began to pull out of Joliet's station. It struck Jared that this was the second time he had left Illinois with a wife. It wasn't a thought that pleased him and so rather than dwell on it, he began to mentally calculate how many tons of hay it would take to get through the next winter.

He had all but forgotten about Glenna when he first felt something nudging him. Glancing over he found her sound asleep and leaning his way. Her head had dropped forward, swinging limply back and forth in a semicircle with the lumbering bounce and sway of the train.

Damn fool woman for sitting up all night in a chair.

She groaned softly, as if something hurt her, and then fell toward him, her head landing against his shoulder. She nuzzled him as if he were a pillow, apparently finding a comfortable spot before settling in.

Jared sat stone still. Every muscle in his body tensed. For a moment he didn't even breathe. Slowly, he swiveled his head so he could peer down at her as if she were a bee just landed there and he didn't want to jar it into stinging him. Exhaling finally, he moved his shoulder slightly to coax her into moving away; but all she did in response was to snuggle closer.

Jared swallowed.

He tried again, barely lifting his shoulder. This time she moaned a complaint but stayed put nonetheless.

He closed his eyes and arched his brows. Feelings were stirring faintly within him—feelings dead for a long time now. Soft feelings; tender things that were hard to shake when there was no longer any call for them.

A long strand of her hair worked free of the knot that held it at her nape. It snaked down his shirtfront.

That hair...

He remembered the feel of it the night before when she had yanked it out of his reach. He couldn't resist taking it between his fingers again, letting it curl around his thumb. It was the silkiest thing he'd ever felt, the texture belying the corkscrew appearance. No, it was not like any hair he had ever seen, and he suddenly had the urge to test the weight of the whole mass in both his hands.

A clean, faintly sweet scent wafted up to him. Curious, he lifted the strand to his nose and breathed deeply of it. It reminded him of something but he couldn't quite place it. And then he remembered the first girl he had ever danced with; that same scent had made him forget his newly learned steps. Wildflower soap, she had told him when he said how good she smelled.

The memory made him smile.

Glenna moved then, her head slipping from the top of his shoulder to his chest. Her hand came up to rest gently on his shirtfront. The warmth of her palm seeped through to his skin.

Jared could feel the fast beat of his heart against the weight of her head. Her hair came unwound from around his finger and he covered her hand with his own, pressing a little so her palm was more firmly against his pectoral.

He'd been without a woman for too long. Too long since he had touched or been touched. He'd forgotten the smell of a woman's hair, the feel of a hand so much smaller than his, so much softer beneath the calluses that hardened his own. He relearned that softness again with his thumb, riding up and down the hills of her knuckles. He traced each of her fingers, thin and delicate, the nails blunt but smooth. Then his own fingers curved around the fleshy heel and slipped beneath, the tips squeezing into her palm in a way that made her take a hold even in her sleep, gently, lightly. He slipped out of her tenuous grip, leaving her hand a fist he cupped and kneaded before sliding his fingers along the back and up her wrist inside the sleeve of her dress. Her skin was warmer there, and downy. Then back out he came to plunge just one finger into the center of her loosely held fist, feeling it clench around him.

Then he stopped. Just like that Jared dropped his hand to his lap as if it were weighted with lead. He held his breath until the sparks inside him were smothered. He wouldn't feel these things about a new hired hand and Glenna was no different. He'd hired her on for the boy. For cooking and cleaning and canning...

But there was no denying that what he'd just felt had nothing at all to do with the position she was intended to fill in his household.

Well, urges were only natural. After all, he was a man, she a woman and his wife; those needs were his right. But the tenderness he was feeling toward her was not part of the plan.

None too gently Jared slipped one arm around her shoulders and slid the other under her knees, moving her like a sack of meal to lay her on her side on the facing seat. Then he sat back in his own.

But that wasn't much better, because he couldn't keep his eyes off her sleeping face. He remembered her saying her stepfather had called her plain, and the thought brought with it a sudden surge of anger. She wasn't hard to look at, even battered and bruised. He didn't believe she was going to be when the man's handiwork was gone.

Jared closed his eyes and tightened his jaw so hard it hurt. He preferred the pain, physical pain, to these other things he was feeling.

He didn't want to feel outrage at the atrocities heaped on her. He didn't want the softness that crept around his heart when he pictured her covering her sister's ears so the blind child wouldn't hear what was happening to their mother. He didn't want the itch that had been spurred to life with that kiss after their wedding ceremony. He didn't want this ache in the pit of his stomach right now, the urge in his hands to feel more of her than he had, the craving to taste and touch her with his mouth, the need to have more of her weight on him than her head and hand on his chest.

He didn't want any damn feelings or any damn urges or cravings or needs. Period.

He clenched his teeth harder still.

He wanted a working arrangement and that was all.

And by God that was all he would have.

Without any conception of time or place, Glenna woke slowly, wondering why her bed was bouncing and where the smell of cigar smoke was coming from. She scratched her nose, thinking to make the acrid scent go away. When it didn't she came more fully awake and reluctantly opened her eyes.

There was only faint light. The first thing she focused on was the thighs of her new husband where he stood between the seats reaching to the upper compartment. His pants were stretched taut by legs so corded and hard they didn't look real to her. Nothing spindly about this man; the thought floated into her head like a dream. She watched him set their box lunch on the facing seat and then take a match from his shirt pocket. His hand was so big the stick was like a splinter held between two fingers into the curve of his palm where he set it aflame with the flick of his thumbnail. Capable hands, she thought, tough and strong. With sudden clarity she remembered the gentleness of his touch both times he had tended her head.

He lit the small lamp above the window and for the first time she realized that it was night.

Glenna pushed herself to a sitting position, getting her bearings and wondering how she'd gotten to this seat when she had started out on the other.

"Finally awake?" Jared's deep voice sounded as he sat across from her.

"Is it the same day?" she asked, still disoriented.

"It is." He took a watch from the pocket of his trousers, flipped open the lid and announced, "It's past eight." Then he replaced the timepiece and opened the box lunch. "I was beginning to think you were going to sleep through the night."

"You must be hungry," she said for lack of anything else to say. "You didn't have to wait for me."

Jared only shrugged as he broke off a chunk of bread and handed it to her. "You needed the rest and I didn't want to disturb you by moving around too much. But by now I figured the noise my stomach was making was as likely to wake you as getting myself something to eat."

Glenna was feeling slightly groggy and relaxed in a way she had not been with Jared before. As she ate she watched him, a feast for the eyes while she filled her stomach. She liked his looks, she realized, preferring his rugged handsomeness to the more refined sort.

It surprised her to find that her thoughtful study of him seemed to unnerve him more than any challenging stare she had yet practiced. His very square brow pulled into a frown and as he ate he looked anywhere but directly at her.

"Did you come to Chicago especially to advertise for a wife?" she asked conversationally.

He blew a short, curt laugh at her. "No, I didn't. Women are scarce in Hays but I didn't have to go as far as Chicago to advertise for one."

"Then why did you come?"

His frown deepened. "I had something to see to there. But things didn't work out the way I thought they would and it put me in need of a woman...." For a reason Glenna didn't understand he seemed to trip over that phrase. He shook his head the way a dog shakes off something caught around his neck and finished. "I decided since I was already in a city full of them I might as well do it there as waste time trying to find one somewhere else."

It gave her a sense of power that her gaze caused him discomfort; she reveled in it for another moment.

Jared broke the silence this time. "We'll be getting off in Topeka. Joseph's sister-in-law and her family have a place outside of it. Two of my nephews have been there helping out since the husband broke his leg. But now that he's healed the boys need to come home. We'll be picking them up."

"Joseph is your brother," she remembered, her curiosity about his family suddenly roused. "Is he older or younger?"

"Older by three years."

"Which makes him..." She had wondered how old Jared was but until now hadn't found a way to ask.

"Thirty-six to my thirty-three."

"And you own your ranch together."

"We inherited it from our father. Six thousand acres."

He had told her that the morning they met. He was obviously very proud of it. "Do you all live together?"

"We have been since ... my wife died. Cally—that's Joseph's wife—took the boy in and it was just easier for me to stay there, too. But there are two houses, one right next to the other. We all share the barns and the outbuildings, no need for two sets of those since we own everything jointly.

Joseph, Cally and their brood have the original house but my wife wanted the privacy of her own.''

"What was your wife's name?" Glenna asked. She watched his jaw clench. His brow puckered and he looked away.

"Janie," he said as if it wasn't easy for him.

Janie, Glenna thought. Not Jane. Janie. The fondness implied by a pet name piqued her.

Then he went on. "Joseph and I built the second house. It's smaller and will take some cleaning and airing before we move in.''

Though she wondered about the woman who had preceded her, it was clear the subject was not one he wished to discuss. So instead she said, "Joseph and Cally have two sons?''

The darkness in his expression disappeared and he laughed. "Oh, no. They have six. And two daughters, and another baby on the way.''

"Eight children?"

"Almost nine. I doubt they'll be sorry to see someone else take over their nephew and the lot of us moved back to our own house and out of their way.''

"Nine children," Glenna said again, astonished.

It took no more prompting than that for him to talk about them. "The oldest, John, is seventeen. He does a man's work so he stayed on to help Joseph while I was gone. Then there's Charity, she's sixteen. Won't be long before we lose her. Girls on the prairie don't stay unmarried much past that. The two we'll be picking up in Topeka are next oldest at fifteen—Matthew and Mark. They're twins. Then there's Luke who's fourteen. Quiet boy, musical like his mother.''

Glenna watched Jared with interest as he went down the list of his nieces and nephews. His face relaxed, his voice was less gruff, and for the first time she saw a warmth in his eyes.

"My brother must have needed a rest," he continued with a smile, "because we had a full four years before the next set of twins were born. Peter and Paul are ten. They're two of the orneriest little toads around. Another six years passed, we were beginning to think Joseph and Cally didn't like each other anymore and then along came little Annie. She'll have had her fourth birthday while I was away.'' He shook his head fondly. ''She's a sweetheart. Keeps telling me when she grows up she wants to marry me.'' That made him laugh again.

It was a sound Glenna liked. It came from deep in his chest and made him seem less formidable. ''Annie's not going to be happy to meet me, then, is she? Maybe you should keep me a secret until she gets over you,'' Glenna teased, smiling at him.

He turned that newly minted warmth in his eyes to her and returned her smile with a genuine one of his own. ''You'd be a hard secret to keep,'' he teased her back. ''But I can't break her heart so I guess you'll just have to share me.''

Now it was Glenna's turn to laugh. ''Such conceit,'' she flirted, surprising herself. ''Someday she'll thank me for saving her for a more humble man.''

''Is that so?'' He feigned offense.

''It is,'' she confirmed haughtily, enjoying herself. ''And what about your son?'' she prompted when it seemed as if he had forgotten him.

Jared's smile faded. ''The boy is nearly a year and a half. He walks and is just starting to talk—or so everyone believes. I can't make out much of it.''

Glenna waited for him to tell her more, to show the same affection she had seen in him when he spoke of his brother's children. When neither of those things happened she asked, ''Is that all?''

Jared shrugged. ''No more to say. He's a baby,'' he answered as if he had been speaking before about his own children and now spoke of someone else's.

Confused, Glenna asked, ''What's his name?''

"Lyden. Do you want more to eat?" He tilted the box toward her.

"No, thank you," Glenna answered, watching him as he closed the lid on what was left for the next day. Even though it was obvious he didn't want to talk more about his son she persisted. "He must think of your sister-in-law as his mother if your wife died at childbirth."

"I imagine so," he agreed distractedly. "But Charity tends him almost as much."

"It must have eased your grief to be left with at least that part of your wife," she surmised, testing.

He stood and replaced the box on the overhead shelf. When he sat back down he slid low and stretched his legs straight out under Glenna's seat. Leaning his head back, he closed his eyes and crossed his arms over his chest. "Blow out the light when you're ready to go back to sleep."

Apparently she wasn't going to get a comment on her supposition. Glenna stared at him, finding that she no longer had the power to make him uncomfortable with mere scrutiny. The more relaxed man she had awakened to had disappeared and the impervious one she had met in Chicago was in his place.

Did he resent the child, she wondered, because the birth had cost him the mother? It seemed so. And Glenna was the replacement for the wife he hadn't wanted to lose—necessary but hardly wanted.

The assumption sat uneasily in her mind. One more thorn in the crown of thistles that was her marriage. Not that she expected love, she was quick to remind herself. But she had seen a different side of Jared as he talked about his brother's family. A side that was easier, nicer, more pleasant to be around. A side that was very attractive. And she would have liked to think that once they got down to the business of living as man and wife that better side would dominate the dark, sarcastic, cold, remote side of the man she had married. But if he still bore a torch for his lost wife so strongly that after nearly eighteen months he didn't even want to speak of his own son, how could she, his wife's replacement, ever hope for anything better?

The answer seemed to be that she couldn't.

And hadn't he warned her of as much when he had told her he would never love again?

It shouldn't matter, she told herself. She had only married him to save herself, to have a place to bring Mary. It didn't matter if he stayed brooding forever.

And yet it did. For some reason Glenna didn't understand, it suddenly mattered a great deal.

Chapter Eight

"Maybe it would be better if I were to take an inexpensive room here in Topeka while you fetch your nephews," Glenna suggested as they were disembarking just after noon the following day. She did not relish the thought of meeting any of his family with her face still bearing her stepfather's marks. But more than that she had decided if Jared would agree to leave her in town alone it would be much easier to try selling the remainder of her mother's jewelry with him out of the way.

"Why would that be better?" he asked her as he led the way to the buckboard the stationmaster had suggested might be for hire.

"I just thought it might be embarrassing to introduce me looking the way I do."

Jared stopped halfway to the buckboard and looked down at her from beneath his frowning brow. "Among a dozen other reasons I can give you for why I would not leave you behind while I pick up the boys is your first lesson in the difference between life here and in that city of yours. Look around you, Glenna," he instructed.

She did, not understanding. She had seen enough from the train window to know this frontier city was certainly more rustic than Chicago. A line of covered wagons lumbering down an unpaved main street of rough-hewn buildings was a far cry from the refined architecture and network of cobbled bustling streets that made up her hometown. But for all of that she saw no reason she could not be left here alone for the single night he had said they would be spending in the home of his distant relatives. She told him as much.

"Look again at the people," he advised. "For every man not carrying a gun there are two who are and half of those are toting them with no good purpose in mind, I can assure you. As for women—we are now in Kansas. While I'll grant you that Topeka isn't as bad as Hays, your sex is a rare breed here. I don't care to come back and find more than my wife's face has been misused and manhandled, the likelihood of which is great for any young woman left alone. And I promise you putting your little nose in the air and proclaiming that you will spend the night in a chair will not save you around here."

That said, he finished crossing the distance to the buckboard, rounded it, kicked the wheels, checked the horses and paid the price to use it.

Sitting atop the wooden plank seat, they were out of town before Jared turned to her and took up their conversation as if it hadn't been interrupted. "Besides, your face looks better. The worst of it is that shiner of a black eye. The bruise on your cheekbone is faded to yellow and green, it'll be gone in no time. You heal fast."

He said it as if it were a compliment. Probably the best she was ever likely to hear from him, Glenna thought. She stared at the open, empty countryside across which they were traveling on a road that was no more than wheel ruts through yellow prairie grass.

"How are your ribs?" His deep baritone voice came after a few minutes of riding with nothing more than the sound of the wagon wheels creaking.

"Better," she answered in a hurry.

"By the time we get to the Johnsons' we'll both need a bath. Afterward I'll wrap them again."

Butterflies took flight in her stomach at that proposition. "I'm sure by tonight they won't need to be wrapped at all. As you said, I'm a fast healer," she was quick to inform him, even though she knew it wasn't true. Every jolt of the wagon shot pain through her sides. The look he gave her told her he knew it, too. But he made no comment.

Instead they rode in silence for another minute. Then Jared glanced over at her, first out of the corner of his eye, then full on. Up came his thumb to run like a feather along her jaw. "Swelling's gone from here altogether, but there's still a mark..."

"That's an old scar," she said, glad for the change of subject. "I got it from falling out of a tree."

His surprise registered in his face. He held the reins in one hand, cupped his knee with the other and looked her up and down incredulously. "What were you doing in a tree?"

"Climbing it," she told him officiously, hiking up one eyebrow for effect.

"You?"

"Yes, me. I was quite a tomboy as a child."

That made him laugh in a mocking way Glenna didn't like.

"Ever ride a horse?" he asked, obviously enjoying himself at her expense.

"No."

"Rope a steer?"

"In Chicago?"

"I'll take that as a no. Shoot a gun?"

"Of course not."

"What exactly do tomboys in Chicago do...besides climb trees?"

"Play marbles and wear britches."

"That must have raised some eyebrows, all right."

''What exactly do tomboys in Kansas do?'' she asked with her temper echoing in her voice.

''Some of them wear britches, too.''

''And ride horses and rope steers and shoot guns,'' she added snidely.

''At least. Come to think of it, it's a lot harder to distinguish a tomboy in Kansas than I imagine it is in Chicago. Girls end up doing pretty much the same things boys do anyway, only most of them wear skirts.'' He eyed her again as if something had just occurred to him. ''What exactly can you do? I should have asked before, but I wasn't thinking too clearly the morning I accepted you.''

''You mean as a tomboy?'' she asked, confused.

''No, I mean as a wife. It strikes me that what girls in Kansas learn—whether they're tomboys or not—prepares them for what wives end up doing. But there's not much call for tree climbing or marble playing where we're going.''

''What exactly is there a call for?''

''Milking cows, killing and plucking chickens, butchering hogs, killing snakes, skinning rabbits, hauling wood, building fires…not to mention just plain cooking. Can you cook?''

Glenna's thoughts were stuck back on snakes.

''I said, you can cook, can't you?''

''What? Oh, well, yes. Some.''

''Some. How much?''

''I make a passable pie.''

''Passable pie. What did you do with yourself once you were too old for tree climbing and marbles?''

''I studied, painted, learned to play the harp and stitched samplers.''

The wagon came to an abrupt halt. Glenna looked over to find him staring at her as if she had grown scales.

''You mean to tell me that you can't do *anything*?''

She met his gaze levelly and matched it in outrage. ''I wouldn't say that I can't do *anything*.''

"Painting pots of pears, playing the harp and stitching 'God Bless This Home' is nothing, lady. Can you make winter woolens or even a dress?"

"Probably."

"Meaning you never have?"

"Well, no, but—"

"Ever can fruit? Put up tomatoes? Dry vegetables?"

"No. But I can learn."

"And who the hell is going to teach you?"

The only sound to answer him was the whicker of one of the horses.

"Good God Almighty, woman, I told you prairie life was a wagonful of hard times. I told you what it involved."

"And I'm willing to work hard."

"You have to know what to do before you can work at all."

"I will learn," she repeated, enunciating each word slowly and precisely, uncowed by him.

With his elbow on his thigh, he dropped his face into his hand and shook his head.

Glenna felt the need to defend herself. "You did tell me some of what was involved, but you did not ask if I already knew how to do it," she told him practically. "I don't know why you're so upset about this. As long as I'm willing to do whatever I need to I can't see why it should matter that I haven't done it before."

He just kept on shaking his head. Glenna looked away, scanning the deserted land around them. She suddenly remembered him saying he would dump her in the middle of the prairie and leave her flat. "It can't be that difficult to learn," she offered.

His dark green eyes shot up at her. "You have a damn lot of nerve, do you know that, lady? When I laid out what this life would be like and you accepted it, I assumed that you knew how to do at least *some* of it. If I advertise for a trail hand and a man takes the job, I expect that he knows how to drive cows. If I advertise for a man to break horses and someone comes for the job, I expect that he knows which end of the horse to rein in. Now what the hell am I going to do with you?''

Glenna swallowed hard but faced him straight on. ''What you aren't going to do is sit there and curse me.''

He stared at her for another moment, his expression dark and forbidding. ''I ought to have the marriage annulled and leave you in Topeka,'' he said more to himself than to her.

''I'd rather you didn't,'' she told him honestly, keeping the fear that he would do just that out of her voice.

For a moment he continued to stare at her, those green eyes of his fierce. Then he turned away from her, picking up the reins, slapped them along the horses' backs and clicked a ''Giddap.''

There were few words said between them throughout the rest of the daylong ride to the Johnsons' place. The quiet left Glenna worrying about being left behind forever in a city in which Jared wouldn't leave her even overnight before.

Then she thought about the kind of home she would have if he did keep her. The country through which they were traveling was unlike anything Glenna had expected. Mile after mile of desolate space without seeing so much as another wagon or a sign of life between the houses they passed—houses that added to Glenna's worries. Never had she seen country so big, so far-reaching and so empty. And never had she seen homes the likes of what she found now.

''I just saw a man come out of the earth,'' was the first thing she said that interrupted the silence between her and Jared.

His answer came with disdain for her ignorance. ''It's a dugout—a house carved into a hill. Those and soddies are what most folks live in out here.''

The road curved nearer the dugout house and Glenna studied it in morbid curiosity. It was no more than a rise in the flat landscape, the front of it flattened, and a rough-hewn wooden door marking the entrance. "It's like being buried alive," she said to herself.

"Hardly," Jared answered caustically. "They're dark inside, but the dirt is smoothed into walls and there's more space than you think. Trouble is, when it rains the roof turns to mud and drips all over things. But out here we make do."

He seemed to know an awful lot about it. Did that mean the home he was taking her to was a dugout? But he had said he and his brother had built his house. The memory eased her mind somewhat. "What's a soddy?" she ventured in spite of his unpleasant tone of voice.

For a moment he didn't answer her, merely staring straight ahead at the horses' rumps, leaning his forearms on his thighs. But then he said, "A soddy is a house made of chunks of earth—sod. There's one way over there." He raised an arm across her and pointed. In the distance, far from the road, Glenna could only make out that the house was a tiny hovel. It didn't ease her trepidations about what her own home might be.

Silence settled again. She hadn't expected to be brought to a replica of Chicago. She hadn't expected a fancy house. She had also not expected to live in a hole in a hill or a home made of dirt. Afraid of provoking him further, she kept her worries to herself.

But worry she did.

It was after dark by the time they got to the Johnsons' farm. Theirs was a soddy and had it not been for the faint, yellow light coming from oiled-paper windows, it would have blended in completely with the soil from which it had been cut.

The sound of the wagon through the stillness of the country night must have been as heralding as a chorus of bells because before they had even reached the place a door opened to flood light and people in the travelers' path.

"Glad to see you're back on both feet, Hal, because I've come to take your two ranch hands home," Jared called as he pulled the wagon to a stop.

"It's Uncle Jared," one of the boys said in a voice that cracked an octave halfway through.

"That you, Jared?" asked a tall, older man in spite of the fact that they all seemed to recognize him.

"Who else would it be coming when you're likely to be on your way to bed?"

Glenna noted that Jared's voice held not a trace of the cold hostility it had for her. In fact, he sounded like the man who had told her about his family the previous night on the train—warm, friendly, happy. It was disheartening to realize that she brought out the hard side of him, while a softer side was reserved for others.

Jared jumped down from the wagon, announcing as he went, "I'm here with a new wife. We're grimy and travel-dirty and in need of a bath. Tend these horses, boys, and I won't make you walk back to Topeka," he teased.

A hearty male laugh sounded. "Well, congratulations and come on in. Dora'll fix you up something to eat first. I expect you're hungry, too."

Glenna moved to climb from the wagon herself but found Jared's hands ready and waiting, catching her under the arms and carefully lifting her down. She watched his face in the moonlight, hoping for a sign of acceptance, even just a glance that told her he wouldn't leave her in Topeka. But even though his assistance was gentle, he didn't so much as look at her, warning one of his nephews over his shoulder about the lead horse's skittishness.

Taking their grips, Jared waited for Glenna to follow their host into the house, but still his eyes wandered around the tiny homestead rather than looking her way.

Giving up her attempt to read anything into his actions, Glenna went to the house. She stopped short in the doorway and looked around the inside of the soddy. It was small and cluttered from the necessities of living. Actually only one room, the front half of the house was taken up by a table and chairs and two rockers in front of a fireplace that served for both heat and cooking. A tall cupboard sectioned off the back where two beds were separated by a blanket hung between, a cradle alongside one of them.

Was Jared's house like this? Glenna wondered. Was it so small, so rustic? Was this the reason he was adamant about taking on only a woman alone?

For herself it didn't matter. She could live in a place like the Johnsons' dugout as well as any, if need be. It was the thought of bringing Mary to such a home that raised her concerns. Not that surroundings were that important to the blind child. But how much more difficult it would be to convince Jared to add yet another person to such a tiny household.

She suddenly realized she was holding things up and stepped inside. In the light of a lamp burning in the center of the table, Glenna came face-to-face with her hosts for the first time. Dora was a large woman, tall, buxom, sturdy looking, her skin as suntanned as Jared's. On her hip was a baby that looked no more than six months old. Hal was bigger and broader than his wife, his face craggy and yet kind looking. As Jared set down their bags and introduced her, Glenna watched them both take in her battered face and choose not to mention it.

Then Hal clapped Jared on the back. "Come and see the calf that came from that cow you and Joseph sent. Can't tell you how much it helped."

As the two men went back outside Dora explained in a confidential and somewhat reverent voice, "Jared and his brother, Joseph, gave us a few head of stock to help us through our hard times. Don't know what we'd have done without them." Then she led the way toward the side of the blanket without the cradle. "You can take the boys' bed. They sleep out under the stars most nights anyway."

"I don't want to put anyone out."

"Why, child, don't give that a thought. We're so glad to have you." The larger woman hung a second blanket at the foot of the bed, completely enclosing the small space where Glenna and Jared would sleep. "And wait till my sister, Cally, sets eyes on you. She'll be so glad. She always was the more sociable of the two of us and she gets lonesome without another woman," Dora chattered as she slid Jared's valise under the bed.

Glenna unfastened the pelisse of her traveling gown and slipped it off.

"Leave your things over a chair after your bath and in the morning I'll have them brushed clean for you," Dora offered.

"Thank you." Realizing that she must look as dirty as she felt, Glenna took out her handkerchief and rubbed at the grime on her forehead.

"Oh, my," the other woman breathed, reaching to finger the lace edge of the handkerchief. "I haven't seen a hankie so fine since my wedding."

Glenna looked at the bit of linen in her hand that she took for granted. Then her glance went back to Dora, finding her staring at it as fondly as if it were a bolt of Irish lace.

"I wore one pinned to my bodice," Dora said wistfully. "It was borrowed—you know, something borrowed, something blue... I always did fancy a nice hankie. Silly, I know. But around these parts such things are treasures." Then she dragged her eyes away. "Well, let's get you and Jared something to eat, and then you can clean up and get some rest."

When she learned that the stew was made from squirrel meat, Glenna lost her appetite and settled on only a slice of bread. As they ate the small cabin seemed to reverberate with the sound of happy voices. She was introduced to Jared's nephews, Matthew and Mark, who resembled their uncle most in the deep green shade of their eyes. They were shy with Glenna but boisterous with Jared, regaling him with tales of the past two months spent there.

Jared listened to all of it, teasing them unmercifully, and then answering a myriad of questions from both the boys, Dora and Hal that illustrated just how isolated they were and how starved for news.

Through it all Glenna watched Jared. He was jovial, animated and relaxed. Glenna was surprised to find herself jealous. There could be no other word for it. She wished mightily for him to turn that genuine grin her way, to tease her with the fondness he did the others, to have that deep voice of his wrap around her without a trace of sarcasm or causticity. And though she didn't want to admit it, she wished for his hand to touch her as easily, as naturally and as affectionately as it did Matthew's shoulder, or the scruff of Mark's neck.

But of course it never happened.

Before she knew it, good-nights were being said, the boys were heading out back to sleep and Jared and Glenna were handed a bar of homemade soap and a single towel. Not wanting to remind him of her ignorance of life on the prairie, Glenna swallowed questions about where exactly they were to bathe as she followed Jared out of the soddy.

But when she found herself off a ways from the cabin at the edge of a pond bordered by two scant trees she couldn't stop herself. Trying to word what she said in a way that sounded helpful, she said, "If you'll show me where the buckets are I'll carry my share."

"Buckets? There's nowhere to carry them. As long as it isn't frozen solid, this pond is the bathtub." He set down the towel and soap and began to unbutton his shirt.

"Out here? In the open?"

"You have the cover of night."

"But the moon is full."

"You could forgo the bath," he suggested, a full measure in his voice of the distaste he would find in her if she did.

"Of course I can't," she shot back. "I've never gone two days without a bath in my life, and now I'm wearing half the dust between here and Chicago."

He pulled his shirttails free of his waistband, finished unbuttoning the shirt and dropped it to a heap on the ground. "Then you'd best get to it because when I'm finished I'm not waiting around."

The moon gilded his broad shoulders, and Glenna jerked her straying gaze away from the sight. They wouldn't all like him so well if they knew what he was really like, she thought as she began to yank at the buttons of her dress.

The sound of his splashing into the water came just before she pulled off her shoes and stockings and let her traveling gown fall around her feet.

"What the hell do you think you're doing?" he called when she headed for the water.

"Taking a bath," she informed.

"In your bloomers?"

And her chemise, but Glenna refrained from adding that. Instead she waded far enough into the pond for the water to reach her chin, keeping her distance from her husband where he watched from the center. "I have no intention of stripping naked out in the open," she informed him imperiously. Then she turned her back to him, held her breath and sank beneath the surface.

No bath had ever felt so good. Glenna stayed submerged until her lungs burned for air, reveling in the cool, clean retreat. Then she dropped her head back so that her face came out of the water first, her heavy hair hanging below.

It startled her to open her eyes and find Jared a scant foot away.

"Soap?" he offered with a half grin that made her wonder if that was actually what he was going to hand her.

"Please," she said, not revealing her doubts in the stern one of her voice.

But soap was what he gave her, and Glenna watched as he plunged beneath the water much as she had moments before. She wondered if he could see anything under there and suddenly felt as exposed as if she actually were naked. In a hurry she put the soap to good use so that when he broke the surface again she was finished with it.

For a moment she didn't hand it back to him the way she had intended. Instead her eyes caught and held on the sight of him emerging from the water, his hair plastered to his head, his mustache flattened and the sharp angles of his face thrown into deep relief by the white glow of the moon. Then he rose even farther, the water reflecting light from his broad shoulders, his massive chest rising in glorious male beauty.

Glenna swallowed with difficulty and shoved the bar of soap his way. "Here. I'm finished with it."

He reached and enclosed her hand in both of his, warm, yet slippery. But rather than taking the soap, there he stayed for a time, his thumbs smoothing up and down her wrist. Sparks began a dance from that spot all the way to her shoulder, and for a moment Glenna was mesmerized by the sensation. Then he slid the bar from her grip and her eyes followed it to his chest.

"You'd best rinse off, city girl," he said in yet a third voice, not mocking or caustic or sarcastic, not happy or friendly or affectionate, but husky and intimate sounding.

Again Glenna stifled emotions she didn't understand and sank below the surface to hide the confusion that seemed so strong she thought it must be reflected in her expression.

The water felt cooler suddenly. Or her skin was just hotter. Either way, the coolness wrapped around her like liquid satin to float away the tightness that had been wound inside her for the past few days, soothing her abused face better than any ointment.

Up she came for air only when her lungs demanded it, and then back down she went, over and over again in a natural rhythm. For a few moments she forgot everything else and just gave herself over to it, letting the water lull her, relax her, wash away all her tension along with the grime of the road.

And then, on one of her bobs up to take a breath, she realized she was alone in the pond. She opened her eyes to find Jared standing on the bank, his trousers on but only partially fastened, waiting for her with the towel. It was an oddly welcoming sight, which chased away any reluctance to leave the pond. Instead she waded out of the water, not even caring that her chemise and pantaloons clung to her.

Jared handed her the towel, moonlight illuminating an expression Glenna didn't recognize. He looked the way she felt, she decided, lazy and relaxed, but something else, too. It was as if heat radiated from the shadow that hid his eyes, a heat she could feel as his chin dipped slightly and told her he was taking in the full length of her body.

She wrapped the towel around herself like a cloak, realizing suddenly that it was dry and unused. She glanced at his shoulders where droplets of water were like sequins on his skin. Strange, she thought yet again at the evidence of his consideration.

Then he gathered his clothes and hers and led the way back to the sod house. They passed the two boys, sound asleep in bedrolls, and went in to the greeting of Hal Johnson's snores. Jared laid their clothes over the seat of one of the chairs. Then he waited for Glenna to join him on their side of the blanket wall.

Tension came back to Glenna. Faced with the small space and single narrow bed, she was at a loss as to what to do and so stood holding the towel around her.

Jared pulled their carpetbags from under the bed and set them atop the mattress. From his he took a roll of bandages the doctor had given him and came to her side. He leaned over and whispered in her ear so softly she barely heard it. "You're going to have to take off those wet underthings and let me rewrap your ribs."

Glenna felt as if every nerve were on the surface of her skin. Her heart was racing like a rabbit's and there was a tingling all through her that she didn't recognize. Arguing was impossible under the circumstances, and so she ignored her embarrassment and gave in to the other sensations that made her situation seem somehow enticing.

She turned her back to him and laid the towel on the bed for a moment while she untied the ribbons that held her chemise. Shrugging out of it was a strain on her ribs and, as if Jared knew that, the moment she began his hands were there to take it off for her. She paused once her pantaloons were untied, realized that to drop them was to expose her bare posterior. But they were cold against her overwarm skin, and since she knew she couldn't sleep in them, down they went. On her way back up from pulling the wet bloomers off she picked up the towel and held it to the front of her, feeling at once modest and something else...free and oddly proud of her nakedness.

She waited for Jared to begin but for a time he just stayed standing there behind her. Glenna glanced over her shoulder at him. The only light in their small space was the yellowed moonglow sneaking in the oiled-paper window; she could see almost nothing but the dark silhouette of him. Still she sensed a tension in him that matched the one in her, not an angry tension or an irritated one, but a tautness in the way he held his body.

Finally he stepped nearer and removed the soaking bandages that were the only thing she wore. His hands never actually touched her as he loosened them from their circle below her breasts. But once the old bandages were gone he took up the clean, dry strip and reached around her, under the towel. Beginning, as the doctor had, at the lowest part of her rib cage, Jared wrapped the bandage firmly but not too tightly. Around and around, Glenna could feel his hands moving ever nearer to her bare breasts. Her breath caught in her throat. One arm brushed just the underside of one breast and those same sparks that had skittered up her arm when he'd taken the soap from her in the pond came to life hotter and sharper now, pinching her nipples into hard, sensitive kernels.

She felt Jared tuck the end of the bandage into one of the folds in back, but rather than that ending it, his hands came to rest on her sides over the wrappings. His fingers curved around to the front of her ribs, just below her breasts, ever so lightly. And there they stayed.

Glenna had forgotten how to breathe. Instead her body was crying out for something it needed more than air; she just wasn't sure what it was.

Then his mouth pressed to that spot where her neck curved into her shoulder, his breath a hot gust there. Reflexively her hands tightened their grip on the towel she still held in front of her, but on its own her head tilted a little to the side, easing his way. Twice he kissed her, the third time making leisurely circles with his tongue and leaving his mark to chill dry as he bent even closer and sucked lightly on the sharp ridge of her collarbone.

Glenna closed her eyes and answered the urge to lean back into him, letting her head fall against his shoulder. And then his hands moved, slowly, all the way around to the front of her, pausing there for just his thumbs to trace the undercurve of her breasts.

Glenna drew breath then, sharply, surprised as much by the pleasure of the sensation as by his touch. Should she move away? she wondered. But she didn't want to. Instead she followed her own instinct and pulled her shoulders back, thrusting her breasts out slightly in much the same gesture of invitation that tilting her head had been.

Answering her, he covered both her breasts with his hands, gently, as if he were allowing her to get used to the feeling. It was glorious. Wonderful. Stirring more than soothing. Then his touch turned more forceful. He filled his hands fully and pressed her back against the length of him.

A hard ridge pushed at the base of her spine but Glenna was only peripherally aware of it. She was becoming accustomed to the leashed strength at work kneading her breasts. For a moment she resented that he let go of her, until he found her again, this time only with his fingers, rolling her engorged nipples with a titillating mixture of tenderness and pressure, teasing them to an even greater yearning.

So lost in the sensations he was giving her, Glenna barely heard him groan, softly, deep in his throat. The thought flitted through her mind that it sounded as if he had just awakened to find he'd done something he didn't want to do. And then his hands fell away. His mouth left her shoulder, and where there had been warm, hard muscle bracing her back there was only a cool gust of air as he moved from her.

Glenna stood straight. She opened her eyes, blinking over and over again as if she, too, had just come out of a trance. But before she had completely regained all of her senses, his arm reached around her, handing her her nightgown.

Shakily, she took it and let the towel drop to her feet. Slipping the soft cotton garment over her head as fast as she could, she no longer felt proud of her nakedness, but was now embarrassed by it, by what had just happened between them, by the craving that was still torturing her. In the time it took her to do up the buttons to her throat Jared had gotten into the extremely narrow bed from the other side. Confused and not a little self-conscious, Glenna glanced there and found him lying on his side, the sheet covering him from the waist down but a corner of it held up for her by one of those same hands her flesh was still crying out for.

"The only way we're both going to fit in this bed," he whispered gruffly, "is like two spoons. Come on."

She called herself every kind of fool for even the flash of a thought that he was inviting her into his bed for more of what he had begun a moment before. She wanted to shout at him, to throw something at him, to hit him, as if activity would soothe the ache that he had roused in her. But of course she could do nothing but sit on the bed's edge, slip her feet under the sheet that concealed him and lie in front of him.

He covered her then, and rested his arm platonically across her waist.

Glenna lay there stiffly, staring into the darkness straight ahead. She willed her body to stop wanting more, to stop waiting for his touch again, because waiting for it never made it come. Instead, after a while she heard his breathing deepen and knew he was asleep. She had expected no more, she told herself.

She lay awake until long after the moon had risen above the paper window, leaving more complete darkness. And in the time it took her to fall asleep she wondered if going to jail really would have been more torturous than this.

Chapter Nine

By half past three the next afternoon Glenna was alone in a room on the second floor of a Topeka hotel. With Mark and Matthew in tow, she and Jared had left the Johnsons' homestead at dawn in order to catch a two o'clock train. But a robbery had sidetracked the train, and it wouldn't be in until the following morning.

The boys were delighted by the delay. A night spent in what for them was the big city was an exciting proposition. For Glenna, the fact that the same train she had ridden into town and would take out again had been robbed was unsettling, and yet she, too, welcomed the delay. Time in the city meant a chance to try to sell off what remained of her mother's jewelry. That the teenagers had persuaded Jared to take them to watch the boxing matches going on in the street below was a further stroke of luck—her husband's absence gave her the perfect opportunity to search the town for a jeweler.

Glenna's only deference to Jared's warning about the dangers of a lawless frontier town was to once more don Aunt Lida's widow's weeds. This time—in addition to disguising her—she hoped the costume might garner some sympathy to aid her cause.

"Maybe someone will feel sorry for the poor tattered widow woman needing to sell off her jewelry to survive," she told her reflection as she stuffed her hair into the back of the hat.

With her costume in place Glenna took the modest jewelry from the velvet box and put it into her drawstring purse. Then she went to the window to peer down at Topeka's main street. Most people were gathered around the roped-off ring where an ox of a man clad only in dusty trousers and red suspenders took on all comers, one at a time. With each victory of his the cheers of the onlookers grew louder, and more people were drawn away from the boardwalk and businesses to witness the spectacle. It made Glenna feel marginally safer in her errand.

Questioning the gangly desk clerk in the lobby as to where she might find someone interested in purchasing jewelry, she was directed to the People's Store. Glenna took a deep bolstering breath and marched outside with a determination that belied the knot in her stomach.

Summer was not giving way gracefully to autumn. The air was hot and dry, and if the dust that blanketed everything was any indication, it had been that way for some time.

Crossing the street, she stepped onto the boardwalk in front of the Topeka National Bank. Two men courteously moved back and allowed her to pass.

Not so different from Chicago, Glenna thought a little smugly.

There was, however, a definite lack of women among the throngs of men milling about. And those she did see were either being escorted or were in pairs; it raised a niggling doubt in her mind about the wisdom of her errand. Still, she kept her shoulders squared and her step measured. She was doing this for Mary.

Even without looking directly at the men she passed Glenna was aware of the difference between them and those she was accustomed to in Chicago. There were whiskers aplenty, most of them in dire need of a trim. The morning suits that clothed most city men were nowhere in appearance here, where buckskin breeches and denim jeans rode low on hips, too many of them weighted with holsters. Sweat-stained Stetson hats were also in abundance, as well as the same heavy leather boots that Jared had taken to wearing since the morning they had left Chicago.

Her heels clicked as she passed an assay office and another establishment called Steinberger & Company. She was aware that she drew the glance of every man lounging against a storefront or approaching her on the boardwalk, but she paid them no mind. Instead she picked up her pace and willed the People's Store to come into view soon, to allow her to escape the watchful eyes and the heat that was dampening her dress with perspiration.

Oh, but it was hot.

And there was no respite in the wind that blew. It was as warm as the air that gusted forth with the opening of an oven door. Glenna's head began to itch unbearably under the black felt hat and she fleetingly considered not wearing it. But each step brought her nearer to the cluster of men around the fight, and rather than lifting her hands to her hat she kept them together around her purse strings.

As she drew up to the assemblage, voices were loud with shouts and calls that were far cruder than anything she had ever heard in Chicago. Money-filled fists waved overhead and the odors of whiskey, beer and bodies were pungent in the air.

She walked even faster to get past the goings-on. But before she had made it a roar went up from the crowd and all at once a body came hurling onto the boardwalk right in front of her. Glenna drew up short, barely stopping before she trampled the sweaty man lying facedown on the walkway where spectators had parted. Catcalls went up all around her, and Glenna found herself being pushed and shoved in the hub of the onlookers.

"Shee-it. Thought that mother-lovin' mountain could take 'im," came a wheedling voice so close beside her that the man could have been speaking to her. "I lost all my whorin' money."

Glenna barely glanced at the man, his head shiny bald. Then she averted her eyes and tried to move outside of the crowd, which was partly disbanding while the fallen boxer was dragged away and someone called for the next to try his luck against the red suspenders. But amid the crush of bigger, harder bodies she could barely move. She tried dodging to the left, then to the right, but was getting nowhere. And then a hulk of a man in front of her stepped on her foot. Glenna jerked backward in pain, losing her balance and colliding with the bald man, who grabbed her reflexively.

"Well, lookee here," came his wheedling voice again. "I got me a widder woman throwin' herself right into my arms."

Glenna regained her balance in a hurry and tried to move out of the man's reach, only to find her arm caught in a tight grip that yanked her back against him.

"Excuse me," she said imperiously.

That made him chuckle and send a malodorous whiff of his breath her way. "Look at that piece of red hair curlin' outside of that hat, will ya, Burt? I never seen nothin' like it."

Just then the felled boxer was removed, another bout began, and the path in front of Glenna was cleared. With more force than before she reclaimed her arm and took several fast steps away from the fight rabble, heading once more for the People's Store. But the bald man and another fell into step on either side of her, and before she knew what was happening the other man snatched off her bonnet and her hair tumbled free. The sight elicited a long, shrill whistle from the bald man while the second tormentor filled his dirty hands with her hair.

Glenna pulled her hair out of his grip but found her arm caught once again by the bald man, who pulled her to a stop.

"I'll be on my way now," she informed them forcefully. It was as if they hadn't heard her.

"I want me a feel of that hair, Burt," her captor told his partner instead.

"Let go of me," Glenna demanded. But still it was as if her words fell on deaf ears.

Again the man called Burt took a fistful of her hair and handed it to her captor as if it were his to give. "What say we take her with us out back of Jersey's?"

That was all Glenna needed to hear. She tried to pull her hair out of his hand and failing that, swung her purse at her captor's bald head, cuffing him hard enough to loosen his grip. Seizing the release in pressure she pulled away but didn't get far before Burt's arm clamped around her and immobilized her against his rocklike front.

"Looks like this'un needs tamin'. Maybe we're just goin' to have to teach her some manners."

With her arms pinned by the vise of his meaty hug the only thing left to fight with was her feet. But the best she could do was kick backward in futility; the man didn't so much as flinch.

"Leave me alone!" she shouted now. Fear was rapidly taking a stronger hold than Burt. When wiggling and fighting had no effect she frantically scanned her surroundings for help. But with all attention on the boxing match, not so much as a glance was spared her.

Her original captor stepped directly in front of her and leaned down until his craggy face was level with hers. His expression was unpleasant. When he spoke it was through the snarl of yellowed teeth. "I don't like no woman hittin' me." Then his hand again closed around her arm, this time punishingly so, and he pulled her away from Burt. Without another word he took off in the direction from which Glenna had come, dragging her stumbling behind him.

"Stop it! You can't do this!" she shrieked at the man's back.

"I can do any damn thing I like," he answered her over his shoulder.

Glenna believed him, since no one they passed made a move to help her. The man jumped down from the board-walk into the first street, and as if his pulling her weren't enough, Burt shoved her from behind. She fell, bringing the man to a halt. He yanked her arm nearly out of its socket to get her back up, but Glenna fought like a cornered cat, kicking and swinging fists and purse at anything she could connect with. For a moment she gained some ground as the man did little more than protect himself from her assault, but then Burt stepped up from behind, took a fistful of her hair and pulled her up as if he were roping a steer.

"We should've saved our money until somebody put *her* in the ring," Burt told his friend.

"That's about enough."

It was Jared's voice. Never in her life had Glenna been so grateful for the sound of anything.

"Let her go," he told Burt in a tone that was all the more threatening for the calm it held.

Glenna winced at the pain that seared her scalp as Burt turned to face Jared and pulled her by the hair with him. Jared stood like a statue only a few feet away, his legs an arch, his left hand hanging loosely at his side while in his right he held a rifle, the butt against his hip.

"She somethin' to you?" Burt demanded menacingly.

Jared didn't take his eyes off the men to look at her. "My wife," he informed them coolly.

For a moment Glenna didn't think Burt believed it, or that it mattered even if he did. But then he opened his hand and let loose her hair. Neither he nor his partner said any-thing, instead merely stepped back from Glenna and then turning around to move off down the street as if nothing out of the ordinary had happened.

For a moment Jared remained just the way he was, watching the two men walk away. Then he lowered his eyes to Glenna, and she found them harder, colder, more contemptuous than they had been as he had faced down her tormentors. He uncocked the rifle and swung it butt first to Matthew where he stood with Mark in the background. "Give this back," he instructed. "I'll see you boys at the hotel." Three long strides brought him to Glenna's side, and when his hand closed around her wrist she wasn't sure if she had been delivered from danger or thrust into worse.

Without a word Jared crossed the street to the hotel. Trailing behind him, through the lobby, up two flights of stairs and down the corridor, Glenna struggled more now to stay on her feet than she had when in Burt's grip.

Once inside their room Jared released her and closed the door behind them. Glenna swallowed hard and forced herself to look him in the eye.

"Thank you," she said frankly.

Jared didn't answer. Instead he stayed staring at her. One of his legs was a little in front of the other, his weight on the one behind. His hands bracketed his hips, all ten fingers digging so hard into the denim of his pants that they were white knuckled. His face was implacable, his eyes shadowed beneath the shelf of his brow.

Glenna's heart was still pounding but she tried to hide her trepidation by moving to the open window and brushing the dust from her skirt.

Still she could feel Jared's gaze boring through her. Did he expect her to explain? Or was he waiting for some self-control before he said anything?

Glenna could only stand it so long.

"You were right about your frontier towns being more dangerous than Chicago," she offered, facing him with the distance of the room between them.

Silence.

Glenna slipped her purse from around her wrist and set it back in her carpetbag. "It was lucky you saw what was going on."

He didn't move. He still didn't speak.

With both hands she picked the mass of her hair off the back of her neck and pinned it haphazardly atop her head. She'd lost her hat, she realized as she searched for more to say. "Next time..." She had to clear her throat. "I thought you were being overly cautious when you warned me not to go out. Now I see what you meant."

That got an answer but in a voice so deep and angry Glenna was almost sorry he finally spoke. "I didn't *warn* you not to go out. I *told* you to stay here."

She moistened her lips. "Yes, I know. I just...well, I didn't really think it was all that dangerous and with nearly everyone watching the fight I didn't expect to draw any attention...and I wanted to have a look at a real frontier town...." Her voice dwindled to nothing. She could see that he didn't believe a word of what she was saying.

"Take off that dress."

That widened her eyes. "Pardon me?"

"I said," he went on louder, each word falling like a separate drumbeat, "take off that dress."

"I don't understand...."

"Now."

Why? Did he mean to humiliate her? Beat her? Keep her some kind of prisoner by taking her clothes? "No," she said defiantly.

"Either you'll do it or I will, but it comes off. Now."

"I don't know what—"

"Now."

For a moment Glenna stared him down. Then he took a step toward her, and almost on their own her hands reached to unfasten the buttons at her throat. She made fast work of them and then slipped the too large black dress down to her ankles, all the while keeping her eyes trained on Jared. When she stood clad only in her chemise and petticoat he crossed the room to her. Involuntarily, Glenna took a step backward, away from him.

Standing directly in front of her, he held out his hand. "Give it to me."

She bent, watching him all the while, picked up Aunt Lida's mourning dress and did as he asked.

Jared flung it out the window just behind her.

"Why?" Glenna confusion was compounded.

He glared down at her. "I don't know what the hell that dress has to do with it, but I know you're up to something every time you put it on."

"I told you before that it's only to make sure I don't attract undue attention."

Both his expression and his tone made it clear he didn't believe that, either. "I won't have a wife who goes out swishing her skirts for other men every time my back is turned."

"Swishing my skirts?" She was incredulous. "How could you even think that's what I was doing dressed in old, shabby, ill-fitting clothes?"

His frown only deepened. "Or is it some sort of sign to one man in particular that you're on the sneak to meet him?"

"That doesn't even make sense. I don't know anyone in Topeka."

"Maybe he's following behind."

Glenna matched his frown. "That's twice now you've accused me of seeking to meet other men or helping one to trail along. I've given you no reason for that."

"You've given me no reason to trust you, either."

"And distrust comes first with you, is that it?"

His silence confirmed it.

"Why?" she asked again, searching for understanding.

"What are you really doing every time you put that get-up on?" he countered instead. "I know damn good and well you didn't go out before dawn the last time for no reason but to take a walk, and if you were just out to see a real frontier town why were you marching down that board-walk like you were headed someplace in particular?''

So he had seen her even before her encounter with the two men. "I just wanted to get past the commotion of the fight in a hurry," she lied quickly.

Jared's disbelief was still evident. He shook his head back and forth, back and forth. "There's a lot of pickings for a loose skirt around here—''

"I'm not a loose skirt," she cut in heatedly, insulted.

He sighed. "No, not with me, you're not. But a woman as prim and proper as you'd like me to think you are doesn't go out walking the street alone before daylight or in a town she's already been warned about."

"And a man who doesn't have cause shouldn't be so suspicious."

"Oh, I have plenty of cause."

"You've had my virtue verified," she shot back at him.

"I've had your maidenhead verified. But virtue and virginity aren't necessarily the same thing."

It was frustrating to be accused of something she was innocent of. But she could hardly defend herself with the truth. She tried reasoning with him instead. "It doesn't make sense that I would put on an old woman's mourning dress that fits me like a sack to go out hunting for someone to cuckold you with. And if anyone were following us all I'd have to do is go right to them when your back is turned. I don't need some clandestine plan for either of those things."

If was Glenna's turn to shake her head. "If you would just think clearly you would realize how unlikely it is that I would marry you with my...virtue...intact only to go walking the streets looking to lose it. And if there was someone else who could follow behind, why wouldn't I have hooked up with him in the first place to get me out of Chicago rather than marrying a stranger?''

He cocked his head to one side and angled a brow up at her. "Why don't you tell me?"

Glenna nearly shrieked. "Because there's nothing to tell! The dress was for safety's sake, that's all."

He continued to stare at her. Glenna watched his jaw clench and unclench. "I don't believe you," he said finally. "There's more going on with you than you'd like me to think."

"And I'd say there's more going on with you to accuse me of such things," she challenged back.

His long index finger stabbed the air in front of her. "I'm watching you, lady." Then he turned away from her and walked out.

For a moment Glenna stood there in her underdrawers staring at the door he slammed after himself. She wished she could feel flattered that he was jealous, but under the circumstances where it wasn't prompted by affection, it was hardly flattering. And what did prompt it? she wondered. Was it merely a case of a man being possessive? Was it the way of men in this section of the country? Or was it, like David Stern's penchant for violence, a flaw in his character?

That was an unsettling thought.

Yet she didn't actually believe he was anything like her stepfather. And she had to admit that there was reason for him to be suspicious of her.

Glenna knelt on the floor beside her satchel and again hid the last of her mother's jewelry before taking out another dress to wear.

The next time she went to sell the jewelry, she decided, she'd just have to be more careful, and not let him catch her at it.

Chapter Ten

Ahh . . . it's good to be back," Jared breathed as they descended the train steps in Hays City at a little past noon the next day.

Following him, Glenna took the hand he offered to help her down onto the long platform that separated the tracks from the small red station house.

"Hee-ya!" Matthew called as he leaped down behind her, obviously as glad as his uncle to be home again. It was Mark who smiled at Glenna and said, "Welcome to Hays," when he finally disembarked.

Glenna answered the quieter twin with a smile and a thank-you before turning to take in her new hometown. As she did, Mark proudly explained what she was seeing.

"This is Old North Main Street—runs east to west from Chestnut Street. Mama says we have more culture than any other prairie town. See, there was a little city 'bout twelve miles southeast of here called Victoria. Bunch of rich Englishmen founded it, aiming to transplant some of their own country over here. They only lasted six years or so, but those that stayed on moved to Hays and brought their fine-and-fancies, and their liking of plays and polo and tennis games and dress-up balls and such with them."

"If you're finished with the history lesson, Mark," Jared broke in with a teasing tone, clamping the back of the boy's neck, "why don't you and Matt go over to the livery and hire us a buckboard. We'll meet you at the mercantile."

Mark's face colored, but he grinned and shrugged out of his uncle's grip. Glenna watched the two lanky boys leave.

"I think poor Mark is smitten with you," Jared said in an intimate tone, leaning down to her ear.

She glanced up at him, surprised to be spoken to that way. He had barely said three words to her since their argument in Topeka. "He's a nice boy. They both are."

Jared's deep green eyes stayed on her for a time. Gone was the harsh suspicion, replaced by what almost looked like warmth. He really was happy to be home, Glenna thought; it even softened his attitude toward her. Regardless of the cause, she was grateful for the easing of the tension between them.

In spite of Mark's description of it as a cultured place, Hays was as rustic as Topeka. The buildings were mainly one-story square-front structures. There were long rails in front of most of them, to which horses were tied to wait for their owners. But still, arriving here meant that Glenna had reached the goal she had set for herself. She was far away from Chicago and the dangers that had forced her to leave, she hadn't been found out or deserted along the way, and now she could settle in to this place, to work toward the day when she could bring Mary here, too. Hays City might not be pretty, but it would do.

Jared took her elbow and they headed up the street past the Leavenworth Restaurant, two saloons and gambling houses, and the justice of the peace. Glenna made a note of the location of the jewelry store next door before Jared steered her past four more saloons and dance halls.

"There must be a lot of drinking here," she mused, spying yet another half dozen such establishments across the street.

Jared grinned lopsidedly, his eyes sparkling with amusement. "I've heard one count come in at seventy-five places where a man can get a drink."

"But it isn't something you know from experience?" she inquired only half-seriously. Since he had shown no sign of a penchant for inebriation after that first morning, she had come to believe it was an isolated occurrence.

He cocked his head and arched an eyebrow. "Oh, I'm familiar with one or two."

"Only one or two?" she persisted, because the tone of teasing between them was as rare as it was pleasant.

"Maybe three," he went on, obviously enjoying it as much as she.

"Well," she said with an exaggerated sigh, "I suppose familiarity with one or two, or even three, out of seventy-five isn't cause for too much concern."

"Were you concerned?" he feigned surprise.

"Mmm."

"Or is it that I've brought in a Woman's Christian Temperance Union crusader?"

"Mmm." She kept him wondering. "Didn't I read that Kansas passed an amendment against liquor?"

"You read that, did you?"

"I did."

"Mmm." This time it was Jared's turn to be enigmatic.

"How can there be so many illegal establishments?"

"It's an unpopular law."

"And so isn't enforced," she finished for him.

"Mmm." His smile was amused.

"Well," she said with an overanimated sigh, "I trust you won't give me cause to become a crusader and insist the law be enforced."

"Well—" he matched her tone "—I trust you won't drive me to drink."

That made them both smile, green eyes meeting aqua in more of that intimacy that seemed to have settled over them along with the Hays City dust.

Several people greeted Jared and tipped their hats to Glenna, their curiosity not appeased as he returned their greetings but didn't stop to talk. Instead Jared kept her headed up the street, passing a boardinghouse and two hotels—one, the York House, with a sign out front purporting to be the best hotel west of Salina. Then they reached the general store, rounding a barrel heaped with apples and a table displaying cookwares to get to the tall front door.

"Ho, Jared," the storekeeper called the moment they walked into the cluttered establishment, which smelled of vinegary pickles, spices and coffee mingled with other, less identifiable scents. "Joseph was just saying at church on Sunday that they expected you anytime now."

"Well, here I am, Sam," Jared called back as warmly. Then he turned to introduce Glenna, and all of a sudden she remembered the shadows of the bruises on her face. It helped immeasurably when Jared stretched his arm along the back of her shoulders as if they actually were man and wife in affection as well as in name.

"How do, how do," the plump storekeeper said with the matching bobs of his head. Then the bewhiskered man winked at Jared. "So you went and did it again, eh? Can't resist these city girls, can you?"

Jared squeezed her shoulders, pulling her in close to his side. "Guess not. Now how about fixing us up with supplies to get us started? Better have two hundred pounds of flour, a hundred of sugar, coffee . . . oh, and tea, Glenna drinks tea, and . . . well, just load me up. But whatever you do, don't forget the licorice whips. If I show up without them Annie will disown me."

"Your own young'un might, too. Charity had him in tow at church on Sunday. Never saw a child with such a sweet tooth. She had to give him little bits of sugar candy so the reverend could be heard over the ruckus he was making. Handsome boy, though. My missus couldn't keep her hands off him. She'll be glad to hear he has a mother all his own finally.''

Just like that Jared's arm was gone from around Glenna, and he was intently interested in a basket of eggs with a sign that offered three dozen for a quarter. Apparently she was not the only one to notice the sudden change in mood. The storekeeper cleared his throat uncomfortably. ''Well, I'd best get your order together.''

Matthew and Mark burst through the door about then, Mark announcing that he needed boot polish and Matthew wanting hair pomade. ''Hair pomade?'' Jared repeated dubiously, laughing before he okayed the addition of both to his order. From that moment his mood was back to what it had been when they left the train.

Once the buckboard was loaded, the teenagers hopped onto the back while Jared and Glenna took up the front seat. Going north out of town they passed the courthouse square and then more saloons, gambling houses, dance halls, and if the muffled laughter coming from the wagon bed was any indication, some houses of ill repute as well. Then they turned into a rutted dirt road that seemed to Glenna to cut a straight path to nowhere.

She had thought west Kansas was flat and dry, but it seemed lush in comparison to the countryside through which they traveled now. At least they had passed an occasional tree on the way to the Johnsons' homestead. But here there was virtually nothing. Flat, dry and barren, the land stretched out to the horizon in an unbroken plane of yellow grass and tumbleweeds.

As if reading her thoughts Jared said, ''It's fair cattle land, but nature's harder on the farmer. There's no depending on the rain and without it water is scarce. Crops dry up and blow away in the wind.''

"I don't suppose there are many people who can afford to start up a cattle ranch, or many who can withstand the hardships of having their work come to naught in farming. Is that why there's so many empty miles between home-steads?"

Jared chuckled and looked over at her as if through new eyes. There was respect in them that buoyed Glenna as much as the tentative closeness between them. "You put things together fast. This is a hard land. It does in a lot of peo-ple."

"But not your family."

For some reason he turned back to staring at the horses' rumps and frowned. "Our roots are pretty deep here." Then he looked back at her, this time pointedly. "That doesn't mean it's any easier, especially on the women. We've lost our share of men and women to hardships not taken seri-ously enough and to false assumptions that life for the Strattons was easier than life for anyone else out here, so don't go expecting things to be smooth sailing."

He fell silent again then, and Glenna let the subject go, wondering if it was his first wife who had somehow crept into his thoughts and if her death had been because of hardships not taken seriously enough or false assumptions that life as a Stratton was easier.

It was late afternoon by the time the wooden arch that marked the entrance to the Circle S Ranch came into sight. To Glenna it seemed stuck in the middle of nowhere and she wondered how anyone could ever tell where one parcel of land ended and another began. Not long after that Jared pointed straight ahead and she could barely make out sev-eral buildings in the distance.

Her heart was beating fast and her eyes were stuck on those buildings. She had learned that soddies and dugouts couldn't be seen from such a distance, and that helped quell some of her fears about what sort of home she was coming to. But replacing those anxieties was an uneasiness about how she would be accepted by this large family.

"Are the bruises still so obvious?" she whispered to Jared, surprising herself by her own intimate tone.

He glanced over at her as if they were something he hadn't noticed of late. There his gaze remained, as if he were taking a fresh look. Then he smiled with one side of his mouth, breathed a little laugh and ran a single finger along her jawline, gently tweaking her chin when he got there. "The swelling is all gone and most of the color. The worst of it is that purple shadow under your eye. I still see some stubbornness to spare but that didn't come from your stepfather. Altogether I suppose you're easy enough on the eyes to look at for a time."

So they were back to the teasing. Glenna was glad, and unaccountably pleased by what passed as a compliment. Still she gave as good as she got. Her glance traveled audaciously over his features. "Your nose is a bit too thin and somewhat pointed, and you've a tendency to look down it like an owl over its beak, but I suppose I can abide it."

One of his eyebrows went aloft, lazily, insolently. "We're in agreement, then? Neither of us is perfect but we'll do?"

Glenna nodded just once, thinking that his rugged good looks were much closer to perfect than she would let him know.

"Since that's settled," he said, "hang on, I'm going to take you home."

He clicked to the horses and slapped the reins against their backs, picking up speed for a moderate dash the rest of the way.

Home, to Glenna's relief, was a whole cluster of buildings, all white clapboard with steep black roofs. They formed a number-seven shape with the houses facing the road and the other structures at a right angle alongside. The first they passed was a huge barn backed up by a paddock that was bordered all around with a three-rail fence.

"That's the bunkhouse," Jared said, pointing to the next building, "and out back you can just barely see the henhouse and the pigsty."

Of the two homes that formed the center of the compound it wasn't difficult to tell which belonged to her in-laws and which would be her own. The main house was twice as large, a three-storied square box. The windows were all shuttered in black to match the roof, and below were shiny red boxes of peonies to break the starkness. Sheets flapped in the breeze on a clothesline along the side, and out front two boys were chasing a white rabbit that proved more slippery than it looked.

The smaller house beside it had a big bay window and a covered porch that shaded the front door. The second story, smaller than the first, was perched like the upper layer of a wedding cake. Directly above the front door was a second door opening to a small white-railed balcony. There were no shutters or window boxes of flowers softening this house, and yet its shape alone gave it a hominess.

There were even trees, Glenna noted with pleasure, two giant elms, one shading the back of each of the houses.

From the rear of the wagon Matthew let out a long, loud howl as Jared steered the horses around a curved drive that took them past the smaller house and right up in front of the larger. They came to a stop a few feet from where the two boys had a tangled hold on the rabbit.

"Uncle Jared!" one of them called, losing his grip and allowing the animal to escape.

"Uncle Jared's home, Uncle Jared's home!" the second, identically towheaded and freckled child called.

All at once the wagon rocked as Jared and the twins jumped down. The older boys began unloading the buckboard, and Jared rounded the horses and came up to Glenna's side. He reached for her, but before his hands had touched her waist a little girl with long golden braids and a pert nose charged out the screen door, leaped off the narrow porch and, with outstretched arms, hit Jared's legs at full speed.

"I didn't think you were ever coming home," she proclaimed gleefully, bouncing up and down.

"What? And stay away from my favorite girl?" Jared laughed down at her once he had regained his balance. Then he lifted her up to one of his hips where she promptly strangled him with a hug and planted a sloppy kiss on his cheek.

"I'm so glad you're home. Where's my licorice?"

That made him laugh again. "You'll just have to wait and see if I brought you any," he teased her affectionately.

"Well, it's about time." A voice as deep and resounding as Jared's came from across the yard, drawing Glenna's eyes from the child she already realized was Annie to a man who could only be Joseph. His resemblance to Jared was marked, though he was less handsome. His hair was lighter, he had no mustache, and around his eyes were laugh lines that made him look somewhat lighter of nature. "Thought I was going to have to bring the stock in to closer ground by myself this year." In spite of the words, Joseph's tone was teasing and his mouth curved into a smile. The two men greeted each other with a rough, back-slapping hug.

"All by yourself and thirty hands," Jared countered.

Just then two more boys, one nearly a man and both of them with the look of the Strattons in their wheat-colored hair and angular faces, came out of the barn. The shorter, slighter of the two climbed the railed fence while the older one scissor-leaped it and came at a run. "Boy, am I glad you're back."

"Working you too hard, is he, John?" Jared answered and then said, "Hello, Luke," to his younger nephew when the other boy caught up.

Since her husband had obviously forgotten her, Glenna climbed down from the wagon herself. Staying close beside it she watched from a short distance as a woman who could only be Cally joined the group, wiping floury hands on her apron as she did.

"Here she is, my favorite sister-in-law. Come give me a hello kiss." Jared called her off the porch and wrapped his free arm around her shoulders. Cally was a naturally pretty woman with shiny brown hair, dark eyes and round apple cheeks that glistened with the pink hue of robust health. Glenna watched the other woman slide her arm around Jared's waist and give him a squeeze and a kiss on the cheek.

"Welcome home, honey," she said with motherly affection.

It was Cally who took notice of Glenna then. The smile she sent was tentative and cool, and Glenna's hopes for a warm welcome were slightly punctured.

"Hello," the other woman, large with child, said to Glenna.

Cally Stratton's tone was so formal Glenna knew her own answering smile was not genuine, tinged as it was with disappointment. Cally's sister, Dora, had been so nice that Glenna had expected the same warm reception. "Hello," she returned halfheartedly.

Charity, the older daughter and last of Cally and Joseph's children to appear, came out of the house then. Slung on her hip as if she was used to it was a toddler. Glenna watched as she walked over to them. Charity was a pretty girl with her mother's healthy glow.

But it wasn't on Charity that her glance stayed. It was on the child Glenna was to mother. Plump, round-faced and rosy-complexioned, he was a beautiful baby, with a head of wavy brown hair and wide black eyes that surveyed the scene over the thumb he was sucking.

But as Charity and the baby joined the group Glenna heard Cally sigh, and her attention went back to the woman with her arm still around Jared.

Cally drew back slightly and looked him in the face, her expression sad. "You did it, didn't you? She's come for Lyden."

Out of the corner of her eye Glenna saw Charity press a protective hand to the baby's back, draw him close and claim him with her cheek against his head. Jared had been wrong, she thought suddenly. Lyden wasn't a bother to these people, he was like one of their own. But mothering him was what she'd come to do, and thinking that, she turned a smile to the toddler, stepped closer and took his tiny fist in her left hand. "Hello, Lyden."

"She's come for the boy, all right," Jared finally said. "She's—"

But before he could finish Cally cut him off. "Don't do this, Jared. It won't wipe everything away as if it never happened. He's your son."

Still holding the baby's hand Glenna looked back at her husband and his sister-in-law, taking in the sudden solemnity of the Stratton family and wondering what was going on.

Jared shook his head. "Cally," he said gently, "this is Glenna. She's my wife."

Instantly Cally's eyes went to Glenna's hand in search of a wedding ring. For some reason Glenna felt naked to have the other woman find nothing there, and it suddenly occurred to her that not having a ring seemed like a denial of her place in Jared's life, as if he had married her but not really accepted her. Pride made her reject the temptation to hide her hand in the folds of her skirt.

"Your wife?" Joseph blurted, voicing the shock that seemed to have settled over the whole group.

Glenna wished fervently that Jared would acknowledge her in the way he had in the general store, with an arm around her or even a glance at her. But instead he merely nodded once to his brother and said, "That's right. We were married in Joliet just before heading home."

"Well, I'll be..." Joseph breathed. Then he came at Glenna with his arms wide open and enfolded her in a bear hug. "Welcome, welcome...what was it? Glenna?"

Glenna accepted his embrace, completely confused by the goings-on. When Joseph released her, the first person she looked to was Cally, finding the woman's brow furrowed with what appeared to be worry while she nodded up at Jared knowingly.

"You couldn't go through with it," Glenna heard the woman say.

Jared sighed and shook his head but didn't answer.

"Good," Cally said approvingly. "It's for the best." Then she left Jared and took both of Glenna's hands in her own. At last her sister-in-law smiled the way Glenna had expected her to in the first place.

"It'll be good to have another woman nearby," Cally said. She hooked her arm through Glenna's and pulled her toward the big house. "Come on in. You'll want to rest and get settled before supper. Plenty of time later to get introduced to this brood."

The evening passed quickly after Glenna changed out of her traveling clothes and went back downstairs to the evening meal. Once she had been formally introduced to each of the Stratton children, the whole family began to chatter at once, each of them as hungry for news of Jared's trip as they were for the fried chicken they devoured.

Through it all Glenna didn't say much, watching her new family with interest. Little Annie was, indeed, smitten with her uncle. She followed him like a lamb, insisting on sitting beside him at the dinner table and taking up his knee the rest of the time. The ten-year-old twins, Peter and Paul, were intent on showing off their newest rope trick, but once Peter had tied up his brother, Paul couldn't get out of the knots quite as slickly as he was supposed to and it took Peter most of an hour to untie him.

As Jared had said, Luke at fourteen was quiet and musically inclined, leaving directly after the meal to play his harmonica on the porch. Matthew and Mark were being pampered by their mother as a welcome back to the nest, and answered all her questions about her sister, Dora, Hal and the new baby. Charity watched Glenna with awe in her expression, asking about city life while she tended Lyden, who was shy of his new mother. Glenna took Cally's advice and left the baby, who walked with an unbalanced waddle, to warm up to her in his own time. John disappeared soon after they had all finished eating, amid merciless teasing from his brothers about his destination, a neighboring ranch where a girl his own age had apparently caught his fancy.

Interspersed with Jared's answers to all the questions he was asked, Joseph filled his brother in on what had happened around the ranch while he was gone, with Cally adding details her husband forgot.

Through it all the dark side of Jared was nowhere in evidence, and Glenna wondered if any of these people had ever seen it. He was patient with Annie's hugs and constant interruptions to gain his attention, and he sat through the younger twins' unsuccessful rope trick as if enthralled, and then laughed heartily when it didn't work. He complimented Charity until she blushed with pleasure, kept up a warm banter with Cally and still managed to pay close attention to everything Joseph was telling him.

There were only two people neglected by Jared through the evening: Glenna and Lyden.

Glenna didn't find it odd that her husband rarely seemed aware that she was in the same room. After all, this was a reunion with his family, and there was a lot of catching up to do. But wasn't Lyden as much a part of that catching up as the rest of them? Shouldn't Jared have been more interested in his own son than in his nephews? Yet not once did he so much as speak to the tiny child or ask Cally or Charity how the baby had been while he was gone.

And as for Lyden, he treated Jared just as he did Glenna—like a stranger.

When bedtime came it was Charity who went up to Glenna's room with her, while Jared and Joseph went out to the barn to see to the stock for the night. The younger girl changed Lyden's diaper and slipped his nightgown over his head, instructing as she went about how he liked things done. Then she rocked him until he found his thumb and his eyelids grew heavy, before laying him in the crib where he curled up on his side and went to sleep.

Left alone, Glenna put on her own nightgown and went to the window to brush her hair and take another look at this land she had come to.

From three stories up she could see past the barn roof, past the bunkhouse and the rest of the outbuildings to the vast emptiness beyond. It made her feel small in comparison, and that brought thoughts of Mary. Even the structures within the compound were far apart, without so much as a fence connecting them. She couldn't help picturing her sister wandering off even just a few feet, losing all sense of direction the way she was wont to do and not being able to regain her bearings. In her mind's eye she saw the panic that overtook Mary when that happened to her, only now that image was of the child in hysterics, wandering farther and farther away, alone in a countryside where surely even sighted people could easily become hopelessly lost. The thought sent a shiver through her.

I'll just have to find a way to make it safe for her, she thought, denying those other frightening images. City or country, Mary would learn to adapt. And Glenna would keep a close watch. They would make it work.

Just then the door opened and Jared came into the room, lit only by the moonlight coming through the window against which Glenna leaned. There was a moment before his eyes were adjusted to the shadows when Glenna knew he couldn't see her. Watching him, she wondered which of his natures he had brought with him—was he Jared the Dark or Jared the Light?

He realized where she was and joined her at the window. She knew when he reached a single finger to smooth her hair behind her shoulder that it was Jared the Light standing beside her.

"Can't sleep?" he whispered.

She shook her head. Remembering him telling Cally that she was here for the boy before saying he had married her, Glenna wondered what it would take to amend his vision of her. What she wanted, she had realized, and what she needed in order to bring Mary here, was a normal life. A life and a relationship like what Cally and Joseph had.

Jared glanced out the window at what she had been contemplating and then looked back at her. "Beautiful, isn't it?"

Daunting, she thought, but instead said, "Yes, it is. And big."

He laughed lightly but said no more for a while. Glenna watched his profile as he seemed to drink in the sight of his land. Then his expression turned thoughtful. "That was a nice thing you did when we left the Johnsons...giving Dora your handkerchief. You didn't have to do it."

Glenna shrugged and glanced away, slightly embarrassed to know he had noticed her press it into the other woman's hand as a gift. "It was a small thing," she answered in a hushed tone so as not to wake the baby.

"Still, you didn't have to bother."

Glenna didn't say anything to that. It was her turn to stare out the window again and his to watch her. She could feel his eyes on her and had the sense that they were taking her in the way they had taken in the landscape moments before.

"I appreciate that you told Charity you'd help her with her hair," he said more softly still. "And that you offered her your dress whenever she might like to borrow it. Those things are important out here—doing for each other, kindnesses.''

His words brought her head around again. Glenna looked into his face. ''We're all family now,'' she told him pointedly, thinking, *Even if I don't have a ring to show it*.

This time it was Jared who didn't answer. Instead he stayed staring at her for a moment, searching with his eyes. Then he tipped up her chin with a single knuckle and dropped his mouth to hers. Strangely, it was a questioning kiss, tentative, as if it were the first time and he wasn't sure she would allow it. Sweet and light and warm. Nice.

Glenna responded in kind, parting her lips in welcome. A normal life, she kept thinking, a normal life.

Jared's arms closed around her, one hand braced the back of her head as he deepened the kiss, his mouth opening wide, his tongue seeking entrance. That, too, Glenna welcomed, raising her own hands to the hardness of his chest, finding that just the feel of him beneath her palms awakened the senses she hadn't known existed before meeting him.

One of his hands slipped all the way down to her side, staying there a moment before curving the rest of the way to her breast. Glenna's breath caught in her throat with the instant desire that assaulted her, remembering too well how good this had felt the night at the Johnsons', how much better without even the thin barrier of her nightgown between his hand and her rapidly engorging flesh. She arched her back to tell him how willing she was for more and his touch deepened, the pressure increasing as his big hand kneaded her firmly, yet tenderly.

His mouth grew demanding, hungry, his pace quickening, and Glenna followed his lead, wondering at the feelings sparking to life all through her body, at the weakness of her knees, at the fullness between her legs.

Jared loosened the front of her gown. It couldn't be soon enough for Glenna, and she let him know by at once drawing slightly away and arching her back. Her breathing was coming fast and shallow, her heart racing. She needed so much more from him—his hands on her bare skin, the feel of his flesh beneath her own palms and more—though she wasn't sure what.

Finally his hand slipped inside her gown and found her breast, high and firm. There was a slight familiarity that she reveled in—the warmth, the leashed strength, the power and the gentle firmness of his touch. Her nipple was hard in his palm, harder still between his fingers.

Just when the wonders he was working at her breast were taking her every thought, Glenna felt his leg nudge between her own. Unsure what he was doing, she nevertheless eased her legs open enough to accommodate him, trusting that he knew better than she what it was she needed. Then his thigh came up between hers and he cupped her derriere, pressing her against him. Her head fell backward, away from his kiss, and Glenna swallowed hard, suddenly unable to breathe at all.

Passion gave her courage. She stared up into his face and then lowered her gaze to find the buttons of his shirt, opening them as if it were something she had done before. His bare chest was broad and magnificent, lightly covered with hair that felt wiry beneath her fingers. Wondering, she covered both mounds of his pectorals with her palms and mimicked his kneading motion, but it seemed to do more for her than for him.

As if her actions had given him license, Jared spread the front of her gown, baring her breasts to the moonlight and his eyes. He took her by surprise when he lifted the thigh that was between her legs, raising it until his boot caught the windowsill and her feet were off the floor. She slid down the hard thickness of his thigh, finding a stopping point in the V where his leg met his hip, and there she rode with that spot of her that was yearning, yearning, for something she still didn't understand, feeling empty and aroused and wonderful all at once. But it was only the first of her surprises, for the real purpose of his raising her higher was so that his mouth could reach the hardened crest of her breast.

Glenna gasped at the first sensation of warm wetness covering, then sucking that which had until so recently not even known the feel of a hand, let alone a mouth. A man's mouth nipping, teasing with his tongue, his mustache tickling just slightly, ever so tauntingly.

She was going to burst, Glenna knew. Feelings, sensations, needs, were building so rapidly, so fiercely within her, that at any moment she was going to explode. And yet instinct told her there was more and she wanted it, all of it. She tugged Jared's shirt from the waistband of his trousers and then slipped her hands up inside, over his shoulders, shedding his shirt as she learned the iron hardness of his back, the bulging of his biceps.

His mouth left one breast only to find the other and shoot new white-hot currents that rocked her hips where she rode his thigh. Fast, they were moving together so fast, as if in a race whose end Glenna could only imagine.

And then from the crib behind them Lyden moaned in his sleep.

Jared stopped short. He straightened away from Glenna and peered over at his son, who was still sound asleep. But in his expression, gilded by moon glow, Glenna saw a change.

He drew a ragged breath and before she knew what was happening he had swept her up into his arms and deposited her on the bed as if she were a child.

"Get some sleep" was all he said, his whisper sounding as ragged as her nerves felt. He snatched his shirt up from the floor where it had fallen and in three long purposeful strides left the room.

Glenna closed her eyes and then opened them again, as if to do so would bring him back where he had been only moments before. But she was alone in the room with the sleeping infant.

Frustrated desire was nothing beside the disappointment that washed through her.

It was clear that he wanted her in whatever way it was a man wanted a woman. But he had brought her here for Lyden. And he seemed determined to keep it that way.

Chapter Eleven

The almanac had predicted an early, hard winter, and as Jared lay on the trundle-backed sofa in his brother's parlor at five the following morning he didn't doubt it. These last days of September still heated up with strong sunshine, but the air was turning cold.

He pushed himself up and arched his back to take the kink out of it, silently calling himself a damn fool. He'd slept in the same bed with Glenna for the two nights before getting home, and yet here he was, sleeping on his brother and sister-in-law's couch. Cally and Joseph would surely have a baker's dozen of questions ready for him when they came down for breakfast.

Jared dropped his head forward and massaged the back of his neck. Sometimes it was so damn hard to forget the things in his past. And other times it was just too easy to lose sight of the vows he'd made to himself because of them. Being home again with his whole family all around had made him forget. Lyden's sleeping moan had made him remember it all again. Pain and grief.

He let out a sigh and got to his feet, heading for the kitchen. It was still dark outside but Cally and Joseph would be up any minute. Jared laid the fire in the stove, lit it and then pumped water into the coffeepot. In the time he'd been living here he had joined Cally and Joseph's morning ritual of sitting around the table with their first cups of coffee and some rare uninterrupted talk before Cally roused the children to start their chores and have breakfast. It was a good way to begin the day. Jared knew he'd miss it when he moved next door into his own house. Somehow the thought of doing it with Glenna didn't seem the same.

That's a good sign, he told himself. It meant these feelings roiling around in him were only lust. Plain, normal lust. Anything more than that wouldn't have him preferring to start his day with his brother and sister-in-law instead. He remembered well that he had been chomping at the bit to get that house next door built and moved into so he and Janie could be alone and carve out their own rituals. It was a reassuring thought that he wasn't feeling any such inclination now.

But there was no denying the lust.

Jared set the coffeepot on the stove and pulled a chair up close in front. Sitting there he hooked his bare toes on the ash lip for warmth, crossed his arms over his stomach and stared at the flames dancing behind the grate.

Glenna's hair wasn't as orange as the fire, he thought, his mind wandering. It was a darker, richer color. Tarnished copper. And with her face almost completely healed she was a beauty. Smooth, creamy skin. Wide, round eyes. Any man would take a second look. And a third. Jared had. Even sitting in the middle of all the commotion around this place last night, his eyes kept getting caught on her. She was prettier in a fresh, natural way than even Janie had been.

Jared threw back his head and looked up at the stovepipe.

It didn't matter how she looked. It didn't matter that she had shown some kindnesses that made him proud of her. It didn't matter that he had felt that strange sense of completion to have her here with him, as if he had his other half, the same as Joseph had in Cally. A kinship like that wasn't for him. He knew too well how hard it was to lose, and he'd never let himself in for that again.

"Morning."

Jared was jerked out of his ponderings by the sound of his brother's voice. "Morning," he returned, knowing that all the questions that hadn't been asked the night before, with the children and Glenna around, would be asked now. Cally's hand came down onto his shoulder as she went past, following Joseph to get cups down from the cupboard. "Coffee's made," Jared offered.

Neither Joseph nor Cally said anything. They were worried about him, Jared knew it the minute he turned his chair back to the table. His brother waited while Cally used the edge of her ever present apron to pick up the coffeepot and bring it with her. Joseph was rocking back and forth just slightly, frowning at the scarred tabletop rather than looking at him. Cally had two vertical lines between her eyebrows that belied her wan smile.

"Winter's in the air." Jared pretended nothing out of the ordinary had happened. "Think you're right, Joseph, we'd better get that fence mended in the north pasture and start planning to bring the stock in."

Joseph nodded his agreement.

"Well," Cally breathed as she stirred sugar into her coffee, "you surely did surprise us."

"I imagine so," Jared returned, tracing the lip of his cup with his thumb. Then, hoping to forestall some of their questions, he added, "The boy needed a mother."

"Is that all she is to you?" Joseph asked bluntly.

"That's all," he answered without hesitation, and a shade too adamantly. He wanted it to be true and he vowed that he'd make it so. "The boy needed a mother, I needed someone to cook and clean. That's all there is to it."

"Is that why you slept on the sofa last night without even taking off your clothes?"

"Joseph," Cally chastised, covering his wrist with her hand. "That's not our affair."

"Sorry," Joseph muttered and took a drink from his cup.

Jared shrugged. "We'll be sharing a bed...." He wasn't sure how to explain why they hadn't the night before, though. He settled on a partial truth. "I was restless last night and didn't want to disturb...things."

"Your wife and baby," Joseph put in pointedly.

The sanity I've finally gotten back for myself, Jared thought but didn't say. "Cally, if you'll help her...Glenna...open up my place next door, we'll move over there and free up that room for the new baby before it comes."

"You know you're welcome to stay," his sister-in-law was quick to say.

"You have enough on your hands. That's the whole purpose in my taking another wife." He hadn't intended for that last word to come out so sourly.

"Does she know about Jane?" Joseph asked.

"She knows all she needs to—that I'm a widower with a child. It suited her own purposes to marry a stranger and leave home."

Cally cleared her throat. "Did she get those marks on her face from home?"

Jared nodded, wondering at the instant anger that image washed through him. "Her stepfather," he said with the full measure of his disdain in his tone, at the same time convincing himself that any man would want to wring the neck of another who had beaten a woman.

"And you married her to save her," Cally finished in a hopeful tone of voice.

"I married her because the boy needed a mother," he repeated yet again. "Don't go getting any romantic notions, Cally. I'm through with that and you know it."

"I know you shouldn't be. I know you were scarred before, Jared. Joseph and I know that better than anyone. But you can't let that keep you bottled up forever."

"I not only can, it's how I want things." His tone had been harsher than he meant for it to be. Jared regretted it and consciously softened it. "Look at the two of you," he teased. "When I left here your heads were hanging with worry over what I had planned to do. Now I come back with a wife and mother for the boy—what you've spent the past year telling me I should do—and you're still not happy."

It didn't lighten their expressions. Instead Joseph said, "We wanted you to find someone you cared about and start over again."

"I am starting over again."

They both looked dubious. "I hope you mean that," Cally said after a moment.

Jared finished his coffee and held his cup out for Cally to pour him another when she had finished pouring her own. As she did Jared caught what looked to be a prompting glance thrown at her husband.

Joseph's answering expression was grim. He cradled his own cup between both palms and hunched over slightly to stare into it. "There's something we need to tell you before you see it for yourself," he said finally, reluctantly.

Jared waited.

Joseph suddenly sat up straight. "There's a new grave out in the family plot."

"A new grave?" Jared repeated.

Joseph scratched his nose with the side of his index finger. "Bill..." He cleared his throat. "Bill died of the influenza and had his body sent without so much as a wire to tell us first. Seems he was determined to be buried here. He'd scribbled a last note saying that since this was the only home he ever knew and since he was all alone in his dying...."

Cally took up where Joseph seemed to have stalled. "We had to see him buried and to do it anywhere but here would have raised a whole passel of questions...."

Jared didn't hear any more of what they were saying. His ears were ringing and his eyes were on the sudden whiteness that circled the knuckles of his hand around the coffee cup.

Bill was dead.

Bill, whom the Stratton family had taken in when both he and Jared were seven. Bill, who had been as close as a twin brother, closer even than Joseph in some ways. Bill, who had been...

Jared's jaw clenched so hard it hurt. Judas.

He tore himself out of his thoughts and looked up to find both Cally and Joseph watching him. He shrugged as if nothing they had said mattered to him. "I can't see anything else you could have done. He was all alone, you said?"

"He wrote in the note that he knew he was dying and there was no one with him who would see his last wish granted, so he had arranged in advance with the doctor to have his body sent here."

Jared nodded and stood up, forgetting his fresh coffee. "Well, I'd better change my clothes so we can get at the north pasture.

"Whew! Let's get some air in here," Cally said. Stuffing her dust rag and beeswax polish in the large pocket of her apron, she flapped her arms up and down and wrinkled her nose as she charged inside the house next door after breakfast that morning. She quickly crossed the entryway into the parlor to the left. The big window that looked out onto the porch didn't open but there were three tall narrow ones on the side wall that did.

Glenna followed Cally, stuffing her own cleaning rags in the waistband of the apron her sister-in-law had lent her. Long disuse made the windows stick, but with their combined efforts they raised all three. Cally fanned the fresh air in. "I should have had Jared come over here before he and Joseph left this morning to air the place out. I didn't think about it."

The musty smell barely penetrated Glenna's senses as she turned from the windows and took in the room. Dust blanketed heavy, serviceable furniture upholstered in brown—a long camelbacked sofa and two square chairs. There was no pattern to their placement; the chairs were at odd ends of the room, and the sofa and a low gateleg table were in the center.

Two massive andirons stood sentry on either side of a stone fireplace with an ash-laden hearth. On the handsomely carved mantel was a box clock with the time frozen at twelve-twenty. Above it was the shadowy outline of a picture that had once hung there. A rolltop desk filled space in the corner, a bookshelf lined the wall to one side of it and a tall glass-fronted gun case stood on the other side.

It came as a surprise to Glenna to find that the home of a wife so dearly loved and lost was not brimming with reminders of her—mementos, hand-sewn samplers, crocheted doilies or braided rugs lovingly crafted by her predecessor's hands. The room was oddly bare of any such personal touches. Not so much as a strip of wallpaper lent the place a homey feeling.

"It looks as if there was a picture above the mantel," Glenna gestured to her sister-in-law.

Cally barely glanced up from running her finger through the dust on the desk. "There was. It was a portrait of Jane."

Glenna had suspected as much but was testing Cally's attitude. Curiosity was eating at Glenna and she wondered if she could find some satisfaction for it from the other woman. Since Cally's tone hadn't been censorious she tried again. "Was it too painful for Jared to keep it?"

"Yes," Cally answered readily and then went on with her assessment of the work they needed to to. "When the men come in for lunch we're going to have to see if we can persuade them to give the afternoon over to us. This furniture needs to be dragged out into the yard and beaten. Let's see about the kitchen.''

Again Glenna followed the other woman through a heavy oak door into a kitchen that ran the entire width of the rear of the house. It was large enough for an oval table at one end circled with six high-backed chairs, an iron stove just like the one Cally used, two white cupboards with tin-punched cutouts decorating their doors and the luxury of an indoor pump. But again there was no sign of its previous mistress in evidence.

''It'll take us a full day just to scrub in here. Everything will have to be taken out of the cupboards and washed or you'll be eating dust.'' Then Cally headed through a second door that opened into the back of the entranceway. ''Let's have a look upstairs.''

''Did Jared's first wife like things plain?'' Glenna asked as she followed Cally's lumbering frame up the oak-banistered steps that rose from the foyer.

''Jane? Oh, no. She liked things fancy.''

''You couldn't tell by looking.'' Glenna's thoughts slipped out.

Cally heard and glanced over her shoulder as they reached the landing. ''Jared was grieved out of his mind. He went through here like a bull and wiped the place clean of anything that reminded him of her.''

''I see.'' *He loved her that much, then.*

Glenna followed Cally down the hall, peering into three empty rooms before they went into one that must have been the nursery, though it contained only a rocking chair and a broken basket.

''We'll move Lyden's bed and bureau back, of course. Poor baby didn't even spend two weeks here in his own room.''

''She died when he was two weeks old?''

"That's why Lyden and Jared came over with us." Cally bustled out across the hall into the master bedroom. "Oh, I'd forgotten about the mattress."

As Glenna went in behind Cally her gaze settled on the empty bed frame. This time she didn't ask, assuming that the mattress on which the other woman had given birth and then died had been destroyed.

"Well, that's no problem," Cally went on. "I have the ticking and enough feathers saved up. All we'll have to do is put it together. We might as well start in here," she finished, taking the dust rag and polish out of her apron pocket and setting to work on the bureau beside the door.

"You save feathers?" Glenna marveled as she began on the spindled headboard.

Cally laughed. "Around here we save anything we get our hands on. It'd be wasteful to throw them away every time we plucked a fowl, especially when my family keeps growing."

"I'm afraid I don't know very much about what it takes to be a wife out here," Glenna admitted sheepishly.

"A willingness to learn is the first step," Cally reassured her. She paused as they went on working and then said, "How did you and Jared get together, anyway?"

Glenna didn't draw a breath for a moment. She had been dreading that subject. Pride made it hard to admit she had been reduced to getting a husband through a newspaper advertisement. For a moment she debated whether or not to tell the truth. But in the end she did.

Cally was astonished. "He advertised for a wife?"

"And I answered it," Glenna reiterated quietly.

"You must have needed to leave home real bad."

Glenna opened a window on the right side of the headboard and then rounded the rope-lattice bed frame to open another. "We had a mutual need," she answered finally, punishing the foot rail with polish.

"Joseph and I didn't expect Jared to ever marry again. Not that we didn't want him to—because we did. We just didn't think he would."

"Yes, I know. He said he loved his first wife." Glenna prompted Cally to say more.

"Like no man I've ever known loved any woman."

For some reason that statement cut Glenna like a knife.

Finished polishing the bed she went to the armoire and opened the doors, finding it empty inside. "Was she...Jared's first wife...from around here?"

"She was from Chicago."

"She was?" Glenna burst out in surprise. Had he been there again this time for something to do with his first wife? But before she could think of a way to word her question, Cally went on.

"Jared went there for the first time ten years ago, stayed longer than he'd planned and came home with a wife."

Except that time he fell in love with her instead of advertising for her. "What was she like?" Glenna had a stranglehold on the dust rag.

It took Cally so long to answer that Glenna stole a glance over her shoulder at her sister-in-law where she shined the globe of a lamp. "Well, Jane was...I don't know...like a porcelain doll. Rag dolls are meant to be slept with and squeezed and dragged through the dirt and patched up again if they tear. Hereabouts those are the best kind to have. But porcelain dolls need to be put up on a shelf just for admiring. I guess Jane was like that. She had a weak stomach, she couldn't wring a chicken's neck or stick a pig or even clean up after what needs to be done around here. She came from a place where women mostly just went to parties and dances till all hours of the night and then slept most of the days away, and she just never adjusted."

"In all that time?"

"I know, I never understood why she didn't come to grips with the way things are around here, either. But she didn't.

She fought it till the last, trying to convince Jared to take her back to Chicago and stay there with her.''

"He must have felt very guilty when she died here, then.'

"Jared didn't have anything to feel guilty about," Cally defended quickly as she wiped down the walls. "He waited on her hand and foot, did nearly all the cooking and cleaning, bought her everything she took a whim to have. I used to feel sorry for him, working as hard as my Joseph from dawn to dusk and then coming back here to spoil and pamper Jane like a child.''

Her he pampered and me he married to be a workhorse, Glenna thought, wishing it didn't rub her wrong to realize it. After all, this had suited her own purpose.

Cally surveyed their handiwork. "Well, that's a start. Peter and Paul can have the window-washing job, and we can come back in here to do the floors later when we're finished with everything else. Might as well hold off and do them all at once when most of the furniture is gone. We can do the walls and windowsills in the other rooms and the banister before lunchtime and then we'll see about getting some male help for the downstairs this afternoon.''

But housecleaning was not what was on Glenna's mind, and her thought found voice. "All that time and he didn't care at all that she didn't keep up her side of the doubletree.''

Cally laughed suddenly. "The doubletree? Oh, these Stratton men. I'll just bet that's what Jared told you he expected in a wife, didn't he? I know because that's what Joseph told me all those years ago when he asked me to marry him. I said if he ever referred to me as a horse again I'd skin him alive." Then she placed a hand on Glenna's arm. "Don't be jealous of Jane. She's gone and no matter how it might sound, there's no cause for jealousy now.''

It was late that night by the time Glenna finished arranging the furniture that the men had taken outside in the afternoon, beaten and moved back in. After the day spent cleaning she alone had come back to the smaller house when the supper dishes were done. With Mary in mind, Glenna had to place the furniture just so and she wanted to be able to do that without explanation. Now that she had, she took a last look from the doorway that connected the living room with the entranceway. Then, even though she knew she was alone, she glanced around to be sure she wasn't being observed and closed her eyes.

With her arms outstretched she took three steps straight forward, stopped and felt for one of the low, boxy chairs. Finding it easily she turned to the right, kept her left hand on its back and proceeded to locate the sofa where it stood at a sharp angle to the chair, then the other chair; the grouping formed a three-sided square around the gateleg table. Still with her eyes pinched tightly shut, Glenna reached out with her left hand and found the desk, from which she followed the walls of the room without difficulty until she was back where she had started.

Glenna opened her eyes. The arrangement was similar to that in the sitting room she and Mary had shared in David Stern's house. The familiar plan would make it easier for her sister to adapt.

Satisfied for Mary's sake, for a moment she looked at the room through her own perspective. Cally had donated a framed mirror to cover the marks on the wall over the mantel, and Glenna already knew just what she would stitch to hang in the bare spot beside the big window. She didn't like the gun case, but her sister-in-law had only laughed at the idea of trying to persuade Jared to remove it. At the very least she made it her goal to replace its clear glass with stained glass, which would not only hide the awful rifles and pistols but add a touch of decoration to the case and the parlor at once.

All in all she was pleased with this new home of hers. She actually preferred her predecessor's personal touches had

NO RISK, NO OBLIGATION TO BUY...NOW OR EVER!

GUARANTEED

PLAY "ROLL A DOUBLE" AND GET AS MANY AS SIX GIFTS!

HERE'S HOW TO PLAY:

1. Peel off label from front cover. Place it in space provided at right. With a coin, carefully scratch off the silver dice. This makes you eligible to receive one or more free books, and possibly other gifts, depending on what is revealed beneath the scratch-off area.

2. You'll receive brand-new Harlequin Historical™ novels. When you return this card, we'll rush you the books and gifts you qualify for ABSOLUTELY FREE!

3. Then, if we don't hear from you, every other month we'll send you 4 additional novels to read and enjoy. You can return them and owe nothing, but if you decide to keep them, you'll pay only $2.89* per book - a savings of 36¢ each off the cover price. And, there's no extra charge for postage and handling!

4. When you subscribe to the Harlequin Reader Service®, you'll also get our newsletter, as well as additional free gifts from time to time.

5. You must be completely satisfied. You may cancel at any time simply by sending us a note or a shipping statement marked "cancel" or by returning any shipment to us at our expense.

*Terms and prices subject to change without notice. Sales tax applicable in N.Y. and Iowa.
©1990 Harlequin Enterprises Limited.

You'll love your elegant 20K gold electroplated chain! The necklace is finely crafted with 160 double-soldered links, and is electroplate finished in genuine 20K gold. And it's yours FREE as an added thanks for giving our Reader Service a try!

"ROLL A DOUBLE!"

PLACE LABEL HERE

SCRATCH HERE

SEE CLAIM CHART BELOW

246 CIH YA3X
(U-H-H-09/90)

YES! I have placed my label from the front cover into the space provided above and scratched off the silver dice. Please rush me the free book(s) and gift(s) that I am entitled to. I understand that I am under no obligation to purchase any books, as explained on the opposite page.

NAME _____

ADDRESS _____ APT. ____

CITY _____ STATE _____ ZIP CODE _____

CLAIM CHART

🎲🎲	**4 FREE BOOKS PLUS FREE 20k ELECTROPLATED GOLD CHAIN PLUS MYSTERY BONUS GIFT**
🎲🎲	**3 FREE BOOKS PLUS BONUS GIFT**
🎲🎲	**2 FREE BOOKS**

CLAIM NO. 37-829

All orders subject to approval.
©1990 Harlequin Enterprises Limited.

Offer limited to one per household and not valid to current Historical™ subscribers.
PRINTED IN U.S.A.

HARLEQUIN "NO RISK" GUARANTEE

- You're not required to buy a single book - ever!
- You must be completely satisfied or you may cancel at any time simply by sending us a note or a shipping statement marked "cancel" or by returning any shipment to us at our cost. Either way, you will receive no more books; you'll have no further obligation.
- The free book(s) and gift(s) you claimed on this "Roll A Double" offer remain yours to keep no matter what you decide.

If offer card is missing, please write to: Harlequin Reader Service®, P.O. Box 1867, Buffalo, N.Y. 14269-1867

DETACH AND MAIL CARD TODAY!

been taken away, leaving Glenna free to add her own, and to not feel so much as if she were moving into another woman's house.

A knot in the middle of her back reminded her just how tired she was; Glenna rolled her shoulders trying to ease it. When it persisted she gave in to fatigue, blew out the lamp and left through the front door.

The air was cool but it felt good on her work-heated skin. The chirp of crickets was the only sound and Glenna paused for a moment on the porch to listen to it.

Standing there she caught sight of someone leaning on the white rail fence that bordered the paddock attached to the barn. There was only a half-moon, and all the men wore the same things—denim trousers and chambray shirts—so at first she wasn't sure who it was. Then he raised a booted foot to the lowest rail, rested his weight on the opposite hip and she recognized him. Tall, broad shoulders, narrow waist, long, thick legs—it was Jared.

Strange how strong was the desire to go over to him. In the day's chores they had been just two more workers, no closer and no more distant than any of the others. Jared had been cordial, the same as he was with the rest of the family. But no more. And suddenly Glenna realized how much more she wanted. How much she wanted what was between Joseph and Cally. And not just in order to have a normal life to bring Mary to. Something inside her yearned for those flashes of intimacy she and Jared had shared to be real and constant, and suddenly she recognized the need in herself to be close to him, to have him want to be close to her.

Glenna took a deep breath and altered her direction, crossing the yard to come up beside him. The rustle of her footsteps on the dry, brittle grass announced her.

Jared glanced over with a questioning, but not unwelcoming expression on his face. ''I wondered how long you were going to be,'' he said in a husky voice.

Had he been waiting for her? Glenna doubted it, but still hope had a life of its own. "I just finished up. The parlor is done now. All that's left is the kitchen and making a mattress." She looked away from him at the mention of that, wondering if he meant to share it with her when it was done.

"Tired?"

Had it really sounded as if he cared? "Yes. Are you?"

"Mmm."

But he didn't move to go in and neither did she. Instead they both stayed staring at the empty paddock.

"Can I ask you a question?" she said after a moment, glancing sideways at him.

He angled her a half smile. "You haven't hesitated to before."

"What did Cally mean when she said you couldn't go through with it?" He looked puzzled, so she explained. "When we got here yesterday, before anyone knew you'd married me, they seemed to think I was someone else, or here for some other reason. After you explained, Cally said you couldn't go through with it."

Jared stared at her for a moment. Then he turned and sat on the middle rail of the fence, crossing his arms over his stomach. "I went to Chicago to see about having the boy's grandparents care for him."

That explained some things. Glenna turned to face his profile, hooking her arm over the fence. "Lyden's mother's parents?"

"Yes."

"Did you want them to raise him?"

"That was the idea."

"Did they refuse?" she asked tentatively.

Jared's head fell back, and he looked up at the night sky. He took a deep breath and sighed. "No, they would have taken him. It was all arranged, in fact."

"But giving him over to them was what you couldn't go through with?" Glenna was unaccountably pleased by that.

If he couldn't abandon the baby, if deep down, underneath the resentment he seemed to feel toward the child that had cost him his wife, he cared enough to keep Lyden, maybe there was hope that he was beginning to let go of old hurts, and in that, that he might eventually let both his son and Glenna into his heart.

"It wasn't right," Jared said after a time, reluctantly, harshly. "The boy is my responsibility."

Letting go of old hurts wasn't close at hand, by the sound of it, but still Glenna had hope. "I..." How hard it was to formally take back the declaration her body had already rescinded. "I would like it if we could be a family...the three of us...since..."

"Since I decided to keep him and bring him home a mother instead?"

"Yes."

"I told you before—"

This time it was Glenna who cut him off. "I know what you told me. I didn't say anything about love. I just said it would be nice to be a family."

"And what does that entail for you?"

She shrugged, not because she didn't know, but because she couldn't say it aloud. Instead she took up his study of the stars.

"Is this an invitation into your bed after all?" he guessed.

Yes, but that wasn't all and it was certainly much too bluntly put. "A family is more than a man and woman in bed," she informed him. It was all new to her and she didn't understand it herself, but she knew that she wanted more of him than a completion of what he had initiated twice in the bedroom.

She could feel him watching her, and the longer it went on the more she expected him to say something snide, to humiliate her by belittling what she was trying to get across to him. But he surprised her instead.

"You're right, a family is more than a man and a woman in bed. You're also right that since that's what I've brought you here for it might as well be what we have."

His agreement seemed to come more out of resignation than out of wholehearted desire, but Glenna was grateful for it nonetheless. "Good," she said softly, looking back into those eyes that quickened her pulse.

"To bed, then?" he asked with the upward query of an eyebrow, in a way that seemed to be testing her.

Glenna nodded, still wishing things were different, that he might have accepted her gladly at least.

Jared stood up and extended his arm for her to precede him. On the way he said, "But only to sleep. This *family* needs to be consummated under its own roof, not under my brother's.

And without another woman's baby in the same room, Glenna thought as she climbed the stairs to that room.

They both undressed in the dark, silently. Glenna slipped on her nightgown before they each lay on opposite sides of the bed. For a while that was how they stayed, he on his back staring up at the ceiling and she on hers.

And then Jared rolled to his side. He reached over and laid his arm across her waist.

Glenna held her breath, hoping for more in spite of what he had said, wishing that he found her irresistible.

But that was all he did. Concession, not passion.

She swallowed a clot of disappointment and exhaled very slowly so he wouldn't guess she had waited with bated breath for something more.

A moment later she heard him sigh into sleep. But she was left awake and wondering what it might have been like to have this man look at her with the love and devotion he'd felt for his first wife.

Chapter Twelve

Glenna began scrubbing the kitchen of the smaller house just after dawn the next day. Cally helped, going back and forth between the houses to oversee Charity's work on the new mattress. By late that afternoon both projects were nearly finished. Cally went home to start supper and Glenna was alone, stocking shelves in the kitchen storeroom when the younger set of Stratton twins appeared at her back door.

"Can we leave Lyden with you for a little while?" Peter, the more outgoing of the ten-year-old twins, was struggling with the baby, who was wiggling and arching his back to be let down. "There's some new piglets over back of the barn and me and Paul want to go see 'em. If we take Lyden he'll try and crawl into the slop, it's one of his favorite things."

Glenna smiled at the older boy's impatient recounting of the nuisances of a toddler. Since it was Saturday and the twins didn't have school, they had been assigned the job of watching Lyden for the day.

"We won't be but a little while," Paul assured her from behind his brother, casting a quick glance over his shoulder to his own house.

This had been timed just right, Glenna realized. If their mother had been here, or if they had gone to ask this of either Cally or Charity they'd have found no sympathy. But she wanted to make friends with both the twins and her stepson. "Just a little while?" she reiterated.

"Won't be more than a half hour, isn't that right, Pete?" Paul grinned impishly.

"I'm going to hold you to that. Let him down."

Peter loosened his two-armed hug around the front of Lyden and let him slide to the floor. Paul tossed the baby's rag doll in after him and then the twins made a fast escape. Lyden eyed Glenna suspiciously for a moment before looking back through the screen at his rapidly retreating cousins. Out went his bottom lip, followed by a wail.

"Poor Lyden," Glenna soothed as she crouched beside him, wrapped her arms around her knees to keep her balance and let the baby know she wasn't going to charge him with open arms. "It's hard to be the littlest, isn't it?"

Lyden turned his chubby face back to her and scowled, but he stopped crying. "No," he pouted, the only word he said clearly and his answer to almost everything.

"Want to come ride my horsey?" she offered hopefully.

"No."

"All right. Maybe your doll wants a ride." She picked up the soiled, love-ragged toy and sat on one of the kitchen chairs. With her legs crossed at the knees she set the doll to straddling one ankle, held its chewed arms with both hands and bounced it up and down, all the while making horse sounds.

Out of the corner of her eyes she could see Lyden's interest. But this was the first time the two of them had been alone and he was still obviously unsure of her. With an exaggerated "Whoa," the doll's turn came to an end and she looked over at the toddler. "Want a ride?"

He thought about it a moment. Then he smiled tentatively and waddled over. It only took a few bounces before Lyden was laughing with openmouthed glee and mimicking the movement to let her know he wanted it to go on when she paused to rest. "Change horses," she said breathlessly as she switched him to her other ankle, pleased that he was warming up to her.

When both legs ached, she stood and held him cradled facedown to twirl him around and around until she was too dizzy to do that anymore either. Then she made a seat out of her clasped hands and gave him a ride around the kitchen, her arms in a lumbering sway she called the elephant's trunk in a singsong along the way.

With a last swoop and twirl she collapsed to the newly scrubbed floor like a deflating balloon, holding Lyden in her lap.

"No," he protested loudly.

"Yes," Glenna answered back firmly, winded but laughing just the same.

"No," he repeated, squirming out of her grip and bouncing up and down to let her know what he wanted.

"How about a cracker?" she said enthusiastically, remembering the small wafers she had come across when stocking the storeroom with what had been brought in from Hays the day of her arrival.

Lyden stopped bouncing and said something that remotely resembled cracker.

"The magic word," Glenna muttered to herself. She got to her feet and crossed the room to the pantry, which was large enough to step into. Flour and sugar sacks leaned against one wall, while shelves lining the other three held canned goods, jars, smaller sacks and a few cooking utensils—pots and pans too big for the cupboards.

"Crackers, crackers, crackers..." she said to herself as she scanned the shelves for the tin canister. "Ah, there you are."

As she took down the can from a shelf above her head Glenna heard an odd sound, like a baby's rattle only more muffled. Her first thought was that Lyden had gotten into something. Quickly she pried the lid off the canister, took out a handful of crackers, replaced the lid and set the can back on the shelf.

Again came the rattle, somehow sounding more efficient than she would have expected from something Lyden might be capable of. Then, in the quiet of the storeroom, she heard a hiss followed by Lyden's elated voice saying the garbled word he used for "kitty."

But it wasn't a kitten Glenna saw when she turned around. Coming up through the floorboards in the doorway between her and the baby was a snake, slowly slithering toward Lyden.

"Calll-lly..." Pure panicked reflex made her call for the other woman before Glenna realized she couldn't hear and couldn't get there fast enough even if she did.

Just then Lyden caught sight of the crackers in Glenna's hand. Trying to say "crackers," he took a few wobbly steps forward, closer to the snake.

"No, Lyden, no! Don't move."

He repeated the word insistently, as if that negated her command.

The snake slithered nearer, the rattle of its tail still coming from beneath the floorboards.

Frantically Glenna tried to think what to do. She didn't believe she could leap over the snake, snatch the baby and run fast enough to avoid it striking out at one of them.

"No, Lyden, stay back," she shouted at the baby, who seemed torn between coming after the crackers or the fascinating creature on the floor.

In desperation, Glenna grabbed up a heavy rolling pin from where it hung from a hook alongside the door. Holding her breath, she raised it like a club, stepped nearer to the snake, and, with all her might, hit the creature over the head. At the same moment Lyden was whisked backward.

The rattle stopped. Glenna looked up to find Jared clutching Lyden protectively against him. For a moment she stared at the sight, as shocked to see it as she had been the snake. Not once since she'd come here had she seen him touch the baby. He'd barely looked at him. He never acted as if the child meant anything at all to him. And yet now his big hands were splayed against Lyden's back, clutching him the way any fearful, loving father would.

Then the rattle sounded again. Instantly Jared set the baby on the floor behind him, and before the stunned snake had moved, he clamped a fist around the base of its head, yanked it the rest of the way through the floorboards and caught it just short of the tail. "Are you all right?" he demanded of Glenna.

She shivered involuntarily. "Yes. Just get it out of here."

Jared glanced back at Lyden, who by that time was crying loudly. "The boy?"

Glenna shook her head. "He's all right, too. He thought it was a kitten."

Jared breathed a wry, relieved laugh. "This is a hell of a dangerous kitten."

Glenna grimaced as she watched him stare at the snake, eye to eye. How could he suddenly treat it with amused curiosity? "Take it away."

He gave her a crooked grin and held it out toward her. "Don't you want to apologize for cuffing it?"

Glenna shivered again at just the thought and stepped back. "No."

"Maybe I should have it stuffed and mounted for you," he teased. "Not many women would take on a rattler with a rolling pin. This is quite a prize." When Glenna stepped farther back into the pantry and waved him away, he chuckled. "No? Well, I guess the pigs get it then."

"No," she blurted out suddenly. "Peter and Paul are looking at the new piglets."

"They'll like watching this a lot better. Pigs are natural snake killers. They have a heyday with one of these and the boys get a big kick out of it."

"That's barbaric."

He laughed, obviously enjoying her revulsion. "No, that's the way things are out here." To Glenna's relief he finally headed for the kitchen door. But with one shoulder holding the screen open he glanced back at her and winked. "You just might make it after all, city girl."

Once he'd gone Glenna went to Lyden, gratified that he accepted her picking him up and comforting him. When he had stopped crying she took him with her into the store-room. After giving him fresh crackers, she set him on the floor and turned to sweeping up the crumbs of those she had gotten for him before.

In her mind's eye was the picture of Jared having snatched his son out of harm's way, holding the baby with the protectiveness of a man who had strong feelings for the child no matter how he tried to deny them.

"Where'd our snake basher go off to?"

Glenna heard Joseph's question as she came down the back stairs into Cally's kitchen after putting Lyden to sleep for the night.

"There you are." Her brother-in-law winked at her as she rejoined the group gearing up for a Saturday night candy pull.

"Want to make sure she's close by to protect you from those rattlers, is that it, Joseph?" Jared goaded. His chair at the table was tipped back on two legs, his thumbs stuck in his trouser pockets.

"You wouldn't believe it, but this big buck of mine is more skittish about such things than most women," Cally explained, stopping her job buttering a platter to hug her husband's shoulders. "Not that I think any less of you for it, mind you," she teased him.

Glenna smiled at Joseph. "I'm with you. If I never see another one it won't bother me in the least." It was heartening to realize that in just these few days here she had been welcomed into the inner circle of the family like one of their own.

"Come on, Jared and Glenna get to do the first pulling," Cally announced then.

Groans of complaint rose from the Stratton children from points all around the big, homey, yellow kitchen.

"I want to pull with Uncle Jared," Annie complained more loudly than her brothers.

Cally gave her youngest daughter a stern, warning look. "Sorry, honey. Tonight Uncle Jared is going to pull with Aunt Glenna."

A knowing chuckle erupted from Joseph and he nudged one of his brother's upraised chair legs with the toe of his boot. Glenna watched the interplay and felt her cheeks heat when Jared answered with a conspiratorial laugh.

Then Jared smiled at her. "Maybe somebody else better go first and show this city girl how it's done."

"I beg your pardon," she said in mock huffiness. "We pull taffy even in the city."

"Is that so?" He grinned at her, meeting her eyes and holding them with the warmth in his own.

"It is." Glenna tipped her chin up at him, but not so much that it cost her losing his glance.

"And I suppose you're pretty good at it, are you, city girl?"

"Passable."

He held out the can of butter for her to slather her hands before she took some. Then he winked at Cally, who watched them with a satisfied smile. "Guess we'll see about that, won't we."

Together they plunged into the first batch of the sugar and molasses concoction cooling on another buttered dish. When they had loosened a glob they worked it to form a ball, their slippery hands sliding into one another, fingers twining and untwining.

"You two ever going to pull that or you just going to keep playing handsies over that candy?" Joseph asked, getting back at Jared for his earlier teasing about the snake.

Cally knocked him in the back of the shoulder with her elbow.

"I don't think Aunt Glenna knows how. Let me do it," Annie put in.

Glenna had finally managed to form a lopsided ball, her hands below and above it. Jared covered both with his own much bigger, stronger ones, his fingers sliding through the buttery slipperiness nearly to her wrists. She looked up at him and found his smile intimate, the one she longed to see from him more and more. Then his hands slid to cup the soft candy on the sides, squeezing it to ooze up through Glenna's fingers.

He answered Annie but his eyes stayed holding Glenna's. "I think we'll give your Aunt Glenna a chance."

She couldn't help hoping that his words had a deeper meaning. And then, just like that, he pulled away, taking his portion of the taffy with him.

All attention turned to the candy. Catcalls and advice boomed around them when they pulled too far and it sagged in the middle or threatened to break. Good-natured teasing was thrown back and forth, with Glenna bantering her share as if she had been at it for a lifetime.

When the group judged the candy pulled long enough Jared and Glenna laid it out on yet another buttered platter and washed their hands, calling their own cheers and jeers to Annie and Peter for the next round. On it went until everyone had pulled their share, with Charity forming her candy into hearts to dry and Paul making canes, even though his twin chided him that they were only for Christmas.

Once both batches were finished and the mess cleaned up, the younger children were sent off to bed and the rest of the family wandered into the parlor. Only one lamp was lit there, leaving the room dim and shadowy. Cally sat before her melodeon, Luke took his harmonica out of his shirt pocket, and together mother and son began a medley of soft, lilting music.

Glenna sat on the end of the sofa, more aware of Jared where he'd come to stand beside her than of the songs. His thigh was at her shoulder, the arm of the couch between them. She felt as if the air around them was charged, but when she looked up and found him watching the performance as if he didn't even know she was there, she thought that she must be imagining it.

The evening was one of the best she had ever spent. She was growing rapidly fond of this family she had married into, and several times tonight had thought how nice it would have been had Mary been there to share in the fun. But now there was a craving in her to be alone with Jared.

Finally he settled down onto the arm of the sofa, as if he had no intention of ending the evening any time soon. Glenna's eyes darted over to his leg, so near now. It was thick and hard enough to strain the seam of his pants. It did funny things to the pit of her stomach.

Are you going to give me a chance? she wondered, and involuntarily fidgeted in answer to the yearnings that seemed to be coming to life inside her like stars appearing in a night sky.

She took a deep breath, hoping it would help, and stole another glance up at his face. This time he wasn't watching Cally and Luke, he was looking down at her. The corners of his mouth turned up slightly.

Glenna smiled back, tentatively, hesitantly. She let him hold her gaze for a time. But all he did was stare until it made her uncomfortable. She broke the tie by dropping her chin and discovered her fingers fiddling nervously with her skirt, plucking up a piece of fabric and smoothing it back again, plucking and smoothing.

Then into her line of view came Jared's hand, palm upward.

Glenna's heart started to pound hard and fast. She was afraid of making a fool of herself, so once more she pivoted her head to look up at him. His smile was gone and what replaced it was a questioning expression. Almost a challenging one, the way his left eyebrow quirked up. When she didn't do more than stare back at him he tilted his head just slightly, as if asking a second time.

Glenna swallowed and looked back at his waiting hand. His palm was callused, his fingers long and thick. She had a sudden flash of what it felt like to have that hand on her, pressing, squeezing, kneading. But just as suddenly she remembered what it was like to have him stop when her flesh was craving more.

Then again, she thought, maybe he only wanted her to take a walk outside with him.

Just then Joseph's booming voice joined his wife's in a love song that filled the room with sound.

Jared bent low to her ear. "Let's go home."

So he did mean to give her a chance. The surface of Glenna's skin went all tingly. She placed her hand in his, settling into his warmth and strength as if it were an old friend. He stood and pulled her with him. Only fleetingly did Glenna wonder if anyone noticed them slip out the front door.

The air outside was cool against her skin; crickets were a chorus to the muted strains of the song still coming from Cally and Joseph's house. Still holding her hand Jared crossed the yard and before she knew it they were climbing the steps to the front porch of their own home.

The silence inside gave Glenna a sudden case of nerves. Her knees felt weak as she followed Jared up the stairs of this place she had cleaned but had yet to feel was her own.

Jared didn't stop to light a lamp, or to pull the curtains on the windows that bracketed the bed in the master room.

White moon glow beamed through the panes and made a checkerboard of light into which he took her to stand on one side of the newly made mattress, which was wrapped in clean sheets, blankets and a quilt.

What had been a yearning in Glenna in the safety of Cally's parlor with all the family around was now cloaked in uneasiness and embarrassment. He really was a stranger, she couldn't help thinking as she stared into his chest.

And yet when his free hand rose to cup the back of her head to angle it until she was looking up at him, he didn't seem so much a stranger after all, and her heart took a skip. He was her husband. Her achingly handsome husband. Moonlight chiseled his features and frosted his golden hair before filtering down to broad, powerful shoulders.

For a time he looked at her as if he were learning her face. The bruises and swelling were gone, she knew, and Glenna wondered if he found her appearance pleasing or not.

"You really are beautiful, you know," he said in a hushed tone, as if he had read her thoughts. "I could tell that first day in my hotel room that you weren't ugly, even with the marks. But I didn't expect this."

Glenna's heart swelled with his words and just a little of her tension eased.

He bent enough for his lips to touch hers, softly, in the way a man might kiss a woman good-night at her front door. But they were a distance from the front door.

His mouth was warm and easy on hers, his lips parted and relaxed. Glenna drew a deep breath and when she exhaled she found in herself a little less stiffness.

A normal life was what she wanted. *He* was what she wanted.

Jared's arms came around her then, wrapping her, pulling her against him. Glenna curved her own up under his and pressed her palms to his back.

When his tongue teased her lips, then came inside and found hers she welcomed it, met it, in fact. He tasted sweet from the candy they had made and eaten earlier, and it was nice. Very, very nice.

A shiver shook her as he unfastened the buttons down the back of her simple shirtwaist dress, not from cold, because her blood was coursing through her at such a pace it kept her warm. Instead the shiver was from anticipation, from knowing how wonderful it felt to have her skin bared to him.

Her dress shimmied down around her ankles and only moments later her chemise and petticoat followed, leaving her naked before him. Odd, but it felt natural and left Glenna with a new sense of freedom she had never known before. It emboldened her and she set her hands to work on the buttons of his shirt while he undid his trousers, shed them and kicked them out of the way.

And then there they were, both of them bare in the moonlight.

Jared's arms went back around her, only now he held her clasped hard to him. Glenna reveled in the sensation of his skin against hers. His mouth opened wide and deepened their kiss, reminding her of the hunger and urgency she had known twice before. Fleetingly she wondered if she should be holding herself in check, resisting the desire so as not to be disappointed if he should stop short again. But something told her this time nothing would interfere and leave her starving, and so she joined in and let her own passions run.

He kneaded her back and then slipped his hands lower, finding her derriere, squeezing and pulling her up to her tiptoes, into his hips. Hard. He was hard all over. His shoulders, his back, his arms, his thighs and that which she found pressing insistently at her middle.

He made a sound deep in his throat, part groan, part moan, and lifted Glenna off her feet to lie back on the mattress with her on top of him. Strange and wonderful sensations were erupting within her, even before he rolled them both to their sides and found her breast with first his hand and then his lips. Her pulse was pounding in odd places, beneath his suckling mouth, his teasing tongue, his teeth gently biting her nipple. It beat in her throat, in her stomach, and much lower, in a spot between her thighs that made her want to part them and arch her hips.

As if he knew, Jared raised his thigh to that spot in the same way he had the night at the window, letting her ride it lying down now the way she had before. And ride it she did, pushing, seeking an answer to the need beating there. She wondered if she alone felt this way, but then Jared pulled her even harder against him, pressing his own lower parts into her hip in a demand that matched her own need.

And then his hand joined his thigh between hers and sharp sparks of pleasure replaced the beating desires there. Like a match to a candle's wick, he found a spot she hadn't known existed and brought it to life, only to desert it and return in a tortuous and wondrous dance, slipping inside her, surprising her, enrapturing her with the sensation that seemed somehow not quite enough. In and out, and then forward and back inside again until every nerve in her body seemed to be right on the surface of her skin.

Jared shifted his weight and rolled on top of her. With his legs he spread her knees ever farther apart. Suddenly that hard shaft that had only pressed against her before nudged at that spot his finger had awakened.

"I have to hurt you," he whispered, his tone telling her how much he regretted it.

Glenna didn't quite believe him when instead he eased into her only a scant inch and retreated. It felt good, so good she wanted more. Again he just barely went inside and left. And again. Glenna arched her hips toward him, telling him with her body how much she needed more, but still he went slowly, deepening his penetration, only to pull out once again. Deeper yet he came, and Glenna felt a pressure this time before he receded. Then, poised above her, he kissed her, tenderly, kindly, before plunging in, hard, sharp, deep.

Glenna gasped at the pain and couldn't help pulling away from it, but Jared held her tightly and kept her from going too far. "Stay still. It'll pass," he promised.

Once more he kissed her, teasing her with his tongue, trailing it down her chin, down her throat, down one breast and around her nipple until Glenna had forgotten the pain in the rekindling of the need she had been feeling moments earlier. Testing, tentatively, she arched up and felt him slip even deeper inside her. Jared's groan told her how much she was straining his control. And then he tested for himself, slowly, carefully moving in and out.

Sparks flickered and passion caught fire again almost instantly. Glenna grasped his back insistently, thinking that now it was his turn to ride her and welcoming him. Soreness was incidental beside the pleasure, beside the sensations and demands that grew with his every thrust. Something was racing within her, faster, faster, she didn't know to what end, she only knew she had to reach it, she had to. And then, all at once, it was as if she burst open, her senses exploded and soared and soared until exhaustion called them back to settle, slowly, slowly, back to rest. Just then Jared tensed above her, plunged to the very depths his body could reach inside her, once, twice, three times, before he shuddered and came to rest.

Languid, lethargic, Glenna was nevertheless astonished. And by more than the physical feelings. She realized that it was as if a door had opened in her heart, as well.

"Are you all right?" Jared asked in a ragged voice.

His question reminded her of his earlier concern and consideration, a side of him she liked. "Yes, I think so" was all she said, when in fact she was tempted to tell him how wonderful she felt. Hope was as alive in her as pleasure had been moments before—they would have a normal life, she felt sure, but more than that, perhaps they would even have what Cally and Joseph had.

"I'm glad," he told her, sounding as if he meant it.

Holding her tightly, he rolled then, leaving them both on their sides, but still joined. With one arm he reached for the edge of the quilt and flung it over them, adjusting it to keep them both warm before holding her fully, keeping her close, wrapped in his arms and legs.

"Go to sleep, city girl," he said into her hair, sighing in a way that let her know that was what he intended to do without ever letting her go.

Glenna was content to do just that, just the way she was. His body around hers and inside of hers made her feel as if she was where she belonged, as if she fit, as if there really was more between them than a marriage born out of mutual necessity. But more than that, being held by him like this made her feel as if he were telling her something he couldn't say in any other way. It seemed to her to be much the same as the afternoon when he had held Lyden close and tight and protectively, as if all he denied with his words and claims and everyday actions, was belied by his body.

And maybe that was a beginning.

Chapter Thirteen

Are you about finished in there?" Jared's voice came to Glenna through the door of their bedroom.

"I'll be down in just a minute," she called back as she buttoned the waistband of her brown skirt. With that done she raised her hands to untie the ribbon that had held her hair atop her head so it wouldn't be dampened by bathwater. As she did, her glance fell to the tub she had left moments before. A kindness was what it was.

A night of passion—particularly the first—was a tiring thing. Glenna had overslept. The sounds of the rest of the family leaving for Sunday morning church services in Hays hadn't done more than mildly disturb her. It had taken Jared dragging the big brass bathtub into the bedroom and filling it from buckets of water he had heated downstairs, to bring her fully awake. But a morning bath in an upstairs bedroom rather than an evening one in the kitchen was indeed a kindness, even though he had masked it with gruff instructions to be quick about it so he could show her how to milk a cow.

Glenna brushed her hair and caught it at the nape of her neck in a brown velvet ribbon that matched her skirt. She tied it into a wide bow, leaving the curly mass hanging down her back. She knew it made her look girlish but she was feeling girlish in a way she hadn't since before her father had died.

"There's bread and jam for breakfast," Jared informed her when she joined him in the kitchen. Sitting in a chair swung outward from the table, he was pridefully polishing the new boots he had bought in Chicago. "We'll set some cream to clabber after the milking and by tomorrow morning you can churn butter. I'm a man who likes my butter."

It sounded like a warning so Glenna refrained from telling him she had never churned butter and hadn't the slightest idea what 'clabber' meant. Instead she spread jam on a slice of bread and sat down to eat it, all the while watching him even though he seemed determined not to look at her.

Odd how rejuvenated she felt this morning. Everything—even Jared—looked different to her, and her heart felt light. Fate had thrust her into a situation that suddenly seemed as if it might just be the best thing that could have happened to her.

Or at least she thought so until she and Jared crossed the yard to the barn and she was introduced to a cow named Hildy.

"I didn't realize they were so big," she said, hanging back a ways from the stall Jared had stepped into.

He smoothed the animal's side. "She won't hurt you."

Glenna wished she believed that and decided on the spot that she didn't like the idea of a pet that was larger than she was—if milking cows were considered pets, and anything she had to touch had better be.

Jared took a three-legged stool from the corner of the stall and set it beside Hildy. Then, for the first time that morning, he looked directly at Glenna. "You can't milk her from over there."

Unfortunately. Still, the last thing Glenna wanted was to rile him. Gamely, she sidled partway into the stall with her back against the rail so as to keep as much distance between herself and the animal as possible.

"Mostly the younger boys take care of the milking, but you can't live around cows and not know how."

"Of course." Glenna kept her eyes on the rusty-colored beast.

"Even Annie can do it."

"I'm sure there's nothing easier."

The cow shifted its weight and Glenna jumped, banging back against the rails.

"Easy, Hildy, easy," he murmured to the beast as if Glenna had scared it rather than the other way around. "An animal can sense fear in people."

It seemed ridiculous to deny she was afraid so instead she said, "Hello, Hildy," as if she meant to be friends.

In answer the animal swung its tail to one side and dropped a healthy pile a scant foot from where Glenna was standing.

"Oh." The word came out reflexively, echoing with her own astonishment.

As if against his will, Jared started to laugh. "You can't live around cows without that, either."

"No, I don't suppose so." Glenna took another step nearer to the stool and farther away from the hind quarter of the animal.

Jared leaned his arm along Hildy's shoulder, braced the back of his head with his hand and stared at her. Glenna glanced over to find him grinning ear to ear.

"Welcome to the country, city girl."

A sudden determination that neither this cow nor Jared was going to get the best of her flashed through Glenna. "Thank you," she said haughtily and then reached a hand out to gingerly stroke Hildy's side the way she had seen her husband do moments before.

Jared chuckled. "Well, let's get to it, then." He took a pail down from a hook on the wall and placed it under the udder. "It's best if you sit on the stool."

Which required being so close to the animal that she had to keep her head sharply turned to the side so as not to have her nose pressed to it. But Glenna did it.

"Good girl."

Was he talking to her or to the cow? Probably the cow.

Jared hunkered down beside the stool and reached across Glenna's lap. "You grab a hold of the teat like so, squeeze at the top, move all the way down and pull."

It looked easy enough. Glenna just wasn't thrilled with the idea of touching the beast at all, particularly on its private underparts.

"Think you can do that?"

"Of course." Rubbing the tips of her fingers into her palms, Glenna reached, hesitated and finally formed fists around the teats. Not so bad. Squeeze, move down, pull.

Hildy lowed a complaint, lifted a hind leg and moved away. Glenna snatched her hands up to her chest and reared back.

"Easy, girl, easy."

This time Glenna knew he was talking to the cow. When he spoke to her his tone was sterner. "Not so hard. You hurt her."

"I'm sorry, Hildy," she said in supplication, hoping the cow didn't intend to hurt her in return.

"Try again."

This time Glenna followed the instructions with such a gentle touch nothing at all happened. Jared reached across her lap again and curved his hands around hers. "Like this," he said, showing her the right amount of pressure. When several squirts had pinged into the pail he let go and Glenna found she had the knack on her own, even if she didn't always hit the bucket. And then, concentrating, she improved her aim, too. By the time she had finished she wasn't even as afraid of the cow as she had been when she'd started.

She clapped her hands clean and sat back to look up at Jared. He nodded his head in grudging admiration. "Not half bad."

Glenna smiled, as satisfied with herself as she was pleased by even his faint praise.

Jared reached down to a curly strand of hair that had worked loose, fingering it thoughtfully. But then as if he remembered himself, he dropped it and jammed his hand into his pants pocket. "Hand me the pail so you don't slosh it all out on the way back to the house, and we'll put it into the churn to clabber. Everybody should be back anytime now."

Glenna did as he said, following a few steps behind as they crossed the yard.

Just keep giving me the chance, Jared, just keep giving me the chance.

Sunday afternoon was spent moving Lyden's bed and belongings to the smaller house before a big dinner weighed everyone down for the remainder of the day, leaving them lazy and content. Glenna helped Charity with a new hairstyle while Jared and Joseph played chess, Cally did a cross-stitch sampler, the older children went off on their own pursuits and the smaller ones amused themselves with the new piglets.

As the evening wore on Glenna found herself watching the hands on the grandfather clock in the corner of Cally's parlor. Was it shameful to be so anxious for bedtime? But anxious she was.

The closeness that she and Jared had shared the night before hadn't followed them into the day. And when he finally stood and stretched, it wasn't to take her home to their bed. It was to announce that he was going to join some of the ranch hands in the bunkhouse for a poker game.

Glenna's disappointment was mingled with embarrassment at what felt like his rejection in front of Joseph and

Cally. Wanting to escape, she quickly gathered up Lyden and went alone with the baby to their own house.

Lying in bed in the dark, Glenna waited until she couldn't resist sleep any longer. She didn't know when Jared came in and he was out of bed before she was the following morning. The only evidence that they had shared the same mattress was his dented pillow and the mussed sheets beside her. Try as she might to convince herself there was no more to his late night than his wanting a game of cards, she couldn't help feeling as if the ground she had gained on Saturday night had been lost.

Without exchanging more than six words with her Jared left after breakfast to work with Joseph. It was with low spirits that Glenna faced her first day of her own chores as wife and mother.

With Cally and Charity's help, she spent the morning tending to the wash. Not too complicated—dirty clothes were swirled around by a long stick in a tub of boiling water and soap, rinsed, run through a wringer and then hung out to dry.

It was Cally who taught her to churn butter once the wash was finished. Churning was a monotonous process that took three-quarters of an hour and left her arms aching from maintaining the up-and-down agitation of the dasher that turned the clabbered—or thickened—cream into sweet butter.

When that was done she fed Lyden his lunch and took him upstairs to put him in bed for a nap. After a morning spent engrossed in trying to put a corncob in a knothole in one of the planks of the kitchen floor, he wasn't ready to be separated from the fascinating toy; Glenna ended up having to put him to bed with his favorite blanket, his rag doll and his corncob. Then she gathered her crisp, dry laundry from the clothesline and took it up to the bedroom to fold.

Washing and hanging Jared's clothes on the line had been done amid the chatter of Cally and Charity. She hadn't really taken notice of the articles themselves. But folding them in the privacy of their bedroom was something else again. The long length of Jared's trousers reminded her of his legs, thick, muscular and hairy. Fresh chambray shirts brought to mind his chest and the feel of his back beneath her palms. The bottom half of a cotton union suit set her stomach aquiver.

Where had these feelings come from? she wondered. When had she gone from being aghast at the drunken man with whom she had struck a marriage bargain to fanciful daydreams about him? No matter, though, she decided. She *was*, after all, married to him and that earned her the right. Better fanciful daydreams and a quivering stomach than revulsion and hatred. Now, if only he could be of a like mind toward her. Then she could send for Mary and they could all live here happily.

With the laundry folded Glenna took it to the bureau and opened the top drawer—Jared's drawer. What was left in it was all askew and she set the clean clothes on the dresser top to straighten it before adding what she had just laundered. From the drawer wafted his scent, a mingling of soap and clean, earthy odors. She liked that, too, she realized.

As she nearly emptied the drawer, refolding more shirts and union suits, she spotted a small cloth sack in the back corner.

She should leave it where it was, she knew. This was Jared's private drawer; what was in it—whatever was in it—were his private belongings.

Then again, it was probably a simple thing. Something silly, like a memento of childhood, maybe marbles. Nothing that would be done any harm were she to see it.

What if he were to go through her private things? a voice in the back of her mind argued. She wouldn't like it.

But she had secrets. He didn't. Did he?

She glanced over her shoulder as if Jared might have somehow appeared to catch her. Of course no one was there.

She was alone in the house except for Lyden and he was sound asleep.

Jared would never know.

She couldn't help herself. The sack was closed by a drawstring and Glenna made quick work of opening it. It wasn't marbles, that much she could tell just by lifting it. Light of weight, whatever was in it was very small. Just a coin, perhaps? Nothing important, certainly.

She upturned the sack and let the contents roll out into her palm. It hadn't occurred to her that it might be something she wouldn't want to see. Something she wouldn't want to know he had. But it was.

There in the middle of her palm was a small silver wedding band. His first wife's wedding band, she had no doubt.

So he had gotten rid of the outward reminders of the other woman, but he had kept one of the most important things, something that had to be the greatest reminder of all, the ring that had joined them.

Glenna sighed and felt her spirits plummet even further at the same moment a stab of the most bitter jealousy struck her. His keeping the other woman's wedding ring and not offering her one at all made her feel as if she weren't really his wife. It reminded her that she was merely a fill-in to do the work of the cherished woman who was no longer there.

"It's silly to be envious of a dead woman," she told herself. But there it was anyway, and with it came some strange urge to go out to the graves she had seen in the distance and assure herself that there was indeed one for the person who seemed like her rival.

With the ring still clutched hard in her fist, Glenna went downstairs and out the back door, marching with determination to the fenced-off plot of ground that sat on a small ridge behind Cally's house.

There were five white crosses marking gentle mounds in the grass that grew there. Two of them were for Jared's parents, one was for a baby born to Cally and Joseph before their oldest living son. Set off from those three, in one corner, was the grave of someone named William McKall, a name she had never heard before. In the opposite corner was that of Jared's first wife. *Janie* was all that was carved into the wood. The affectionate name Jared alone used for her. There were no dates of birth or death, no loving sentiment. And yet to Glenna the simplicity of that pet name seemed striking, as if that said it all.

Staring at the cross Glenna felt guilty for resenting the woman, but resent her she did. Why couldn't he let go of her? Why did he hold on to his grief, taking it out on his own son and keeping his distance from Glenna the way he had before Saturday night and since?

She's dead, Jared. Dead and buried right here. Let her be and give both Lyden and me a chance.

"Glenna, honey?" Cally's voice came softly from behind her and made Glenna jump. "What are you doing out here?"

Glenna took a deep breath and hoped her feelings weren't plain on her face. "I just got curious," she answered in a hurry, the wedding band burning into her palm within the fist that clutched it.

"Curious to see a grave?"

Glenna shrugged and held out her hand to show her guilty plunder to the woman she had come to regard as a friend. "I was putting Jared's clothes away and found this. It got me to thinking about . . . things."

"About Jane." Cally took the ring and looked closely at it. "This was Jared and Joseph's mother's ring."

Glenna looked hopefully at her sister-in-law. "It wasn't hers then?"

Cally shook her head sadly. "It was Jane's, too. Joseph bought me one of my own, so Jared used their mother's. I didn't know he still had it . . . that he hadn't buried it with Jane. I imagine it must have been a hard decision for him to make, whether to keep it because it had been his mother's first, or to bury it.''

"He kept it because he still loves her.''

"Is that what you think?''

"It's what I know.''

"Did he tell you that?''

"He didn't have to. He kept her ring and he didn't give me one at all. What would you think?''

Cally frowned, first at Glenna and then at the grave in the corner of the family plot. "I think that none of us ever really knows what's going on in anyone else's mind.''

Because she disagreed, Glenna didn't answer that. Instead she changed the subject. "Who is the man buried in the other grave?''

"That's Bill. The Strattons took him in when he was a child, raised him the same as they did Jared and Joseph. He lived and worked here like one of the family until not long ago. When he died last month it was only right that he be buried here.''

"I see. Jared never spoke of him.''

Cally didn't say any more. Instead she curved her arm through Glenna's, turned them both away from the graves and headed back to the houses. "Come on away from here. If you don't believe anything else, believe that there's nothing out here for you to think about.''

Glenna wished that were true.

She burned supper that night. It was the first meal she had ever cooked, a stew Cally said no one could ruin, but Glenna scorched it black. The kitchen was full of smoke and stench when Jared came in for the day. Glenna was using her skirt to fan it out the open window beside the big iron stove.

He didn't say anything, and even though it was senseless, she felt inclined to confess. "I'm afraid I've ruined supper.''

Jared shed his sweat-stained shirt. With one hand he slipped a basin under the pump spout while with his other he reached for the handle. "There's jerky in the pantry" was all he said before pumping water into the basin.

Was he thinking that marrying her had been a mistake? Glenna wondered as she kept on trying to clear the kitchen of the smoke. Most likely. Jane might not have been adept at a wife's chores, but at least he had loved her.

Glenna's eyes went to Jared. Bending at the waist, he cupped his hands together and threw water over his face and hair again and again, letting it run in rivulets down his neck, back, shoulders and chest. Then he took the bar of soap he'd brought with the basin and washed up.

All the while Glenna watched. She followed the soap's path where it zigzagged up and down the thick column of his neck, then across each shoulder.

Why did you stay away from our bed?

She stopped fanning her skirts as he again bent over the basin and splashed water to rinse off. She watched the glimmer of wetness replace soapsuds and had the urge to let her palms slide along the surface of his skin. It seemed unfair that he had awakened this awareness in her and could remain so impervious himself.

He reached for the towel he had set beside the pump and caught sight of her standing there, staring. As if jolted back to life, Glenna went back to flapping her skirts at the waning smoke. But even out of the corner of her eye she could see the rough strokes of his big hands wielding the towel to dry off, and she couldn't help wondering why it was that just the sight of him had such power over her pulse.

Jared was still quiet through dinner and so was she. Only Lyden chattered as he ate the meal of jerky, corn on the cob and bread with Glenna's first lumpy attempt at butter. As a result both adults tended to look from their own plate to the baby and back again rather than at each other.

When they were finished eating Jared's gaze seemed stuck on Lyden as the baby squished buttery bread through his fingers. As she cleared the table Jared's study of his son was something Glenna took note of and couldn't help watching as intently as she had his sponge bath.

Ordinarily he didn't spare the child more than a sidelong glance. Never did he show any real interest. And yet he seemed so lost in his thoughts that even he didn't realize what he was doing. There was definitely interest in his expression. His eyes weren't remote; he didn't look detached at all. Instead, for one brief moment he smiled at the baby's delight in the mess he was making. He even reached an index finger over and wiped a smear of butter off the toddler's nose.

Then as if he remembered himself, Glenna saw him frown and push away from the table to take what was left of the dishes to the sink before he strode through the house and went out the front door.

She's heavy in the air today, isn't she? Glenna mused, doing the dishes. *She's taking up your thoughts and haunting mine.*

With the kitchen clean and Lyden in bed, Glenna went back downstairs and found Jared standing with his back against a post on the front porch. That he was facing Cally and Joseph's house, staring at the yellow light coming through their curtains, was suddenly too much for Glenna to suffer on top of everything else that had been on her mind today and tonight.

"Lyden isn't to blame, you know," she said before she realized her thoughts had found voice.

Jared glanced over at her. "What?"

For a moment she considered the wisdom of pursuing this and then decided to take the bull by the horns. "I said Lyden isn't to blame for your wife's death."

He cocked an eyebrow her way. "Have I ever said he was?"

"You didn't have to say it."

"And what makes you think I blame the boy for that?"

"'The boy,'" she repeated. "He has a name. Do you know that I've not once heard you use it? That's part of what makes me think you blame him. But it isn't the baby's fault when the mother dies giving birth."

"I never thought it was."

That surprised her. "Then what is it? Is he just too much a reminder of his mother? He shouldn't be punished for that. I'd think you'd love him all the more for it."

There was only silence between them for a time. Jared watching her, his expression showing confusion. "Are you looking for a fight tonight?"

"Of course not. It's just that you told me that I'd have need of making the best of things out here, and I'm wondering why you don't do some of that yourself."

"Is that right?"

His easy drawl, the half-amused tone of his voice didn't help her mood any. "Yes, that's right."

"Funny, I thought that's what I was doing by bringing you here."

"By going right on rejecting your own son because he reminds you of his mother? By pining away with thoughts about her still? By standing out here looking longingly at your brother's house and family, and wishing you were a part of their life instead of taking up your own?"

At leisure he took his hands from his trouser pockets and crossed his arms over the clean shirt he'd donned after drying off. Glenna had a sudden flash of what she had watched so intently before. It was a disconcertingly intimate image that clashed with the turmoil roiling around inside her.

"Let me see if I have all this straight," he said. "I married you and brought you here to mother him rather than sending him to be raised by his grandparents in Chicago, but I'm rejecting the boy. You've read my mind and know I either blame him for his mother's death or that he reminds me of her. That sets me pining for her. And I couldn't just be standing out here against this pole because it feels good, it has to be because I'm wishing I had stayed next door with Joseph and Cally. Is that about it?''

Defending her point, she shot back an answer before thinking about what she was saying. ''If you aren't pining for your first wife, why did you keep her wedding ring tucked in with your private things?''

''What were you doing in my private things?''

''Putting away your clean clothes. That's what I was hired to do, wasn't it?''

Silence fell heavily after her raised voice stopped, and Glenna glanced quickly next door to see if anyone had heard. When she looked back she found Jared studying her. He took a breath, sighed it out long and slow and turned his head the other way, looking out at the barn across the yard. She had succeeded in sobering his amusement. ''You don't know what you're talking about.''

''Working here last week to clean the place up, you had the distraction of your family all around. Sleeping here Saturday night was…well, it was something new…because it was with me. But yesterday, moving Lyden's things over and settling in to living here the way you did with her stirred up all your feelings for her. That's why you spent last night playing cards instead of sleeping here. That's why you've been so quiet tonight. You can't stop thinking about her.''

That made him laugh wryly. ''You're wrong.'' He pushed off the porch post and stepped down the stairs. Glenna thought that was all he was going to say, that he was merely going to walk off. But then he turned halfway toward her, looking up at her over his shoulder. ''It isn't Janie that I haven't been able to get out of my mind, though to tell you the truth, I expected to have some trouble that way. Instead it's a sharp-tongued, curly-headed snake basher who's skittish of cows and damn near burns my house down making a simple stew.'' His voice grew quiet, and he looked away from her. ''I'm not a man who ever wanted any woman to take up so much of his thoughts again. I can't help that it doesn't sit easy.''

Then he walked away, going in the direction of the barn in long strides.

And Glenna was left with the wind knocked out of her sails.

Chapter Fourteen

It started as a distant rumble just before dusk on the following Saturday. Jared and Joseph had come in from their work early, Jared had just settled into a long soak in the tub in the kitchen and Glenna was changing into a clean cream-colored shirtwaist dress in the bedroom upstairs. She was looking forward to the first meal they were to share with Cally's family since moving next door. Pity for Jared's stomach had spurred Cally's invitation, Glenna thought, but she was so anxious for the evening of socializing that she didn't care what had prompted it.

The sky had been overcast all day, and when Glenna first heard the rumble she thought it was thunder from a long way away. Jared kept saying the weather was going to change any day now. He'd seen the fast approach of winter in the thicker hair on the horses and cows, the cows' hooves breaking off early and the fact that there had already been two frosts, in spite of the warm daytime temperatures. In the moments they met and spoke each day in passing, Cally had confirmed the prediction with news that her carrots were growing deeper, her sweet potatoes had tougher skins and there were more layers on the last of the onions she had picked from her garden—sure signs of a harsh winter ahead.

Fastening the last buttons on the high, tight collar of her dress, Glenna went to the window for a look. In the waning light she could see that the clouds still hung heavily in the sky, but no different than they had all day long. Yet the rumble grew louder and she realized it wasn't intermittent the way thunder would have been, but rather a constant sound.

From next door she heard a whoop of excitement, recognizing the voice as Matthew's. It was the same sound the fifteen-year-old had made on their arrival here and repeated whenever he was exuberantly glad of something.

In the distance Glenna saw a cloud of dust before she made out the racing wagons that were causing it. Had it not been for Matthew's hoot she would have thought something terrible had happened. As it was, she didn't know what to think.

"Put on your dancing shoes." Jared's voice came from behind as he strode quickly into the room. His chest and feet were bare, and the waistband button of his brown trousers was open. His hair was wet, and smoothed back by only his hands, a few strands falling onto his brow rakishly. The expression on his face was one of unveiled pleasure. He went on as he snapped the folds out of a clean white shirt, "There's a surprise party coming."

"A surprise party?" she repeated dubiously. At home surprise parties didn't come in racing wagons.

He nodded over his shoulder in the direction from which the rumble was becoming louder still. "With everything and everybody so far apart around here, any occasion is cause for friends to gather together and invade a place without warning for a party. My bringing a new bride home is certainly cause, and unless I'm mistaken, here comes the celebration."

"But we aren't ready," she said, wide-eyed and thinking about the weeks of preparation that preceded every party she had ever known about.

Jared laughed as he jammed his buttoned shirt into his pants and slipped a leather vest over it. "They'll come prepared. That's the way of it. Happens a lot here even without a new Stratton being brought in. Cally's melodeon and Luke's knack with a mouth harp are big attractions." He pointed to her stockinged feet with a jab of his chin, obviously as excited at the prospect of a party as Matthew was next door. "You'll want to hurry, Glenna. I'll go over now and start to help move the furniture out of the way for dancing."

He ran a brush hastily through his hair, grabbed up a pair of socks from his bureau drawer and left as hurriedly as he'd come in.

So he likes parties and dancing, does he? Glenna thought. She was pleased with the revelation, not only because she did, too, but because maybe it would lift the solemnity that had dominated his manner the whole week long.

Within half an hour the center of Cally's parlor was cleared of tables, chairs and sofa, the rug had been rolled up and the house was filling with neighbors, friends and ranch hands. The kitchen table and drainboards were cluttered with meats, cheeses, freshly baked breads, canned goods and sweets brought by the revelers. A nursery was set up in Annie's room where older children tended the younger ones, Lyden included, and the cool evening air was suddenly a blessing coming in through open windows.

With Cally on one side of her and Jared on the other, Glenna was introduced to what she decided must be everyone in the county. Some names she had heard before and those she was glad to put faces to; but most were strange to her and all she could do was hope those people didn't think too unkindly of her if she didn't remember everyone's names afterward.

One of the ranch hands, Scott Bradley, made a particular impression. Rather than moving past after he had been introduced to her, the tall, thin man who looked not much older than Glenna herself, lingered in front of her, staring at her with an ear-to-ear grin on his face.

Another man peered over Scott Bradley's shoulder and said, "You'll have to excuse old Scott here, Miz Glenna. Every time he gets all Saturday-night slickered up he falls in love."

Scott Bradley jabbed the other man in the ribs with a backward shot of his elbow and cleared his throat. "If there's anything I can do for you, you be sure and let me know," he said to Glenna.

Still he didn't move, and out of discomfort Glenna asked, "What is it that you do here, Mr. Bradley?"

"Call me Scott, please, ma'am. When they don't need me for bringing up the tail end of a cattle drive I'm the carpenter 'round here. T'was my daddy's job before mine so I been on the place since I was knee-high. About anything you want made I can do."

That sparked her interest. "As a matter of fact I've been thinking how nice it would be to have a fence put up around the house. And painted white," she added. Feeling the attention of both Cally and Jared drawn to this delay in the introductions and her idea, she explained herself. "Then Lyden could go out of the house without the worry of him wandering off."

"With wood as scarce as it is..." Jared began to discourage the idea.

But Scott Bradley cut him off. "I think there's enough left from that shack we took down last month. Isn't good for anything else. That old wood'd drink a lot of paint, but I'd be happy to do it for you... as a wedding present."

Glenna looked up hopefully at Jared. She had been mulling over this idea all week. As she worked she had put her thoughts to what could be done to make life here easier and safer for Mary, and she had decided that a fence would provide the perimeters her sister needed to find her way from one house to the other and even out to the barn if it was built just right. That it would also allow Lyden some freedom was an added benefit...and hopefully a strong selling point. But she hadn't known how to broach the subject with her husband. The offer from Scott made this seem like as good a time as any.

Her cause was aided when Cally put in, "If there's enough we might as well put it around both houses—one big fence. I wouldn't want Lyden not to be able to get to his Aunt Cally's anytime he has a mind to."

Jared gave in with aplomb. "Wallpaper and fancy lace curtains are what most women want. But not my wife. She's after a fence." He shook his head. "We'll be gone four days next week to drive those fifty head of cattle to that buyer, but I suppose when we come back we can spare you."

With that decided Scott had no choice but to move on. "It'll be my pleasure," he assured Glenna, not taking his eyes off her even as he left.

When the introductions were finally complete the music started up. It was the first time Glenna had seen quiet Luke animated. He blew out the holes of his harmonica and took up the space between the melodeon—tonight played by an older man rather than by Cally—and two more men, one who jammed a fiddle under his chin and another who placed thimbles on all five fingers of one hand and tapped on a hollow drum.

Since the party was in honor of their marriage, no one would dance until Glenna and Jared did. When the four musicians struck their first harmonious chord, Jared's arm went around the back of her waist. Glenna looked up at him, wondering if he was going to be unhappy about her victory over the fence. But instead what she found was that same warm, happy expression that had been on his face when he announced the party earlier. As if he hadn't given the fence another thought, he swung her into the middle of the floor, caught her hand in his and started the dancing for the evening with a rousing reel.

Joseph had the second dance with Glenna, and she teased him about how he and his brother had become so good at it. By the third it was clear that because they were so outnumbered, no woman in the room would be left without a partner for any dance, so Glenna took a deep breath and stepped into a polka with a man whose name she couldn't remember.

And then back came Jared, to her pleasure, for the fourth dance. He smelled faintly of the corn liquor that had been brought in a heavy crockery jug and was being enjoyed in small cups by the men while the women sipped dandelion wine. His face radiated his enjoyment of the festivities, and Glenna couldn't suppress a laugh at the sight. But rather than question her about what she found amusing, Jared merely grinned down at her and swung her into a schottische—a dance resembling a polka but done in the round, with one couple following another to circle the room.

He kept hold of her when the strains of "The Blue Danube" followed, pulling her in close and slowing their steps to the waltz. His body was warm against hers and it felt good in spite of the fact that she, too, was heated from the dance. Caught up in the moment she indulged the urge to rest her head lightly against his chest, where she could hear the rapid, strong beats of his heart and feel those of her own matching them. It felt wonderful to be in his arms like that, and Glenna was immensely disappointed when the music came to an end and yet another stranger claimed her for the next dance.

But it was a short lapse. After that Scott Bradley argued his way into the next waltz only to be cut in on halfway through.

"Sorry, but the slow ones are all mine tonight," Jared said to the younger man, sounding, in a friendly sort of way, very possessive. He kept his eyes on Bradley's back as he reached for Glenna. "He's a randy buck, that one. With an eye for you, if I'm not mistaken."

Unlike the previous times Jared's jealous streak had shown itself, there was nothing accusatory in his tone, so Glenna teased him. "Do you think so?"

He smiled down at her slyly, obviously seeing the game. "Well, no, now that you mention it, I might be mistaken. He could be trying to cover up thinking that you're the homeliest woman he ever set eyes on, so he doesn't lose his job."

"Oh, in that case, I'm glad he's hiding it so well. I'd feel terrible knowing my looks cost a man his livelihood," she said flirtatiously.

"That could weigh on a person, all right," he agreed with mock sincerity. Then he chuckled, shook his head and pulled her so close she had no choice this time but to turn her head to his chest as they finished their dance.

Six more times Scott Bradley asked her to dance and six more times Jared cut in, until the very sight of her husband made the ranch hand groan and Glenna laugh. After a while the rest of the party realized what was going on. It turned into the joke of the evening, with half of the group cheering on Scott Bradley and trying to distract Jared so the younger man could finish just one dance with Glenna, and the other half goading Jared on. Since it was all in good-natured fun Glenna reveled in it, glad of the fact that it put her in her husband's arms for most of the night.

It was well into the morning hours when the party wound to a close. The younger children and babies were left sleeping in Annie's room, and the adults divided up, some to spend the night in Cally and Joseph's house, some to go next door to Glenna and Jared's to throw bedrolls onto the floors of the unfurnished rooms.

As the group of them walked across the yard to the smaller house Glenna lagged somewhat behind, wondering what was going to happen now. Every night during the past week Jared had loitered in the barn or the bunkhouse until so late that she had fallen asleep before he came to bed.

With so many celebrating their wedding she didn't think he would do that tonight, and yet she was loath to have her husband's attention in bed only because he didn't want to evoke rumors of discontent among his friends and neighbors by staying away.

It didn't take long to see to their guests' needs, and then Glenna and Jared were alone behind the closed door of their bedroom, awash in the soft yellow glow of a lamp on the table beside the bed.

Neither of them said anything. Jared sat on the bed and Glenna crossed the room to stand near her dressing table. As he lazily pulled off his boots, she slowly untied the ribbon that held her hair atop her head. As he dragged his shirttails from his trousers she sluggishly plied the buttonhook to her shoes and took them off. At a snail's pace he unfastened his shirt buttons. With great deliberation she unrolled her stockings. He shrugged out of his shirt and laid it over the foot rail; she tilted her chin and began to slip pearl buttons out of their holes. Then, with nothing remaining to be removed but his pants, Jared stood and went to the window, leaning his shoulder against the edge to stare out at the night as if he were the only one in the room.

It riled Glenna suddenly to see him like that, to feel ignored. She didn't want his attentions just for the sake of outward appearances.

With her back to him she made hasty work of the rest of her disrobing and donned her nightdress. Then she yanked the quilt off the bed and billowed it out onto the floor at the foot of it. As she returned for her pillow Jared turned from the window to look at her.

"What are you doing?" he asked in a hushed voice.

"Sleeping on the floor," she answered in a normal tone as she sat cross-legged in the center of the quilt and began to brush her hair with angry strokes.

He turned and sat on the window ledge, his back against the glass, his legs outstretched, one ankle over the other; he folded his arms across his bare chest. "Why?"

"To make it easier for you," she lied when she knew full well it was to make it easier for herself. "You can't bear to come to bed with me at night until I'm already asleep, but with so many people around you can't very well do that tonight. So I'm giving the bed over to you. That way you don't have to sleep with someone you don't want to sleep with."

"That's what you think, is it? That you're someone I don't want to sleep with?"

Glenna didn't answer.

For a moment the only sound in the room was the crackle of the brush going through her hair. Then Jared pushed away from the window and crossed to her in three long, confident strides. He lay down on his back on the quilt directly in front of her, clasped his hands behind his head and stared up at the ceiling as if he were lying in summer grass contemplating clouds. But the expression on his face was a long way from relaxed. Instead he looked very serious, very disturbed. He took a breath that raised his bare chest and then sighed as though in surrender.

"I told you right off that I'd never love another woman, Glenna."

The reminder stabbed her too sharply to comment. As if she hadn't heard him, she went on brushing her hair with even more fervor than before.

"Damn," he said softly, to himself.

Glenna divided her hair into three lengths and began to braid it with hard yanks, trying not to look at Jared but looking just the same. He was shaking his head back and forth, as if in denial. Of what? she wondered.

"I didn't think it could happen again," he railed suddenly at the ceiling. "There were barely feelings enough left in me to go on living when Janie..." He paused. "There sure as hell wasn't enough left to love someone. And I didn't want to.'' In the dim lamplight Glenna saw his jaw clench and unclench. ''Still don't.''

''It doesn't need to be said,'' she told him firmly, wanting to stop him before he went any further. But he didn't seem to hear her.

Again he sighed, long and deep, almost angrily. His bottom lip disappeared under his mustache. Then he turned his head and captured her eyes with his stern look. ''But God help me, here it is. I think I'm falling in love with you, and I know I can't stop it because I've tried this past week.''

Glenna froze, her hands in mid-braid. Had she heard him right? She struggled to concentrate on what he was still saying.

''I didn't stay away from your bed because I didn't want you. It was because of these damn feelings, Glenna. I told you they don't sit easy and I meant it. If we went to bed together I knew I wouldn't be able to keep my hands off you and that it would only add fuel to the fire. So I'd wait up until I was so damn tired I could barely see. But it didn't matter. The fuel's there anyway—in that damn wild curly hair of yours, in the curve of your backside, in the stubborn tilt of that chin, in the all-fired determination in your eyes that makes you charge into things around here like a bull, in the way you've made my family your own, even in the way you've taken to the boy....''

It was as if he were thinking aloud and caught himself. ''God, you don't know what I went through after...'' His voice trailed off but his eyes still searched her face. Then he reached up and clasped her nape. His thumb feathered into her hair a moment before he pulled her down to him, straining upward to catch her mouth with his.

At first Glenna was too dumbstruck to do more than react to his kiss, his touch, to what she had been thinking about all week long, especially at night as she lay alone in their bed. But after a moment her mind began to spin. Breaking away, she straightened. ''Do you mean that?'' she asked.

But rather than say anything he pulled her back into a kiss more firm and insistent than before, and Glenna realized that was the only answer he intended to give. She sensed that he had admitted all he could. But there was confirmation in the hunger of his mouth on hers, the tenderness, the consideration when she could feel urgency in him.

He loved her.

For a moment she reveled as much in that as in his kiss. But then she thought again.

He hadn't said he loved her. He said that he *thought* he *might* be falling in love with her. *Tonight*, when they were once more sharing a room without a choice.

Again she pulled away from him, sitting back on her heels. "And what about tomorrow?" she demanded.

"What about it?"

"I don't want to be just what you use to...to slake your thirst, and then once it's quenched you're fortified to deny it all again. I don't want to be what you're wanting and fighting against at the same time."

For a long moment he stared at her from beneath a furrowed brow. Then he said in a voice deep and sincere, "I'm not fighting against it anymore."

Glenna stared down at him, so handsome it made her ache. It wasn't heartening to know his feelings for her were something he didn't want. Yet maybe that, too, was a beginning, however begrudged. And maybe even begrudged beginnings could find happy futures.

He didn't pull her back to him. Instead he waited, watching her, clearly letting her know it was her move.

She could reject his less than wholehearted proclamation for the sake of pride, and have a semblance of revenge for the rejection she had felt all week. But what would that serve in the end? And when she wanted so much more from him, perhaps she should take any beginning she could get.

Glenna blinked back moisture that had somehow gathered in her eyes. Then slowly, she bent over and kissed him, gently, just a little sadly, to let him know she would accept what he was giving her. For now.

Jared's hand slipped up into her hair and held her tenderly to the kiss he answered with his own lips. In that instant Glenna's senses came to life and gained strength over her thoughts. Now was not a time for pride or revenge, her body seemed to say, and Glenna couldn't resist it.

His hands left her head and went to her hip to tempt her to lie beside him. There was no resistance in Glenna.

Lying next to him, she felt his arms go around her. She reached hers around him, holding him as tightly as he was holding her. Passion washed through her with more force than she had yet known, quieting the inhibitions that had been with her before. She met his tongue with her own, parried and danced and teased. She filled her hands with his back, reveling in the sensation of its broad, hard expanse.

When he tipped her head backward she willingly arched her throat to his exploring tongue and learned the silkiness of his sun-washed gold hair with her hands. As he worked her nightdress off she rained kisses across his collarbone, into the hollow at the base of his throat and down into the deep cleft between pectorals honed with hard work. She learned the feel of his ribs beneath her flattened palms, the tautness of his belly, and then slid her hand around his narrow waist and ventured just her fingertip into the back of his half-unfastened pants.

Bare to him, she even forgot to be embarrassed that the dim light exposed her to eyes that unabashedly devoured the sight. Instead she grew bold enough to finish opening the buttons of his fly, telling him she, too, wanted to look.

When Jared had shed his britches, look she did, finding him as magnificent to the eye as he was to the touch. And when with one hand he pulled her cheek to rest against his chest and with the other he guided her hand to mold around that long, thick shaft, she even did that with a new sense of freedom and daring. Silk and pulsing heat was what she found, and the response her touch elicited gave her a sense of the power she could wield over him.

He shifted and his mouth dropped to her breast. She melted into the splendid torment of his nipping teeth, flicking tongue and suckling lips. Then power didn't matter anymore, not his over her or hers over him. All that mattered was that they came together, that he came into her in one fluid motion, embedding himself to the core of her. Like a flock of fluttery winged birds alighting in a treetop, desire and need settled deep, deep inside her and waited to be assuaged. Glenna arched her hips to have as much of him as she possibly could, going so far as to clamp her legs around his massive thighs to hold him tight.

He pulsed inside her and Glenna answered with the flex of her own hips. Again and again he spoke with his body and hers answered, until his rhythm grew to such a pace that she could do no more than accept. She let him carry her along in his climb, up and up until hot sparks shot all through her, igniting an explosion so intense she wasn't sure she would survive, or that she wanted to once something so wondrous ended. But end it did, and the spasms that seemed to rock Jared as strongly, as profoundly, ceased as well.

Glenna could hear her heart pounding, and she could feel Jared's, fast, hard, strong. She reached to caress his hair where it curled damply at the base of his head and for a time that was how they stayed.

Then all at once he was gone.

Kneeling on the quilt beside her, he scooped her up into his arms and took her to their bed where he gently set her in the very middle of the mattress. He blew out the light and climbed in beside her, reaching for her. With her lying against his long, taut body, he wrapped his arms around her, cupping the back of her head to hold her cheek against his chest in the same way he had before. He settled his chin atop her curly hair and sighed, now calm, replete.

"Go to sleep, city girl," he said in a raspy voice. "I'd better take you to church tomorrow morning and let the rest of Hays get a look at you."

But sleep didn't come instantly to Glenna. Instead she lay in his arms wondering what it was that she felt for this man. There were feelings, she knew, but she had been holding them at bay rather than allowing them to blossom, for fear that he would never care for her. It was hard to let those feelings flourish now and know what they were. Harder still to entrust them to an unpredictable man who didn't want to love her at all.

Chapter Fifteen

Glenna and Jared took up the rear of the parade of wagons from the Stratton ranch into church the next morning. It was a jovial group with friendly gibes called up and down the line and several lone riders nudging their mounts to a canter to aid the teasing along and pass messages.

The church in Hays was a white clapboard structure with a high spire housing a bell that was ringing when they arrived. As they filed in Glenna was gladdened by the arm Jared kept around her, his hand riding the small of her back. It was a possessive gesture that claimed her as his, even though once again she was all too aware of her lack of a wedding ring.

It wasn't a rousing service, and as they all sat down for the sermon Glenna watched a little girl in the row ahead of her. Sitting very primly, obviously on her best behavior, she looked to be Mary's age. In fact, she resembled Mary in coloring and stature.

Glenna's heart gave a twist at the thought of her sister. She'd written twice since arriving in Hays, but there hadn't been time enough to receive a letter back. How was her sister faring? Glenna wondered for the thousandth time since she'd left Chicago. Was she sad and melancholy with missing Glenna? Or had she bounced back almost instantly the way children do? Glenna hoped she had bounced back and gone on with her everyday life. To picture Mary moping was hard.

Soon, Mary, soon.

The congregation gathered outside the church when the service was over. It seemed to Glenna that she was introduced to every single person; again names and faces became a blur. All through the introductions, Jared remained at her side, his arm around her waist or her shoulders or his hand at her elbow, but unlike the times before when it had been for the benefit of onlookers, now there seemed to be a naturalness to it. Was she imagining it? She didn't think so. Instead it was as if they fit together, a matched pair, a couple, and for the first time Glenna honestly felt like his wife.

Cally had come prepared with food enough for all the Strattons for the picnic that followed. With the weather on the cusp of changing this was to be the last picnic of the season, a daylong affair in the churchyard. Lyden was tended by Cally and Joseph's children while the four adults shared a blanket and a leisurely meal of fried chicken, potato salad and pickles.

"Becker's brought in his bulls," Joseph said when they had finished eating.

Cally rolled her eyes. "You two can't be thinking about bulldogging in your Sunday best."

"Bulldogging?" Glenna asked from where she sat with her feet tucked up under her dark blue skirt.

"They ride a horse at full speed and jump off its back to grab the horns of a bull and twist it to the ground," Cally explained, clearly disapproving. "You know how men love to show off."

Joseph ignored his wife's comment and answered the basis of her objection instead, winking at Jared. "Doesn' matter what you're wearing to watch."

"And bet," Cally put in slyly.

"How was it you came by that fancy new winter coat last year, Cally?" Jared asked with a half grin. Lying on his side, his head braced on his hand, he wore his gray three-piece suit as easily as he did his dungarees and chambray shirts. He ignored Cally's censorious glare and went on anyway. "As I recall Joseph split his winnings with you, wasn't that it?"

"And how much did the two of you lose the rest of the time?" she countered good-naturedly.

"We come out winners more often than not," Joseph defended.

"Not since Bill left you haven't—" Cally caught herself, cutting her own words short.

Silence fell for a moment, and Glenna accounted for it as grief over the sudden reminder of their old friend. Then Jared answered his sister-in-law, but the levity in the debate had evaporated. "She's got us there, Joe. Not many bull-doggers as good as he was."

Joseph lit his pipe and Cally busied herself with picking up the remnants of their picnic.

"You all must miss him very much," Glenna put in. "Cally told me he grew up with you both."

Cally looked at Joseph, Joseph at Cally, and then, out of the corner of his eye, Joseph glanced at Jared. It was Jared who answered Glenna. "There are times" was all he said to confirm her remark.

Joseph cleared his throat. "Well, sir, what do you say we go *watch* some bulldogging while these womenfolk get themselves caught up? Leddy Marra's headed this way with her new grandbaby—if we don't get out of here we're going to have to listen to how this one's the handsomest yet. And I don't know about you, Jared, but another session of how many yards of lace it's going to take to make Laverne Watkins's wedding dress and I just might strangle that woman with that hankie she flaps around like a flag."

Jared looked to Glenna. "Do you mind?"

Did she mind? She didn't mind much of anything when he showed her the consideration of asking if she did. She smiled. "I think you'd better. We can't very well have Joseph strangling someone in the churchyard."

Then he surprised her by reaching up to kiss her lightly before pushing himself to his feet to follow his brother.

"Well, well," Cally said as the two men left, her tone full of insinuation. But she didn't get a chance to go on before Leddy Marra reached their blanket.

"Looks like you're going to get your fence sooner than expected." Jared closed the bedroom door behind him and crossed the room to where Glenna was just beginning to braid her hair for bed that night. He reached a hand to the curly strands to stop her. "Leave it loose," he ordered softly.

Glenna ran her brush through it again and did as he said. In the mirror she looked up at him where he stood behind her, still dressed in the gray trousers, matching vest and white shirt of his Sunday suit, his jacket and tie having long since been discarded. When Joseph had called him to come to the bunkhouse an hour earlier, Glenna had worried that he would stay away until she fell asleep as he had the week before, that in spite of the genial closeness they had shared all day and through the evening's drive home, he would distance himself from her again. But her worries seemed to be for naught as he pressed a kiss to the crown of her head while he unbuttoned his vest and began to undress.

"What happened?" she asked, referring to his announcement of a moment before.

"Seems that after we left town today, Scott Bradley got brave and tried to bulldog. He missed and caught a horn up high on the inside of his leg. He'll be all right for putting up your fence, but he's no good for sitting in a saddle to come with us on the drive."

"But he is all right?"

"Damn lucky, actually. An inch higher and it would have gelded him."

That embarrassed her. Trying to hide it, she said, "Did a doctor see to him?"

Jared had moved out of the reflection in her mirror so Glenna only heard him get into bed. "Doc was out delivering a baby. Cally saw to it."

Glenna set her hairbrush on the dressing table and swiveled on her stool to face him. "Cally tended to it?"

He laughed. "Shocked?"

Glenna didn't want to seem so. She stood and went to blow out the lamp on his side of the bed. "I would have thought a man would prefer another man to tend a wound so near . . . like that." She was floundering.

In the dark Jared reached for her wrist and pulled her onto the bed. "His privates were covered up."

"Well, I'm glad he wasn't hurt any worse."

"Good, then maybe we can quit talking about Scott Bradley's lower parts and start thinking about mine."

Gladly, she thought, but couldn't say anything with her mouth so busy under his.

There was a growing familiarity in their lovemaking that made it more relaxed. Tonight Glenna needed no prompting to explore every inch of his taut, well-honed body, most particularly that long, steely length of heat and power that was so new to her. At first Jared concentrated on kissing her, allowing the exploration while he held her head in both hands, his fingers combing through her hair as if the silky texture intrigued him. But he seemed to know just when her actions had awakened a need to be touched herself, and touch her he did—with his hands, his fingers, his mouth and lips and tongue, even with the tip of his nose tracing featherlight circles around the outside of her nipples.

When at last he came into her Glenna welcomed the fullness of him. Knowing the heights to which he could take her only increased her need and anticipation. She rode with him on waves of ecstasy until every nerve in her body exploded into white-hot pleasure.

Afterward, lying in his arms, her legs still entwined with his, Glenna remembered that he was leaving in the morning and regret stabbed her.

"How long will you be gone?" she whispered.

Jared rubbed his cheek against the top of her head and then pressed his face there and spoke into her hair. "Most of the week. We should be back Thursday or Friday."

She thought a moment before admitting softly, "I'll miss you."

He didn't say anything but he kissed her head and she could feel his lips broaden into a smile there.

"I've brought you a glass of lemonade, the last we're likely to see this year—or so they tell me."

It was midmorning. Jared had been gone for two days, and Scott Bradley was more than halfway through putting up the fence around the two houses. But it wasn't concern for Scott Bradley's thirst that brought Glenna outside with her offering. She had an ulterior motive.

The ranch hand accepted the libation, draining it in one long pull. Then he smiled down at Glenna, showing a dimple in one cheek. "That was thoughtful of you. I appreciate the kindness."

She smiled back. "Actually, I've come to ask a favor. Do you think you might stop for today and take me into Hays?"

His smile broadened into a grin and his voice lowered. "Why, I'd like that very much. Just let me clean myself up."

"It won't be too much trouble, will it? I mean, with your wound and sitting and all?"

"No, ma'am," he was quick to reassure her. "No trouble at all. And even if there was, it'd be worth it."

"Good then. I'll just get my things and be ready when you are."

Pleased with herself, Glenna went into the house to ask Charity if she could extend her visit with Lyden to watch him until she got back. With that seen to, she made sandwiches filled with slices of beef and packed them in a small basket. Then she went upstairs to don gloves and a bonnet that matched her brown traveling gown and pelisse. Lastly she took the lavender velvet box from where it was hidden in a drawer beneath her neatly folded underclothes.

The time was nigh, she had convinced herself, to broach the subject of Mary coming to live with them. For the two days since Jared left she had thought about little else. It was sooner than she had thought she might chance mentioning it, but since they'd gotten to the ranch everything seemed to have moved quickly. And though she wasn't exactly secure in her place in Jared's life, he had spoken of love, and after this past week, she was no longer afraid he would turn her out at the very suggestion.

In her mind's eye she kept seeing him as he'd been with Mary the morning they left Chicago, hunkering down low enough for her sister to feel his face. She remembered that he hadn't seemed uncomfortable with the little girl's disability, that he had been kind to her.

And then there was Jared's affection for Joseph and Cally's children, helping to convince her that he wouldn't reject the idea. All together, Glenna believed that her husband would accept that she wanted to bring Mary to live here. They might be only starting, but they really were making a life for themselves. He knew her now, he had feelings for her. Before long, she felt confident, she would have completely replaced his first wife in his thoughts and his heart. And suddenly she couldn't see any reason to wait any longer to include Mary.

What she wanted to do before Jared got back was to sell the remainder of her mother's jewelry so that she would have all the money to back up her claim that Mary would not be a complete financial burden to him. With Scott

Bradley close at hand and a means of getting her into Hays, everything seemed propitious.

Glenna was waiting on the porch when Bradley drew up in front of the newly erected fence in the small two-seater rig. She barely noticed that he had a freshly scrubbed appearance, or that he wore a clean shirt and his hair had been slicked back. Her only real thought was that she was glad he had chosen the buggy with the padded seat for his own comfort.

Distracted by her plans, Glenna didn't say much on the ride into Hays. Once there she instructed Scott to take her to the jeweler near the train station. Rather than wait for his help, while he gingerly lowered himself to the ground, Glenna climbed down herself and went to the small store whose single window was stenciled with H. M. Muensheimer, Jeweler and Gemologist on the outside and barred like a jail on the inside.

A man with a sharply pointed chin greeted her. "The new Mrs. Stratton, isn't it?" The jeweler nodded to the ranch hand who followed Glenna in. "Glad to see you up and about, Scotty, even if you did cost me two bits by taking that horn."

"I'll get that ornery pile of fur next time," Scott said with a laugh.

Then Mr. Muensheimer turned his full attention to Glenna. "What can I do for you?"

"I've a few pieces of jewelry I want to sell," she told him without giving an explanation why.

When Scott Bradley held the door open for her to leave the jeweler's fifteen minutes later Glenna was only richer by twenty dollars. The amount was a disappointment, but one she tempered with thoughts that her relationship with Jared was on a better footing than she had hoped for.

"Would you like to eat before we head home?" she asked Scott on the boardwalk in front of the store.

He pulled his head back on his neck like a turkey and looked at her from beneath arched eyebrows. "You mean this was the only reason you wanted to come into town?"

"Yes."

"You came all the way into Hays to spend a few minutes selling twenty dollars' worth of jewelry?"

"I told you I did."

"You aren't even going to spend the money now that you have it?"

"No." She didn't understand why this all seemed so odd to him.

For a moment he just stood there staring at her. Then his expression erupted into a slow, one-sided grin. "I see. Well, in that case, no, I'm not hungry for those sandwiches you brought. I'd just as soon head back."

Rounding the buggy Glenna was surprised to find Scott close on her heels, his hands circling her waist to help her back into the carriage. Once she was there he lingered, grinning up at her. "Is there something wrong?"

That made him laugh. "No, ma'am. Not a thing in this whole wide world."

Confused, Glenna had no idea what she had done to so amuse him, but since he finally climbed into the opposite side and slapped the reins across the horses' backs to get them into motion, she didn't think any more about it.

Bradley's happy whistling blended with the muted clop of hooves and the clatter of wooden wheels on the washboard rutted road until they were well out of town. Then, without a word, he steered the horses off the road and over a small ridge.

"Do you want to eat now?" Glenna asked, confused by their detour.

He grinned.

Taking that for an answer, Glenna bent over to retrieve the basket she had set under the seat. But Scott reached a hand to her wrist to stop her.

Jolted by the contact, Glenna sat back up straight and eyed him strangely. All at once Scott's arm was around her, he pulled her near, and his mouth clamped down over hers.

Stunned, it took Glenna a moment before outrage set in. Then she pushed herself out of his grip. "What do you think you're doing?"

Scott frowned at her as if he was the one who was confused now. "What you made up that excuse to get us out here to do."

"I beg your pardon?"

"Nobody makes a special trip into town just to sell some old jewelry for no good reason, lady. And they don't make a point of getting a man they've been watching and smiling at, bringing lemonade to and asking after, to take them unless they have something else on their mind."

"Well, you're mistaken!"

"That so?"

"It is. Everything you think was some . . . some invitation, was nothing more than being friendly. I asked you to take me to town because you were the only person around to do it. And as for making a special trip to sell that jewelry . . . I had a reason for that that's none of your business."

He breathed a short, disgusted chortle. "And none of your husband's business, either. That's why you're sneaking around behind his back."

"I was not sneaking," she lied. And then, adopting an imperious air, she demanded, "Just take me home, Mr. Bradley."

Again he snorted at her. Then he picked up the reins and made a clicking sound to start the horses into motion again. Out of the corner of her eye, Glenna saw him shake his head.

"Yes, sirree, that Jared Stratton sure does know how to pick 'em. You ought to count yourself lucky that I'm not a man who makes a tease follow through."

Chapter Sixteen

"You've been in the damnedest hurry this whole trip and now that we're an hour from home you want to stop at a jeweler's?" Joseph complained.

Jared reined his horse around and went back to where his brother had suddenly stopped in the middle of Main Street. "Getting too old to drive a few head of cattle fifty miles without turning cranky, are you, Joseph?" he goaded, unperturbed.

"I'm getting too old to do it without so much as a night's stopover to sleep in a real bed."

"Well, go on home. I didn't ask you to come with me. I just said I was going to Muensheimer's before I do."

"I didn't say I wouldn't go with you," Joseph groused. "Just that I wanted to know what for."

Three days' worth of stubble itched, and Jared scratched his jaw without letting his brother's mood rile him. Joseph had every reason to feel tired and out of sorts. Jared had pushed them at a breakneck speed in order to have this trip over and done with so he could get back home. Home to Glenna. It wasn't something he wanted to admit but it was something that kept him patient.

"A wedding ring." He finally answered Joseph's question the same way he might have announced he was about to buy a new saddle—bluntly, devoid of the sentiment he was still not comfortable with.

Joseph's eyebrows shot up. "For Glenna?"

"No. For Beula Jordan's half-bald spinster aunt."

Joseph nudged his mount with his boot heels and went on past Jared in the direction of the jewelry store. "It's about time" was all he said.

Jared didn't comment, merely turning his horse around again and falling in behind his brother. He wasn't altogether sure it was about time. In fact, it seemed as if his feelings for Glenna were washing in over him like a tidal wave, and he wondered if he should be putting up more of a fight to keep them under control. But wondering was as far as he got. For some reason he was disinclined to fight the feelings anymore.

Maybe it was because Glenna was trying so hard to fit in, to learn everything she needed to know about living out here. She wasn't as weak as Janie had been, and he hadn't heard a complaint out of her about the job she'd taken on.

A wedding ring was something that he hadn't even thought about before Joseph had relayed the message from Cally that Glenna should have one. He knew why it hadn't occurred to him, even though it wasn't a reason he was proud of; it was because he hadn't actually thought of Glenna as his wife.

Did he now?

Now he couldn't think about much else. Now he was anxious to get home to her, to get back to her bed, to have that normal life she talked about. Now he didn't like the idea of her being without a wedding ring while he was gone. Those were thoughts of her as a wife, no denying it.

"Three Strattons in two days," Muensheimer said in greeting to Jared and Joseph as they entered his store a few minutes later. "Your new wife was just in yesterday, Jared."

"She was?" Jared leaned a hand on the glass case that separated him and Joseph from the jeweler.

"Scott brought her in. I bought some small pieces of jewelry from her. She didn't seem inclined to tell me much about them, just that she wanted the money right away." Harold Muensheimer winked at Joseph and then teased Jared. "Yessir, you're a more trusting man than I am, leaving a looker like your wife with old moon-eyed Scott."

Jared stood up straight and narrowed his eyes at the pointy-chinned jeweler. "Did she say what she wanted the money for?" he demanded.

Harold Muensheimer shrugged and showed his surprise at Jared's unfriendly response. "No, she didn't say much at all."

"And Scott Bradley was with her?"

"He just drove her into town, far as I could tell."

"Where'd they go after that?"

"Jared..." Joseph put a cautioning hand on his brother's arm.

But Jared ignored it, repeating his question in a more menacing tone.

"I don't know. I told you she didn't say much at all. It isn't so unusual for a woman to come in and sell off something to buy her husband a surprise gift—that's what I thought she was doing. Maybe she's planning ahead for Christmas," he suggested too quickly. "Now, what can I do for you?"

But Jared didn't answer him. Instead he turned on his heels and left the jewelry store and his brother behind.

Glenna leaned far over her kitchen sink and craned her neck to look at the overcast late-afternoon sky. Lyden was still napping and Cally had just left after drinking a cup of tea with Glenna. Rain, maybe turning to snow, was what Cally predicted, and Glenna wondered if Jared would be home today before it started. If not, Cally had said the men would probably hole up somewhere until it passed. It wasn't what Glenna wanted to hear.

Cally had thought Glenna was just plain lonely and Glenna hadn't disabused her of the idea. But loneliness was not why she was so anxious for Jared to come home. She missed him, yes, more than she had expected to. Somehow her bed seemed even emptier these past nights than it had the week before when he had been out at the barn or the bunkhouse. At least then she had known he was nearby and that sometime during the night he would join her.

But added to simply wanting him home was her eagerness to broach the subject of bringing Mary here. She had been rehearsing what to say for hours on end, when and how to start, mentally debating every argument she thought him likely to make.

A knock on the back door took her away from the weather watching. She knew it wasn't Jared—he wouldn't knock. Probably Cally had forgotten something.

But it wasn't Cally on the other side of the screen when she opened the door. It was Scott Bradley.

"I know you've finished the fence, Cally told me," she informed him curtly before he had said a word.

"I didn't come about the fence. I need to talk to you." He swung the screen wide and stepped into the kitchen.

Glenna backed up in a hurry, unnerved to see him after what had happened the day before and unsure what he wanted now. "We don't have anything to talk about."

Scott took two steps into the room and faced her squarely. "Look, about yesterday—"

"There's nothing to say about yesterday. You misinterpreted the situation. Now please get out of my kitchen." Glenna turned away from him, pumping water into the teakettle as if that would make him leave.

"I want to apologize, but you sure aren't making it easy."

And she had no intention of doing so. With fresh water in the kettle she moved to put it back on the stove. Bradley stepped into her path and stopped her with his hand on her arm. Glenna jumped and then cast a scathing look up at his face.

"I been working this place most of my life and I don't cotton to the idea of losing my job now because... Well, I'd have never done what I did if I didn't think it was something you wanted, too. And besides, the way things seemed, there was Jared spending most of the nights out with us instead of in here with you like there wasn't anything between the two of you, and him saying he'd just married you for the boy every time somebody joshed him about it.... You're right, I saw things different than they were. It won't ever happen again."

Jared had told the ranch hands that he'd only married her to give Lyden a mother? It was a blow to the tenuous confidence that had grown in the time since he had admitted he had feelings for her.

"Did you hear me?" Scott demanded. "I said it won't ever happen again."

Glenna forced her attention back to him. "So you're here for assurance that I won't have you sent away?"

"That and to apologize," he said with a sharp nod of his head.

Glenna sighed and relented, knowing that to do anything else would only prolong this. "I won't be the one to tell Jared about yesterday."

Just then the screen door flew open and crashed on the outside wall.

"Jared!" Glenna said in surprise.

Scott let go of her arm and stepped away guiltily.

Jared's deep green eyes went from the ranch hand to Glenna, where they stayed to bore into her as he reiterated her last words with a snarl, "No, you won't be the one to tell me about yesterday. I heard it from Henry Muensheimer."

The mention of the jeweler confused Glenna. For a moment she just stared back at Jared.

Then Scott's voice broke the silence. "It won't ever happen again, Jared. I swear to God. It was just a kiss.... You know I couldn't do anything else in the shape that goring left me...."

"You have ten minutes to pack up your gear and get the hell off this place," Jared said so menacingly that the other man flew into motion and nearly ran out of the house without even trying to salvage the job he had come here to protect in the first place.

Then her husband's narrow-eyed glare turned back to Glenna. "Caught in the act this time," he sneered through clenched teeth.

"Caught in what act? I don't understand—"

"Ah, innocence," he said, cutting her off sardonically. "You're good at that, as I recall. Do you think because I didn't find you in bed that you can just deny what's going on here? What's the plan, Glenna? Marry me to get yourself out of Chicago and then once you're on your way hunt for someone else to take you farther than Kansas? Somewhere faster and fancier and flashier? Was Scott going to do that for you? And what did you sell to bankroll it? Something you stole from around here, maybe from Cally?"

Glenna's mouth dropped open, shock at his accusations turned quickly into outrage. "What's gotten into you?" she demanded as she set the teakettle she was still holding on the stove.

"I can't believe I was actually beginning to trust you."

Her own anger lashed out. "I can't believe you would actually think I could ever take something of Cally's—for any reason! And I don't know what makes you so suspicious of such things but I had nothing to do with your ranch hand. It was he who kissed me and me that stopped it. You have no cause to accuse me of any of this."

His hands went to his hips, his weight shifted onto one leg. "No cause? I took you on your word when I accepted you—that proved worthless, and even your second story could have been a lie for all I know. Twice I caught you in those damn widow's weeds, and twice I know you were doing something behind my back and lying about it to hide it. Now I hear you've been into Hays with a man the whole town knows has eyes for you, selling off jewelry. No cause? Where did that jewelry come from, Glenna? If you had something of value why did you need to marry me to get yourself out of Chicago? Why are you selling it off now? Why do you want money when everything you need is provided for? And if all that isn't enough, I come in here and find you nose to nose with Bradley, promising him you won't be the one to tell me about your little jaunt yesterday. That sure as hell seems like cause to me."

"Cause to wonder about what I'm doing with other things maybe, but not with your ranch hand."

"What exactly are you doing? Selling things to raise a dowry to offer me?" he shot back with cutting sarcasm.

This wasn't the way she wanted to tell him. Calmly, reasonably, rationally, was how she had pictured it. Presenting him with the idea and the money in a way that would make him the most inclined to hear her out and agree. But what else could she do now? It was either tell him the truth or have him believe she had other, unsavory motives.

Glenna swallowed and raised her chin to him. "In a way, a dowry is just what it is."

"Don't take me for a bigger fool than you already have."

Glenna turned on her heels and went to one of the tin-punched cupboards. From a drawer there she took out the dented, battered jewelry box and brought it to him. "There's $327 and some odd change in this," she said as she handed it over to him.

"Then you've been at this for some time."

"I want to bring my sister here. The money came from selling my mother's jewelry. Most of it that first morning to a man Aunt Lida knew in Joliet. I was going to try to sell what I had left in Topeka when those men assaulted me.

Since I didn't accomplish anything then I asked your ranch hand to take me into Hays yesterday. He got the wrong idea, and thought I was just using it as an excuse to be alone with him. Today he was apologizing so I wouldn't tell you and cost him his job."

Jared frowned down at the box and then at her. "You told me that jewelry had been confiscated."

"If I had told you I still had it, you would've said the law or David Stern would be following after me to get it back. I knew that wasn't going to happen but I also knew you wouldn't believe it."

"Then you're admitting to another lie. Could be you're just lying about Scott Bradley, too."

Frustration raised her voice another octave. "If I had said straight out that I wanted to bring my sister along, would you have taken us both?"

He answered her with silence.

Glenna put it into words. "You wouldn't have."

She could tell some of the steam had gone out of his rage. Without opening the lid of the box or looking inside, he held it toward her. "And what the hell is this for?"

"To help pay her way here and her keep."

"You had this planned from the start?"

There was stern accusation in his tone, and being guilty on that count backed her down some. Glenna looked at the jewelry box in his hands rather than at his face. "Yes." Then she forced herself to meet his eyes again and took up her cause. "She doesn't belong in Chicago living off an old woman's charity. She belongs with me."

"Not out here, she doesn't. The prairie is no place for a blind child, even one born to it."

"She'll adapt. She's good at that. I've looked after her most of her life, what does it matter if it's here or in a city?"

He let out a derisive laugh. "You can't even look after yourself out here. You think a few weeks of floor scrubbing and baby tending and cooking—most of which isn't even edible—means you could take on your blind sister to boot? You don't even know enough not to flirt with women-starved cowboys."

Glenna took a breath and held it long enough to keep her temper under control. When she spoke again it was a tone that illustrated the depth of her determination. "Mary is my sister and my responsibility. I promised her."

"You're going to have to break that promise. You knew when you agreed to be my wife that I was taking you and no one else. I made that clear. And even if I was inclined to change my mind, it wouldn't be over a blind child. This country swallows up even strong, healthy, sighted children. It's for her sake that I won't let you bring her here."

"She belongs with me."

"You belong here—that's the bargain we made—and she doesn't. Now leave it." He turned on his heels and walked out, slamming the door behind him.

"Are you over being mad or are you out here still stewing?"

Jared looked over his shoulder at his sister-in-law as Cally came to stand beside him at the paddock fence. He'd been out there long enough for it to get dark, and her white bib apron was the only thing about her that wasn't just a shadow. "Did you come out here to meddle, Cally?"

"Me? Meddle?" She laughed and angled a hip onto the middle rung of the fence.

"What brings you away from cooking your supper? Joseph, or hearing what went on at my house?"

"Both. Joseph's worried; the sound carries."

"Did you hear the whole thing?"

"Most of it."

Jared just nodded, looking out at the two horses lazily nibbling hay a few feet away. When he didn't say anything Cally did.

"I came to tell you not to fault Glenna for whatever went on with Scott Bradley. She wasn't playing loose with him. There wasn't anything she did that I wouldn't have done."

"You're sure about that?"

"Sure enough. If you took the time to look at what's really there instead of being suspicious, you'd see that she's in love with you, that you're all she wants."

"I'm not *all* she wants."

"It came as a surprise to you that she wants to bring her sister here, did it?"

"It did." But it shouldn't have, he had realized since he'd come out here and done some thinking. Glenna's staying in a household where her mother was brutalized in order to protect Mary was telling in retrospect. Her ties to her sister were strong. He had seen it himself—Glenna's arm wrapped so tightly around the child that it looked as if she were squeezing the life out of her the morning they'd left. He should have known better than to think she would abandon Mary. But he'd had other things on his mind, other things he was watching for.

"I saw it coming," Cally went on. "Glenna talks about that little girl in every breath."

"Not to me."

"No, I don't suppose so. She's trying too hard to please you."

"She didn't want to give away her plans."

"That, too."

"Well, I won't have it. The child is blind. Remember the Watsons' boy? He was blind. Remember what happened to him?"

"Mmm. Wandered off and fell down that well hole, poor little thing. But he was so much younger than Glenna's sister."

"Do you think that would have made her any better able to see a hole in the ground and not fall into it?"

"Of course not. I'm just saying an older child might be more cautious."

He shook his head. "The girl stays where she is. Where she has teachers and familiar surroundings..."

"And no family."

Jared looked slowly to his sister-in-law. "Are you out here to tell me I should let a blind child who's never known anything but city life come here to be cared for by a sister who's no better off except that she can see what's coming at her?"

"No, I'm not." Her voice quieted. "It's your decision, Jared, and you have good reason to be against the idea. But I understand how Glenna feels, and I think that it wouldn't do you any harm to understand it, too. It isn't going to be easy for her to accept this."

He blew a disdainful sigh. "So, here I am with another wife who can't accept things the way they are."

"It isn't that she can't, just that it won't be easy for her. Don't mix her up with Jane when there isn't call for it."

Jared didn't say anything to that.

Cally stood up and patted him on the arm. "Go on into supper and talk to her without accusing her of anything. Listen to her feelings. She missed you," she told him. Then she left.

Jared stayed at the paddock fence for a few minutes more, staring down at the tufts of field grass yellowed for winter.

When he finally went in, Glenna was just coming back from putting Lyden to bed. She barely glanced at him as he came in the back door and then she went to the stove. "Are you ready to eat?" she asked in a voice without inflection.

"Glenna..." He took a deep breath before he continued. "I know Mary is your flesh and blood, the only family of your own that you have. But she can't come here to live. It wouldn't be any good for her, it'd be dangerous and foolish and... The wide-open prairie is the last place on earth for a blind child. For her sake it's better if she stays where she is. If she could see it would be different—not easy even then, mind you, but something that wouldn't put her life at risk. As it is, whether you realize it or not, coming here is just too dangerous."

She didn't look at him as he spoke. Jared knew enough to realize that words alone wouldn't convince her, that only time spent here and lessons learned would do that, so instead he took another tack. "I'll pay anything it takes to make sure she's well cared for in Chicago, that she has the schooling she needs, that she isn't a charity case. Even if that means we have to set her up in a small house of her own with someone paid to live with her. Write to... what was his name? Carter? Write to Carter and ask him to arrange for everything, maybe even have him appointed as her guardian—he seemed kind and genuinely fond of Mary. But for her sake, I can't let her come here."

Glenna picked up a pot of potatoes and took them to the table. "I never meant to make Scott Bradley think I wanted his advances. And I didn't accept them when he made them."

"I know that now. Cally told me. But that isn't what we were talking about."

"I don't know why you think such things of me...maybe because of the way we came together...maybe you think that the only kind of woman who would answer an advertisement for a wife is some sort of..."

"That isn't what I think of you. I wasn't thinking at all. I was out of my head. About Mary..."

"You'd better eat before it gets cold." She went to the sink where the creak of the water pump made it impossible to go on with even this disjointed conversation.

After some debate with himself Jared decided to let it all lie. Given a little time she'd see for herself why the child couldn't come here under any circumstances. He could only hope that when she saw it she could accept a future without her sister.

Chapter Seventeen

During the last two weeks of October winter crept in like a shadow. For both Glenna and Jared it was a bone-wearyingly busy time. Jared left each morning before dawn, bringing in the last of the cattle to closer ground, stocking the winter supply of hay and feed and bracing fences and outbuildings against the winds and snows to come. He came in long after dark each evening, ate supper and fell asleep about the same time Lyden was put down for the night.

Glenna couldn't stay awake much later herself.

She was convinced that the timing had been poor when she broached the subject of Mary's coming to live with them. Anger had spurred Jared's opposition to it. But in no way did she accept that as the end of the matter. Now that the seeds were planted, she decided to throw her energies into what she felt would help win him over to the idea when she brought it up again. To that end she set to work adapting what she could of their surroundings to Mary's benefit.

The rugs were her first undertaking. When she had originally cleaned the house after its long disuse she had left in place the circular braided one in the living room and the long, thin runner that covered the upstairs hallway. No sense chancing questions, she had thought then. But now her secret goal was known, and so up came the rugs, leaving the hardwood floors safe for the blind child to traverse.

Mary would need a bed, and with the excuse of wanting to begin furnishing some of the other upstairs rooms, Glenna persuaded Jared to have a bedstead made. Cally showed her how to thread rope through the holes in the frame, weaving a support for the mattress that Glenna sewed and stuffed from the other woman's stock of feathers. Cally offered her an old armoire and bureau from the attic, both pieces of furniture dilapidated and scratched. Glenna took them gladly, doing what she could with polish on the outside and lining the drawers and bottom of the armoire with scraps of wallpaper—also Cally's leftovers.

The fall rains softened the ground and Glenna used it to her advantage. She gathered stones and pushed them deep and evenly into the earth to form two pathways—one leading from the kitchen door to the outhouse and a second that led from the porch steps directly to the gate in the new fence. Mary felt almost as much through her feet as she did with her hands, so keeping to the paths would be easy for her and allow her to find her way unaided.

Glenna counted off the distance from the front fence to the barn. There she found one of the stable hands and asked for a piece of rope the same length. Her plan was to tie the rope to one of the pickets of the gate where Mary could slip it around her waist and learn her way to the outlying grounds and buildings while still safely moored, in no danger of wandering into the vast openness of the prairie beyond.

Within the perimeters of the fence Glenna put her attention to organization, pounding nails to hang the ax safely above the woodpile rather than merely leaving it wedged into the chopping block. Likewise, she found a spot for the washtub against the side of the house, up and away from where it could be tripped over. And when she discovered in a windstorm that the fruit cellar door flew open and left a gaping hole that Mary could fall into, she fixed the latch to prevent it.

Through it all no one commented on her efforts. Cally sometimes looked on with sadness in her expression, often relaying stories of this child or that person who had perished from getting caught in razor-wire fences that were difficult to spot, who had fallen down a well or stumbled into a wolf trap or stepped in a snake hole. Glenna could only assume that Jared and Joseph realized what she was doing as well. She sensed an air of indulgence in them all, as if they knew something she didn't and they were just waiting for her to accept the inevitable. But she paid them no mind.

November came with the gently falling flakes of the second light snow of the season. Sitting with Lyden on the sofa in the living room late in the morning, Glenna was trying on a new pair of winter woolen coveralls she had made him. Playing peekaboo to get him to cooperate, she was surprised to look out from behind her hands and find Jared leaning against the doorway leading from the kitchen, his arms crossed over his chest, an amused smile on his lips.

"I didn't hear you come in," she said, a bit embarrassed to be caught playing baby games so energetically.

"I came to take you into town, but if you're too busy…"

"You want to go into town in the middle of the week?" she asked in astonishment.

"Mmm-hmm. I have some things to tend to in Hays. Cally and Charity will watch the boy. I thought it was about time you learned to drive a rig and find your own way, so next time you need to get there you don't have to persuade one of my men to take you. Besides, it seems like we haven't seen much of each other for a while now."

She had thought she was the only one to notice. Now it seemed that not only had he noticed, but maybe he hadn't been any happier about it than she was. With a smile that felt too big, Glenna snatched Lyden up in a hurry. "I can be ready in five minutes."

Jared took his son out of her arms. "I'll take him next door. You just tend to yourself."

"Bundle him up, his nose has been running all morning," she called as she held her skirts high and headed upstairs.

It took her ten minutes instead of five to get ready, because she changed out of her plain brown shirtwaist into a plaid wool skirt with a matching pelisse that covered a high-necked white blouse. Then she brushed out her hair, twisted the sides back and caught them at her nape with a ribbon, leaving the rest to curl down her back. She put on her heavy winter coat and slipped on her leather gloves, but decided she'd rather have cold ears than wear a hat or even the dark muffler Cally had knit for her.

Jared was waiting in the entranceway when she finally came down. Glenna had the sudden sensation that she hadn't seen him in a long time and drank in the sight of him greedily. He wore a bulky, sheepskin coat buttoned to his neck, the collar turned up in back. Dark tan britches encased his thick thighs, and tobacco-colored leather boots climbed nearly to his knees.

His eyes never left her as she descended the stairs, and when she reached him his face broke into a smile that lifted just the right side of his mustache. "I don't think I've ever pleased anyone so much with so little. It's only a trip into town."

She didn't want to tell him that the destination had nothing to do with it, that it was the company alone that lightened her heart. So instead she sashayed past him out the front door, purposely swishing her skirts at him.

"Turning sassy on me, are you?" he teased as he followed, lightly swatting her rump as he did.

The small black rig was waiting for them outside the fence. Jared lifted her up and then went around to the other side to climb in himself. Once he was beside her on the tufted seat he settled a lap robe over them both, tucking in Glenna's side around her.

A little shiver skittered through her but not because of the cold. It occurred to her that this was the first real courting-like thing they had ever done, and it set off a tingling, excited, very feminine feeling in the pit of her stomach.

"You see that small rise there." He pointed as they turned out onto the road. "If you always keep sight of that off your right shoulder you'll know you're headed into town. Off your left for home."

Glenna nodded, forcing herself to pay attention in spite of the feelings that were making her mind wander. The air was crisp and clean, the countryside quiet, and her senses were all alive and filled with Jared.

When he handed her the reins she took a breath, squared her shoulders and told herself to quit being fanciful and get down to business.

"Hold them loosely," he instructed as he pulled on gloves that matched his coat.

Glenna did as he said, holding them so loosely the horse slowed to an amble.

"Not that slack, city girl, or it'll take us all day long to get there and you'll miss the lunch I'm going to buy you."

After that she got the knack of it, and Jared lounged back and left her to it. For a while she concentrated hard and then realized that the horse did most of the work, so she relaxed and let her gaze wander beyond the rig.

Barely an inch of snow blanketed the ground like a sheet thrown over a lumpy mattress. There was a whispered crunch as horse hooves and wagon wheels cracked the frozen surface of the road. The cold and a sudden sense of freedom invigorated Glenna, and she tested her prowess as a driver by urging the horse to a trot.

Out of the corner of her eye she glanced at Jared to see if he disapproved. But he was watching her in the same amused way he'd been when she had looked up from her game with Lyden.

"Feeling your oats, are you, Glenna?"

"Mmm. It feels good to just let go sometimes."

"I didn't think city girls knew how to just let go. All prim and proper..."

She slapped the reins along the horse's back to speed up more still. "I haven't seen too much frivolity in you," she challenged.

He went back to looking out at the countryside, unperturbed. "Oh, I've been known to do one or two foolhardy things."

"Such as?"

"Such as placing advertisements in newspapers and marrying a willful woman," he said wryly, without rancor.

"What about kicking up your heels? I'd say of the two of us, you're the more serious."

That made him laugh.

"It's true. I can't picture you even as a devilish boy."

"I wasn't," he said in a way that told her he was lying.

"What were you like?"

"Serious and studious."

"Did you tease the girls and wrestle with the boys?"

"Mmm."

"Did you lure unsuspecting young women into haylofts and race horses on this very road?"

"My share."

"And then you grew up to be sober and somber and grim," she teased, making a face at him.

"Not until I met you," he said, teasing her back.

"I beg your pardon. You were somber and grim the day I met you."

"But not sober," he filled in for her.

"And you smelled bad."

"I was driven to drown myself in the stupor of whiskey after looking over the other women who had answered my advertisement."

"I had competition?" she asked coyly.

"One or two."

"But you chose me."

"And lived to regret it."

She knew he was teasing, but the remark stabbed just the same.

Her expression must have shown it because Jared reached a gloved hand to the back of her neck and squeezed. When he spoke again there was only sincerity in his voice. "I was joking," he said to reassure her. "What about you? Do you regret marrying me?"

Again she looked at him out of the corner of her eye, liking the teasing that had been between them better than the serious tone. "I do when you steal my blankets and leave me to freeze in the middle of the night." And then she spurred the horse into a full gallop the rest of the way into Hays.

They had lunch at Molly Ring's Café, a small restaurant on Old North Main Street with white linen napkins and tablecloths. As they ate a sumptuous meal of pot roast, potatoes and carrots, Glenna declared that Jared's real reason for the day's outing was to get himself a good meal. He didn't deny it.

Afterward they took a pair of his boots to be repaired, delivered a recipe Cally had promised to the dressmaker, bought Joseph a new pipe he had asked for since he'd bitten the end right off his old one and then went to the mercantile, where Jared surprised her by announcing that she could pick out wallpaper for the parlor while he went to run one last errand.

While he was gone she chose a paper with a cream-colored background and stripes formed by tiny vines of blue flowers. She was waiting when he came back.

"Done already?" he asked when he had reentered the general store.

"I'm a woman who knows her own mind," she informed him.

"Did your own mind remember Annie's licorice whips?"

She grimaced. "No. I forgot."

Jared bought the candy and then took Glenna's elbow to lead her out.

They headed home through the gently falling flakes of a midafternoon snow. This time Jared drove and Glenna merely enjoyed the ride. Once they were back she thought he would probably go to work with Joseph stacking hay bales, but instead he handed the buggy over to the stable hand, stretched his arm along Glenna's shoulders and went with her across the yard.

"Shouldn't we go get Lyden?" she asked as he bypassed the main house and headed straight for their own.

"Cally can keep him for the afternoon."

"Oh" was all she said, curious about what he had planned for the remainder of the day. It became clear when he closed the front door behind them, took her hand and started to climb the stairs.

"But it's broad daylight, Jared," she said in a whisper as he took her to their bedroom.

"What was all that talk about frivolity and just letting go?"

Jared faced her and began to unfasten her coat. "But it's broad daylight," she repeated, albeit without much conviction.

"Just like I said, prim and proper." She'd misplaced one of her gloves and her cold fingers were nestled in her pocket; he pulled her hand out of it and as he slipped her coat from her shoulders he leaned to whisper in her ear. "It doesn't always have to be night, city girl."

The warm brush of his breath seemed to run through her. Finger by finger he pulled off the single glove she wore and then divested himself of his own snow-dusted outer clothes.

"I could go stack hay with Joseph if you'd rather," he suggested in a challenging tone.

Glenna glanced in the direction of the window at the mention of her brother-in-law, and then back to Jared. He stood before her with one eyebrow quirked up in question, his broad, flannel-encased shoulders towering above her, narrowing to that firm belly her mind's eye could see clearly, and those hips...

"Glenna?"

She couldn't stop the slow smile that curled her own lips. "Joseph didn't look like he needed any help." And with that she unfastened her pelisse, her eyes staying on Jared as he raised those big hands of his to the buttons of his shirt.

She wondered peripherally if she would ever get tired of looking at him, if his body would ever cease to excite her and send her blood racing through her veins. She couldn't imagine such a thing.

When he was completely undressed he came to her. Her chemise and petticoat had yet to be shed and he gently moved her hands aside before she could accomplish it. He pulled the ends of the ribbons between her breasts. Glenna gave the job over to him willingly, pressing her flattened palms against the hair-roughened expanse of his chest. His skin was warm and firm over muscles.

And then he slipped her underclothes off and pulled her with him to the bed where he lay beneath the quilt and held it up for her to join him.

She did so gladly, lying beside him so that when he dropped the blanket and encircled her with his arms there was very little distance to be closed between their two naked bodies. His mouth found hers then, open and soft and seeking right off, and Glenna met and matched him. Since this had not yet become a steady diet she hadn't realized how hungry she was for him, for his touch, for his kiss, for his body. But now the craving welled up in her and demanded sating.

His hand slid around from her back and molded the side of her breast, his thumb alone reaching to just the edge of her nipple, tormenting for a moment before he took her fully into his palm. Glenna couldn't stop the groan of pleasure that rumbled in her throat when he slid his thigh up between hers. Feeling bold, she did likewise, raising her leg up between his. It pleased her to discover that he couldn't control his moans any better than she.

She missed his mouth when he broke away from the urgent strivings of their kisses, but forgave him a moment later when he closed his lips around her nipple, flicking it with his tongue and gently pulling with his teeth. She held his head, raking through the silkiness of his hair with her fingers while his hand found her other breast and gave it equal time.

Yearning, craving, Glenna rocked against him. She needed him inside her more than she needed air to breathe, but while she was still achingly empty he reached a hand there, plying her with tender, thrusting fingers until she could barely draw air, so desperate was her desire.

Finally Jared rolled her to her back and found his place between her thighs, pressing home into the moist, welcoming heat of her. Glorious. His body belonged to her and hers to him. Together they moved in perfect unison, meeting, drawing away, meeting again. Faster, harder, deeper, until Glenna felt Jared stiffen with ecstasy and plunge into the core of her, once, twice, three times, and with his final shudder her own body exploded with passion and bliss and love.

When the waves had subsided and Glenna remembered to breathe again, she opened her eyes. It seemed strange to find cloudy gray light in the room, strange that the rest of the earth had gone on undisturbed.

Too soon Jared left her. She didn't want him to go. She watched as he reached for his coat where he had thrown it on the floor beside the bed, but all she thought was that she wished he would lie still and hold her. She needed him to hold her. Then he settled beside her, his head propped on one hand.

"If you had it to do again, would you marry me?" he asked in a passion-roughened voice, nuzzling her temple.

Odd question. But she didn't need to think about it. "Yes, I would."

"Then I think it's time we do it right." He set a small black box between her breasts.

Glenna took the box and opened it. Inside was a thick gold wedding band, shiny and new. For a moment she just stared at it, there in its nest of velvet.

Jared kissed the spot on her temple that he had nuzzled before; his mouth stayed pressed there and she could feel the heat of his breath. Then he took the ring, slipped it on her finger and pulled her hand to his lips where he kissed both ring and finger at once, reverently.

It was in her heart and in her mind to tell him she loved him because at that moment she knew it was true; but her throat was so full no words would come out.

Jared laid his head beside hers on the pillow. "Now it's done the way it should have been in the beginning," he murmured and fell asleep.

For a long time Glenna lay there, feeling the ring around her finger—finally. Periodically, when just feeling it wasn't enough, she held her hand up to look at it to convince herself it was there. His ring. And she realized it wouldn't have meant so much if he had given it to her the day of their wedding.

Sleep was impossible, and so rather than disturb Jared by staying in bed with him, she slipped out. As she dressed in her brown shirtwaist again her eyes never left him. So this was what it was like to love a man, she thought. A fullness inside so large it seemed she might burst. Did he feel the same way? He had to. Feelings this strong, this big, must be answered in kind.

She would have stayed there watching him sleep if a knock hadn't sounded on the front door. Hurriedly she tied up her hair, embarrassed that Cally or Joseph or one of their children would see her and realize what she and Jared had been up to this afternoon. She hoped it was Cally, for of them all her sister-in-law would be the easiest to face.

But it wasn't Cally.

Glenna could tell that by the time she had descended half the stairs. Through the oval glass of the front door she could see the midsection of a woman wearing formfitting burgundy velvet. Rather than Cally's large, sturdy hands were delicate black-gloved ones holding a beaded drawstring purse.

The reverend's wife was the very next thought Glenna's conscience conjured up. It stopped her short for a moment as she pressed cold hands to her cheeks, hoping to fade the color she had seen there when she'd looked in the mirror to tie back her hair. But then she realized that there was no reason in the world why the reverend's wife would come to call. And so long as it wasn't anyone who knew them as well as Cally, or who had seen her and Jared come home, whoever it was would never guess she was coming straight from her husband's bed to answer the door.

With a glance down at the shiny gold band on the third finger of her left hand for reassurance, she went the remainder of the way to the foyer.

Glenna didn't know the woman who stood on her front porch when she opened the door and came face-to-face with her. She was taller by several inches, statuesque and regal. She wore a small black hat at a jaunty angle atop shining brown hair, not like Glenna's corkscrews but naturally wavy the way Lyden's hair was. Her complexion was rosy, and her wide black eyes struck a chord of familiarity in Glenna, as if she recognized this woman and yet couldn't place her. That didn't strike her as odd; she had met so many people since she had come here.

She smiled her greeting, waiting expectantly.

After a moment during which the visitor overtly sized Glenna up, she smiled tightly. "I take it you're Jared's second wife."

"Yes," Glenna said, less an answer than a prompting for the woman to say more.

She gave a breathy smirk of a laugh, eyed Glenna up and down yet again. "The second Mrs. Stratton," she mused. "Well, I'm the first."

Chapter Eighteen

I'm Jane Stratton.''

Glenna stared at the woman on her front porch. She couldn't have heard rightly. "Jared's first wife is . . . Jared was a widower." But even as she spoke Glenna realized why the woman was familiar. She was staring into an older, female version of Lyden's face.

Jane Stratton cocked her head and laughed ironically. "Yes, I know that's what he told people. But as you can plainly see, I'm quite alive." She paused for a moment as if waiting for Glenna to realize the fact for herself. Then she said, "May I come in? It feels like it's getting colder out here by the minute."

Glenna's first thought was to refuse, as if not letting her in the house might make this all untrue. But courtesy demanded that she step aside. She watched as the other woman glided into the entrance, paused to glance around and then went into the living room. When Glenna followed she found her sitting in the center of the sofa as if she were the one receiving Glenna.

Jane Stratton looked around the room assessingly. "I don't like the furniture this way," she declared, as if to say so was to have it changed posthaste.

Still dazed, Glenna ignored the comment. "I don't understand what's going on."

"Don't you? Well, I'm certainly not the one to tell you why Jared would pretend to be a widower when he's not. What I do know is that to the best of my knowledge, Jared and I are still married and I've come home to my husband and son." Then, as if the matter were settled, she said, "I assume Jared will have to be sent for, but where is Lyden?"

"The baby isn't here," Glenna said in a rush. Until that moment she hadn't realized how much she had come to think of Lyden as her own. Protective maternal instincts seemed to blaze to life in her.

"Where is he?" Jane demanded as if she had the right.

It occurred to Glenna that she did. And yet she couldn't bring herself to say that Lyden was just next door where a dozen steps would put him in the other woman's arms. Rather than answer she made a demand of her own. "How do I know you're who you say you are? I've seen the grave of Jared's first wife with my own eyes."

"You have only to send for him, or Cally or Joseph or any one of their children to verify who I am. They'll recognize me."

It had been a feeble attempt on Glenna's part to refute what she only hoped was untrue. The more she looked at the woman the surer she was that this was Lyden's mother. And yet how could that be? "Do you expect me to believe Jared is a bigamist?"

"I think that's a question we should both have answered."

Confusion. There was so much of it whirling like a dervish in Glenna's mind that she didn't even know what to ask. "If you're still married to him then where have you been?"

Jane smiled enigmatically. "I'm really not obliged to answer any of your questions." She stood and went to Jared's desk, running her fingertips lovingly across the top of the chair pushed into it.

Glenna felt small and plain in the face of the other woman's stature and beauty, and her imperious air didn't help matters. So this was the beloved Janie. The cherished Janie. A nightmare come to life. "Why..." Glenna's voice had lost its power.

"Why am I not obliged to answer your questions?" Jane asked snidely.

"Why are you here?"

"I told you, I've come home to my husband and son."

It was a quiet, steely declaration, but somehow it didn't have the ring of truth to it. It seemed almost like a goad. "He's my husband, and Lyden is my son now," Glenna said just as quietly, in just as steely a declaration.

"And you want to keep them, do you?" she asked matter-of-factly.

"I do."

Jane Stratton shrugged her very straight shoulders confidently. "I've been without them for a long while now. It would take a great deal to persuade me to give them up again."

"But you could be persuaded?"

"Perhaps," Jane said coyly, moving from Jared's desk to the mantel. She stared up at the mirror that was covering the marks left from the painting that Cally had told Glenna used to hang there. "My portrait..." She seemed to have had the same thought as Glenna. "I remember when Jared insisted that I sit for it. Weeks and weeks with that artist. But it was worth it, Jared treasured it so." She breathed a satisfied sigh and said wistfully, "Oh, but it was wonderful to be loved so much. To have such devotion, such adoration...such power over a man...."

"If any of that were true you'd still be together," Glenna shot out defensively.

Jane Stratton turned to face her, staring her straight in the eye and saying bluntly, "I couldn't bear it here. As much as I loved him and as much as he loved me, this country wore me down. The isolation, the tedium... I was immature then.

I thought it was driving me mad." Then she finished very pointedly, "Jared understood."

"It's still isolated and tedious."

"Yes, but I'm more mature now. I've seen what the world has to offer.... It's left me with a new appreciation of certain things." Of Jared and Lyden and this life, she said by implication.

It seemed to Glenna that they were playing cat and mouse. but Glenna was at a disadvantage. More so when her attention drifted to the fact that Jared was upstairs, just a few feet away from this woman whom Glenna believed he might still love. "You said you could be persuaded not to pursue it," she reminded, working to keep the desperation she felt from her tone.

"I do have friends in San Francisco," Jane said whimsically. "But of course it would take money to get there and to keep me until I could get settled and find employment of some sort...."

"Then you would consider taking money to leave here again?" Glenna asked, trying to contain her repugnance.

Jane sighed and stared up at the mirror once more. "I just don't know. There's so much to be sorted through, isn't there? Jared claiming to be a widower when he isn't, and taking a second wife—why, they put men with more than one wife in jail.... I think we need to have a long talk, he and I. And then, well, then we'll just have to see. Why don't you send for him?"

The idea of calling Jared downstairs to face this woman right before her eyes was intolerable to Glenna. It raised panic in her, and whether it was wise or not, she suddenly wanted to do anything she could to avoid it. "He can't be sent for. He's out on one of the far ranges and won't be back until tomorrow," she lied, buying herself time to think this thing through. "Are you living in Hays?" she asked before the woman could pursue the matter of Jared's whereabouts. She headed back toward the foyer to let her predecessor know this visit was at an end.

To Glenna's relief, Jane followed her. "No, I've been in periodic contact with a friend who lives in Hays—Eliza Perkins. It was she who wrote and kept me up on what was happening in my husband and son's life. I'm just visiting her—discreetly, of course. The last thing I'd want is for Jared to be suddenly arrested for having two wives."

"It's best if you go back there now."

"Yes, I suppose you're right. We couldn't both stay here and wait for him, now, could we? But you will tell him I've come back, won't you? I'll expect him to call on me sometime tomorrow." She glided out past Glenna much as she had glided in, regally confident.

Glenna closed the door, and the moment she did she heard Jared coming down the stairs behind her. Her first impulse was to press her back against the oval glass to block his view, but by the time she turned to do it he had already seen.

"Janie."

To Glenna his voice sounded reverent and his expression didn't ease that impression. His face was pale and his eyes were wide beneath a knitted brow.

"Is that who that was?" he demanded.

"I guess that's something you should tell me," Glenna said softly.

With his boots in one hand he leaned on his other forearm arched above the oval window and stared out. Over her shoulder Glenna followed his gaze, watching the velvet-clad woman climb into her carriage and drive away. For a moment after she'd gone Jared just stood there staring out at nothing. Was he staring longingly after her? It was hard to tell. But Glenna was afraid it was so.

"Is that who she was?" she demanded with more strength than she felt.

But he didn't answer her. He pushed away from the door and walked through the living room into the kitchen.

Glenna trailed behind him, her stomach lurching at the lingering scent of the other woman's perfume in the living room. She stopped in the doorway to watch Jared.

At the sink he pumped water into his cupped palm and splashed it over his face, again and again. Then he held his wet hand to the back of his neck, his head hanging far down between his hunched shoulders.

"Christ!" he exclaimed under his breath.

Pride kept Glenna from repeating her question. Instead she merely waited as he lifted his head, sighed and let it fall backward so that he spoke to the ceiling. "Yes. That was Janie. Didn't she tell you who she was?"

Janie. The affectionate name grated on Glenna. "She did. But for all I know she was lying. After all, you told me she was dead."

He gave a mirthless laugh at that but he didn't say anything.

"She believes you're still married," Glenna challenged.

Jared turned and leaned back against the sink. He smoothed his mustache contemplatively and then began to button the cuffs of his black flannel shirt. "She's wrong. But it isn't something she'd have any way of knowing. Kansas law has it that when a spouse has been gone a year they can be divorced. I did that quietly before I went to Chicago. Since I didn't have any idea where she was, there was no way for her to be notified. And it wasn't something I let be known to anyone except Cally and Joe. But it's legal. And so was marrying you."

But it wasn't his first choice, it wasn't what he wanted, Glenna couldn't help thinking, even though she was relieved to hear that her marriage to him was valid. "She told me living here wore her down, that you understood why she had to leave—as if maybe the two of you had agreed to it."

That brought a derisive snort from him. "We didn't agree on it." Then he finally looked at Glenna, as he stood up straight to tuck his shirt into his denim jeans. "Life here was too hard for her, all right. She wanted parties and teas and grand balls. She wasn't going to hunker down and work. Pampered and petted, that was how she saw herself. It takes a woman with a core of iron to make it here. And she didn't have it."

He spoke flatly and the statement hurt Glenna. Given the choice of having him see her as a beautiful, feminine woman who deserved to be lovingly adored and doted on, or as an iron-clad workhorse, she'd choose the former. "So she left," Glenna prompted.

He picked up his boots from where he had dropped them and went to sit on one of the kitchen chairs. Hard yanks pulled on each boot in turn. "Ten days after the boy was born she ran off with another man."

Of all the things Glenna had thought, that hadn't been one of them. She could do nothing but stare, slack-jawed.

"I went to bed beside her and woke up the next morning with a note," he said disgustedly.

"Did you have any idea?" Glenna asked in amazement.

He shook his head. "I knew she was unhappy. She'd been trying to talk me into leaving with her for a long time—for years, in fact. But this was my home. She knew that. Knew I wasn't going to leave it. I kept thinking that if only she'd get pregnant..." He stalled there for a moment. "I figured it would give her roots here the way I had them. That a baby would cure her restlessness, give her more to occupy her time. For five years it didn't happen. And then it did."

He was staring into space again. Glenna thought about the doubts that must have arisen when his wife had finally gotten pregnant.

"Who was the man?" she said quietly.

"Bill."

The other grave in the family plot. The man who had been raised alongside Jared and Joseph, she thought.

"It wasn't something I would have expected of him any more than of Joseph. The three of us were like brothers, Joseph and Bill and I. I would have lain down my life for either one of them, but Bill and I were . . . well, we were the same age, went all through school together, did everything together. We had more the same temperament than Joseph and me. . . ." The reminiscences made his voice dwindle. Then he seemed to force strength back into it. "I thought Bill and Janie didn't even like one another. She complained about all the time I spent with him or all he spent here with us. She said she thought that if I had to choose between Bill or her I'd choose Bill. Maybe she just bewitched him. . . ." He stood up quickly and raked his hands through his hair. "She wrote in her note that Bill was doing what I wouldn't, that he was taking her away from here. He had gone to Durango two days before—I thought for business, and she left sometime during the night to meet him. I never knew what happened to them from there. . . ."

"What about the graves?"

"Hers is full of the belongings she left behind. I wanted no part of a scandal for myself or the family. I said she'd died from complications after the birth. No one but Cally and Joseph knew the truth—or at least no one else ever faced me with it. I overheard some talk about burying her without a funeral, about Bill disappearing at the same time, but it didn't come to anything. I just went on as if she really had died. I never thought she'd come back. Divorcing her . . . well, that only ended it legally."

He seemed to have forgotten the other grave. "What about Bill's grave?"

"Apparently he died while I was in Chicago and had his body sent back here. To keep up appearances Joseph had to bury him where he would have been if he hadn't stuck a knife in me. . . ."

For a moment Jared was stock-still, staring into space. The silence between them was palpable. And then Glenna couldn't help asking, "And Lyden?"

Jared shrugged but the lines in his face were taut. "He's most likely not mine, though I've never been told one way or the other. And since he's the image of his mother...there's no way of telling whether it's me or Bill in him."

Again neither of them said anything, with Jared staring off that way and Glenna watching him do it. Then, as if he'd been brought from the past back into the present, he frowned over at her. "Why was she here?"

For you, was the first answer that occurred to Glenna, but she wouldn't tell him that. "She said someone named Eliza Perkins had written to her about you and Lyden...about our marrying..."

He nodded. "Eliza Perkins. I thought all along that she knew but she never said anything."

Silence again. Once more Jared seemed to be lost in memories. Or was he lost in feelings? she wondered. "She wants to see you," Glenna said reluctantly.

"Then why did she leave? You could have called me down."

Was she imagining disappointment in his tone? Glenna raised her chin. "I didn't want to be witness to it."

Again he nodded. Was it understanding? Pity? Or an agreement that it was just as well that he meet with his first wife alone? Glenna's heart sank with belief that it was the last when he took his sheepskin coat from the hook beside the back door.

"You don't have to go right to her...I told her you were away, that you wouldn't be back until tomorrow."

"No sense putting it off. Where is she?"

"With her friend. She said she's been very discreet so you don't get arrested as a bigamist." The words had come out harshly and Glenna wished she could call them back.

But Jared didn't seem to notice. Instead he put on his coat and left. Just like that. Without so much as another word to her, as if in his preoccupation he had forgotten she was there.

And Glenna couldn't fight the thought that in nothing he had said had there been any reassurance for her.

It was dark by the time Jared reached Hays City. Light flooded out onto the boardwalk outside the saloons and gambling halls as he passed them to get to Eliza Perkins's small clapboard dwelling. It was the first in a line of houses inhabited mainly by women of a less than virtuous nature, those keeping private residences—and a small, private clientele—rather than openly selling themselves in one of the whorehouses. Jared had always found Janie's friendship with Eliza strange. After she left him, he'd thought it should have told him something about her real nature.

He didn't go directly to Eliza Perkins's house. Instead he stopped across the street and tethered his horse outside a place called the Gaming Parlor. It was freezing cold and he considered going in for a drink to warm up, but he decided against it. Instead he leaned on one of the poles that braced the boardwalk overhang, crossed his arms and stood staring at the inside of Eliza's ornate parlor through her big front window.

The images in his memory were as vivid as if they had happened yesterday instead of nearly two years ago. Twenty months to be precise. The boy was twenty months and two weeks. Her boy.

He had stood in the same spot the night after Janie left. Hope and despair were warring within him that night. Hope that maybe she hadn't left town yet, that maybe she was at her friend's house, that he might catch sight of her and rush in to persuade her not to leave. He'd stood there nearly until dawn. He'd seen Muensheimer go in and share a drink with Eliza before they disappeared into the bedroom. He'd seen the jeweler come back out two hours later. But there was no sign of Janie.

It was that night that he had concocted the story that she had died. And once it was told, he couldn't go to Eliza and question her about Janie's whereabouts even had he wanted to. She had never said a word to refute it. But there was something in the way she had looked at him on the few occasions when their paths had crossed since then, something that told him she knew Janie wasn't dead. That she knew where she was.

As he stared at the house now, he saw Janie come into the parlor. She had on that same burgundy velvet dress he'd caught a glimpse of in the afternoon. She was as beautiful as she had always been, he thought in a remote way.

He remembered the very first time he'd seen her. One look at her and everything else had faded from his vision as if she were a blinding beam of light. Mesmerizing.

Now he could only laugh bitterly at himself.

He remembered the last time he'd seen her—not during those ten days after the boy was born when the midwife had said she needed to stay in bed—but during those last weeks of pregnancy. He'd thought she was even more beautiful then, big with his child.

That memory was a thistle in his gut.

He'd been so damn happy when she told him she was finally going to have a baby. So damn happy...

And when the boy was born it didn't seem that life could get any better.

It hadn't. It had gotten so much worse.

Right after she left it had seemed as if he would go out of his mind. Sometimes he'd wished he would—a cocoon of insanity. One minute he damned himself, the next her, the next Bill. So many things had gone through his head. He'd thought of tracking them down, of bursting in on them and shooting them in their lovers' bed. He'd thought about leaving the ranch himself—taking off where no one knew him or Janie or Bill, where someone else's bastard son wasn't crying all night long, where he didn't have to lie to save face or pretend grief when what he really felt was murderous rage.

He'd thought he didn't want to go on living without her.

Jared jammed his gloved fingers together like the prongs on two forks intertwining.

Want to or not, he had gone on living. The pain and anger had gone away, even if some of the bitterness had remained.

And now she was back.

What did she want? The boy? Somehow he doubted it.

Or was she here for Jared himself? Now that Bill was dead, had she come back with apologies and pleas for forgiveness? Did she think he would welcome her with open arms?

Or was there some other reason?

Impossible to tell. A woman who would do what she had done would do anything.

There was only one way to find out.

Jared pushed away from the pole and stepped off the boardwalk. The crunch of snow beneath his boot heels seemed to echo in the deserted street. A few steps, a knock on the door, and he would be in the same house with her, in the same room, face-to-face with her again after all that had happened, after all this time.

He wondered what he would feel.

Glenna retrieved Lyden from Cally's house not long after Jared left. Joseph was there, and the hush that fell between husband and wife when she went in was evidence that they knew the infamous Jane had reappeared, that Jared and his two wives were the topic of their conversation. It was also apparent in their uneasiness that neither of them was any surer than Glenna of what Jared's response to the other woman would be.

As much as she loved both Cally and Joseph, Glenna couldn't bear their pity, so she said very little and took Lyden home.

Feeding him his supper, she couldn't help studying the baby. He was his mother's child, there was no doubt about it. But who had fathered him?

Living with the doubt must be a constant thorn in Jared, she thought. Was this baby the evidence of his first wife's infidelity? No wonder he resented the child. No wonder he shied away from loving him.

"What's going to happen to us all?" she whispered to Lyden as he plunged his hands into his bowl of bread pudding.

Glenna's fear that Jane would take him was almost as great as the fear that she would take Jared.

How could Glenna just hand over the child to a woman who had left him behind to run off with her lover? she asked herself as she cleaned up the toddler and took him to his room to get him ready for bed.

But fast on that thought was the reminder that the choice might not be Glenna's. The possibility existed that she might not do any handing over at all, that she might be told to pack her bags and go now that the woman she had replaced was back again.

She rocked Lyden long after he had fallen asleep, loath to let him go, comforted by his warmth and softness. But when being held made him restless she conceded and put him in his bed. Then she went downstairs and gave the kitchen floor the scrubbing of a lifetime.

All the while her mind raced. She loved this man and she loved this child and she wasn't going to give them up.

But what if Jared loved Jane? The most he had said to Glenna was that he *might* be falling in love with her. Not that he did love her. Even in giving her the ring he hadn't said the words. What if he decided he and Jane and Lyden should be the family they had begun to be before? The family he had wanted them to be?

Logic told her that Jared would never want a woman who had already deserted him and Lyden once. Surely he would know better than to trust her again.

But what if Jane was determined to win him back regardless? What if she had her cap set for him? She was still the woman he had loved devotedly once. She was still a woman he might yet harbor feelings for.

Was Jane so determined? Or could money rid Glenna of the threat the other woman posed?

It was possible, or why would she have brought up the possibility at all?

But there was no ease in that. If it was true it left Glenna with another dilemma, for the only substantial amount of money she had was for Mary.

It was past midnight by the time Jared came home. Glenna was in bed. She hadn't wanted him to think she had been so worried she couldn't sleep. And yet, as he undressed in the dark she knew she couldn't keep up the facade.

"Jared?" she said softly as he got into his side of the bed, taking pains not to jostle her.

"It's late" was all he answered, a full measure of weariness in his tone.

"Did you see her?" she asked in a whisper.

"Yes."

And? she wanted to shriek, but she bit her tongue to hold back the sound.

After a moment he sighed heavily. "In the morning, Glenna. It doesn't bear talking about now."

Pride wouldn't let her say any more so instead Glenna lay silently on her back, staring into the darkness. Why didn't it bear talking about now? Was it because the middle of the night was no time to tell her he was taking back his first

wife? Was Jane in bed with them now in his thoughts? she
wondered.

After a while she heard Jared breathing deeply in sleep.
But Glenna had no such luck with slumber. Instead, all
through the night she wrestled with her choices. If, indeed,
she had any, they would have to be made quickly, before
Jane's hold got too strong. To use the money to send her rival away was to risk never bringing Mary here. But not to
was to risk Jane staying and taking Jared from her.

She felt her love for Mary as strongly as she had since the
day her younger sister was born. Mary was Glenna's to look
after, to care for, to raise, almost as if the little girl were her
own child rather than her sister. And the promise she had
made to her was inviolable.

But at the same time Glenna's heart felt swollen nearly to
her throat with love for Jared. Was buying Janie off a self-
ish choice?

It seemed like it. And yet a future without him seemed too
bleak to bear.

She'd promised Mary, the voice of her conscience argued.

But without Jared and his home Glenna had no place to
bring her.

And so it went all through the night.

Jared . . .

Or Mary.

Chapter Nineteen

Jared's deep breathing was the only sound in the room when Glenna slipped out of bed before dawn the following morning. As she dressed, Lyden coughed in the next room. She paused to listen, willing him to stay asleep, to stop coughing before he woke Jared, too.

The baby quieted a moment later. Stillness resumed and so did Glenna's dressing. Quiet determination. Sometime during the night she had resolved not to sit and wait for her future to be decided for her. She had decided to do what she could to salvage it for herself—if, in fact, there was anything she could do. She had to try.

Downstairs she took the purple velvet box from the cupboard drawer. Hurriedly she stuffed its contents into her drawstring purse and put that into the pocket of her skirt. Then she replaced the empty jewelry box. Dented and soiled, it was the only thing she had left that had belonged to her mother, and even without a use, she meant to keep it.

She went for her winter coat where it hung beside Jared's on a hook near the back door. Putting the heavy wool outer garment on, she fastened it all the way from her throat to the last button just above her knees. Next came the muffler Cally had knitted for her. She wrapped it around her neck and ears, tying it just below her chin. Then, since she still

had only one glove, she reached into Jared's coat pocket fo
his.

What she found there were not only his big sheepski
gloves but her missing one as well.

Her first thought was that he had found it. Then she re
membered her new wedding band and realized he must have
taken the glove to give the jeweler an idea of her ring size
For a moment she paused to glance at that which had bee
so dear to her and then so quickly forgotten in the turmoil

Thoughtfulness was evident in the pains he took to bu
the ring without her knowing. He could have just marche
her into the jewelry store, picked one out and had it size
right there. But instead he had planned how to do it quietl
and chosen a special, intimate moment to surprise her.

That touched her. But more it lent strength to her con
viction that there was enough between them to fight for, t
take a risk for.

And a risk was what she was taking.

She stuffed her gloves into her empty pocket and wor
Jared's anyway; feeling connected to him bolstered he
spirits.

All of the ranch was still asleep when she stepped ou
side. Two inches of snow had already fallen from the storn
everyone was so sure was going to be the first big one of th
season. The white powder and low-hanging clouds the colo
of new Bible pages lightened the predawn darkness.

Glenna crossed the yard to the barn. She had to rouse th
stable hand who slept in the tack room, because althoug
she felt sure she could drive the small rig by herself sh
didn't know how to hitch the horse to it.

"Shouldn't head out with the kind of storm that's con
ing," old Morty advised, but Glenna didn't answer him. Th
weather was the least of her concerns.

Frigid morning air bit her lungs as she breathed it in onc
she was on the road that led to Hays. She had to stop th
horse, take off Jared's thick gloves and readjust her mu

fler to wear it like a scarf—covering her head and wrapping it fully around her nose and mouth. Before she replaced his gloves she took her own from her pockets, put them on and then put Jared's over them. But never did it occur to her to turn back.

Hays City was barely rousing by the time she got there. She stopped at the hotel—one of the few establishments actually open—to ask if the desk clerk knew the whereabouts of Eliza Perkins's house. He did, though he looked oddly at Glenna before he shared the information with her.

Of all the names of townsfolk heard mentioned by the Strattons, Eliza Perkins didn't ring a bell, and when Glenna found the house she realized why. Even in her brief time here she had learned enough to know what part of town was the seedier section and that the people who inhabited it were unlikely to socialize at church picnics.

The small clapboard house was still dark, but that didn't keep Glenna from pounding on the door. It wasn't Jane who finally answered, but a plump woman whose eyes were puffy slits and whose yellow hair was sticking up out of its topknot. She held a wrapper closed at her throat and leered at Glenna.

"I've come to see Jane Stratton," Glenna informed her.

"She's asleep."

"She'll have to get up, then." Glenna took a step into the doorway and after a moment's hesitation, the woman she assumed to be Eliza Perkins backed up and let her in.

"Liza, did I hear someone ask for me..." Jane came into the entrance in much the same condition as her friend, obviously awakened by Glenna's arrival. One look at her and Jane stopped short. "Oh," she said before regaining her haughty air. "This is an odd hour for a social call."

"It isn't a social call," Glenna informed her curtly.

For a moment both women merely stared at Glenna. But then Jane slowly drew her gaze away and said to her friend, "It's all right, Liza. Go on back to bed."

Eliza Perkins seemed to need no more encouragemen
than that. She left them alone. Glenna followed Jane inte
the parlor where her nemesis poked a log and some kin
dling into the fireplace and lit a match to it. Then Jane
huddled down on the hearth and looked across the room a
Glenna. "Jared was here until very late last night," she saic
with heavy insinuation.

It was in Glenna's mind to ask the questions Jared had lef
unanswered, but she wasn't altogether sure she wanted to
know what had happened between the two of them the nigh
before. What she was sure of was that she wanted thi
woman out of Hays and out of her life as soon as possible
if she could manage it. She supposed the outcome of thi
meeting would tell her something about the events of the
previous evening. "You said yesterday that you needec
money to get yourself to San Francisco and to tide you ove
until you could find work."

"Did I say that?" The other woman's tone was coy. He
gaze stayed on Glenna, who felt as if she was being studiec
or gauged for something. Was her rival wondering just hov
serious she was, perhaps? Or was Jane merely indulging her
knowing that she had already won Jared back?

"I have two hundred dollars. If you'll leave with me righ
now I'll buy your train ticket and then we'll go to the tele
graph office to have the rest of the money wired to a banl
in San Francisco so that it's waiting for you when you ge
there," Glenna said straight out. In thinking about thi
meeting, she had worried that the other woman might tak
the money and stay anyway. This plan had occurred to he
as a means of insurance.

"So, you want to rush me out of town."

"And I want your word that you won't come back."

Jane prodded the log in the fire with a poker. "Does Jared
know about this?" she asked tentatively, looking at th
flames rather than Glenna.

Glenna hesitated. "No, he doesn't. He . . . we didn't talk when he came home last night. The money is mine."

"I see." She looked back at Glenna. "You must want me to leave very badly."

"I don't think you really want to stay or you wouldn't have brought up having friends in San Francisco and what it would take to convince you to go there."

Again Jane poked at the fire as she mused, "I never was very fond of Hays. I like a big city so much better."

Encouraged, Glenna still couldn't help wondering if this was only a mean-spirited game on the other woman's part. "Then you'll take the money and go?"

"It isn't really all that much, when you think about it. I could be a long time without any more coming in. . . ."

Glenna had been afraid of this. It was the reason she had started low. "How much do you think would be enough?"

"Well, now, I don't know. What do you think?"

For a moment Glenna considered explaining her situation, hoping Jane had even a shred of conscience that would leave some money for Mary. But in the end she knew that was too much to hope for, and she wouldn't stoop to it.

"Two hundred and fifty, then," Glenna dickered.

"There would be lodgings, meals. . . . At least in Hays I have Eliza's generosity housing and feeding me . . . and of course Jared . . ."

"Three hundred."

"I've never actually been employed. What do you suppose I would do? My friend there has written about needing a partner in opening a dress shop, but of course that would involve an investment. . . ."

Glenna held her breath for a moment. Then she sighed it out. "Three hundred and twenty-seven dollars. It's every penny I have in the world."

Jane glanced out the big front window at the gray daylight dawning outside. "That's better but it still isn't very much, is it?"

"It's all I have," Glenna said firmly, with finality.

Jane seemed to think about it. Then she took a breath that lifted her shoulders into a coquettish shrug. "Well, then, I suppose I'll just stay here in Hays the way I told Jared I would...."

"Yes, I suppose you'll have to." Glenna spun around to leave before she lost her temper and her pride with it. She wouldn't beg and she had already bartered all she could.

Jane's sigh sounded loudly behind her. "No, wait."

Glenna's heart was pounding. She turned around but said nothing.

"All right. But I want all the money now." The woman stood up, and when she spoke again her tone of voice had lost all semblance of nicety. "I'll get dressed and we can go. Even Jared isn't worth staying in Hays."

At 8:23 Glenna stood on the station platform and watched Jane board the train for Denver where, after a two-day stay, she would leave for San Francisco.

It was snowing harder by then, big fluffy flakes that collected quickly on her shoulders, but Glenna stood there until the train whistle blew for the last time and the iron wheels finally made their first turns. She stayed watching until the caboose was nothing more than a speck in the distance, as if the other woman might jump off the train the minute she turned her back.

I'm sorry, Mary. I'll make it up to you. I'll still get you here. Some way. I promise.

"What have you done, Glenna?"

Jared's voice sounded from behind her, startling Glenna who had thought she was alone except for the stationmaster chalking in the day's arrivals, departures and destinations on a blackboard beside the ticket window. She turned to find the man she had just risked so much to keep.

He was standing there, frowning at her. Snow dusted the top of his head and tiny ice crystals tipped his mustache. The collar of his sheepskin coat was turned up around his ears, framing a jaw stubbled with unshaved whiskers.

Had he come after Jane?

His hands were in his pockets and Glenna suddenly remembered that she had his gloves. They no longer lent her strength.

"What have you done?" he repeated when she didn't answer him.

"I've sent her away," she finally said, poking her chin out of its nest of muffler.

"'Her' being Janie," he surmised. He shook his head with a sigh that gusted a cloud into the frigid air. "I guessed you'd come to see her when I found out you'd taken a rig into town. Eliza said I'd find you here."

Was he hiding rage behind that flat tone of voice? she wondered.

He squinted up at the sky. "I'd like to go in somewhere and get warm, but if we don't head straight home we won't make it at all. You should never have come here in weather like this."

That was all? Just this halfhearted chastisement about the weather? Maybe she should be grateful that he had at least half a heart left for her.

Jared pulled his bare hand out of his pocket and took her arm. "Come on," he said as he guided her off the platform to the buggy where the horse he had ridden to town was already tied to the rear.

When they were in the small rig Glenna pulled off his gloves and handed them to him. He put them on and tucked the lap robe around them both. Then he took up the reins, slapped them across the horse's back and called a "Giddap" that set them into a race against the storm.

Glenna didn't know what she had expected, but it felt strange for him to just pick her up and take her home again. He drove through the storm without talking, every so often glancing up at the clouds or readjusting his collar to keep his ears warm.

By the time they reached the ranch a violent wind was whipping snow into ground clouds so thick the horse pulling the wagon was nearly obscured from sight. They were only a few feet from the barn before Glenna could see the faint glow of lanterns hung on hooks outside the great door. Jared shouted the stable hand's name, and after a moment the huge wooden panels parted in the middle to allow them to drive straight into the well-lit interior.

Helping Glenna down, Jared gave instructions for seeing to the horses and then hurried her out again. Through the blowing snow the house was indiscernible. She was surprised to find that a rope tied from the barn to her fence and from there to the porch post led them to the front door. She had thought her idea for a similar solution to aid Mary was unique.

Once inside they stomped snow from their feet and brushed it from their heads. Jared went directly to the big stone fireplace and started a roaring blaze there.

"Come over here and get warm," he ordered, his tone telling her nothing.

Glenna perched sideways on the hearth, hugging her bent knees and looking up at her husband where he stood directly in front of the flames. His ears were beet red from the cold, and after he had warmed his hands he placed them over his ears. The fire melted the ice on his mustache and turned it into beads of water that he wiped away with his shirtsleeve, then replaced his hand over his ear. But still he didn't speak.

Glenna was rapidly becoming less aware of the cold and wet than she was of the silence. "How was Lyden when he woke up this morning?" she asked, both because she wanted to know and because she wanted to make Jared talk.

He took his hands away from ears that were now merely bright pink and sat down on the hearth, his thigh covering just the tips of her toes. "His cough is worse and he was feverish. I wrapped him up in three blankets to take him to Cally." He pulled off his boots and roughly rubbed first one stockinged foot and then the other between his hands. Finally he looked over his shoulder at her. "What did you do?" he repeated yet again.

"I told you, I sent her away," Glenna said with less boldness than when she had told him on the station platform.

"And how did you manage that?"

Glenna looked into the fire. "When she was here yesterday she let me know that she would take money to go to San Francisco. So I gave it to her."

"What money did you give her?"

"Mary's," she admitted in a near whisper.

She saw him shake his head, only this time his disgust was clear. "Why the hell would you do that?"

"Because..." She couldn't bring herself to say it was because she loved him, not now. So she settled on, "If you and Lyden were genuinely what she wanted she wouldn't have settled for any amount of money to leave."

He shrugged. "Once she agreed and you knew what she was really after, you could have rescinded the offer and kept your money."

"That wouldn't have proved it to you, and it still would have left her here to—" Glenna caught herself.

For a moment Jared's eyes bored into her. Then, in a low, rough voice, he said, "What have you been thinking, Glenna?"

"You loved her," she shot out defensively. "You said so yourself the night we were married, Cally told me just how much, and yesterday Jane made it clear all over again. Or should I call her 'Janie' the way you do? What I think is that you might not have seen through her."

"I told you what she'd done."

"And then rushed out of here after her like your tail was on fire."

"I didn't rush out of here. Hell, I told you the whole story before I left."

"And then stayed a long time with her, only to come sneaking home and not tell me anything."

"I did not come sneaking home. Until you let me know otherwise I thought you were asleep, and I was trying not to disturb you. I would have explained everything this morning if you'd given me half a chance. I told you that."

"Half a chance to tell me to pack my bags."

"That's really what you think, isn't it?"

Glenna didn't answer him. She could feel Jared's eyes boring into her, but she didn't budge.

"Do you want to know what went on between us last night?"

She quirked an eyebrow but didn't look at him. "She wanted you."

"You're right, she did. Partly."

Glenna's stomach took a turn.

"She wanted me now the same way she wanted me before—if I left here and went off to some fast, fancy city with her."

Glenna knew him well enough to know he wouldn't agree to that now any more than he would have before. But what if Jane had wanted to stay here with him? Would he be sitting here telling her this? Or would he be telling her to leave?

He went on. "When she realized I wasn't going to do that, she thought she'd force me to pay her not to let anyone know I had two wives. She figured she could extort a lot of money out of me to keep a thing like that quiet."

Nothing surprised Glenna about the other woman. But that didn't matter to her. What mattered was how he felt about his first wife. "What if she had wanted to come back here and be a family?"

"Do you think I'm a fool?"

"I think that love makes fools out of the best of us."

He let out a short, wry laugh. "It certainly made one out of me the first time around. But not now. I never thought Janie . . . Jane . . . coming back would be a good thing. But it was." Jared reached over and cupped Glenna's chin, turning her face to his. "It was a good thing because it showed me that I really didn't have any feelings left for her. I saw her for what she was and the only thing I felt was contempt. If she had begged and pleaded to come back here, I still wouldn't have wanted her." He smiled just a little. "And calling her Janie is just a habit. It doesn't mean anything. It's what I always called her. I never even noticed it until you said it."

"Then how was it left last night?"

"With her knowing there was no chance that I would have anything to do with her, that since my marriage to her was dissolved I had no reason to pay her blackmail, and that I didn't give a damn what she did, where she went or how she paid to get there."

Which was why she had accepted Glenna's relatively small payoff. "Then I gave Mary's money away for nothing," she said softly, more to herself than to him.

"I never thought you would do something like that."

Glenna turned out of his grip, away from his eyes. She swallowed hard. "I was afraid I was going to lose you."

He hadn't taken his hand away. Instead he fingered a loose strand of her hair, his forearm braced on her upraised knees. "Would that have been so bad?" he asked softly.

"Yes."

"Why?"

"You know why. It's obvious."

"But you've never told me."

Because you've never told me, she thought.

But then she realized that she had been more close-mouthed about that subject than he had. She took a deep breath and looked him in the eye. "I know we didn't start

out in a way that would seem like it could ever happen. And
I know you don't want anything to do with it...." She
paused and then finished quietly, "But I love you, Jared."

He laid his palm flat against the side of her face and
smiled, a slow, lopsided thing. "That's all part of why it was
good that Janie came back. For me, I realized not only that
I do love you, but that it's stronger and more real than anything I ever felt for her. Coming face-to-face with her
showed me that even though I was a damn sight too old for
it, what I'd felt for her was immature infatuation, not this
that I feel for you."

He reached for Glenna then and pulled her into his lap.
He captured her mouth with his as if the words needed to be
sealed. Glenna was only too happy to reciprocate. Her heart
was full and so was her throat, with relief and happiness and
hope.

He loved her. He loved her more than he had ever loved
the cherished Janie. Were it not for one thing her spirits
would have been soaring, her life perfect.

But she wouldn't think about having needlessly given
away Mary's money. Instead she held tight to the wealth of
knowing Jared loved her as much as she loved him. With
that, the rest could be overcome, she felt sure.

Slowly their kiss ended and for a moment Glenna merely
stared at his handsome face, for the first time actually feeling as if he belonged to her.

And then Joseph burst in through the back door. Calling
frantically for Jared, he charged into the living room.
"We've got trouble. You'd both best come right now."

Chapter Twenty

The wind blew in a section of the barn roof," Joseph explained hurriedly as Jared pulled his boots back on and Glenna grabbed up both of their coats. "It crashed through part of the loft and trapped John, old Morty and three horses underneath."

At the sound of Joseph's eldest son's name Glenna stopped in her tracks, noticing for the first time that her brother-in-law's face was ashen as he went on.

"I wish to God we had more than four men hired on for winter. We're going to need every strong back on the place to raise it. John is answering our shouts. He's hurt but alive. There's no sound from Morty—can't tell what kind of shape he's in."

Morty was the oldest man on the ranch. He'd been one of the original hands hired by Jared and Joseph's father. His jobs now were light, mucking out the stalls, keeping hay in them, general upkeep. He was a short, thin man with a near toothless grin who had supplied Glenna with the length of rope she had hidden away for Mary.

Then Joseph's gaze fell to Glenna. "And Lyden is bad sick. He's convulsing with fever."

As Jared and Joseph ran out the front door Glenna left through the back. Since the two houses sat close beside each other no rope was needed to link them through the storm.

With her head tucked against the wind that blew snow like icy shards of glass against her skin she made her way to Cally's kitchen door and went in without knocking.

What she found was Lyden lying in the center of the big round table, his small body shaking and twitching with muscle tremors. With one hand Cally held his head from banging and causing him any damage, and with the other she clutched her own protruding abdomen.

"Trouble comes in threes," Cally breathed when the pain had passed and she could glance up at Glenna.

Glenna stood just inside the door, staring at the overwhelming scene, not knowing what she should do.

"Come on over here, honey, it's not as bad as it looks," her sister-in-law coaxed. "But it is a bad time for Charity to be off visiting that friend of hers in Topeka."

Glenna swallowed and raised stiff arms to take her coat off. She had never seen anyone in convulsions and regardless of Cally's reassurance, Lyden looked frighteningly ill.

Her thoughts must have shown in her face because Cally said, "This sometimes happens with small children. They're more prone to high fever when they've first taken sick and the convulsions come with that. Won't last long...see, he's already calming down."

"What can I do?" Glenna asked as she neared the table where, after a few last jerks, Lyden was lying still now, his eyes opening with heavy-lidded lethargy.

Cradling her belly with both arms Cally left Lyden to Glenna and began to pace. "Get those heavy clothes off of him. We have to bring his fever down. Joseph brought the washtub in and filled it before word came about the barn. Test it to make sure the water's tepid and then put Lyden in."

Glenna started to take Lyden's heavy flannel nightgown off, her fear not aided by the limpness and glassy-eyed stare of the toddler. As she did she caught sight of Cally doubling over once more. "Your baby's coming?" she asked faintly when her sister-in-law again seemed to have weathered the worst of it.

"A month early and without it being ready. This baby isn't in the right position yet—same as my first, God rest him. I can feel the head over to my side."

Glenna knew very little about the intricacies of birth. She did know from talking to Cally about the one buried out in the family cemetery that a baby not born headfirst had a greatly diminished chance of survival. "We'll send for the midwife," she said in a hurry.

Cally shook her head. "She's too far away. Nobody could get to her in this storm. It's up to you and me."

The first thought that came into Glenna's mind was an exclamation of her inexperience in such matters. But she didn't voice it. Cally knew she was inexperienced, and what Cally didn't need to contend with at that moment was Glenna's panic. So instead she said, "You'll need to tell me what to do as best you can."

Picking up Lyden, she took him to the washtub. On her way she passed Cally and realized how pale the other woman's face was. "Everything will be all right," Glenna offered, trying to sound as if she believed it. "Joseph said John was answering their calls, so that's a good sign. And you told me yourself that if that other baby hadn't been your first he might have had a better chance. Being the *ninth* ought to help considerably." She tried to make a joke out of it with her exaggerated tone of voice. She succeeded in making Cally laugh, albeit feebly.

Cally pointed with her chin at the tub half-filled with water. "If it makes him shiver it's too cold."

But Lyden didn't seem to have the energy to shiver even if the water was too cool. Holding him securely, Glenna bathed him for a few minutes before Cally went out the back door and brought in a bucketful of snow.

"Put some of this in the water. Once he's been in a while he can stand it a little cooler and that's what we need."

It seemed cruel, but Glenna did as she was told. Lyden didn't shiver with the addition of the snow, but the cold did rouse him to say an angry "No," and attempt to get out. Glenna didn't have to be told that a show of even rebellious energy was a good sign.

But her pleasure at his revival was shortlived; the hand Cally reached to feel his brow was abruptly drawn back with the onset of another labor pain.

Again Glenna waited until it passed. "Shouldn't you be in bed?"

"Not yet. I'm hoping if I keep moving the baby will turn."

The sound of the front door opening stopped both of them. Glenna hadn't realized that Peter, Paul and Annie were in the other room until she heard them asking Jared for news. His answers didn't carry but a few moments later he came into the kitchen.

"We need your medicine bag, Cally. Morty's out from under the rubble but it doesn't look good. His leg's gone and he's unconscious. If we don't get the bleeding stopped he won't make it. Hell, he may not make it anyway."

"John?"

"We haven't gotten to him yet, but he's still talking to us. I don't think he's too bad off, he's making jokes."

Cally went for the medicine bag and Jared came to Glenna, but his gaze was on Lyden. "How is he?"

"Cally says convulsions aren't unusual, that this bath will bring his fever down." She glanced back over her shoulder to see where her sister-in-law was. Seeing she had gone into the storage room off the kitchen, Glenna said more urgently, "Cally's baby is on the way. And it isn't in the right position—like her first."

He murmured a curse.

Glenna went on, "I understand that there's nothing to do for it. But I thought Joseph ought to know."

Just then Cally came back with the small satchel she used to hold her medicines. Another labor pain stopped her before she reached Jared and Glenna, illustrating what Glenna had told him.

Jared rushed to her. "Let me get you to bed."

Cally shook her head but couldn't speak. Glenna explained why the other woman didn't want to lie down. Then the pain ended and Cally stared Jared firmly in the eye.

"Go get my son out from under that damn woodpile. We'll tend to things in here."

Jared looked to Glenna. She nodded, hoping her own apprehensions and self-doubt didn't show. He took the medicine bag and headed out again. "Send one of the twins if you need us."

Cally continued to pace as Glenna took Lyden out of the water and dried him. Leaving him in only a diaper and wrapped in a light blanket, she rocked him to sleep, all the while worrying and watching the woman whom she had come to think of as a sister.

Morning turned into afternoon and the pattern progressed. The cool baths lowered Lyden's temperature for about an hour before it would begin to spike again. Then Glenna would rush him into the water before the convulsions would start.

Cally continued to pace, the pains staying about the same time apart. Although Cally didn't voice her concern Glenna could see it in the lines of the other woman's face, which suddenly looked years older. Somehow it didn't seem possible that two of her sister-in-law's children could be lost today, and yet Glenna remembered too many of the stories Cally had told her about the quickness of death on the prairie; she was afraid that was just what would happen. But she tried hard not to let any of her own fears, worries or frustration show.

Periodically throughout the day Luke was sent in from the barn to see how they were faring and to report on what was happening outside. By midafternoon he came to tell them Morty had died without regaining consciousness, and still John hadn't been reached. It seemed that the eldest of Cally and Joseph's children had been at the head of one of the stalls when the roof had blown in. They thought that he had missed the worst of the weight, but he was the farthest away from being rescued. Still, Luke assured his mother, John was answering their calls, and it was only a matter of time before they got to him.

By dusk Cally took to her bed, no longer having the strength to stay on her feet. Fearful of leaving her alone, Glenna moved the washtub upstairs into the master bedroom so that she could tend to Lyden and still watch over Cally. In the process she relegated sandwich making to the younger twins and reassured a wide-eyed Annie that everything would be all right.

During a time right after Lyden's fever had been reduced, Glenna helped Cally out of her clothes and into a fresh nightgown. Then she followed her sister-in-law's instructions, looping two belts around the headboard posts of the bed, gathering clean sheets, towels and blankets, scissors and twine. She built a fire in the hearth and set water to heat there. When the first potful had boiled she used it to sterilize the basin she would need to use.

But with the baby's head still at Cally's side, Glenna didn't know how it was ever going to be born at all. As the hours passed without change or relief she began to worry that more than Cally's child might be lost.

The evening was half over when a commotion sounded downstairs. Cally struggled weakly up onto one elbow, watching the door. "Go see, Glenna," she beseeched, her fear mingling with her pain.

With a glance at Lyden where he slept on the seat of an overstuffed chair, Glenna hurried out into the hall. Jared

Joseph and two other men were each at a corner of a blanket that supported John, carrying him upstairs.

"He's all right," Joseph called, loud enough for Cally to hear. "His arm and leg are both broken and he's cut here and there, but he'll be just fine."

Glenna stepped out of the way as they reached the upper landing and took John past the door to the master bedroom into his own.

"I'm just fine, Mama," he called in a shaky voice that was barely audible.

Cally's "Thank the dear Lord" was stronger.

It took Joseph only a few minutes before he left his son's bedside and went to Cally's. Leaving them a few minutes of privacy, Glenna stepped into the doorway of the other bedroom where Jared was giving the other two men instructions about disposing of the horses that had either been killed in the collapse or had had to be put out of their misery when they were reached. Glenna turned aside to allow them through the door on their way out.

"How's the boy?" Jared asked.

"The baths keep him from convulsing but his fever is still high."

"And Cally?"

Glenna shook her head. "No change. What about John?"

"I'll need to help Joseph set his broken bones. Then I'll take over tending the boy so you can just see to Cally." His gaze searched her face, his expression showing new concern on top of the old. "Are you all right?"

"Just worried."

He grasped both of her arms and pulled her to his body for a moment, as if to give her some of his strength.

Against his chest she said, "Has the storm let up any at all? Is there any way to go for a doctor?"

"None."

Just then John groaned from the bed. It was loud enough to bring Joseph out of Cally's room.

The cocoon of Jared's body was a wonderful respite, but with Joseph needing to get through the doorway and Cally and Lyden to look after, Glenna couldn't stay. She took a deep breath and straightened away from him. "We'll just have to do the best we can," she said in a tone that sounded much stronger and more resigned than she felt.

He gave a last squeeze of her arms and let her go. Glenna turned to face Joseph where he waited to be let into his son's room and her heart gave a lurch for the worry that was in his eyes. She reached a hand to his, pressing a moment's reassurance before she went back to Cally and Lyden.

Lyden was still sleeping, and a touch of his brow told Glenna that he didn't yet need to be bathed again. She could only pray that this time the fever would stay down, that he might sleep the night through and wake up tomorrow with nothing more than sniffles.

Then she went to Cally's bedside.

The longer Cally labored the more her strength had waned. When the pain she was enduring ended she took two breaths and said, "This baby's not going to turn on its own. Let's see if it'll do it for you."

A fresh surge of nervousness washed through Glenna. "Can that be done?"

"We can try. We have to."

For one brief moment Glenna considered calling for Joseph to do this. Then she steeled herself and forced false confidence into her voice. "What do I do?"

Cally placed her own hands on her abdomen, one on the right side just above her hip and the other near her rib cage. "The head is down here, and the backend is butting against my ribs. Just try turning it the rest of the way. Don't force it, just..." Another pain struck, cutting off her words.

Glenna's hands were as cold as ice. As she waited for the pain to subside she rubbed them together to take some of the chill off.

Cally relaxed out of her pain and breathlessly finished what she had been about to say. "Just try to guide the head straight down."

For a moment Glenna hesitated, wondering how much damage she could do. What if she hurt the baby or Cally?

But what if she didn't do it? another voice in the back of her mind asked. Cally and the baby both would die if something wasn't done. And one look at Cally's drawn features, at the perspiration dotting her brow, and Glenna knew she had to try to do whatever Cally told her.

"My hands are cold," she warned as she touched the hard mound of Cally's stomach, finding the melonlike lump of the head and the softer mound of the baby's rump just where Cally had shown her. "Tell me if I hurt you," she said weakly as she tried to turn the two mounds like the hands of a clock. With the first pressure the baby rebelled and Glenna lost the rump. She was filled with amazement at the living movements inside Cally.

"This is a stubborn one," Cally said, a weak smile of encouragement on her face.

Glenna swallowed and applied more pressure to the head. *Please, God, don't let me hurt either one of them.*

Then, suddenly the head slipped out of her grasp and only the hardness of another contraction replaced it, taking both her and Cally by surprise.

Glenna pulled her hands away, tight fists clutched to her chest as she waited and prayed that she hadn't done something fatally wrong. When the pain ended this time Cally smiled up at her, and for the first time in the past few hours the expression looked genuine.

"I think you did it." Then another pain struck.

From that time on Cally's labor progressed more normally, the pains growing stronger and closer together.

Sometime during the night the rest of Cally and Joseph's children came in from the barn, put the younger ones to bed and went to sleep themselves.

Still Lyden's fever raged, and Glenna had to divide her time between bathing him and watching over Cally. But the space between baths lengthened, telling her that although the fever wasn't broken, she was winning the battle by slow measures.

From the room next door John's pain was carried to Glenna's ears in moans he couldn't seem to stifle as his father and uncle worked to set his broken bones. Finally, just past midnight, they finished, and Jared came to take Lyden back downstairs to care for him while Joseph cleaned and stitched the last of John's cuts. That still left Glenna alone to deliver her sister-in-law's baby when the time came.

After so long and hard and fretful a labor, the birth was surprisingly easy as Cally's third daughter slipped out into Glenna's waiting hands and brought relief to both women with her immediate gusty cries. With the sound Joseph rushed in to make sure both mother and baby were all right. Once he was convinced of it and had briefly met his new daughter, he went back to tend John, leaving Glenna to finish.

She bathed the new baby and swathed her in fresh smelling, soft blankets before cleaning up Cally. Once that was finished she changed the bed linens by rolling her sister-in-law from side to side. Then she laid the tiny, bundled baby in Cally's arms.

"Well, we did it, didn't we?" Cally murmured exhaustedly before thanking Glenna.

Glenna took her hand and squeezed tight. "I'll look in on you through the night. Go to sleep now."

In the hallway Glenna pressed both of her fists to the small of her back and arched the kink out of it. Then wearily, she went downstairs.

At the door that led into the kitchen she stopped and leaned for just a moment against the jamb. In profile to her, Jared sat in a carved wooden rocker. He dwarfed the chair, his denim-encased legs spread wide, his knees higher than the seat. The flannel shirt he had been wearing before, blood-soiled and torn, had been discarded. What was left was the top half of his cream-colored union suit, the sleeves pushed up nearly to his elbows, the top two buttons open at the throat and exposing just a few tufts of wheat-colored hair. The woolen knit fit his hard biceps and finely honed pectorals like a sausage skin. And against that broad, hard chest, in those long, thick arms and massive hands, he cradled Lyden.

The rocking chair whispered a creak as he kept it in a slow sway back and forth. His head was bowed to the sleeping toddler in what looked like absorbed, intent study.

"You're the uncle of another girl," Glenna told him to announce herself, her voice soft.

Jared glanced over his shoulder at her and smiled tiredly. "I heard the wails. Is she as healthy as she sounded?"

"As far as I can tell."

"And Cally?"

"She's fine, too. And relieved. It's been a worrisome day and night." Glenna nodded toward Lyden. "How is he?"

"I think the fever is finally broken. He's still warm but not the way he was when I first brought him down here."

"Good." She pushed off the doorjamb and went to see for herself, bending over the two of them to feel Lyden's forehead. "Why don't we put him to bed upstairs?"

Jared shook his head. "I think we better watch him a little longer."

He made no move to give her the baby, but stayed rocking him. That surprised Glenna, since he usually avoided all contact with Lyden. But she didn't say anything or reach for him. Instead she pulled a kitchen chair over to face them. As she sat down she saw Jared go back to his study of the child, frowning.

"I asked his mother who fathered him," he told her then, out of the blue. "Strange. I didn't intend to. I meant to jus' tell her to take her son when she left. But when I got to i' that isn't what came out of my mouth. Instead I asked the question I had sworn I never would because it would giv' her the advantage of throwing in my face that he was Bill's that the two of them had dumped their bastard on me."

Reflexively, Glenna reached for the toddler's tiny hand "Don't call him that."

Jared looked up at Glenna, arching an eyebrow at he chastisement. "That's what he'd be if Bill fathered him."

"I don't care. Don't call him that." When he didn't go or she prompted, "What was her answer?"

Jared breathed a mirthless laugh. "She didn't know. Or maybe she did and wouldn't say for fear that I wouldn' keep him if I knew he was Bill's."

"If she was really afraid of that I'd think she would have said he was yours to make sure you kept him."

That made him give that humorless laugh again. "True I guess it didn't occur to me that she could be honest."

"So you'll never really know."

"I will if he grows up to look like Bill."

"And you won't if he grows up still looking like hi mother."

He didn't answer that. Instead he glanced down at the sleeping toddler again. "I was worried about him." He saic it as if it seemed odd to him.

"I know you were."

"I wasn't easy to work with all day and night, itching to get in here and see how he was. I kept thinking about him dying. If he had . . ."

"It would have hurt you," she finished for him.

He raised his head, but rather than looking at Glenna he turned the other way. "I don't want to love him," he admitted reluctantly, his voice deep and gruff.

Glenna's eyes filled with tears that she blinked back. "A baby is a clean slate," she told him, her own voice quiet because it came through a throat clotted with emotion.

In much the same struggle she had watched in him since she'd come there, he seemed to fight against his softer feelings. His tone hardened and he frowned down at Lyden blackly. "He's the embodiment of the betrayal of the two people I loved most in the world at the time."

"He's no such thing," Glenna shot back. "Regardless of who fathered him, he's no more guilty of what happened than you are. He took the brunt of it just the same." She hadn't meant to sound so harsh and so she softened her tone. "Who do you punish by resisting loving him? Yourself and Lyden, not Jane or Bill. What's the good in that?"

"There's no good in any of it," he said wryly.

"I know it's hard, Jared." For a moment Glenna didn't know what else to say to him. "You care for Joseph's children as if they're your own. If something happened to Joseph and Cally you wouldn't think twice about taking their whole brood—raising them and loving them, would you?"

"Of course not."

"Well, you thought of Bill as your brother for all those years. Even if Lyden is his, can't you find it in yourself to do the same?"

He seemed to mull that over in his mind.

"Just let it go," she implored. "You let go of Jane and your feelings for her. Bill is gone. It's all in the past. The only way you keep it alive is by pushing Lyden away. Only you can't really push him away. You can ignore him and avoid him, but there's something in you that makes you worry about him when he's sick, that won't let you give him away to his grandparents in Chicago or even to the woman you know is his mother. Accept your feelings for him. I think it matters less that he has your blood than that he has your heart. At least that's how it is for me. I don't care that he isn't from my body. I love him anyway.''

For a moment he didn't say anything. Then he sighed. ''I guess I'll have to think about it.''

''Yes, please. Think about letting us all be a family the way we should be.'' But it wasn't only the three of them that were on her mind just then and he seemed to know that.

''Glenna...'' He shook his head and looked at her with a sad expression on his face again. ''That can't be. Mary can't come here and be a part of this family. That's something *you* have to let go of.''

For a moment she considered denying that Mary had been as much a part of her plea as Lyden. But then she decided that since he had already brought it up she might as well pursue it. ''I know you think you're only considering Mary's welfare. But I've made it safe for her to live here.'' She outlined all she had done, from the rope she had hidden away to tie onto the fence, to the path to the outhouse and everything in between.

Then she went on earnestly, ''I understand how you feel, Jared, I do. All sighted people believe there are dangers around every bend for a blind one. Why, we didn't even let her feed herself until long after she could have, because we just didn't think she was capable. But once you watch how able a blind person really is from hearing and feeling and sensing things that we don't notice, you realize that not being able to see makes things harder but it doesn't make them impossible. She'll do all right. She'll stumble and fall and get bruises, yes, worse at first while she's learning her way. But that's not enough to keep her from coming here. She can't be put in a cage because she's blind. She doesn't need to be.''

''Glenna...'' He sighed again and then said softly, compassionately, ''It just can't be. Don't you think I've seen a you've been up to around here? Don't you think I know how much this means to you?''

"No, I don't think˜you know how much this means to me.''

"I do. But what I know that you don't is that ropes and rock pathways and taking up rugs still doesn't make it safe for her to live here. It still doesn't change how hard the life is. These past hours should have taught you some of it, but even this is only a taste. Don't you see all that can happen to able, sighted people in the snap of a twig? There are so many more dangers for a blind child. And look what happens when something does go wrong—we're isolated here. We had four people that desperately needed a doctor and there was no way to get one...."

"And we managed anyway, didn't we?''

"Morty might have lived had there been a medical man waiting when we pulled him out from under that rubble. Who knows if John's bones will mend right, though we did our best to set them? It's just too hard out here to add being blind to it. This is only the start of winter, Glenna. It can get worse. Blizzards and windstorms can leave us snowed in for a month. We can get so low on supplies that we have to cut back and ration them just to eke out enough food to last. We can run so low on even cow chips for fires that we'll have to move into Joseph's home rather than try to heat two places. And that's only the winter. There's still spring rains and floods and tornadoes.... How is a blind child to find her way to the privy through two feet of water or save herself by spotting a tornado on the horizon? You, yourself faced a snake and there's more of them where that one came from. There can be locusts and drought and..." He stopped. "Isn't being blind hardship enough for her?''

Still cradling Lyden in one arm he reached to clasp Glenna's nape with his other hand. "I love you. But I can't let Mary come here. I can't." He made it sound so final.

"I promised her," Glenna said through a tight throat, her voice a bare whisper but her tone as implacable as his.

He shook his head. "You're tired. This is no time to argue." Then he stood with Lyden and reach for Glenna's hand. "Come on. The fever's been down for a long time now. We'll put him in bed between us, but we both need some rest."

There was a knot in the pit of Glenna's stomach but she couldn't refuse. She put her hand in his and let him lead her upstairs.

He was right, she was tired. Bone weary. Exhausted.

But nowhere in that was there acceptance of the unacceptable.

Chapter Twenty-One

The wind had blown the storm all the way through by the next morning, leaving dull gray clouds that seemed mirrored by the drifts of powdery snow. The newborn woke everyone up early. Having taken on the chore of delivering Morty's body—lying in a freshly made coffin—into Hays, Jared was on the road shortly after dawn. As was the usual practice in winter, the coffin would be put in the icehouse until a warm stretch thawed the earth enough for Morty's grave to be dug in the church cemetery.

Bundled up against the cold, Jared sat atop the buckboard seat thinking of what he had left Glenna doing. She had just changed the new baby into a dry diaper, clothes and blankets and given her over to Cally for feeding. Lyden had awakened without fever but with a bad cold and a hoarse throat that put him in a whiney mood. Glenna had been holding him on her hip with one arm while she flipped pancakes with her free hand for the tribe of hungry Strattons, none of whom had eaten well the previous day.

The image was vivid in Jared's mind on the deserted road to Hays. It made him smile and shake his head. The past twenty-four hours had been nothing if not a test of Glenna's mettle. And yet she had come through it still wanting to add the burden of her blind sister. That was either fool-hardiness or a loyalty even greater than he'd realized she felt.

Since he didn't believe her to be a fool, loyalty seemed to be the answer, and a new vision of just how deep her feelings for her sister were left Jared's mind troubled.

"The prairie is no place for a blind child," he told the horses forcefully. Every argument he'd given was valid. He should know, he'd lived here all his life and seen enough of the hardship and calamities.

But Mary was Glenna's only sister, an inner voice poked at him. Her only sister, to whom she had a duty, a responsibility, to whom she had made a promise....

A promise she shouldn't have made, the argument went. Even in his advertisement he'd been clear about accepting only a woman alone. She had known before she even headed for the hotel that morning that Mary couldn't go along. And then he'd told her himself.

Jared dipped his nose into the upturned collar of his coat and breathed the warmer air for a moment.

Glenna would accept it in time, he told himself.

Or would she?

How often had he said the same thing about Janie? That she would get used to the life here, that she'd come to accept it, even love it one day?

He hit a hidden bump in the snow-covered road, and the coffin behind him bounced. Jared cast a glance over his shoulder to make sure it was not in danger of falling off the wagon. Then he turned back to the horses.

Much as he didn't want it, again came the image of Glenna as she'd looked that morning, along with the voice he was beginning to recognize as that of his conscience. She worked hard, he couldn't fault her for that. And without complaint, even when the work involved the whole of Joseph's family. And Lyden...she'd taken him on as if he were her own, a child Jared couldn't even say for sure was his. She'd taken it all on for him, accepting everything that was a part of his life.

And he was refusing her the only part of her own life that she wanted.

"But dammit, this is no place for a blind child," he told the horses again as if they'd said it was.

The fence and a rope tied to it, pathways, bare floors, furniture situated just so and an organized, orderly yard meant nothing when it came to what could happen out here. Look at Morty back there. Look at John lying in his bed with broken bones. Look at that blind boy who fell down the well....

Look at Glenna doing so much for him, for Lyden, for all the Stratton family....

Would she come to accept the way things had to be... needed to be... should be?

She would, he told himself.

But Janie never had.

"Land, but you've done enough now." Cally pulled the dishrag out of Glenna's hands. "Charity can do those dishes later on. She's had two whole weeks of being waited on hand and foot. But right now we're going to have butter cake."

Glenna grabbed up the dessert plates and followed her sister-in-law into the parlor.

Ten days had passed since the storm and the new baby's birth. What with her christening after church services and the welcoming home of Charity from her visit, the Sunday afternoon was a festive one.

Joseph and Jared had helped John downstairs, where he sat on the sofa with his leg propped on one bed pillow and his arm on another as Charity regaled the entire family with news from Topeka. The name Simon Smithers was peppered so frequently throughout all she recounted that it became apparent she had a beau.

But Glenna couldn't keep her mind on the lively banter that warmed the parlor. The new baby had been christened Marie Christine on this, only the second day Cally had been up and out of bed. During her sister-in-law's recuperation Glenna, Jared and Lyden had stayed in the main house so that Glenna could tend to everything. She hadn't minded the work. The good thing about being so busy was that it had left her little time and no energy for fretting about Mary.

But now Cally was her old self again, taking over the full care of her new daughter, her injured son and her own household. Charity was back to help, Lyden was well and after this celebration Glenna, Jared and Lyden were moving back into their own home next door. And Glenna was no longer distracted.

With yet another mention of Simon Smithers by Charity, Joseph took his pipe out from between his teeth, his other hand cradling Marie as he rocked near the fire blazing in the hearth. "Now listen here, missy. Just because I have a new daughter doesn't mean I'm ready to let go of my old one," he told her, pointing the stem of his pipe her way.

"Papa!" Charity blushed becomingly.

"She's nearly seventeen, Joseph," Cally reminded him gently. "If you'll recall, the day after my seventeenth birthday was when we married."

"Hush, Cally, she doesn't need to be reminded of that. You were older at seventeen than Charity is."

"Well, Charity," Jared put in, obviously goading his brother, "looks like your father wants to make you an old maid. What does this Simon Smithers do?"

From behind her Peter sang, "Simple Simon, Simple Simon."

Charity threw a crocheted pillow at him and turned back to answer her uncle. "He's a blacksmith."

"Hays already has a blacksmith," Joseph said as if that ended it.

But Jared wouldn't let him off that easily. "Stringer is old as dirt, Joseph. We could use a little new blood."

It was his brother who had Joseph's pipe stem pointed at him this time. "I'm going to live to see you regret this,

Jared. You'll have a daughter of your own one day, remember that."

"Is Glenna going to have a baby?" Charity blurted out ecstatically.

Glenna could feel her face heat. "No. One child in diapers is enough, thank you," she answered quickly, feeling sad that it wasn't so and yet knowing at the same time it was for the best with the way her thoughts had been heading.

"You'd better get busy, Jared." Joseph was taking his turn at goading. "I'm way ahead of you."

"Poor Glenna," Cally said, laughing. "After these past ten days she probably never wants to see another houseful of children."

Joseph laughed, too. "We might have scared her right out of your bed, Jared."

"I didn't scare Glenna," Annie put in.

Jared winked at his wife. "No, not our Glenna. You're not afraid, are you?"

Just then Marie Christine began to wiggle in her father's arms, screwing up her face and yawning wide. Half the people in the room went over to watch.

Glenna took in the scene, hearing Jared's "our Glenna" echo over and over in her mind. There was an unmistakable air of closeness and warmth in the room, an air of family. A family she belonged to. It was something she hadn't experienced before coming here, a sense of safety, of security, of belonging, of being loved and accepted. It was like open arms that could be trusted to be there waiting whenever she might need protection or comfort or reassurance or strength. This place and these people had become a haven for her, a home.

Guilt was an odd companion to those warm feelings, and yet there it was. Guilt. Strong and burning bright.

Here she was in the center of all of this with a man she loved and who she knew loved her. And to get it for herself she had had to abandon Mary to an old "aunt" who wasn't even a real relative.

Glenna felt like a glutton feasting before a starving child. Her glance fell to Jared where he still bounced Annie on his knee. *You mean it, don't you? You won't let Mary come here.*

They had spoken about it often since the night of the storm. And each time he hadn't minced words in refusing her. He honestly believed life here was too dangerous for Mary. He believed he was doing what was best for her sister. And that wasn't going to change.

She had to accept it, Glenna realized. And with that acceptance came the resolution to do what she had been thinking about so much in the past day.

"Can we have cake now?" Annie said loudly to draw the attention away from the new baby.

Cally left the group and picked up her other daughter from Jared's lap, cuddling her. "Yes, we can have cake now."

Without being asked, Glenna went to the table and took up the knife to slice the two-layer concoction. It allowed her face to be averted from everyone as she blinked back moisture from her eyes and took several deep, silent breaths.

"Aren't you having any?" Jared asked when twelve pieces of cake had been served and everyone was enjoying it.

Glenna shook her head and busied herself by taking Lyden from Luke and feeding him his. "I'm not hungry," she said softly through a lump in her throat.

The time had come, but this was not the moment to bring it up. They'd had privacy the morning they had struck the bargain that united them. It would take privacy again to undo it.

Glenna was waiting for Jared in the kitchen of the small house when he came downstairs the next morning. His coffee was made, and she sat at the table warming her hands around a cup of tea.

She had been up most of the night. Somehow it had seemed deceitful to sleep beside him knowing what she was going to do this morning, and so she had pushed his arms away when he would have pulled her to him to make love. She had used the excuse that she wasn't feeling well. Not altogether a lie when she considered that she was heartsick. Then, when he was asleep, she had gotten up and gone to the bed she had intended to be Mary's. But there had been little rest for her even then. Long before dawn she had given up trying to sleep, straightened the bed and come to sit in the kitchen.

"I need to talk to you," she told him as he poured himself a cup of coffee.

"If the look on your face is any indication it must be something bad." He brought his cup to the table, pausing to kiss the top of her head before sitting down in the chair beside her. "Are you still not feeling well?"

"I'm fine."

"I'm going into town this morning, if there's anything you want."

I want to stay here with you and still keep my promise to Mary. But the time for that discussion was past. Glenna took a deep breath and sighed. "I want to borrow some money from you."

That stopped his coffee cup halfway to his mouth. Then he took a drink and set it down. "What would you need to borrow money for?"

Glenna stared at him, her gaze stuck to the sun-washed gold of his hair, to the handsome planes of his face, to those riveting deep green eyes, to that thin nose above that mustache that tickled like a feather when it brushed against her skin.

How could she leave him? her heart moaned.

The Doubletree

How could she not and leave Mary abandoned? her mind answered.

"I want to borrow enough to bring Mary here, to set her and me up in someplace small to live in Hays," she blurted out, averting her gaze from the face she loved too much to look at and still say this.

"I see" was all he answered.

Glenna looked at him again, imploring him with her eyes. "I know you don't understand but I made Mary a vow I can't break."

His gaze was on her, his brows drawn into a V. "You made vows to me, too, as I recall."

"And I've kept them."

"Until now."

"We'll still be married," she said feebly, knowing that although it might be true in the legal sense it wouldn't be so in any other way.

"With you living in Hays with your sister, and me here?"

She didn't answer that, but instead tried to make him understand. "I love you, Jared, I do. And I love Lyden. But..." Her throat suddenly constricted and she had to swallow before she could go on. "I love Mary, too. She's my family, but more important, I am the only family she has. I just can't go back on the promise I made her. I just can't leave her in Chicago with strangers—or even Carter and Aunt Lida—paid to raise her while I flourish here with all of your family around me. She has a right to be with me." She tried to sound less frantic. "I know you won't change your mind about bringing her here. I know you believe it would be too dangerous for her. I can't change what you think and this is your home—"

"It's your home, too," he cut in.

"But it's your decision in the end about whether or not Mary lives in it. And you've made it clear what that decision is. So I'll bring her to Hays and live with her there."

"You've thought all of this out, have you?"

She nodded, curving both hands around her cup now because they were frigid. "I know you married me to be a mother to Lyden, so that Cally wouldn't have the burden of him. If you want, I'll take him with me. You can pay for his keep—at first you can deduct it from what I owe you and then later when that's paid back—"

Again he interrupted her. "You've just convinced me that I should accept Lyden as my son regardless of who fathered him, and now you want me to give him up."

"I'm just telling you that I'll still care for Lyden in order to keep up my half of the bargain we made in marrying in the first place. I intend to take in wash and sewing and whatever else I need to do to support Mary and myself."

For a moment their eyes remained locked together.

Then Jared said, "No, love. I'm sorry, but I won't do it."

It came so offhandedly. "What do you mean you won't do it?"

"Any of it. I won't loan you the money in the first place. I won't let you leave me and I won't let you take Lyden. I've held on to him twice when I might have given him away. You were right about my feelings for him, about his being a clean slate. And I'd do anything in the world rather than lose you—"

This time it was Glenna who cut him off. "But you'd force me to lose the person in my life who is equally as important to me? To whom I am that important?"

"I won't loan you the money," he repeated. "You're my wife, Lyden's mother, and you belong here."

"And Mary belongs with me." Anger, especially in the face of his calm, would not serve her, so Glenna took a breath and tried to reason with him again. "Maybe once she's in Hays you can visit us and see for yourself how really able a blind person can be. You might change your mind about her living here. I only want to borrow a hundred dollars, just enough for Mary's train fare, for a small place to live and to get us started. A hundred dollars, Jared."

He stood up and carried his cup to the sink. From the hook beside the door he took his sheepskin coat and put it on. "The answer is no, Glenna, I will not loan you the money," he repeated. "So put it out of your head."

For a moment after he had walked out Glenna merely sat there.

In her mind's eye she had the image of Mary as she'd left her—hurt, upset, so afraid that Glenna would not make good on her promise.

Glenna loved Jared.

But she had come to him with other ties that couldn't be severed and she had to make good on her word. No matter what it took to do it.

Chapter Twenty-Two

Not long after Jared left Glenna went upstairs. She packed her single satchel stoically, trying not to think about the wedding celebration at which she had worn this dress, or the way it had felt to have Jared unfasten the buttons of another. She tried to block out memories of nights on the bed that now held her valise, and the image of the babies of her own she might bring into the world on it.

It was a strange, painful limbo through which she moved—fighting back thoughts of things that had actually happened and trying not to remember dreams she had had of what might be. She'd had such high hopes here for a life unlike the one her mother had lived, for years and years within the warm circle of the large Stratton family, hopes of giving that to Mary as well.

But it wasn't to be. She had left Mary too long already, and even if she couldn't give her this home and this family, she could at least give her the love and care no stranger could.

When all her belongings were in the satchel she took it downstairs to the entranceway and then went back to get Lyden. She had heard him stirring as she packed, but he awoke in good spirits in the mornings and often played in his bed for a short time before demanding his breakfast.

Glenna felt as if a fist had clenched around her heart when she went into his room and he greeted her with his version of good-morning, which sounded like "mooring," and held out his arms for her to pick him up.

"Hello, sweet baby," she answered him, holding him close.

Would he miss her?

Glenna's eyes filled and stung. A lump blocked her throat. But she forced herself to think of Mary at this age, of how much she had loved her. At least Lyden would be left here among a wealth of people who cared about him.

She kept him on her lap as she fed him his oatmeal, wanting the last few minutes close to him. Her hair was tied simply at the nape of her neck and left down her back, and the toddler captured a corkscrew strand of it that had gotten caught on her shoulder. Fascinated, his eyes crossed to study it close up as he opened his mouth reflexively for his breakfast, like a trusting little bird. And suddenly Glenna wondered how she was going to bear being so near and seeing both father and son on the occasions when their paths crossed without being a part of their lives.

Was it possible, as she had suggested to him, that Jared would relent once Mary was here and he saw that she was not as handicapped as he thought?

But that was another hope she was too afraid to hang on to for fear it would be dashed.

Best not to think about it. Or plan on it. Or dream on it. She was leaving him and she had to consider that final—and surely it would be once she had done it, for wasn't she doing very nearly what his first wife had? And she knew better than anyone the scars that had left.

When Lyden refused to eat any more Glenna took him back upstairs and dressed him. Quickly now. She told herself she had wasted enough time, though the truth was that she was afraid if she didn't hurry she might never go.

Then she bundled him up and took him next door.

"You can't mean that," Cally said when Glenna told her what she was doing.

"I mean it, all right. I'm leaving. But Jared doesn't want me to take Lyden, so you'll have to keep him."

"Glenna...don't do this—"

But Glenna cut off her sister-in-law with a frantic shake of her head and thrust Lyden at her. "I can't talk about it anymore," she said in a rush, fleeing the warmth of the yellow kitchen before she lost her nerve and the floodgates on her feelings at once.

That left her a single chore.

She had come to Jared accused of being a thief. Now she was going to make the accusation true, and it wasn't something that sat well with her. But she knew of no other way to do what she felt she had to.

Back once again in the smaller Stratton house, Glenna went directly to Jared's desk in the parlor. She had seen him taking money from the strongbox he kept in a bottom drawer there often enough, but she had no idea how much might be in it. The lock on the metal chest itself was open. Somehow the trust that symbolized made her feel all the worse for doing what she was.

She counted more than two hundred dollars there, but took only one hundred of it, leaving a signed IOU in its place. How long would it take her to repay that money? Much, much longer than it would take to spend it.

She closed the strongbox, replaced it and put the money into her skirt pocket.

That was that. Nothing now but to leave.

Rather than standing up, though, she stayed where she was.

Was it only her imagination or could she really smell the scent of Jared in the air?

Imagination or not, it was there. The mingled odors of soap and man and horse and earth. Again her eyes filled with quick tears.

Go. Leave before it gets any harder.

But still her body wouldn't move in response.

Maybe she should stay, take only enough money fo[r] Mary's train fare and gamble that when her sister got her[e] Jared wouldn't send her back again.

Somehow that seemed more dishonorable than what sh[e] was doing. Certainly it would be harder on Mary to com[e] into a situation like that. At least this way Glenna woul[d] have a little time to find them a place to live, to prepare fo[r] her sister.

Finally, Glenna forced herself to stand up. She'd made he[r] decision and she had to follow through with it.

Her legs felt weighted as she went into the foyer, her arm[s] stiff as she pulled on her coat and fixed her muffler aroun[d] her head and neck. When she lifted the valise it seeme[d] heavier than it had when she'd first brought it downstairs[.] She stepped outside onto the porch and closed the door be[-] hind her firmly, as if that would convince her she was leav[-] ing for good.

Cold winter air bit her cheeks. The sky was as gray as he[r] spirits. It had snowed twice since that first bad storm and th[e] ground was blanketed in white, smooth and rolling where n[o] one had trodden upon it, and packed down hard wher[e] booted feet, horses' hooves and wagon wheels replaced b[y] sled runners had traveled.

Glenna stepped carefully down the icy porch stairs an[d] followed the stone walkway to the fence. The house seeme[d] to call to her from behind but she steadfastly resisted th[e] urge to look back at it.

She headed across the yard to the barn where she ha[d] every intention of using a rig she would later have returne[d.] But the sound of an approaching wagon stopped her in he[r] tracks. It couldn't be Jared back so soon, she thought as sh[e] stared down the road, the distance too long for her to mak[e] out who was coming. She had worried about meeting u[p] with him in Hays but not about leaving before he was hom[e] again. She had learned for herself after the incident with Scott Bradley that no one went all the way into town without at least half a day's worth of errands to run. For Jared to be back so soon would mean he had gone there, spent not more than half an hour and then come home.

But what if it was Jared?

She would just have to face him down.

Glenna took a few more steps toward the barn but curiosity got the better of her. She stopped again and looked off in the distance at the approaching wagon.

It had drawn near enough for her to recognize her husband more by the color of his coat and his stature than by actual features. A shiver went through her.

What would he do when he found her packed and leaving him the way his first wife had? What would he do when he found she'd stolen from him?

Should she make a run for the stable and try to race out the other direction and circle around to the road? She'd never make it. There was no avoiding him. She took a breath of arctic air for bolstering, resigned to the confrontation.

The wagon approached steadily. There was something on the seat beside him, a smaller form wrapped in bright red.

Confusion and curiosity kept Glenna standing where she was, halfway between her fence and the barn. Who was sitting next to Jared?

She squinted her eyes. It was a small person. A child perhaps?

A child.

Her breath caught and her pulse picked up speed, but she was afraid even to think the thought that popped into her mind. It couldn't be.

Mary's coat was blue, she reminded herself.

Maybe her eyes were playing tricks on her. Surely, if it were true, when she was telling him she was leaving him for her sister's sake this morning he would have told her she didn't have to do that, that Mary was coming.

Glenna was hardly aware of the valise dropping out of he
hand. No matter how she reasoned it away, hope was a fi
inside her, keeping her warm and giving her energy.

On came the wagon.

The red-clad child was slight but Glenna could tell not
ing more than that.

"Glenna?" It was Joseph's voice as he walked up behir
her. "Cally told me what you're doing and you can't leave.

"Is that Jared coming?" she asked him without takir
her eyes off the wagon.

"I expect it is."

"Who's that with him."

"Well, now . . ." Joseph drawled slowly.

"Who is it, Joseph? Is it my sister?"

"Never tell . . ."

It had to be Mary. It had to be. Cally must not ha
known.

The wagon drew nearer, nearer.

And then she could finally see clearly enough to reali
who it was sitting so erectly beside Jared.

Mary's cheeks were almost as red as the coat and hat sl
wore. Her mittened hands were clasped primly in her la
her chin was tilted up in that way she had when her sens
were being bombarded with many new things at once.

Mary. He'd brought Mary here.

It took Glenna a moment to realize that tears were ru
ning down her cheeks. But not the sad tears she had be
fighting all morning; these were from joy and gratitude ar
a love for Jared that had multiplied tenfold in that instan

"Mary!" she called, waving her arms as if her sister coul
see them.

It was Jared who waved back, one arm arching over h
head just before he pushed the horses to a faster pace.

And then there they were, right in front of Glenna on tl
wagon seat above her.

"Mary?"

"Glenna? Is that you? Doesn't it smell wonderful here? There's not even any factory smoke in the air," her sister said as if only a few hours had passed since they'd last been together.

All Glenna could do was laugh at that, because her throat was too choked for words. It was Joseph who stepped up and reached for her sister.

"I'm Joseph, Jared's brother, Mary," he told her as he touched her.

"Hello, Joseph. Jared said there are lots of cats here and that I might have one," she said matter-of-factly.

Jared dropped the reins, kicked the brake into place and jumped down from the wagon. He came around to Glenna's side. Bending to her ear he said, "Were you going somewhere, city girl?"

Glenna looked up at him, finding him smiling. She touched his cheek with her palm, thinking she might burst for loving him so much. "Thank you" was all she could manage at that moment, an understatement of her gratitude.

He winked at her and then dropped a kiss to her lips for the briefest of moments. "Hadn't you better get Mary out of this cold?" he suggested as he brushed at the dampness on her face with his gloved finger.

"Oh, I'm not a bit cold," Mary answered him. "But where are you, Glenna?" she finished impatiently.

"I'm here," Glenna said as she stepped to her sister and took her into her arms. "Oh, how I missed you."

"I didn't think I was ever going to get to come. Aunt Lida kept saying I was just too impatient. Carter would tell me I could have a home with them as long as I needed, and then *finally* Jared sent a telegraph wire with enough money for my ticket and even for this new coat. Feel it, Glenna, it's soft as cotton. That's why I got it. There wasn't another one that felt this way."

Glenna laughed at her sister's excited ramblings a
placed Mary's hand in the crook of her elbow. "You'll ha
time to tell me everything, but let's go into the house now
She still spoke to the little girl, but back over her should
her eyes stayed on her husband. "I'll show you the way."

For Glenna the day seemed to fly by in a flurry of intr
ductions as all but John came over to the smaller house
meet Mary. Cally scolded both Jared and Joseph for lea
ing her out of their secret and hugged Glenna tightly, war
ing her never to even think about leaving again.

As he did with all new people, Lyden studied this ne
member of his family from a distance at first, but when
offered her his new ball it seemed a friendship had beg
between them.

Glenna helped Mary learn her way around the hous
though not without bumping into several things. Practi
would make perfect, she told Jared when he lunged to sa
her from walking into the corner of a wall once, assuri
him it wouldn't have been the first one she'd hit.

Cally invited them for supper that evening. When it w
time to go next door Glenna guided Mary while the chi
counted off the steps. Once there Mary let go of Glenna
arm, turned around and found her way home and then ba
again, just to see if she could.

Throughout the meal Glenna drank in the fact that he
she was again, in the center of this family she loved, on
now it was complete because Mary was a part of it, too. A
as if to imprint that on her mind, she couldn't keep her ey
off her sister for longer than a few moments at a time.

After supper Mary instigated a game with the younger s
of twins whereby she learned their very similar faces wi
her hands and then tried, without the help of their voic
to tell them apart. When she'd won the game she told the
it was the grimacing antics of Peter that had given it aw

because she knew Paul was not ornery enough to try to fool her.

When the evening was over Mary made it back home unaided, ahead of Glenna and Jared, who carried Lyden. But the little girl's fatigue showed when she forgot to take three steps straight into the kitchen before she turned and she banged into the tin-punched cupboard.

"It's been a long, busy day," Glenna said as she stepped in to get Mary upstairs to bed while Jared did the same service for Lyden.

Mary was asleep almost the instant her eyes closed, but for a time Glenna stood beside her bed, watching her. And then, when she heard Jared leave Lyden's room for theirs she tore herself away and went to face her husband alone for the first time since he'd found her with her bag packed ready to leave him.

He was just lighting the lamp on the beside table. She wanted to walk into his arms and tell him how happy he'd made her, but she knew there were other things that needed to be said before she could do that, not the least of them being that she had to tell him she had stolen his money.

"I looked in on Lyden but he was already asleep," she said by way of opening the conversation as she began to unpack her satchel.

"Um-hmm." Jared turned to her, shaking out the match as he did. "So, where were you going this morning?" he asked, making it obvious that the same things that had been on her mind had been on his.

"To Hays," she answered evenly. "I . . ." How did a person tell her husband she had stolen from him? Glenna cleared her throat and took the money out of the skirt pocket it had been in since she'd put it there. "I took a hundred dollars out of your strongbox and left an IOU."

He crossed his arms over his chest and shrugged one shoulder. "The money is as much yours as it is mine. It's there for you to use, without considering it a debt."

"Yes. Well. I didn't think that was the case if I was using it to set up housekeeping somewhere else." Glenna hazarded a glance up at him as she hung a dress back in the armoire. He surprised her by looking amused. "You're not angry?"

"No."

It was a great relief to her. Then she asked the question that had been on her mind all day long. "When did you decide to bring Mary here?"

He smiled lopsidedly. "When I started to think about what you had taken on for me—Lyden and all of Joseph's family—while I was refusing you your own. And when I realized that I should honor the kind of loyalty you feel for Mary. The kind I'd be grateful to have for myself."

Her eyes misted yet again. "I don't suppose you'll believe me since I was ready to leave this morning, but you do have my loyalty. And my gratitude. And my love."

He came to her and smoothed her cheek with the backs of his fingers. "Don't ever leave again and I'll believe it."

She smiled up at him. "That's a promise I can make."

"And we know how you keep your promises."

She turned into his arms then, wrapping her own tightly around him and pressing the side of her face to his chest. "I didn't want to go."

"I know you didn't. Cally told me how it was." He cupped her head and held her close.

"Mary will do all right here. You'll see."

He breathed a little laugh and lowered his face into her hair. "I hope you're right. I decided that was another thing I had to trust you on."

"And you really can trust me, you know."

"I know."

He tipped up her chin and pressed a warm kiss on her lips for just a moment before letting go of her. He took her satchel off the bed and turned the quilt down. Then he began to unfasten the buttons of the traveling gown she still wore.

Glenna reached up to caress his face lovingly. "Thank you," she whispered.

"You're welcome," he said without looking at her face, earnestly undressing her.

"For marrying me," she went on. "For my wedding ring. And for bringing Mary here."

He raised his gaze to her face and smiled tenderly. "My pleasure."

For a moment their eyes held, and then it was Glenna who broke the bond by pulling his shirt free of his trousers and unbuttoning it.

Only seconds passed before each had removed the other's clothes. Jared picked her up and swung her onto the bed, following close behind to lie with the length of his body against the length of her.

"I love you," he told her sincerely as his mouth captured hers.

"I love you, too," she answered between kisses.

With mouths and tongues and hands they roamed each other freely, finally unfettered by the past or distrust or fears. Slowly, languidly, openly, they courted and teased. His lips to her breast. Hers to his hardened male nib. His hands to her derriere. Hers to his. His fingers to her depths. Hers closing around his hardness. Tenderly, firmly, tormentingly, they played, until need demanded a stronger, closer meeting. And when his body came into hers this time it seemed that more had been joined than his flesh with hers and hers with his. It was as if their spirits and maybe even their souls merged into one to seal their union for good. It was a fusion that stayed with them even afterward when

Jared fell back on the mattress and pulled Glenna to meld into his side, her head on his chest.

For a time she listened to his heartbeat as if it were her own. "It's perfect now, our life," she said then. "Just the way I imagined, with Lyden and Mary both sleeping in the other rooms. A family."

"Mmm," he agreed tiredly. "But it could be even more perfect."

She craned her head back to look up at him. "How?"

His mouth stretched into a slow smile. "We could have a few more of those rooms filled with sleeping children."

Glenna rested on his chest again. "A bigger family?" she mused as if it hadn't occurred to her before.

"A little."

"So you are in a rivalry with Joseph," she teased.

"No, I'd just like to have a few of our own making. Wouldn't you?"

"Mmm. But if we never do I'll still be happy."

"Will you?"

She laughed at even the thought of doubting it. "I count the day I first saw your newspaper advertisement as my luckiest. Strange how so much good came from bad."

"Cally used to tell me that. I didn't believe her."

"And now?"

"Well, you still need to learn how to cook." But he hugged her tight, softening the complaint. "I guess I was meant to have a city girl from Chicago. I just picked the wrong one the first time and had to go back to get it right."

"I'm certainly glad you did."

"So am I, love. So am I."

Silence came over them then. Beneath her ear Glenna heard Jared's heartbeat slowing, his breath deepening into sleep. Her left hand was on his chest and on her third finger was his ring, gleaming in the lamplight. Good from bad, she thought again. Only this was better than good. And she knew with certainty that she could spend the rest of her days yoked together with this man in that doubletree he had spoken of when they first met. Contentedly. Blissfully. Lovingly.

Forever.

*   *   *   *   *

Take 4 bestselling love stories FREE

Plus get a FREE surprise gift!

PASSPORT TO ROMANCE
SWEEPSTAKES RULES

1. **HOW TO ENTER:** To enter, you must be the age of majority and complete the official entry form, or print your name, address, telephone number and age on a plain piece of paper and mail to: Passport to Romance, P.O. Box 9056, Buffalo, NY 14269-9056. No mechanically reproduced entries accepted.

2. All entries must be received by the CONTEST CLOSING DATE, DECEMBER 31, 1990 TO BE ELIGIBLE.

3. **THE PRIZES:** There will be ten (10) Grand Prizes awarded, each consisting of a choice of a trip for two people from the following list:
    i)   London, England (approximate retail value $5,050 U.S.)
    ii) England, Wales and Scotland (approximate retail value $6,400 U.S.)
    iii) Carribean Cruise (approximate retail value $7,300 U.S.)
    iv) Hawaii (approximate retail value $9,550 U.S.)
    v)   Greek Island Cruise in the Mediterranean (approximate retail value $12,250 U.S.)
    vi) France (approximate retail value $7,300 U.S.)

4. Any winner may choose to receive any trip or a cash alternative prize of $5,000.00 U.S. in lieu of the trip.

5. **GENERAL RULES:** Odds of winning depend on number of entries received.

6. A random draw will be made by Nielsen Promotion Services, an independent judging organization, on January 29, 1991, in Buffalo, NY, at 11:30 a.m. from all eligible entries received on or before the Contest Closing Date.

7. Any Canadian entrants who are selected must correctly answer a time-limited, mathematical skill-testing question in order to win.

8. Full contest rules may be obtained by sending a stamped, self-addressed envelope to: "Passport to Romance Rules Request", P.O. Box 9998, Saint John, New Brunswick, Canada E2L 4N4.

9. Quebec residents may submit any litigation respecting the conduct and awarding of a prize in this contest to the Régie des loteries et courses du Québec.

10. Payment of taxes other than air and hotel taxes is the sole responsibility of the winner.

11. Void where prohibited by law.

COUPON BOOKLET OFFER TERMS

To receive your Free travel-savings coupon booklets, complete the mail-in Offer Certificate on the preceeding page, including the necessary number of proofs-of-purchase, and mail to: Passport to Romance, P.O. Box 9057, Buffalo, NY 14269-9057. The coupon booklets include savings on travel-related products such as car rentals, hotels, cruises, flowers and restaurants. Some restrictions apply. The offer is available in the United States and Canada. Requests must be postmarked by January 25, 1991. Only proofs-of-purchase from specially marked "Passport to Romance" Harlequin® or Silhouette® books will be accepted. The offer certificate must accompany your request and may not be reproduced in any manner. Offer void where prohibited or restricted by law. LIMIT FOUR COUPON BOOKLETS PER NAME, FAMILY, GROUP, ORGANIZATION OR ADDRESS. Please allow up to 8 weeks after receipt of order for shipment. Enter quickly as quantities are limited. Unfulfilled mail-in offer requests will receive free Harlequin® or Silhouette® books (not previously available in retail stores), in quantities equal to the number of proofs-of-purchase required for Levels One to Four, as applicable.

PR-SWPS

OFFICIAL SWEEPSTAKES
ENTRY FORM

Complete and return this Entry Form immediately—the more Entry Forms you submit, the better your chances of winning!
- Entry Forms must be received by **December 31, 1990**
- A random draw will take place on **January 29, 1991**
- Trip must be taken by **December 31, 1991**

3-HH-1-SW

YES, I want to win a PASSPORT TO ROMANCE vacation for two! I understand the prize includes round-trip air fare, accommodation and a daily spending allowance.

Name_____

Address_____

City_____ State_____ Zip_____

Telephone Number_____ Age_____

Return entries to: **PASSPORT TO ROMANCE**, P.O. Box 9056, Buffalo, NY 14269-9056

© 1990 Harlequin Enterprises Limited

COUPON BOOKLET/OFFER CERTIFICATE

Item	LEVEL ONE Booklet 1	LEVEL TWO Booklet 1 & 2	LEVEL THREE Booklet 1, 2 & 3	LEVEL FOUR Booklet 1, 2, 3 & 4
Booklet 1 = $100+	$100+	$100+	$100+	$100+
Booklet 2 = $200+		$200+	$200+	$200+
Booklet 3 = $300+			$300+	$300+
Booklet 4 = $400+	———	———	———	$400+
Approximate Total Value of Savings	$100+	$300+	$600+	$1,000+
# of Proofs of Purchase Required	4	6	12	18
Check One	———	———	———	———

Name_____

Address_____

City_____ State_____ Zip_____

Return Offer Certificates to: **PASSPORT TO ROMANCE**, P.O. Box 9057, Buffalo, NY 14269-9057

Requests must be postmarked by **January 25, 1991**

ONE PROOF OF PURCHASE

3-HH-1

To collect your free coupon booklet you must include the necessary number of proofs-of-purchase with a properly completed Offer Certificate

© 1990 Harlequin Enterprises Limited

See previous page for details